Prai

"Riveting. Veteran Ken Andrus has written a tale of military intrigue that draws the reader into a new reality. Fast moving, *Arctic Menace* keeps the reader immersed in this thriller, rushing to a dynamic conclusion. This one's a page-turner."

Col. Robert St. Clair USMCR (Ret.), author of
Saving Stacy: The Untold Story of the Moody Massacre

"If you're looking for a suspense thriller that will grab you, spin you around, then pin you to your chair until you finish, this is it. *Amber Dawn* is terrific entertainment by a writer working at the top of his game."

William Martin, *New York Times*-bestselling author of *The Lincoln Letter*

"*Amber Dawn* is for everyone who loves action-packed international thrillers that pit a talented but fallible protagonist and his team against a complex yet completely intriguing opponent for the highest possible stakes."

Rick Ludwig, author of *Pele's Fire*

"[Amber Dawn] is a great action-packed novel. It lets you in on the complexities of the United States intelligence community in our war on terrorism. The author obviously knows his way around the territory!"

>Robert Miller, former Navy intelligence officer

"Intrigue, action, terrorist plots, political maneuvering. *Amber Dawn* has it all. Ken Andrus weaves an intricate, complicated web as this tale winds toward its exciting climax."

>George Wallace, author of *Warshot*

"A great read. Don't start *Flash Point* unless you have the time to finish it in one sitting. Andrus knows the region, the politics, the militaries and the importance of the South China Sea area. Today's news headlines mirror the "fiction" he began writing several years ago."

>Adm. R.J. "Zap" Zlatoper, USN (Ret)

"*Flash Point*...will make your day."

>All Reading World

THE CURATORS

THE CURATORS
The Defenders Series

KENNETH ANDRUS

Copyright © 2022 by Kenneth Andrus

All rights reserved.

No part of this book may be reproduced in any form or by any electronic or mechanical means, including information storage and retrieval systems, without written permission from the author, except for the use of brief quotations in a book review.

This novel is dedicated to those Wounded Warriors who returned home, confronted and over- came their own ghosts to find their way to both heal their bodies and their souls.

Chapter One

THE STATION APARTMENTS
COLLEGE STATION, TEXAS
WEDNESDAY 16 SEPTEMBER

Nick Parkos' head jerked up, his concentration broken by the sound of his iPhone singing out the first bars of Aerosmith's "Dream On." Dressed in a tattered pair of tan shorts and an old T-shirt, he'd been working on his family genealogy prompted by the discovery of an ancient burlwood keepsake box in his grandparents' attic. He slid his finger over the answer bar without glancing at the phone's screen, expecting the call to be from his wife, Michelle. "Hi there, kiddo."

"Please hold for the director."

He clenched the phone at the sound of the detached, officious voice. *Director? What the hell?* He only knew one *Director*. The Director of National Intelligence. Bryce Gilmore came on the line before he could gather his thoughts.

"Nick, we need you," Gilmore opened without preamble.

Nick stiffened, the voice dredging up a jumble of suppressed emotions. He'd heard nothing from the Agency for three months. His last contact? A frustrating call to HR about his benefits. And now? A personal call from the Director? Nothing good would come of this.

His jaw tightened, his mind clouding with foreboding at the intrusion into his new life. He had to escape…no. Another imperative in his life took precedence. He glanced at the stack of "Thank You" notes he'd just finished for his and Michelle's wedding. Since moving to College Station, Texas so she could attend A&M, he had devoted his time to forgetting, puttering around the apartment, struggling to keep his mind occupied. A man without a cause.

Does the name, Anton Král, mean anything to you?" Gilmore asked.

"The only thing I can recall is that he was a minor player in the Czech Republic," he replied, struggling to ignore the churning in his gut.

"We thought you might have more. Putting that aside, things are going to hell in the Balkans and there's spillover to a narco-terrorist outfit in northern Mexico. The Mendez cartel."

Nick's brows knitted in consternation. *Mexico*? *Mendez*? He knew nothing about either. His thoughts jumped to Austin Mack. Mack had been his assistant in the Analytics Department, specializing in Balkan Transnational Crime Organizations (TCO's), and had moved up to replace him when he'd left the agency. "What about Austin?"

"He's the one who suggested the call. We've got a hiring freeze and couldn't backfill." Gilmore stopped. "I'll reset. You could give a damn about my personnel problems."

"I care about what happens to Austin."

"Fair enough," Gilmore continued. "Mack's swamped and you've got field experience."

Chapter One

Nick shook his head in disbelief. "You want me to go to the Balkans?"

"I can't overstate the importance of what I'm asking you to do. You're the only one I trust to get the job done. Mack—"

Nick eyed the plate of cooling leftovers he'd warmed in the microwave and put his phone on speaker, preparing for the worst. "What's happening?"

"I can't say over an open line. Talk things over with Michelle. If you agree, I'll arrange for a plane."

"Is Geoff involved?" His friend, Geoffrey Lange, led The Curators, a black ops unit of the NSA's Special Operations Center. Buried within the Special Operations Group, the unit's mission paralleled those covert direct-action groups within the CIA. The Curators operated under deep cover, conducting clandestine operations that the government officially distanced itself from, missions that were not suitable for the CIA, Delta Force or SEAL Team Six. And if their mission failed and the operators were captured? The government would disavow any knowledge of them. The Curators were not listed on the organization chart or even acknowledged.

"Lange can be, if you want him on your team."

Nick cocked his head at the DNI's response, his mind visualizing Gilmore's eyes peering over the top of his half-glasses and down the length of his nose like sighting a rifle. *My team?*

"Call Strickland with your answer." Three tones sounded on his phone. Gilmore had terminated the call.

Strickland? That son-of-a-bitch. I'll be damned if— He stood, then dropped back into the kitchen chair, staring at the refrigerator door festooned with colorful, vegetable-shaped magnets holding in place the snapshots of his new life. "Crap."

Chapter Two

THE STATION APARTMENTS
COLLEGE STATION, TEXAS
WEDNESDAY 16 SEPTEMBER

Where your life's particular circumstances place you sets up your reality. And for Nick? His new reality centered on three things; a five-by-seven-inch journal he'd placed to one side of the dinette table, the ancient burlwood keepsake box next to it, and Gilmore's call. He reached for the black-leather Le Vin spiral notebook that Michelle had given him the day before and tapped out a syncopated rhythm on the cover. She understood his need to find purpose in his life after leaving the Agency, and that to do so, he had to come to grips with his past. He decided to start at the beginning with his family's genealogy. The notebook to annotate his journey was the first step.

Where to start? He opened the journal and stared at the blank page, searching his mind for a hint of inspiration. He printed PARKOS/PATYKAOVI in large caps at the top of the first lined page. His pen halted at the bottom of the "I," his eyes settling on the framed needlepoint Michelle had crafted that graced the wall, celebrating their marriage.

His gaze drifted to their modest living room with its seldom watched flatscreen and the mix of Midwest décor from their old apartments. Michelle had explained the look was *eclectic*. And the new recliner? Her wedding present. She had insisted that he trash the ancient, stained chair, burdened with its memories of the dark times in his life. The mental image wrenched him back to the present.

Why would I even consider Gilmore's request? He's playing the damn guilt card. He dropped his head, struggling to wrap his mind around what had just happened.

Something the FBI's Agent-in-Charge of the Miami Field Office had said several years before speared his consciousness. "It's always complicated with you guys." Nick's lips tightened. He acknowledged that basic truth. The complications, the unanswered questions. That realization focused his thoughts, and he began to jot down a list of pros and the cons on the blank page below the two family surnames, his and the other, Patykaovi, that hinted of his past.

He set his pen down some fifteen minutes later, studied the columns, then began another list—his demands if he agreed to return. Topping the list? He'd insist his old supervisor, Ned Strickland, be sidelined. Marriage hadn't been the only thing that prompted his departure from the Agency. He'd been burned. He'd become a persona-non-grata despite being cleared of the charges of financial maleficence and treason manufactured by the Chinese in his last operation for the Agency. He suspected Strickland. Perhaps leaving was fortuitous. His career as an analyst had led to a dead end, and he hardly stood out as a leader destined for executive service or even a senior GS-15 level position, despite Gilmore's expressed confidence in him. Those positions were beyond his reach.

His attention drifted to the keepsake box, which he'd abandoned on the coffee table the night before when he couldn't locate the key. The walnut box was burnished with age, the joinery exceptional. The filigreed latches and the ornate escutcheon surround of the keyhole were bronze. On the lid, he could make out a Coat of Arms with the faded white image of a lion. He lifted the box to his ear and gave the contents a gentle shake. A faint rattle. He had nothing else to hint at its contents, and without a key, he didn't want to try to open the lock, to literally unlock the secrets inside.

He set the ancient box down with a sigh. He'd have to place his genealogy research on hold if he returned to Washington. Until the call, he'd almost begun to feel normal, although he had no firm concept of what *normal* was after nine years at the Agency. The sound of the apartment door opening prompted him to look up. Michelle.

Michelle gave her head a toss to put in place an errant lock of red hair despite keeping it cut short to conform with Texas A&M's Air Force ROTC requirements. His heart softened at the gleam in her emerald-green eyes and the splash of freckles across her cheeks and nose, the features that had drawn him to her when they first met. She wore faded jeans and a garnet and white long-sleeve plaid shirt hinting at her upbringing on a small farm—and she looked great.

She touched the crucifix hanging on the living room wall as she passed through the door, another of her mannerisms he adored. He'd been raised in the church, but her faith was much stronger...perhaps strong enough for both of them. They'd met in Paris, not at a romantic café, but at a French air force base on the outskirts of Paris, when the president had offered him a ride home on Air Force One following the terrorist incident he'd been investigating. Michelle was one of the aircrew, and they'd immediately made a connection.

They'd shared their upbringings in rural America, his in Indiana, hers in central Ohio, but she had an intact family.

And him? His mother had died two days before his fifth birthday and his dad had inexplicably disappeared from his life when he needed him most. If it weren't for his grandparents, he would have been orphaned. As it was, he'd always felt adrift with no firm sense of place or self-value, especially after his grandparents died. Then Michelle had entered his life.

Over time, he eased into a comfortable platonic relationship with her, discovering that what he needed was a friend, not a lover. He could talk to her, experiencing a resonance he'd never felt with anyone else, nor could he understand why. They would talk about all manner of things including the painful years of his childhood, something he hadn't been able to do with his ex, Marty. They'd married just after graduating from Ohio State, divorced a few years later, and Marty had returned to Florida with their young daughter, Emma. He rarely saw his child despite being awarded joint custody and having the best of intentions.

"Hello, sweetie," Michelle said to their pet, her eyes sparkling. She swept up the limp, purring cat who'd been asleep by the front door, waiting for her.

A smile appeared at the sight of his bride of two months. Michelle's voice pushed the annoyance of Gilmore's call and the painful memories from his mind. Her greeting, meant for the cat, not him, had become a private joke when they first began to date. He'd named the stray he'd adopted years before "Bill," after the frazzled feline featured in the Bloom County and Opus comic strips. "How were classes?"

Michelle set Bill down by his cat food bowl and dropped her backpack by the kitchen table. Weighted down by books, it landed with a heavy thud. "Fun—Newtonian Mechanics. I gotta go back for lab this afternoon."

He shook his head, marveling at her drive. She was now deep into her Aerospace Engineering studies at Texas A&M, working toward a commission in the Air Force courtesy of the

Airman Scholarship Program. "That can't possibly be fun." He stood and accepted her hug.

She detached herself from his embrace and cast a skeptical eye at the leftovers. "Whatcha eatin?"

"Red beans and rice. Want some?"

She picked up his fork and gave a bean a suspicious poke. "They won't poison me?" she teased.

"Geez."

Her eyes settled on the journal pages covered with his scrawled notes filling the columns under the headings of 'Pros and Cons.' "What's that?"

He made to cover the pages, then pulled his hand back, hesitant to break the news. She peered over his shoulder. "I got a call from Bryce Gilmore."

Michelle dropped the fork. "What on earth for?"

"He wants me to come back."

"To D.C.?"

"Yeah."

"Oh." She wobbled and reached for the table, staring at the two columns. "What did you say?"

"That we'd talk. I didn't commit." He noted the corners of her mouth drop, her eyes beginning to glisten. He reached for her hand. "I won't do anything you're against and I'll only use the journal for my genealogy research."

She swept her finger across the corner of her eye, rubbing away a tear, regaining her composure. "Do you want to go?"

"Truthfully, I don't know. There's a lot of broken glass left on the ground."

"Strickland?"

"And others. I need to call Geoff."

"Good idea. Think about it and we'll talk this evening."

Nick scrolled through his contact list after Michelle left for the A&M campus. He picked up his phone and tapped in the number of a burner. What he needed at the moment was to talk to a trusted friend.

"Lange," his friend said after picking up on the second ring.

"You know what's going on?" Nick asked

"Well, it's good to talk to you, too," Geoff Lange, the chief of The Curators responded. "How's Michelle?"

"She would be a whole lot better if it weren't for Gilmore's call."

"He called her?"

"No. Me. He wants me to come back."

"What the hell for?"

"I was hoping you'd know. He asked if the name 'Anton Král' meant anything."

"Never heard... No, wait. Could be the Král Group. I hear they're making a move in Czechoslovakia."

"Gilmore did mention that the Balkans were going to hell and a possible link with the Mendez drug cartel."

"He wants you to clean things up?"

"Can you test the waters?"

"I'll check around."

Chapter Three

DULLES INTERNATIONAL AIRPORT
WASHINGTON, D.C.
FRIDAY 18 SEPTEMBER

Nick shifted his weight from his left to his right leg, waiting for his bag at the American Airline's carousel, catching snippets of conversation. The other passengers clustered around him flashing their calling cards, laughing at lame jokes, boasting of their positions. Several of them cast him a glance but kept their backs turned. The unvoiced signal, intentional or not, angered him. These self-absorbed millennials with their inflated egos had created their own fantasy world within a Washington full of deceit. An unceasing House of Cards.

He wondered how many of them would leave their jobs, like him, with unfinished business, loose ends festering in their subconscious, victims of a merciless world.

And what about me? The sound of Gilmore's voice intruded in his thoughts, forcing him to acknowledge that he must

Chapter Three

confront his past; the way he'd left the Agency, the trauma of being orphaned at five, his divorce three years ago, the flashbacks of his past missions.

Michelle had stayed up late with him Wednesday night discussing what he should do. What they should do. In the end, she understood better than he. He had to return. To expunge the demons. To make things right. She assured him that she would be fine. "Go," she'd said. "End of discussion."

The corners of his mouth curled up in a chagrined smile at how Michelle had dealt with the issue. *Ah, laddie.* The mixed Scotch-Irish blood of Michelle's small ancestral clan, the McClungs, brooked none of his nonsense. *If only he were so self-assured.* He spotted his bag sporting its yellow priority label, snatched it from the conveyor belt, and made his way outside to the passenger pickup lanes, searching for the promised government vehicle. The black GMC SUV sat idling at the curb.

He was shocked to see Ned Strickland appear from behind a pillar, his jowls sagging in quarrelsome discontent, rimless glasses sweeping away any vestige of sincerity from his eyes. "Good to have you back." He didn't offer his hand. "Toss your bag in the trunk."

Nick slid across the rear seat after hefting his bag and carry-on into the rear storage compartment. Strickland slammed the door after him and climbed into the front passenger seat. His old supervisor twisted and spoke over his shoulder as the driver exited the terminal, accelerating onto SR 267. "We've got you booked at the Tyson's Corner Marriott, but the DNI wants to see you before you check in."

Their subsequent small talk trickled into a strained silence during the remainder of the sixteen-mile trip to the National Counterterrorism Center's Liberty Crossing campus located near Tyson's Corner. He gazed out the rain-dotted window at the passing countryside, welcoming the silence.

NATIONAL COUNTER TERRORISM CENTER LIBERTY CROSSING CAMPUS, MCLEAN, VIRGINIA

Nick felt an utter sense of unreality as his and Strickland's footfalls echoed in the empty halls of the National Counter Terrorism Center's headquarters building. His uneasiness increased as Strickland pushed open the double doors leading to Gilmore's reception room. The lamp from the DNI's office cast a blurred rectangle of light across the darkened reception room floor. Wendy, Gilmore's secretary whom he'd befriended over the years, had gone home.

Strickland reached for the package she'd left on her desk and handed it over. "Temporary ID. Sign the security clearance. Same with your computer access. You know the drill."

Nick turned at the sound of Bryce Gilmore's voice, tired of Strickland's crap.

"Welcome home." The DNI extended his hand in greeting. "Have a good trip?" He didn't wait for an answer. "Figured you'd enjoy the upgrade."

"Yes, sir." He suppressed a grimace at Gilmore's crushing grip. "Thank you." The DNI looked different. He realized he'd never seen him without a coat. He also didn't detect the reek of stale cigarette smoke. *Must have given up his Marlboros.*

Gilmore gestured to his office. "We've got a few things to talk about."

Strickland made to follow, but Gilmore stopped him. "I'll let you know if we need anything."

Nick suppressed a smile and followed the DNI into his office. *New ballgame, buddy, and you're out.* His eyes lit on the credenza with a large coffee maker set to one side. He'd seen one like it at Williams Sonoma. He also knew that he'd

Chapter Three

politely decline a cup if offered. The director's coffee was so strong, it was undrinkable. A framed picture of the Marlboro Man, a gift from his staff, stood guard over the coffee pot. The hard-bitten cowboy, who'd never smoked, fit Gilmore's self-image of the American male: Rugged, his own man, never backing down. The DNI was the zealous guardian of the nation's secrets he'd sworn to protect. No threat escaped his scrutiny. And his world view? Machiavellian.

Gilmore settled behind his massive desk, adjusted his half-glasses, and waited for Nick to take his accustomed chair. "*Jak se máš češtinu?*"

"*Trochu rezavé.*" Nick responded to the DNI's opening of: *How's your Czech?* before adding in English. "A bit rusty."

In truth, his family's language came easily, as did Russian, the other Slavic language he'd learned. What didn't come as easily was the reason he'd really come back to Washington, to the Agency. He relaxed his hands and rested his forearms on his lap.

"You haven't missed a beat," Gilmore said. He gestured to a thick folder in front of him. "Operation Switchback: Drug Trafficking and Money Laundering Operations in the Czech Republic and the Balkans. This report contains the findings from the Attorney General's investigation specifying the DEA's failure to exercise due diligence in the oversight of their operations in Czechoslovakia. It wouldn't have come to my attention except for Mack. He picked up on something we missed. Something else appears to be going on in Prague. Something we don't fully understand that could threaten the security of the country."

Gilmore anticipated Nick's question before he could ask it. "The DEA failed to manage undercover money laundering ops through various fronts that were authorized under an AG's Exempted Operation. When I queried, the Attorney General admitted to the DOJ's weak oversight. That admission led him to conduct his own investigation. The results are now in our hands."

"I spoke to Geoff."

"Good."

Nick noted the DNI's face didn't reflect any reaction to this revelation. *Had his friend already spoken with Gilmore? If so, what hadn't Geoff told him?* He pondered the significance of the DNI's response, or lack of one, and moved on. "Geoff mentioned the Král Group. Before I left the Agency, I didn't think the activities of this small-time operation warranted a deeper look."

Gilmore tapped his finger on the seventy-two-page report. "You had other things on your mind." He opened the cover. "It's all here. Stings, record keeping, lax control of informants. You name it. The Balkan Transnational Crime Organizations have expanded their operations reaching out to the Mexican and Central American cartels. Case-in-point? The recent Croatian intercept of close to a ton of methamphetamine in Novi Sad worth two billion on the streets. The shipment originated in Guatemala. The relevant piece that bears scrutiny is the reports we've received from our agents in Mexico."

"Operation Koštana Prašinco?" Nick said, not focused on Gilmore's mention of Mexico and the link to the Mendez cartel he'd mentioned on their phone call. When he'd left the Agency, he'd just begun work on operation Koštana.

"Bone Dust," Gilmore added. "Then you may know the Serbian kingpin is awaiting trial while cooling his heels in Sremska Mitrovica Prison. The landscape has shifted since his arrest. One of the Mexican cartels is making a move and the DEA thinks it has reached out to Král's organization. The cartel's leader, Carlos Mendez, fancies himself as the next *Tlatoani*, and he appears to have grandiose visions of empire."

Nick nodded, making a mental note of this new player, Mendez, and the odd name Tlatoani. This was the world he felt comfortable in and he was already constructing a Venn

Chapter Three

diagram in his mind, a tool he had attained some notoriety for within the Agency. He had also just let it slip that he still followed events related to his old job. Gilmore's voice broke through his thoughts.

"Mack has a good start on sorting through the known players and compiling estimative intelligence."

"Anton Král?"

"Suddenly, he's big time," Gilmore affirmed.

"What about the Organization for Security and Cooperation in Europe? They must have something."

"I don't give a damn about the EU. They can take care of themselves. Something else is going on. Something linked to the cartels and all the baggage they carry: Drugs, weapons, trafficking. The Attorney General and his IG structured their summary to ensure we'd have investigative authority."

"Yes, sir," Nick said, still not sure where Gilmore was headed.

"This is where you come in."

"Why me?"

"The same reason I picked you for the al-Khultyer and Win-Lu operations: Your ability to analyze seemingly disparate events and link them to a common element. We're assembling a team. We've elected to use a broader definition of *flexibility* than the one cited in the IG's summation."

"Geoff Lange?" Nick ventured.

"Correct."

Nick reached his hand out. "I'll—"

Gilmore pulled the report back, placed it on top of another folder, and stood. He followed Nick's eyes. "The second report is the DEA's Sensitive Activities Review. These can't leave the building. I'll get them to Austin tomorrow morning. Consider this an advisory tasking. He walked Nick to the door. "I've got a bad feeling about this, Nick. Find out what's going on and put a stop to it."

Chapter Four

NATIONAL COUNTERTERRORISM CENTER
LIBERTY CROSSING CAMPUS, MCLEAN, VIRGINIA
SATURDAY 19 SEPTEMBER

Nick lowered his hand just before knocking on the doorframe of his old office, a wave of conflicting emotions washing over him: Self-doubt, remorse, anticipation of seeing Austin, the excitement of plunging into a new adventure. Overriding them all, though, was the emotional baggage he'd left strewn about after his abrupt departure from the Agency. He raised his hand and rapped out a double-knock.

Austin Mack looked up from his keyboard, a smile lighting his face. "Dang, aren't you ever a sight for sore eyes. I wasn't expecting you for another half-hour. How you guys doin'?"

Nick took a cautious step. "Great, until I got the call. Michelle took it pretty well, all things considered."

"Well, I'm sure glad you're here." Mack made to stand and offer his chair.

Chapter Four

"No, that's yours." Nick settled into the one next to the desk. "Seriously, a tie?" he continued, intent on deflecting any more questions about Michelle and his decision.

"Strickland insisted."

"Figures. Make you any smarter?"

Austin looped his index finger under the knot and gave it a tug. "Nope, cuts off the circulation."

Nick concluded Austin's relationship with Strickland wasn't optimal based on what he'd just heard, but it would be dangerous to presume and drag the kid into his private feud. He cast a look around the office. Austin had transformed the place. His old desk and the cork board with a few green index cards still pinned to it were all that remained from his last investigation. The desk was uncluttered and dotted with family pictures. A DeLonghi Espresso machine rested on a new table set by the window overlooking the beltway and a dull-gray sky.

Nick felt a pang of jealousy. Austin's square-jawed good looks and deep baritone voice were the very image of a country singer, and he'd grown up on a working farm near Eagle River, Wisconsin in an intact family. His family had made a name for themselves, producing award-winning artisanal chèvre cheese. Austin was also a closet gourmet, catering the celebratory party Lange had thrown at The Nickolas following their last operation. The same party where Nick and Michelle had announced their engagement and his intent to leave the Agency. His jealousy turned to guilt. *What the hell's wrong with me?* His eyes settled on the espresso machine.

"Beats the Starbucks from the canteen," Austin said. "Make you a cup?"

"That'd be great, thanks."

Austin waved his hand toward his desk after tapping down the coffee grounds. "I leafed through the AG's report. Looks like we have our work cut out." He stopped to study the dark, bubbly brew filling the cup. "How about a Cappuccino? It's no trouble."

"No, thanks," Nick said, anxious to get started.

Austin handed over the cup of steaming espresso and settled in at his desk. "You have a chance to read it?"

Nick sat down, trying not to spill the brimming cup, grateful it wasn't a demitasse. "No, but the Director gave me the thumbnail last night."

"I was reading the Scope of Objectives when you knocked. There's no doubt the operatives lost control of a money laundering operation designed to cripple the major players. Millions of dollars are unaccounted for."

"That's why Justice conducted their Sensitive Activity Review." Nick took a sip of his espresso, savoring the flavor. "I'm curious. Where do I fit?"

"Anton Král."

His eyebrows knotted. That name kept popping up. "What's his significance?"

"I'll back up a step," Austin said. "After you left, I ran a query through the Document and Media Exploitation Center. One report got my attention. An investigative reporter affiliated with the Organized Crime and Corruption Reporting Project was murdered. The rest was pretty much what you'd expect in the Balkans. Same Transnational Organized Crime stuff you were tracking."

"Not an accident?"

"No. Her death was meant to send a message. She was tortured. Lots of knife cuts. When they were done, they dumped her body outside the Czech Center for Investigative Journalism's Prague office."

"Gruesome. Sounds like a Mexican cartel's work. You know what she was investigating? Trafficking, contraband?"

"It was who she was investigating," Austin said.

"Let me guess. Král?"

"Yeah. Whoever did this broke into her apartment, took

Chapter Four

her computer, notes, phone. Anything that would indicate what she'd found. Several of her colleagues said she was on to a major scoop."

"You find anything?"

"Nothing solid," Austin replied. "The DEA's been working with the Czech Republic Intelligence System and the *Státní Tajná Bezpečnost*.

Nick glanced at the remaining index cards on the corkboard, recalling the Chinese agents he'd confronted. "The Czech State Security Service plays hardball."

"They've linked Král to narco-terrorists."

Nick gave his chin a thoughtful rub. "The Director also mentioned Král and another player named Mendez."

"The boss is an ex-field agent. He's got good instincts," Austin said. He spun his chair, brought up a document on his computer, and hit the print key. "While you gents were sipping tea, reminiscing about the good old days, I was working my fingers to the bone." He snatched the sheet of paper off his printer and handed it over. "Not one of your Venn diagrams, but it's a start. You have access?"

"Working on it. Strickland didn't do much to expedite the process."

Austin made a circular motion with his right hand, index finger extended. "He is not the droid you seek, Jedi Master. But not to worry. I have connections within the Galactic Republic."

Nick set the empty cup down. "Who?"

"Need-to-know."

"Give me a break."

"More espresso?"

"You wouldn't happen to have some biscotti stashed in your desk?"

"Costco." Austin pulled open the bottom right drawer and handed him one. "Don't push your luck."

Nick removed the plastic sleeve, took a bite of the chocolate-covered biscuit, leaned across the desk, and grabbed a couple pieces of paper from the printer. "For my notes and a Venn diagram. Did you see anything else that caught your attention?"

"A number of things that don't seem to mesh. How about you put a fresh set of eyes on the reports, then we'll compare notes? I'll start on the Suspicious Activities Review and see what the DEA has to say."

Nick took a crunchy bite of biscotti and opened the report. "You're on."

"Oh, if you need computer access, I'll—"

"No need." He wasn't about to let Austin break a cardinal rule and share his passwords. He brushed a scattering of biscotti crumbs off the title page and onto the floor. "There's more than enough here to keep me busy."

Nick grabbed a pen and drew a series of circles on one sheet of paper, the first step in creating his diagram. In truth, there was more than enough to keep him busy. Unable to sleep the night before, he'd lain awake thinking about the ancient burlwood box and had already decided what else he needed to do in Prague besides fulfil Gilmore's tasking. The Agency owed him that much.

He tapped the pen on the diagram, deep in thought, framing how he'd pursue his investigation, then set to work drawing five interlocking circles. He inscribed "Anton Král" in the open circle he'd labeled "'Leader.'" His lips tightened, his head nodding in affirmation. He'd taken the first step in meeting Gilmore's challenge to find out what was going on in Prague and eliminate any threat this Král presented to the United States.

Chapter Five

**THE NICHOLAS
3136 M STREET, N.W.
GEORGETOWN, WASHINGTON D.C.
SATURDAY 18 SEPTEMBER**

Nick paused before the sage-colored door of The Nicholas, the private club Geoff Lange frequented. *Or owned?* It was hard to believe six months had passed since he'd last stepped through the door. He waved at the security camera tucked in the upper corner of the sill, then gave the ornate doorknocker three thumps. The door opened an instant later to reveal the formally attired doorman. He stepped aside to allow Nick to enter the parquet-floored foyer.

"Welcome back, sir," the doorman said in his native Scottish brogue.

"Thank you, Edmund. It's good to be back."

"Will you be having your usual?"

Nick hesitated, running the names of half-a-dozen Scotch whiskies through his mind laboring to decide what might be his favorite. He'd been served any number of very expensive ones, but he couldn't recall a *usual*. *The Macallan?*

Edmund scrunched his lips. "Perhaps you would like to try the Auchentoshan Three Wood? I believe it would suit your palate. If you permit, I will pair it with some Stilton or perhaps a selection of truffles from our Scottish chocolatier, Iain Burnett."

"Surprise me."

Edmund smiled. "Of course, sir. You know the way."

Nick studied him. The title of "doorman" didn't match, nor did "maître d'hôtel." There was more to this man and to this club. Pondering what those might be, Nick made his way toward the stairs and the second-floor drawing room. He stopped on the first tread and tossed a salute to the formal portrait of a Colonial-era Naval officer mounted on the far wall: Major Samuel Nicholas, the first commandant of the United States Marine Corps and the club's namesake.

He stopped again at the top of the stairs. The ultimate man-cave. Oak wainscoting topped by embossed, English-green silk wallpaper; original leaded-glass windows; a picture above the hearth of America's first frigate, the *Alliance*, Marines in her main fighting top. He closed his eyes and inhaled, absorbing the woodsy smell of the fire, the rich undertones of leather emanating from old books, the bouquet of an expensive cigar, before making his way toward a pair of tufted red-leather chairs in front of a crackling fire.

"Feel at home?" Lange said, rising from his place of repose, flashing a welcoming smile. Lange presented a figure that could have sprung straight from nineteenth-century England. A touch of gray dusted his dark-brown hair. Tortoise shell glasses perched on a prominent nose set off steel-blue eyes that missed nothing. Knotted around his neck, a gold paisley-patterned ascot accented a vintage burgundy smoking jacket with black velvet lapels.

Nick offered his right hand. Instead, Lange wrapped him up in a crushing man-hug.

A raucous laugh burst from Lange as he released him. "What? No back thumps?"

"No need." He replied, echoing Lange's laugh.

They'd first met when Nick decided to visit the Upper Crust Tap and Grill, a new pub hyped in the *Washington Post's* "'Lifestyle'" section, instead of going home to his condo and another meal of leftovers. He'd found an open seat at the bar next to Lange and that happenstance meeting had led to a strong friendship.

Lange led him to the chairs. "How's married life treating you?"

"Couldn't be better."

"Except you're here."

"Yeah, that's a problem." Nick settled onto the deep leather cushion of his wingback. "The weird thing? Michelle understands."

Lange selected a cigar, lit it with a wooden match, and took a thoughtful pull. "She would. She knows we gotta clean up the loose ends. This operation is as good a place as any to start."

"What would you do in my position?"

"Not my decision," Lange said.

"But what if I fail?"

"Do you even know what Gilmore is looking for?"

He reflected on Lange's question. "I've got a—"

"Excuse me, sir," Edmund said, placing a Glencairn glass filled with a generous portion of the Auchentoshan on Nick's end table. He set a selection of gourmet chocolate truffles next to it, then took a respectful step back, his face expectant.

Lange eyed the plate. "You eat all your dinner?"

"This is dinner." Nick hefted his glass and held it up to the fire, commencing the expected ritual. Golden copper. A swirl and several short sniffs over the rim. A *touch of toffee*. A wee taste to coat the tongue. Another. *Hints of rum from the aged oak barrels. A long finish.* He set the glass down. "Incredible, Edmund."

"Thank you, sir. Will there be anything else?"

Lange held up his half-empty glass, then settled back in his chair and took a long pull on his cigar. A comfortable silence between them gave Nick some space to enjoy his Scotch and chocolates and get into the right frame of mind.

"Got a cryptonym for your op?" Lange opened.

"I haven't got that far. That, and I don't know how they're constructed."

"Well, Little Grasshopper, permit me to explain."

Nick emitted an amused snort at the reference to the '70's TV show, "Kung Fu." "Enlighten me."

"We'll start with the first two letters, DI, of your digraph that indicate the region for the op. DI stands for Czechoslovakia. The rest of the identifier is tagged on at the end and often spells out a common word. But you don't want to give away the target with something obvious. For example,—Diatribe."

He countered after a moment. "Diabolism."

"'An action aided by the devil'? Good choice, but it won't do."

His jaw dropped in disbelief. "How'd you know that?"

"Remember, my cover? I'm an investigative reporter."

He also recalled Lange had a Master's degree from Northwestern University's School of Journalism. "How about Diagonal."

"Possible. Want to try Dichotomy on for size?"

"Maybe," Nick said, warming to the mental gymnastics. He looked up at the ceiling deep in thought. "Got it. Diddly-shit."

"Not a chance, Dimwit."

"Touché," Nick responded.

"I'd go with Diagonal," Lange concluded.

Nick bit his lower lip in thought, then hefted his Glencairn glass. "To 'Diagonal.'"

A log in the fireplace broke, collapsing the stack and sending a flash of glowing embers up the flue. Lange pulled a poker from a stand of fireplace implements and gave the pile a stir. A burst of red-orange flames leapt from the logs. "What's your cover?"

Nick paused, wondering if Lange would see through the deeper reason behind what he'd already chosen. He hedged, his answer tainted by only a tinge of guilt. "I haven't thought that through."

"In our business, there are two. Diplomatic and Nonofficial Cover. For our op, Diplomatic is off the table. Too many people involved. You'll have to operate under NOC. And that means, if you're arrested, you're on your own. There's not much the Embassy can do …. No, that's not entirely correct. We'll cover your ass."

"Like my botched break-in at Lin-Wu's house?"

"I'd say that wasn't one of your better moments."

Nick's eyebrows bunched at the memory. He'd been knocked unconscious and imprisoned in an old root cellar of the home he'd planned to case. Lange and his team had rescued him. "Yeah, pretty dumb."

"Let's not plan on doing that again," Lange said.

Nick took a sip of his scotch, his mind returning to the mission. Lange's brief tutorial was sobering. He hadn't thought enough about the specifics of the operation, immersing himself in sorting through Gilmore's admonition: "Find out what's going on and put a stop to it." He'd been focused on going to Prague, to his family's country. He tossed out his idea. "A genealogy tour. We could get the whole team in."

Lange tapped the ash off his cigar, studied the fire, then nodded. "Brilliant."

Nick warmed to his idea. "We shouldn't use a known outfit."

"Ask Austin to create one?"

"I'll need a good alias." He swirled the last of his whisky, sorting through the possibilities. "I started a query on Ancestry a couple of weeks ago. Figure it'd be fun to find out where I came from. The name, 'Nikola Patykaovi,' popped up."

"He part of your family tree?"

"No idea. I could Americanize it to Nikola Partyka."

"Go with it. We'll need to start creating your backstop…" Geoff stopped at the quizzical look on Nick's face. "The false identity for your Mr. Partyka. Work history, home address, accounts on Google, Facebook, Apple. And something easy to hack that can track your locations, enable WPS and Wi-Fi. I'd suggest using an ESP8266 microcontroller to create your fake networks."

"Who can do that?"

"Our CIA friend."

"Ferguson?" His hand tightened around his glass. The addition of Taylor Ferguson to the team, while not unexpected, elicited a rush of ambivalent feelings. While Fergusson had proven helpful in his two previous operations, he felt the agent was a loose cannon and a narcissistic ass not worthy of his trust. *No way.*

Lange took a pull of his cigar, leaned his head back, and blew out a large smoke ring. "Yeah, your buddy."

Chapter Six

PLAZA LOS REYES
MICHOACÁN PROVENCE, MEXICO
MONDAY 20 SEPTEMBER

Carlos Mendez lifted his binoculars and scanned the barren expanse of Michoacán Provence's *Tierra Caliente* from his sand-bagged lookout. The sun-scorched, airless plain stretched out before him, and in the distance, the town of Plaza Los Reyes. Soon, in one audacious act, the world would know his name.

A stocky, five-foot seven, with penetrating dark-brown eyes and a trimmed goatee, he wore faded jeans and an open-collared blue shirt, fashioning himself as a man of the people. There was some truth in that. He'd grown up in abject poverty, his family subsistence farmers, but he had found his place with the local cartel trafficking opium and fake gold jewelry, before becoming a hitman. He had risen through the ranks because of his superior intellect and ruthless efficiency in completing any task assigned him.

He was also cultivating an image that would lead to his ultimate goal, the resurrection of the *Tlatoani*, the ancient chief priest of his ancestors. He, Carlos Mendez, would soon be the supreme ruler, a descendant of the ancient Meso-Americans, and he would reclaim his nation's stolen land.

Mendez adjusted his binoculars, bringing the distant images into focus. Several of his advance vehicles dotted the scrubbed landscape like so many scurrying black beetles, kicking up contrails of dust as they headed toward the twisted alleyways of the small town. He emitted a satisfied grunt. The plumes were calculated to attract the attention of the town's defenders. The five *Valentes*, the Brave Ones, in the lead vehicle mounting a Russian 12.5mm DShK heavy machine gun were the bait.

He held the local army garrison, an insignificant unit of the Guardia Nacional, in contempt. They were protecting his weaker rival, the Lupo Cartel, violating the President's "Hugs, Not Bullets" non-aggression pact developed to keep the warring cartels apart. The garrison commander favored his rivals and was interfering with his attempts to extort the local farmers. Mendez also had to ensure the supply routes from the port of Mazatlán remained open for the shipments of Chinese-manufactured precursor chemicals for the production of methamphetamine and fentanyl that he shipped across the border into the United States.

The targets of his operation, though, were the two American Drug Enforcement Agents reportedly holed up in the town. The orders from his Russian benefactors were to capture the two and interrogate them about what they knew of his links to the Czech, Král, and the FSB. If they knew nothing, no matter, they would die to send a message to the American and Mexican presidents that he was not one to be ignored. There was also another matter he was considering, one that his compatriot, former Defense Minister, Juan Carlos Alvarez, had suggested.

Chapter Six

Alvarez had suggested taking a page from ISIS and reaching out to the MS-13 gangs to engage in asymmetric warfare along the U.S. border, thus shielding his own nascent army from American scrutiny. Of course, and unknown to Alvarez, he had already been in contact with the leader, the *corredores*, of the Los Angeles clique enticing him with promises of weapons, power, and prestige. Mendez spat, giving vent to his disdain for Alvarez, vowing that he would soon eliminate the greedy *pinche*.

Twin plumes of black, oily smoke smudged the distant skyline. A tight smile flattened his lips. Another piece of his plan had been executed. Soon, several more plumes would appear from the burning trucks blocking the gritty roads into and out of the town. He had also recruited the villagers, who had no alternatives, to act as human shields to prevent the army troops from exiting their barracks.

The high-pitched whine of a helicopter's twin turbine engines underlain by a rhythmic dull *Whop-Whop-Whop* sound interrupted his thoughts as a government Blackhawk appeared over the horizon. The helicopter, armed with a lethal Gatling minigun, would have proven troublesome if not for his plan. He swung his binoculars toward a camouflaged arroyo. Several of his men were hidden beneath a spread of sand-colored canvas topped with brush, armed with 50caliber sniper rifles and rocket propelled grenades, But his real surprise? A two-barreled ZPU2 anti-aircraft cannon mounted on the bed of a flatbed truck he'd commandeered.

The ZPU was sourced from Syrian rebels desperate for funds, but soon he would have weapons from a more reliable source: AK-47s, anti-tank RPG-75s, and NSV 12.7mm heavy machine guns obtained from his supplier, Anton Král. He sweetened the deal with the Czech by including 500 kilos of cocaine and a gallon-sized zip lock bag stuffed with Fentanyl tablets with his cash payment for the weapons. And the cost? A pittance compared to the amount he would earn from the recent trans-shipment of tons his product through Guatemala, bound for Král's Prague network.

Mendez shifted his binoculars to study the advancing helicopter, calculating the time for a probable intercept. *Now.* He turned to his deputy, Major Alfredo Sanchez. "Order the lead vehicle to feign panic and head for the arroyo."

A hail of 14.5mm rounds erupted from the ZPU's twin barrels when the helicopter was within range. Mendez tracked the undulating, snake-like trails of the gun's tracer bullets, his scowl replaced by an elated fist pump as they impacted near the tail rotor. The fatally wounded helicopter spun counter-clockwise in increasingly erratic circles before pitching nose down, exploding in a red-orange fireball as it hit the ground. The sound of the aircraft blowing up reached him a second later.

He lifted his radio. "Now"

His *droneros* toggled the controls of their quadcopter drones which were rigged to carry explosive grenades that would rip open the thin metal roofs of the garrison's barracks. The explosives would cause little other damage. They were intended to sow another layer of confusion and terror among the town's defenders. An assorted collection of SUVs, trucks, and even an old school bus lead by four technicals, their door panels embossed with FEM in black letters, stood in readiness to attack. Mendez's Special Forces, his elite.

He gave the order for them to engage the enemy, the hundred-man company of the National Guardsmen that had the audacity to confront him. Those who choose not to join him, would lose their lives. The resulting attack bore little resemblance to organization, the haphazard collection of vehicles racing across the plain instead giving the appearance of a crazed snarl of drivers freed from a highway traffic jam.

He waved for his driver and jumped into the Ford Grand Cherokee SUV to join his men roaring into the center of town, indiscriminately firing their Kalashnikovs into the air, peppering the front of the police station. They found the DEA agents a short time later hiding in a dilapidated barn among the sheep, cowering under a pile of hay.

He approached the agents, their faces bloodied, their arms pinioned behind their backs. "What do you know of Anton Král?"

They stared back in defiance.

"I will give you one more chance." Still they said nothing. Perhaps they did not know, but no matter. "*Lástima, amigos míos, moriráns.*" He merely shrugged at the one who spit on the ground and addressed Sanchez. "Kill them."

He turned, indifferent to the executions of the two Americans, deciding on the spur of the moment that he would add "El" to his title: El Tlatoani.

Chapter Seven

NATIONAL COUNTER TERRORISM CENTER
LIBERTY CROSSING CAMPUS, MCLEAN, VIRGINIA
MONDAY 20 SEPTEMBER

"What's new?" Nick asked.

Austin hefted his cup of espresso in welcome.

Nick held out a white bakery sack. "Croissants."

"I'll buy tomorrow," Austin said.

"What's going on?"

"I'd hoped you could tell me," Austin said. "You get access?"

"I'm good to go. An old buddy from IT is setting me up this afternoon." Nick scanned the cramped room. "You have any preference where we put the station?" He paused noting the expression on Austin's face. "The DNI wants to keep me as low a profile as possible. I don't get my own office. Hell, I'm not even going to appear on HR's rolls."

Austin pursed his lips and surveyed his office. "Hmm, maybe across from the espresso table."

"I did some work over the weekend," Nick said, pushing through the awkward moment. "I met with Geoff, and we came up with a name for the op, Diagonal. And my alias, Nikola Partyka. We figured I'd automatically answer to 'Nick,' instead of some made up first name."

"Makes sense. How'd you choose Partyka?"

"I modified my grandparents' surname. I had just started a genealogy search on Ancestry before the director's call. My grandparents emigrated after the war and settled in Indiana."

"Timing's everything. You come up with a cover?"

"Fell right into place: 'Prestige Genealogy and Heritage Tours.' We can get the entire team in under the guise of a tour group. Geoff's working the support angle and deciding where his group will locate."

"Poland?"

"Probably Dresden. It's almost a straight shot north from Prague."

Austin cradled his chin on his thumbs and index fingers. "It'd be best to make it a start-up. You'd be the company's first tour. That would account for screw-ups that will give your mission flexibility in case you have to improvise."

"That's great," Nick responded.

"I'll get on it."

"Can I pick your brain first?"

"Sure," Austin said.

"I started my Venn diagram by asking myself a basic question: What incentive would compel the rival ethnic groups in the Balkans to cooperate?"

"Form an alliance? I haven't seen any indicators."

"That's just it. I can't see that happening, either. The old hatreds from the region's years of civil wars run too deep. The other thing is the Czechs, as a whole, are individualists. They're not big on unity or solidarity."

"Would profit, power, or keeping the Russians out be enough? You know, your old friends from the Novorossiysk

Business Group appear to be making a move." Austin stopped. "I'd focus on what got the DNI stirred up."

"Besides your report?" Nick asked.

"Well, yeah, there is that."

"He told me he has *a bad feeling*. Something he spotted in the IG's review."

"Not much to go on."

"No, it's not." Nick picked up a pen, wrote "NBG" in large caps, and underlined it twice. What were the Russians up to? Or could the oligarchs of the NBG be operating on their own? He'd pursue this lead once he accessed his old databases, provided they hadn't been erased. "Then again, if you were the DNI, what would get you spun up?"

"Something new that presents a clear and present danger to the United States."

"'New' excludes Russia, China, Iran, and Radical Islam."

"How about drugs? Central or South America? Mexico?" Austin suggested.

"The link between Král and Mendez is topping my list because of the director's concern but I'm wondering where the NBG fits."

"Trafficking would be a reach," Austin said, "but it's high profile: indentured servitude, construction and domestic workers, sexploitation."

"Nothing new there, but we shouldn't dismiss trafficking. It's the third largest crime industry in the world after drugs and arms."

"Trafficking wouldn't present a 'clear and present danger,' but I'd still ask what links them?" Austin said.

"Or who?"

"Chicken or the egg?"

"Exactly." He tapped out a staccato rhythm on the intersecting circles of his diagram. The pen stopped on: Leader. "Let's go with the chicken."

Chapter Eight

OFFICE OF THE DIRECTOR NATIONAL
INTELLIGENCE
LIBERTY CROSSING CAMPUS, MCLEAN, VIRGINIA
TUESDAY 21 SEPTEMBER

Nick pushed open the suite's right-hand door and strode into Gilmore's office. The summons by the DNI did not catch him unaware, but the word of his visit to Gilmore's office would be all over campus by close of business. *That said, he did wonder what had gotten the boss stirred up.* He'd know soon enough. Wendy ushered him into the Director's office with a knowing arch of her right eyebrow.

"Come up with anything?" Gilmore asked, ignoring Nick's glance at the thin, red-hashed folder set to one side of the desk.

"Nothing solid, sir."

Gilmore digested that bit of information. His expression soured. "You may not until you're in Prague." He redirected his next question. "Got a cryptonym for your op?"

"Diagonal."

"Good one. What's the status of your team?"

"We'll be ready to go in two weeks. Austin put in the dates for our tour package on Prestige Genealogy's website. We've got our airline and hotel reservations lined up."

A frown appeared on Gilmore's face, then vanished. "Understood. There are a lot of pieces to get right. We can't afford a half-ass operation. Let me know if you need anything. That said, I don't want you to contradict the official narrative."

Nick was beat and didn't want to play mind games. "Narrative, sir?"

"You haven't figured that out?" Gilmore snapped. "No, that was out of line. You're simply here to provide Austin an assist." He paused. "There's something going on within the agency. I don't want you to get entrapped. Lange will fill you in. We've got other issues to discuss."

Gilmore's admission confirmed Nick's suspicion that he'd been burned. But why? He couldn't even begin to fathom the reasons.

"Why did you leave, Nick?"

"You, sir, of all people should know that."

"You're right. We thought it best to let you go."

"That doesn't make any sense."

"Do you recall the message that popped up on your computer last year?" Gilmore asked.

Nick rocked back in his chair, stunned by Gilmore's statement. "'*It's Not Over?*' How did you know about that?"

"Geoff told me that part of the message alluded to your difficulties after the al-Khultyer mission. He also needed your assistance to take down that Chinese cell."

Gilmore cast a glance at the framed picture of the Marlboro Man. "Part of being your own man is knowing when to ask for help." He leaned back in his chair. "You know I'm an old field agent."

Chapter Eight

Nick nodded, not sure where this conversation was going.

"I still carry baggage from some of my missions. Things that still come back to haunt me. It took a long time to get through the worst of it. I sought help, Nick." He leaned forward. "Denying what happened to you, what you saw, is lying to yourself, not to others."

"Why'd you bring me back?"

Gilmore fixed his eyes on Nick. "You want out?"

Nick hesitated only a moment. He understood on a deeper level that it was too late to back out even if he wanted to. "No, I'll see this through."

"The bad blood between you and Strickland is an open secret. Don't overthink the internal stuff at the Agency. I'll take care of it. If there's something going on that endangers you or the mission, I'll put a stop to it. I want you and Geoff to go in clean."

"Thank you, sir."

Gilmore's lips tightened into a decisive line. "I should have kept you off campus. Austin's office is too close."

"Sir, this place is full of spies. It wouldn't have made any difference."

Gilmore emitted an amused snort. "True enough." He set his pen on the table, his prompt that the meeting was over. "Anything else?"

"I'd like to stand up a Principle's committee. I could use the help."

"The short answer is, no. We have to keep this op black. I can't risk exposing the Curators. Or you, for that matter."

"Understood."

"Good." Gilmore stood.

Nick made his way out of the office sorting through what had just happened. He needed to talk with Geoff, but another meeting remained on his agenda. One he'd reluctantly scheduled out of necessity.

Gilmore watched Nick stop by Wendy's desk to exchange a few words before taking his leave. Both he and his secretary had taken a liking to Parkos, but he couldn't let that dissuade him from taking those precautionary measures to protect the Prague operation. He grasped the red-hashed folder, opening it to a single typed page. The brevity of the report undermined its import, and the contents left him conflicted. At one level, he'd hoped Parkos would take his offer to back out, but at another, he knew that both he and Parkos had to see the mission out.

He re-read the last, operative, paragraph:

"While there are compelling arguments to include both Parkos and Ferguson on the mission, significant risk may be incurred if Parkos discovers the connection between his father's death and Ferguson. Furthermore, I am of the belief there is more to Parkos' choice of a genealogy tour as the team's cover than mere coincidence. In the event these factors should impair the successful execution of the Operation Diagonal, I will take appropriate action."

Chapter Nine

MARRIOTT TYSONS CORNER
TYSONS CORNER, VIRGINIA
TUESDAY 21 SEPTEMBER

Nick stretched out on the huge bed of the Marriott's Executive King Suite, listening to his favorite country band. He picked out a square of Swiss cheese from the plate of snacks he had filched from the Concierge's Lounge just down the hall and popped it in his mouth. He needed time to decompress. Gilmore's admission that something was going on within the agency came as no surprise, but the confirmation did little to assuage his concerns, nor did his upcoming meeting with Taylor Ferguson.

He glanced at the bedside clock. Twenty minutes. Enough time to call Michelle with his nightly check-in. She should have the results of her finals by now. He picked up the burner Geoff had given him and entered her number.

"Hi, stranger," Michelle answered.

The sound of her voice calmed him. "Hi to you, too. How'd you do on your mid-terms?"

"Me first," Michelle said. "Wait … is that *Still Waters?*" She didn't wait for a response. "It is. You're listening to 'Stay by Me.'"

He turned down the Country Music Channel's sound on the room's TV. "Guilty as charged."

"You so totally have a crush on Jennifer."

"Not. I just think she's got a great voice."

"Uh huh."

"Have I told you that I miss you?"

"Yesterday. So, how was your day?"

"Interesting."

"Good interesting or bad interesting?"

"A bit of both." The unvoiced part of his response was that he couldn't say anything about what he was doing and talking in vague codes to Michelle made him nuts. The only redeeming factor? She understood. As a prior Presidential Flight Crew member on Air Force One, she knew the drill: Keep your mouth shut when *friends* try to pry out tidbits that would expand their Twitter hits. "Have I told you I can't stand this place?"

"More times than I can count," Michelle answered. "What happened?"

"Nothing out of the norm. How 'bout I just say, 'I miss you.'"

"That'll do for starters. I miss you, too. So does Bill. He keeps looking at your chair and meowing at me. I told him, 'Don't go talking to me like that, Mr. Cat. You gotta talk to Nick.'"

"How'd you do on your mid-terms?" Nick repeated, not wanting to think about Bill wandering around looking for him.

"I did great. So far, all A's and one B. And I aced my lab. Major Costa has really been a big help."

"How about your research?" he responded, trying to block

the mention of the handsome, single, Major Andy Costa from his mind.

"He's been encouraging me to pursue a Master's at the Squadron Officer's School. He's going to be an instructor there next year."

"How's that factor into pilot school?"

"It doesn't. Our next stop after I'm commissioned is Pueblo, Colorado. Undergrad pilot training."

"Wheww whoo. Refried beans."

"Perish the thought." Her voice brightened. "Hey, I forgot to tell you yesterday. Mom's coming for a visit. Isn't that great?"

"I'll say. When?" His reply was sincere. He really liked Michelle's mom, Melissa. They'd become close while she coped with her husband's losing battle with Alzheimer's. After his death, she'd adopted him as her own.

"The first of November. We're planning on a couple of weeks."

"You'll be well fed," he said, hoping he'd be home before Melissa left.

"You betcha. Oh, and speaking of food, I found the last of your red beans and rice hiding out in the back of the fridge. Ew. I tossed them."

"Another biohazard neutralized."

The song changed to another of his favorites. A two-step. His mind registered the quick-quick, slow-slow rhythm, his head bobbing to the beat. Michelle had overcome his resistance to learning the dance after he protested that he had two left feet and that the distance from his brain to his legs was too great. He smiled, recollecting her patient instructions. "No, your other left foot."

In the end, the dance suited him perfectly, as Michelle had insisted it would—a strong foundation of the basic steps, balanced by the 'there are no rules' style that allowed him to do whatever steps flowed from his mind. Fortunately for both of them, she was an expert dancer, who could follow his erratic steps, and lead when he lost the beat.

Michelle picked up on the new song. "We'll go dancing at Hurricane Harry's when you get home."

"You've got a date." He glanced at the bedside clock. "Dang. I've gotta go. I have a meeting."

"Now?"

"Yeah, couldn't be helped."

"All right. Take care of yourself."

"Will do."

"Love you."

"Love you too."

Ferguson would be here any minute. Nick swung his legs over the side of the bed and paused, his right hand massaging his chin. At the very least, Ferguson held his fellow men in contempt and perhaps even his own life. Nick paused in his assessment. He had first met the CIA agent in Somalia and the guy's sole focus had been on rescuing a fellow agent from a terrorist camp, even to the point of choking up with emotion. Nonetheless, he dreaded the upcoming meeting. He walked to the bathroom and splashed some water on his face, dropping the towel at the sound of the room's doorbell.

He opened the door and started at the sight of the man standing before him. *The guy had the wrong room. No.* The man he knew as Taylor Ferguson stood before him, transformed. A neatly trimmed gray beard and mustache covered his worn face and a pair of fashionable dark-rimmed, square-framed glasses offset a receding hairline. "Taylor?"

Ferguson flashed a smile. "A win for vanity, don't you think?"

"Dang. I barely recognized you."

Ferguson offered his right hand. His grip firm, assured. It meant something.

"Great look," Nick responded. "Come on in."

Chapter Nine

Ferguson's eyes swept over the two-room suite. "You must be off the shit list."

Nick raised his hands. "I—"

"Yeah," Ferguson interrupted. "The word on the street is you were burned. I know the feeling. This time around, though, both of us appear to have our asses covered."

"Appear?"

"You never know." Ferguson looked around, taking in the luxurious furnishings. "Nice. I'm also assuming you're back in the Director's good graces."

"Appears so." Nick steered Ferguson to a small conference table, wondering if he'd ever been on the Director's *shit list. Ferguson's revelation, true or not, shook him. Had that contributed to him being pushed out?* He recovered, pulled out one of the table's two chairs, and pushed a bowl of fruit to one side. His gathered up his notes and a Venn diagram that were scattered on the table.

Never one for formality, Ferguson selected a red McIntosh from the bowl, took a crunchy bite, and sat down, ignoring the other item on the table—Nick's wooden box with its faded, white imperial lion embossed on the lid. "I've done some advance work. The Station Chief has an asset in Prague who'd be ideal. She works for a legit tour agency, but moonlights."

"For?" Nick asked.

Ferguson took another bite out of the apple. "Us."

Nick cringed at the chomping and looked at the diagram, focusing on the circle inscribed, LEADER. *Who's running this damn operation. Me or Lange?* He looked at Ferguson wondering if he'd read his thoughts.

Ferguson didn't react. Not much escaped him, which was the reason why he was still with the CIA after having survived the fallout of a previous mission that had gone sideways when his source, Bashir al-Khultyer, went rogue. "Trust us, Nick. There's a lot riding on this op. That's not an excuse. We got ahead of ourselves…Yeah, we should have run this by you first."

Somewhat mollified, Nick spun his diagram around and pushed it across the table. "What do you think?"

Ferguson traced his finger over the interlocking circles, stopping on the name, Carlos Mendez. "Who's this guy?"

"A bad actor vying for dominance with the Sinaloa cartel. We've got intelligence suggesting he may be working with Král."

"To what end?"

"Unknown, but I saw something in the news where Mendez's guys ambushed a Mexican army unit."

"Weapons?"

"Maybe."

Ferguson took a last crunchy bite of the apple and set the core on a plate. "I'd say we need to get down to work."

Chapter Ten

NUMBER 10 UVOZ STREET
PRAGUE ADMINISTRATIVE DISTRICT FIVE
WEDNESDAY 22 SEPTEMBER

Lieutenant Colonel Aleksandra Kuzminova Grekov, the Federal Security Service's lead operative in Prague, capped her pen and set it on the red-leather blotter of the antique desk. She looked out the curtained window at the sweep of orange-tiled roofs. Her oak-paneled office in Administrative District Five was near the western bank of the Vltava River, a short walk from her comfortable apartment via her favorite stopover, Café Tone. "After all," she'd explained to headquarters, she had to maintain appearances as the wealthy CEO of Meycek Imports, part of the Novorossiysk Business Group.

Now an accomplished business owner, she had achieved a reasonable degree of competence running this multinational company. Like many of the foreign-owned companies in Prague that the Formative Agent, Dyna Pospisil, had guided through the Czech bureaucracy and legitimized. Meycek had lain dormant for two years, taking advantage of the laws that allowed foreign nationals who owned a business in the country to obtain Czech, and thus, European Union residency status. The *Federalnaya Sluzhba Bezopasnosti*, the FSB, had bided its time, a*t least on the surface*, she reminded herself. For the better part of the past eighteen months, she and the others in Moscow had worked tirelessly to put their plan together.

Their plan was complicated, each layer adding additional risks of discovery—or failure, she cautioned herself. The same laws that had permitted Meycek to establish a foothold in the Czech Republic, had also unwittingly permitted Prague to become home to dozens of these silent companies, many linked to transnational crime. The country had become a logistics hub for illicit drugs, human trafficking, and arms shipments throughout the world. Like many other Transnational Crime Organizations, Meycek had been invisible with no business address, financial reports, or anything else that would have exposed its very existence beyond its name.

Grekov dismissed her brooding and savored a sip of strong Russian Black Caravan tea, taking a moment to collect her thoughts. She'd been entrusted with an enormous responsibility and a number of recent developments threatened her operation. She steeled herself, accepting that these things were bound to happen, and turned back to her work.

Topping her "To Do" list was the message she'd received alerting her that an American special operations team, cryptonym Diagonal, was headed to Prague to investigate the DEA sting operation she had undermined. She frowned. The report also mentioned that Anton Král's name had surfaced as a suspect. As near as she could determine, Král was unaware of the full implications of his company, Alpite Import and Export, fronting for Moscow's initiative to provide sophisticated weaponry to the Mendez cartel. And if he was? That would be his problem.

Chapter Ten

To ensure her operation was not exposed, she'd also dealt with another risk by eliminating the reporter from the Czech Center for Investigative Journalism, Brid Krejci. Krejci had befriended Pospisil and had stumbled across a story that would have made the reporter famous within her tight circle of friends. But that knowledge had led to the reporter's untimely death at the hands of Král's assassin. Grekov's pen skipped over the next entry, the meddlesome Rajif Mohammadi, the local front man for the Iranians and their bungling efforts to arm the Mexicans, and focused on Dyna Pospisil.

Ah, and Ms. Pospisil. What to do with you? She set down her cup, knowing the answer. She, too, had served her purpose and would have to be eliminated. She turned her thoughts to the American National Security Agency employee, Ned Strickland, whom she detested. He too had served his purpose by alerting Moscow to the arrival of a clandestine American team in Prague. The alert provided her an advantage over Král, who would require extra vigilance to ensure he didn't make an amateurish move and expose her role in the arms shipment to Mendez.

Grekov picked up her pen and jotted down another name, Katerina Vasek. They hadn't been able to turn the tour director, who she suspected was doing bit work for the CIA. Under Vasek's name she wrote, "Dexter Coleman." She'd been able to disrupt the DEA's sting operation that threatened her own, discrediting him with his Washington bosses. One more name followed, one of Král's lieutenants, Julius Delezal. He was the weak link. She had decided to test him, and had her deputy inform him that an American investigative team was scheduled to arrive within the week. She would know soon enough if Delezal could be trusted.

Setting her notes aside, she picked up the message from Moscow Center about Mendez's attack on the Mexican army detachment. The Center's analysis concluded that if properly armed, Mendez would provide a credible threat to the security of the southwest United States. The final paragraph of the report was operative. She had the final authorization to proceed with her operation. President Srevnenko's patience had reached the breaking point with the American's meddling in his designs to restore the grandeur of the former Russian empire. Srevnenko would provide a counter operation to distract them. Indeed, she thought, two could play this game.

Chapter Eleven

THE NICHOLAS
3136 M STREET N.W.
GEORGETOWN, WASHINGTON D.C.
WEDNESDAY 22 SEPTEMBER

Nick took a step toward his usual chair at The Nicholas and halted mid-stride. There was a third wingback and an extra side-table forming a tight crescent in front of the hearth. He caught a glimpse of auburn hair above the new chair. An elegant hand, accented by dark-red nail polish reached for an hors d'oeuvre plate set on the table beside her. *What the...?* He glanced at Edmund. The gentleman stood discreetly to one side of the arrangement, holding a server set with two bottles of Scotch, his face a mask of pure innocence.

Geoff Lange leaned over to the stranger and said something before they both rose and approached. "Nick, I'd like you to meet the newest member of our team, Marie Lynne. Marie, Nickola Partyka."

Nick's surprise at Lange's use of his new alias evaporated

at his first sight of Lynne. *She's an absolute knockout.* Tall. A good inch taller than him. She wore calf-length brown leather boots and designer jeans, her ensemble pulled together by a stylish asymmetric buttoned jacket over a cream-colored silk blouse. Her long auburn hair was tied in a ponytail, unlike Michelle's short, regulation haircut. She'd moved with confident ease as they crossed the room to greet him. An athlete? She reminded him a bit of his friend, Jessica, at the FBI.

"Marie made a name for herself in Manila a couple years back," Lange said. "We poached her from the CIA's Special Operations Group."

Marie approached as Nick grappled with this turn of events. An unexpected scent charged the air, immersing him in an elegant fragrance. *My God. Her perfume. What is that? Bergamot?* Whatever it was, the perfume's peppery scent complemented the library's ambiance.

She offered her hand. "Hi. I'm your new wife."

Nick's jaw dropped, his own hand frozen in midair, perfume forgotten. "My what?" He glared at Lange. "I don't need a new wife!"

Lange raised his hands in supplication. "Yeah, yeah, I know. Taylor told me we may have overstepped and made a few presumptions."

"May have? Damn, Geoff. A few....?"

Marie observed the two men, a bemused smile on her face. "I guess we should have broken the news a bit more gently."

"News?" His stare switched from Marie to his friend. "Okay, I give up. What's going on?"

Lange turned to the chairs. "Perhaps we should all sit down and enjoy the Auchentoshan Edmund just poured."

Edmund emitted a discreet cough and nodded to Nick's glass. "Sir, I took the liberty to pour you a glass of our Laphroaig Ten-year, cask strength. It's from Batch 007. I believe it will pair well with your discussions."

Nick cast a curious look at Edmund, then turned his attention to the plate set on the middle table. Arranged on it was a large wedge of blue-veined Stilton cheese, English crackers, and a mound of something he didn't recognize.

"Mango chutney, sir," Edmund explained. He couldn't suppress a chortle as he eased his way by and exited down the stairs.

"I may need to try that one next," Marie said, eyeing Nick's glass.

"You like Scotch?" Nick said, trying not to stare.

"Among other things," Marie teased. She turned to Lange. "Does he always get so flustered?"

"Mostly when he's surprised."

"I suppose we did give him ample reason." She studied Geoff's cigar, then hefted her Glencairn glass. "Confusion to our enemies."

Nick struggled to recover, trying to decide how to respond to her toast. At the very least, he was confused. "Don't tell me you like cigars too?"

"Can't stand the things. Present company excepted, of course."

"Of course," he said. "Care to tell me what's going on? That might provide me at least the appearance of still being in charge."

"I suppose that means I'm up," Lange said.

"I'm listening," Nick said.

"I'll begin with a note of explanation."

"Please do."

"We figured you'd have more pressing matters to think about than how the tour group will come together. Austin suggested three couples. You and Marie. George and—"

They've been talking to Austin? Damn. He recovered. "George?" George had been his controller the past February teaching him the basics of breaking and entering, among other things. He'd also been the 'assaulter' on Geoff's team who had rescued him, breaking down the reinforced door to the carriage house where he'd been imprisoned

"You'll need his experience."

"Anybody else I know?" he demanded, ignoring the implications of including George.

"No. We felt it best to have the group mostly unknown to each other like these tour groups normally are. Figured it'd provide some realistic interplay. Getting to know each other, perhaps getting into some conflicts which would be an excuse to split up the group if someone happens to be watching."

He nodded, his anger abating. "Makes sense."

"I've worked with all the others except Marie," Lange continued. "I selected them because of their complimentary skill sets. You know what George can do."

"I'm glad to have him. What about the support team?"

"That's been trickier. We have a safe house picked out in Dresden, but the team's too big. I've got to pare it down."

Nick listened to Lange ticking off the support requirements and how best to structure the team, realizing his anger about not being in charge was misplaced. He didn't have the expertise to manage and execute this mission. The more he thought about Lange's work, the more he realized that in the past, he'd pretty much been in charge of one person: Nick. And that, he reminded himself, was challenge enough. He also recalled Gilmore's words from their first meeting. He'd said *your team*, but he had also said, *We've assembled a team*. True enough. He snuck a look at Marie, wondering how she'd fit.

Lange turned to the newest member of their team as if responding to Nick's unvoiced prompt. "Marie, what are your thoughts?"

She set down her glass and studied the glowing embers in the hearth before answering. "I wouldn't have survived in Manila if the Station Chief's team hadn't covered my ass. Will we have people in Prague? A counter-surveillance team?"

Chapter Eleven

"George and I have been working the overlook piece," Lange said. "I'm thinking of adding Vincent Cade."

George? Vinny? Nick studied the 1776 French Charleville musket mounted on the far wall. Since his last time in the club, a long bayonet had been attached. He thought the addition appropriate considering he'd been stabbed in the back, completely sidelined in an operation he was supposed to be leading.

"Vinny was another member of Nick's rescue team," Lange went on. "Considering what Nick told me about the reporter from that Organized Crime Reporting outfit—"

"The woman who was dumped in front of her agency's headquarters?" Marie asked.

"Yes," Lange said. "It'd be prudent to have a team in Prague. Vinny's prior Delta Force. He also learned Czech at the Defense Language School. We have to presume someone will be watching your group."

"Has anyone picked up her torch?" Marie asked, referring to the reporter.

"Not that we know of," Lange answered, "but if someone has, we have to steer clear of him."

"Or her," Marie amended.

Lange addressed Nick. "That brings me to another unknown, the tour director. What do you know?"

"Other than she's legit and does some moonlighting, not much."

"For the Agency?" Lange asked.

"Yeah. Taylor's running another background check. Parts of her story didn't line up."

"Maybe the Station Chief should spread some chicken feed and see if we get some playback," Marie suggested.

Lange addressed the quizzical look on Nick's face. "Marie's suggesting, we try to smoke out our tour director to see if she's a double agent. Feed her some misinformation to pass to Král that's accurate up to a point, but not particularly damaging."

"Does the Chief of Station have a deep-cover agent?" Marie asked.

Lange opened the top of his Italian humidor, the lid inlaid with exotic woods in the shape of a tobacco leaf. He chose a cigar and clipped off the end. "Unknown."

"Perhaps we should go in naked?" Marie suggested.

Naked? A totally inappropriate image of his *new wife* flashed through Nick's mind and exited just as fast.

Lange almost choked on a piece of soppressata he'd been eating, clearly trying to suppress a laugh at the expression on Nick's face. He managed to collect himself and said with bemused tolerance. "Nick, Nick. What-on-earth am I ever going to do with you?"

"What?"

"'Going in naked' means going in without cover or backup."

Nick clenched his glass, embarrassed that they had picked up on his reaction. "Yeah, I know."

"No spy could fake that reaction," Marie said. "Bringing Nick along will be all the cover I need."

Nick studied the newest member of the team. "I thought we were the ones bringing you along?"

"Details," Marie said.

He couldn't help but smile. "If you're my wife, I'll need to class up my act."

"Not necessarily."

Marie's response prompted a loud guffaw from Lange. "Okay, on that note, we're done. I believe it's safe to say you two have been introduced."

Marie reached for Nick's plate.

"Oh, no you don't," he said, making to slap her hand away. "You keep your mitts off my cheese."

"Ah, the happy couple," Lange said.

Nick ignored the comment, cut off a large chunk of Stilton and popped it into his mouth. The pungent, salty cheese melted on his tongue like softened butter. He decided this newest member of his team would be a very good fit. *La femme fatal.*

Chapter Twelve

BENEDIKTSKA APARTMENTS
OLD TOWN, PRAGUE
MONDAY 28 SEPTEMBER

By any measure, Anton Král was a handsome man, displaying few outward signs of his thirty-eight years. A dark-red ribbed sweater accentuated his broad shoulders and flat abdomen. His brown hair was cut in a fashionable comb-over fade, sideburns blending into a sculpted full beard. The beard accentuated the soft blue eyes that belied the hardened man behind them, brutalized by what had happened to his family—to all the Jewish families during the Holocaust and the Russian occupation that followed the fall of Nazi Germany.

He closed his new iPad OS Pro, reached for a Baccarat crystal decanter, and poured a generous measure of the Australian 23rd Street Distillery's Prime 5 brandy into a balloon snifter. He normally eschewed alcohol this early in the afternoon, but he, well, his financier, was close to tapping into 300 million dollars in Venezuelan government funds the United States had supposedly frozen in a monitored forfeiture account at their New York Federal Reserve Bank. He corrected himself; $289,331,020.17, to be precise.

The goal justified a celebratory drink. Not for the money per se, but for the chase. No. That was not true. He would use part of the money to restore his wife, Natálya's, family castle that dated to the fourteenth century—the castle of her ancestor, Count Vilém Patykaovi, that predated Charles IV of Bohemia. And to achieve those ends, he had made a deal with the devil. He felt no compunction admitting that his goals were not all together altruistic. If some misfortune would befall Natálya's brother, Petr Hájek, he would stand to inherit the castle. And for that reason only, he'd included Hájek in the leadership of the Král Organization

He swirled the snifter and held it up to his nose, indulging in the brandy's Interplay of vanilla, oak, and spice while looking across the shadowy back alley separating the Ketva Department store from his small business office in the Benediktska apartments. Built in the 1930's and recently refurbished, the apartment complex in Old Town was advertised as trendy. That may well be true, he thought, but at night the surrounding neighborhood was…what had he heard an American tourist call it…? *Sketchy.*

Aside from his love of brandy, Anton cared little for the trappings of luxury and planned to relocate to the tawdry Modrany district on the outskirts of Prague, known for its tall slabs of drab Soviet-era apartments. The buildings had morphed since the ouster of the Communists into clusters of anonymous gray hulks. Perfect for his needs. They would also make a good setting for a movie about the mythical Jewish monster, "The Golem of Prague." He sipped his brandy and glanced at the small carving of the monster he had set on the credenza. *Perhaps Golem should be my moniker?*

He dismissed this thought as pure foolishness, stood, and made his way to the free-standing vault set in the corner of the room. He punched in the access code and spun the spoked wheel engaging the gear drive. He heard the six heavy steel locking bolts disengage and pulled open the door, exposing a small armory, bundles of cash, and various documents. His eyes fell on an ancient silver Etrog box set on the second shelf.

He removed the object and carried it to his desk. From what he'd been told, the box would have held a yellow citron, an etrog, to be given as a Sukkot gift on the Jewish celebration day of the Sukkot. Hájek had agreed that it would be best if the family heirloom was secured in the safe. Anton smiled at the naivety of his brother-in-law. The Etrog and the objects it contained where worth far more than their weight in gold.

Anton had traced the box, now containing small relics instead of the citrus, to Natálya's and Petr's great-great grandmother, Anya Mrazik. Her first name meant "God was Gracious" or "Jehovah's Cloud," depending on whom you asked. Aside from Natálya and Hájek, nobody else knew the box's contents. He lifted a Sephardic hamza earring that could be centuries old and studied the relic linking to her family's past. He set it aside and examined two shallow blue goblets that once would have held saltwater for Seder and a tefillin, a small leather prayer box stained black with age. One of his own Jewish ancestor's would have tied a similar box to his forehead or his arm.

The year before, when Natálya had told him of the treasures, he'd opened the tefillin. It was divided into four compartments, each holding several scraps of paper inscribed in Hebrew, verses from Exodus and Deuteronomy. There were also two curious items in the box. The first, an old key with a tasseled red cord attached was of obvious import. The other, an inscribed fragment of ancient parchment, was stained a mottled brown-yellow and had been torn down the center. One day he would have it translated…when it was safe. The odds of determining what the key would have opened were low to none.

His research into Natálya's family's past had confirmed, as

near as he could determine, that Petr Hájek was the sole surviving male of his lineage after the atrocities committed by the Nazis and Communists. And what of the family castle built by Vilém Patykaovi? One day it would be his home. His family's home. He paused. As long as there weren't any remaining family other than the ancient one and Hájek's mother, Ida. And of that, he was not sure. He refocused on what he knew. Soon he would have an heir to continue the family line and he must lay the foundation for the child's future.

He replaced the box, locked the safe, and returned to his desk to review the salient points he wanted to address at the upcoming meeting with his lieutenants: Cartel shipment, NBG, mole, surveillance, Formative Agent. His plan was falling into place, but he couldn't afford to be complacent. Or, he reminded himself, to bring the others in by revealing the full details of his audacious plan and its implications for the new world order. He tapped out a thoughtful rhythm on his desktop with his index finger. His gut told him that one of his lieutenants, Julius Delezal, no matter how long the odds, may have surmised his intent.

A frown crossed his face at the thought that someone else, someone outside his organization could also derail his intricate plans: the Formative Agent, Dyna Pospisil, whose job had been to set up the fronts for his business, Alpite Import and Export, LCC. His plan had almost fallen into disarray due to her clumsiness. And, because of that clumsiness, he'd had no choice but to order the death of that reporter from the Czech Center for Investigative Journalism and the Organized Crime and Corruption Reporting Project (OCCRP) who'd nearly exposed his network and his ultimate intentions.

The reporter had befriended Pospisil and had come too close to revealing the Russian, Grekov, and connecting her to his front company. Anton had been left with no choice but to eliminate the threat. Perhaps her death would also stop the meddling from the American Drug Enforcement Agency's investigation into his operations.

Anton's enforcer, Ondrej Reznik, had silenced the reporter. He couldn't even recall the woman's name. *No, I do remember. Brid Krejci.* He paused at a fleeting moment of regret. Her first name translated to "Warrior."

Reznik had desecrated the corpse, emulating a measure taken by the Mexican cartels or that of a deranged sexual predator. Anton pushed the image out of his mind. No matter how distasteful both he and Hájek had found the atrocity, they both agreed that the probability of any of the woman's co-workers would soon be asking questions about the Král Group's affairs was remote. He'd also taken the extra precaution to ensure that his contact in the State Security Service, the StB, had dampened any investigation of the murder beyond a cursory look for appearance's sake. After all, these things happened.

His StB source, whom he had compensated for his diligence with an outrageous sum of money, also kept him appraised of any new developments pertaining to the arrest and incarceration of a major competitor, the Serbian kingpin, Radenko Ćetković, and the seizure of one ton of the Serb's methamphetamine at a Croatian port.

Anton swirled the snifter, deep in thought, pondering another possible complication. Perhaps he had moved too quickly to partner with Grekov's company, Meycek Imports and Exports, and its parent, the Novorossiysk Business Group. Initially he had thought the partnership a shrewd business decision, that is, until that damn reporter had linked Pospisil's activities to Alpite Import and Export. He'd recruited Pospisil because of her expertise in registering the foreign owners of various companies with the Czech government to obtain permanent residency status. How she'd been compromised remained a mystery. *Perhaps Reznik should have a conversation with Ms. Pospisil?*

Chapter Twelve

Anton set down the snifter and glanced at his watch at the sound of his brother-in-law entering the office. He motioned Hájek toward a chair set to his right with a sweep of his hand, a gesture reflecting his nascent jealousy. Hájek was far from handsome, his face was narrow, set off by a sharp nose, a pointed chin softened by a clipped beard, and his lips? Thin, hard set. Hájek's one redeeming feature were his deep-set brown eyes, compelling you to question what thoughts were held behind them.

"Ah, Petr, we have a few minutes to review our plans before the other's arrive." He made to pour Hájek a brandy.

"Thank you, but no," Hájek said, his response accompanied by a reticent smile. "I will be meeting Natálya for lunch."

Anton stiffened at both the rebuff and his surprise. Natálya had said nothing to him about meeting her brother. He did not care for the idea of the two meeting without him, especially if they were to compare notes about his designs on the castle.

His mind flashed to one of the few portraits remaining in the castle's gallery. Hájek could have been the man who stood in the painting, resplendent in a renaissance era red and gold patterned heavy brocade doublet with cap sleeves and cape topping a pleated garment that girded his waist. A direct descendant of Count Vilém Patykaovi.

Anton suppressed a flare of jealousy. "The others will join us any minute."

Chapter Thirteen

BENEDIKTASKA APARTMENTS
OLD TOWN, PRAUGE
MONDAY 28 SEPTEMBER

By design, Ondrej Reznik was the first of Král's lieutenants to arrive for the short meeting. Král noted Reznik's three-day stubble and newly shaved head which revealed a jagged five-centimeter scar crossing his left temple, allegedly from a knife fight. Reznik's eyes travel to the brandy decanter.

"Ah, Ondrej, please be seated," Král said without offering any. "We will talk."

Reznik looked at Hájek, who also ignored him. He dropped heavily into the room's best chair, pouting at the rejections. "What is it you want to discuss?" he asked, his tone reflecting a demand versus a question.

"Pospisil," Král countered, not giving an inch.

"I did nothing wrong. It was the others."

Král knew there were no others. He decided to play to the

man's narcissism. "You did well. I would like you to have a conversation with her." He also noted Hájek suppress a grimace at the sudden gleam in Reznik's eyes.

"That w—"

The arrival of Julius Delezal and Karel Sokol interrupted Reznik's declaration. Král toyed with the idea of offering them both a brandy to gauge Reznik's response but discarded the thought. There was nothing to be gained by antagonizing a man who stood just shy of two meters in height and one-hundred kilos…and whose last name translated to "Butcher." He waved the two men to the remaining chairs.

Julius Delezal's round face and bulging waistline had earned him the nickname, "Lazy," but his physical appearance belied his usefulness even though Král did not completely trust him. With that caveat, there was minimal risk that any task he assigned Delezal would go awry…like Reznik.

Karel Sokol's nickname, "The Falcon," also fit. Sokol's black beard softened the contours of a shrewd, pinched face. Král could count on Sokol no matter what his assignment. He addressed Sokol. "What of our dealings with Meycek?"

"This Grekov is shrewd and I've also been told she has connections with the FSB."

"Do you know of any problems I need to address?" Král asked.

Sokol appeared circumspect. "She is holding her cards close to her chest."

"You've taken her to the casinos, then?" Hájek said.

"I would not," Sokol answered. "She would know I was trying to play her. But, no, she said they are prepared to deal if we are prepared to roll the dice," Sokol responded, playing with Hájek's metaphor.

Král met Sokol's reply with a tight smile, one selected from a repertoire that he reserved for such meetings, but beneath his response lay concern. Was he prepared? He decided it best to move on. "Julius, what of our surveillance? We must assume the Americans will make a move after the amateurish bungling by our source within their embassy."

"We are watching the airport, and our source within Customs will alert me of any suspicious visitors," Delezal said.

"And the OCCRP?" Hájek asked.

Delezal glanced at Reznik before he responded. "It is safe to presume Ondrej has silenced any reporter who may have wished to continue Krejci's investigation."

"For now," Král cautioned while he held Reznik's eyes with his own, the enforcer's eyes suggesting that at the least provocation the thug would erupt in unchecked violence. He relented and broke his gaze, not wishing to unnecessarily trigger his enforcer's smoldering rage.

"I have eyes on a new tour operation, Prestige Genealogy and Heritage Tours, but have nothing solid," Delezal volunteered.

Král leaned forward, his interest perked. *How would he know that?* He had no firm indication the Americans were anything more than they professed to be, a tour group, but he wanted to explore all possibilities, including betrayal by those within his own circle. "Are they a cover?"

"A source contacted me," Delezal said. "My own background check has turned up nothing. It seems the owner is doing a bit of freelancing and started her own business."

"An entrepreneur, then. And this person's full name?" Hájek asked.

"Katerina Vasek," Delezal said. "Perhaps she can be turned."

The name meant nothing to Král. He tapped is pen on his desk and chose to end the meeting without addressing the remaining items on his list, not commenting further on Delezal's revelation. Perhaps he'd stumbled across something, but the odds were long. "Then, we are done, my friends. I commend you all for your efforts. And Petr," he added,

Chapter Thirteen

dismissing his brother-in-law as well. "I believe you have another meeting."

Král rubbed his chin in thought after the four left, considering another business opportunity, the unlikely alliance he had forged across the Atlantic. One he did not plan to share with his brother-in-law who would undoubtedly reject it. He'd made a deal with someone who'd fashioned himself after the *Tlatoani*, an ancient meso-American leader who could best be described as an amalgam of Commander in Chief and head priest. He pondered the title. This alliance could well have unknown consequences.

A son of history, Král had read about the infamous Zimmermann Telegram. While the United States strove to remain neutral during the European war of 1914, Germany's Foreign Minister, Arthur Zimmermann, had proposed a secret alliance with Mexico. His telegram to his ambassador in Mexico City was intercepted by the British, who, in turn, passed it to the Americans. The message contained the details of his proposal that Mexico align itself with Germany and receive funding, munitions, and diplomatic support to regain their territories lost during the Mexican-American War of 1846.

The incentives for Mexico at the time were great. The country had lost one third of its territory. Territory that now included significant parts of the States of Texas, Arizona, New Mexico, Utah, and Nevada. It was this history that Mendez was drawing on to foment rebellion and further his own cause.

Král had also sensed an opportunity following the chaos of the recent U.S. elections tainted by interference from China, Russia, and Iran. He held no personal animosity toward the Americans, but Mexico's President Salazar was weak, his government in disarray, the loyalty of his military and the Federal Police problematic. And Carlos Mendez had positioned himself to force the issue, having fashioned himself as the supreme leader of a resurgent Mexican State. The root of his name translated to: Son of Mexico.

He leaned back in his chair, cautioning himself. This Mexican and those who chose to deal with him were not to be trusted—nor was Hájek. While he'd invited Hájek into the business, he could not dismiss his doubts about his brother-in-law's loyalty.

Chapter Fourteen

RESTAURANT ZVONICE
JINDRISSAKÁ TOWER, NEW TOWN
SATURDAY 10 OCTOBER

Petr Hájek jogged across the street, slowing at the base of the Gothic-era Jindrisšaká Tower. Multiple venues nestled within its ancient walls, including one of his and Natálya's favorite restaurants, Zvonice. He took the elevator to the eighth floor and made his way to their preferred table located in the far corner under a dark-beamed oak gable, overlooking Prague Castle. Natálya awaited, a bottle of Armand de Brignac Brut and two glasses set by her right hand.

Natálya looked fantastic. Her cobalt-blue ensemble amplified the colors of her raven- black hair and expressive, clear-blue eyes—eyes that pulled you in. But there was something else about her today; she looked radiant. He leaned over and gave her a light kiss on her cheek before taking his seat. *"Jak se má moje oblíbená sestra?"*

"I'm your only sister. And to answer your question, I am fine."

"Just fine? You look fantastic and you've ordered a bottle of Champagne."

She reached for his hand. "I have news. Something to celebrate."

"Oh, and what could that be?"

"I am pregnant."

Her three words staggered him. He managed to recover, abandoning what he had planned to discuss with her, and motioned for their waiter. While he understood the nature of his brother-in-law's business, Král's latest revelations about the reporter, Brid Krejci, had left him shaken. What else hadn't Anton told him?

Petr sought to bury his misgivings. His concerns about his sister's husband and whatever other dealings he'd kept hidden would have to wait, perhaps indefinitely. "Then we must celebrate." He paused as they both watched the waiter wrap the bottle in a white cotton towel. "But can you…?"

"Just this once. And only one glass," she said to the pop of the cork.

"Have you talked to Mom and Pádriac?"

"I plan to drive to the castle on Monday." She paused. "Is there something troubling you?"

Petr collected himself. She'd always been able to read his face. What troubled him—what troubled both of them, was the future of the family line and the fate of the castle. Their mother, Ida, then an infant, had been spirited away from the advancing Nazis by a sympathetic Christian family just before Ida's own parents and her brothers, Pádriac and Jakub, were sent to the Theresienstadt Ghetto. When Ida's own parents had perished in the camp, all knowledge of her whereabouts had disappeared. Ultimately, Ida had made her way back to Prague and married, but her husband had died prematurely, a continuation of the string of family tragedies that further decimated what was left of the family.

"There is much to think about," Petr replied to her

appraising look, "but now, we must celebrate." He lifted his glass. "*Na zdravi vase i vaseho miminka.*"

Natálya rewarded his toast to her and her baby's health with a radiant smile. "Thank you, brother." She took a sip of the champagne then pointed to his menu. "I've already selected. The Preštic piglet with morel sauce beckoned."

"That is hardly kosher," Petr quipped.

"It is another of God's foods. I don't consider it *trief.*"

"Then I will order the pork tenderloin with blackberry sauce and flat pancakes."

She chatted happily of family while they lingered over desert, but his thoughts were morose. When he and Natálya were gone from this world, her child would stand to inherit the family castle—Castle Král. Could he justify in his mind Anton's bad deeds balanced by good intentions? Perhaps, but there was no truth in that. He suppressed a shudder. He must find a way to thwart Král. He could not permit him to inherit the castle and, with it, his own family's heritage.

Chapter Fifteen

MARRIOTT TYSONS CORNER
TYSONS CORNER, VIRGINIA
SATURDAY 10 OCTOBER

Nick set his new Samsonite suitcase on the bed, packing for the next afternoon's KLM flight to Prague. He hesitated at the remaining item. Should he take the oak keepsake box or have Austin send it back to Michelle? He had no idea of the contents, but the ancient crest suggested his family's connection to nobility, and his quest for his family, for his own identity that were a large part of his ultimate decision to lead this mission to Prague.

His hand lingered, then set the box aside. If his new partner, Marie, knew what he was doing—well, he wasn't sure what she would do. She'd likely conclude the box would be a distraction and impact the execution of their mission. *Well, so what?. The Agency owed him one.* Besides, the quest for the contents of the box would provide a legitimate cover for the operation. He placed it in his carry on.

Chapter Fifteen

Packing done, Nick headed down the hall to the Concierge's Lounge with his laptop, tour package, and the Le Vin notebook containing his genealogy research. He'd filled in a few blanks by tapping the Agency's resources as well as exploring the links on the Ellis Island Foundation and the Genealogy website. He'd used his alias, Nikola Partyka, making sure he'd left a digital trail on the hotel's Wi-Fi in case somebody was tracking his new identity.

He pondered, once again, why he'd really accepted the mission to Prague. There would be no question in his mind that he would find the answer to Gilmore's tasking, the risk posed to his country, and he would clear his name. But he would also pursue the shrouded history of his family and perhaps discover a clue about what had happened to his father.

He showed his room key to the maître de hotel guarding the Lounge's door, found an open table by the windows overlooking the courtyard and settled into his chair, then opened the folder from Prestige Genealogy and Heritage Tours.

Austin had done an incredible job of creating their front company, including a Web page and the tour packet: "Discover the formative elements of your family's past. We specialize in the exploration of out-of-the-way places and the fascinating history of the Czech Republic."

Nick's last conversation with his father flashed through his mind. His own history remained obscure. After a night of drinking, his dad had once mumbled something about his grandparents having to change their family name when they emigrated to the United States in 1948, settling in Greenville, Indiana. He'd also mentioned something vague about making their name more pronounceable, more American. His father had never offered any explanation of what had happened to his own parents.

But those weren't the only gaps in his life. Nick's mother had died days before his fifth birthday, and he'd essentially been orphaned when his dad had also disappeared from his life. What had tormented him over the years was that he had no recollection of his mother, just a few pictures that failed to stir any memories except for the one—a faded Polaroid of a little boy standing next to his mommy, happily holding up a pastry for the camera to see.

Nick stifled an unexpected sob. *What had happened to her?* His dad had never said, and Nick's own searches had ended in frustration. Her absence in his life haunted him and, like so many other children who'd lost a parent, he blamed himself for her death, not knowing if she had died of cancer, or some other disease, or even an accident. In his darkest hours, he even wondered if she'd ended her own life because of something he had done, a thought that left him adrift in guilt.

He blocked out the memories and the noise from the late-night, west coast college football game blaring from the flatscreen in the adjacent room. His best bet to finding the answers to his family's history was to use the same analytic processes he'd used in his old job investigating Balkan TCOs. *So, where do I start? With what I know.*

One known was that he'd been named after his great-grandfather, Nikola. But his grandfather's surname? Partyka? Not Parkos. There had to be more than what his father had said. Why the change? One of his searches on Genealogy had traced his family's surname to another name: Petr Patykaovi. Irrespective of the spelling, could this man be his great-great-grandfather? Nick chewed on his pen pondering the unknowns. His family's origins remained frustratingly obscure.

He put down his macerated pen and typed in a search on the Ellis Island Foundation's website, an incredible resource for those tracing their origins. The site offered passenger lists; immigrant documents; birth, death, and marriage certificates; and arrival records. The amount of information available was overwhelming. But if you had the time—which he didn't— you could find answers to the nagging questions that plagued

Chapter Fifteen

your consciousness. Time notwithstanding, he decided to begin with a search of arrival records focusing on the 8th of June 1948. The motor vessel, *Roma* caught his eye.

What he found on the ship's passenger manifest verified what his father had said. His grandparents and an infant–his father–had arrived at Ellis Island on the Cosulich Lines vessel *Roma*. The ship's manifest also listed his grandparents as Moravian. A clue to his family's origins. That is, he cautioned himself, if his grandfather hadn't lied on the application.

The emigration documents substantiated what he'd discovered. Nick wrote down the probable ages of those family members he'd found to verify the various generations. But there was still a huge gap in his family tree. What had happened to his great-grandparents? And why had his grandparents changed their name? Were any of his relatives still alive and could he find them?

Another conversation he'd had with his dad surfaced from the recesses of his mind. One he'd tried to suppress. He'd once said to his father, *"You're never satisfied with me, so I've never been satisfied with myself no matter what I do."* To which his dad had responded: *"You are my son. You must be better than me."*

And what of his father? After his mother died, he had disappeared. Years later, when Nick was able to understand, someone had told him: "Your father was the victim of a carefree life." *What did that even mean?*

Nick didn't have many memories from his early life, except for one more, a faded picture of a sad little boy clutching his Star Wars lunch box on his first day of school. He polished off his bourbon, the antidote for the sorrow filling his heart. All that remained in the glass was a melting, solitary ice cube. The finality seemed fitting. He remained in the shadows of his family's past, his past. Or so it seemed if he surrendered to the unknowns of his own life. He braced himself, gathered up his things, and returned to his room intent on calling Michelle.

Chapter Sixteen

VÁCLAV HAVEL INTERNATIONAL AIRPORT
PRAGUE, CZECH REPUBLIC
MONDAY 12 OCTOBER

Nick watched the uniformed officer stationed at *Celní Kontrola* stamp his passport after asking him the routine questions: "Reason for your visit to the Czech Republic? How long do you intend to stay? Where will you be staying?"

The agent studied Nick's face, stamped his passport, and handed it back after confirming his return flight to the States on the twenty-eighth. "Welcome to the Czech Republic, Mr. Partyka. Enjoy your stay."

What made this entire drill tolerable was that KLM's World Business Class service had exceeded his expectations, leaving him well-rested. He made his way to baggage claim with a shake of his head, where, to his great relief, neither the customs officials nor their dogs alerted on his keepsake box. He grabbed his bag, caught up with Marie, and headed for the exit.

Chapter Sixteen

They made a beeline toward a waving sign inked with large black letters: Partyka, Prestige Tours. The sign waver stepped forward to greet them. "Mr. and Mrs. Partyka? Welcome to Prague. I am your tour director, Katerina Vasek. It is a pleasure to meet with your acquaintance."

He could barely speak; she was the very definition of a classic Slavic beauty. Thin, fair skin, light brown hair, strong cheekbones, a nose that some might consider a bit long. She wore minimal makeup, just enough lipstick and eyeshadow to accentuate her mouth and intense green eyes—like Michelle's. He managed to utter a few polite words. *"Rád vás poznávám."*

Vasek smiled, revealing a set of perfect teeth. "Ah, you speak Czech. And Mrs. Partyka?"

"I'm afraid not," Marie answered. "Nikola will speak for the both of us."

He cast Marie a quick look. *Yeah, if that were only true.*

Marie returned his skeptical look with an adoring one of her own, prompting him to roll his eyes.

Vasek tossed a beckoning wave at a man in chauffeur's attire standing beside a black Mercedes CLA Coupe. "Dusa will take care of your bags," she said flashing an enigmatic smile, while ushering them to the car. There is bottled water in the console if you are thirsty."

He gave Dusa a quick once-over, as did Marie. The driver was a detail they'd overlooked, but he couldn't worry about that now. He'd call Geoff later.

"Did you have a pleasant flight?" Vasek asked as they pulled away from the curb. "If you are not too tired, I will give you a preview of our beautiful city. Not the tourist traps. It's just a little out of our way, but well worth the extra time." She didn't wait for a response. "Dusa, the Staré Mēsta."

Nick translated. "Old Town."

Vasek provided a running commentary as Dusa wove through the congested quarter's worn cobbled streets, whose origins dated to the 12th century. Nick was transfixed by the

Gothic architecture and the pastel colors of the buildings. He tried to imagine what life would have been like hundreds of years ago, any sense of danger far from his mind.

He caught a glimpse of the Mihulka Powder Tower, an anchor of the town's early fortifications and one of its original thirteen gates. *Perhaps members of my family passed through its portal?* His musings were cut short as they passed over the Vlatava River on a modern span. In the distance loomed the city's famous Charles Bridge.

"This is New Town," Vasek said as they crossed the river heading west. "Its origins can be traced to the fourteenth century. Perhaps it is not so new, yes?"

Nick gazed at the passing vistas swarming with tourists sensing a sudden undercurrent of tension. New Town's name stuck him as appropriate. A city, perhaps, still searching for its identity after the bedlam it had endured over the past eight decades. Within this context, Prestige Tours was ideal. Their tour was not designed for those American tourists seeking the sterile make-believe foundation of their lives. A Transylvanian city of horrors. What troubled him was that they were heading away from their hotel. *Why?* He kept swiveling his gaze from one side of the car to the other, alert for anything suspicious, only relaxing his vigil when Dusa reversed direction back toward Old Town and their hotel.

His first impression of the Alcron Hotel was its discordant design. The Art Deco property's façade and the adjacent buildings on Stepánská Street were a fusion of styles. And the one immediately to the hotel's left? Its stonework was a weird orange color that reminded him of the old marshmallow Circus Peanut candies he'd eaten as a kid.

Vasek noted Nick studying the building. "That is the Galeria Lucerna. The interior is breathtaking. We shall see it tomorrow morning before we begin to explore the rest of the city. Ah, here we are."

Appearances could indeed be deceiving. He suppressed a groan, climbed out of the van, and made his way past a silver and black Bentley and a top-hatted doorman into the hotel's lobby. The interior's Art Deco design appealed to him. The photos on the internet did not do the lobby nor their two-room junior suite justice.

"Good lord," Nick blurted at his first sight of their surprisingly modern room. "You think this is big enough?"

"I guess," Marie responded before making her way to the bedroom.

He caught sight of the king bed from the door. "I'll take the couch."

"You sure?" Marie answered.

"Very."

"Flip for it?"

"Best two out of three," he agreed.

Two flips later, Marie looked at her watch, having won the king. "We've got over five hours until we meet the others. How about we unpack and get acquainted with the neighborhood?"

"I don't suppose we have to hold hands?"

"Nope," Marie said over her shoulder. "You want the top or bottom dresser drawers?"

"Doesn't matter."

"Well, then. We're off," Nick said, heading for the door after unpacking. "How 'bout we take a look at the Galeria?"

"Great idea," Marie said. "I'm not sure we need to spend our first morning tied up in a museum."

HOTEL ALCRON
RESTAURANT LA ROTONDE

"Well, here goes. Kick off," Nick said as they approached the La Rontonde restaurant's maître d'hôtel podium.

"Our chaperone awaits," Marie said.

He wondered at her word choice. *Chaperone?*

Vasek greeted them with two glasses of champagne. "Good evening, Partykas. Shall we join the others?"

Nick paused. "Katerina, Marie and I used our open time to visit the Galeria."

Vasek met his statement with a wisp of a frown, then brightened. "We have so much more to see. If the others wish to see the museum, I will make arrangements." With that, she escorted them to a quiet table in the far corner of the restaurant, where two other couples were chatting. Both gave polite nods to Nick and Marie.

"Now that we are all assembled," Vasek opened, "let me introduce everyone. Nick and Marie Partyka from Washington D.C., this is Tom and Ann Balek from Chicago. And for our tour," she added for clarification, "Tom said he would like to go by Tomáš. Yes?"

"Yes," Tomáš affirmed as he lifted his glass in a welcoming salute. "Ann and I thought it might be fun to use my old family name."

Nick studied the couple. As Lange had planned, he didn't recognize either of them. Tomáš, as he called himself, stood in a relaxed stance. A set of bushy eyebrows perhaps a bit too big for his face topped dark eyes that conveyed he was ready to react to any threat. Ann was a petite brunette with long fashionable bangs framing intelligent, observant eyes. Nick suspected nothing much escaped her. She too, could be Slavic. They were matched well.

Chapter Sixteen

"And this is Adam and Jennifer Myska from Atlanta," Vasek said.

Jennifer flashed a radiant smile. "I don't suppose you two are Falcon's fans?"

"I'm afraid not," Marie said. "Nickola graduated from Ohio State. We're Buck Nuts."

"Ah," Jennifer said a deep, southern accent. "I suppose we can make allowances."

Nick was impressed. Not only would Jennifer be fun, she looked as if she could easily take care of herself in case of trouble. He offered his hand to George, one of the men who had helped rescue him in their prior mission, pulling him a bit closer. "You've got your nickname."

"What are you talking about?" George whispered back.

"*Myška* is Czech for *Mouse*," he replied a bit too loudly.

"Yes, I must agree," Vasek affirmed, looking at the six-foot, muscular man. "I think it is a good, funny name for you."

Marie hefted her glass. "To our Mouse."

George cut off an expletive, but he wasn't the only one who suppressed a swear word. Nick chastised himself over his gaff. Vasek had overheard his comment. He'd have to exercise more caution. For a supposed first encounter, he'd been overly familiar.

Vasek saved him, directing the conversation back to Tom. "Tomáš, it appears you are enjoying the music. It is Martinů."

"Yes. His Fourth Symphony. A masterful work, although I prefer Jan Zelenka, a contemporary of Bach. His Missa Votiva in E minor is sublime."

A look of delight lit Vasek's face. "*České, hudebník.*" She translated the Czech saying alluding to her countrymen's love of music. "'The Czech, the musician.' We will have to adjust our city tour to show you our Museum of Music."

Nick shared her surprise. This guy knew his music or had really done his homework. Probably both.

"Do you sing as well, Tomáš?" Vasek asked.

"Only in the beer halls."

She responded with an easy laugh. "You have the makings of a true Czech."

"But we shall have to speak in English," Tom added.

Nick noted Marie take Jennifer to one side, speaking quietly to her. He took a sip of champagne, concluding that on first impressions, they had the makings of a good team. They'd better. They only had sixteen days. Marie confirmed his assessment when she made her way back to his side.

"Jennifer's spent time with the Agency and has a blackbelt. I wouldn't mess with her."

"What? Me?" Nick protested. "Not a chance. I've already got two wives."

Chapter Seventeen

SAFEHOUSE
OBERGRABEN STRASSE, INNERE NEUSTADT
DRESDEN, GERMANY
MONDAY 12 OCTOBER

Geoffrey Lange leaned his bicycle against the wall next to the apartment complex's front door. The light-gray limestone building was set along a tree-lined street of colorful baroque townhomes only a short walk from the Elbe River. The surrounding neighborhood with its restaurants, wine bars, and trendy shops reminded him of Georgetown.

He had decided it best not to accept the Station Chief's offer of the Agency's safehouse. Instead, he had opted for the unobtrusive two-bedroom flat advertised by Airbnb's European branch. Besides keeping the whereabouts of his support team and its location secret from the Embassy staff, many of the adjacent flats in his unit also appeared to be rentals. His team's appearance would be accepted by the locals as just another group of tourists.

He took several steps before halting at the vibration of his iPhone. He pulled the device from his pants pocket and slid the bar to connect. *"Ja?"*

"I got confirmation of our friend's message."

"Danke." He disconnected and locked the bike while checking to see if anyone had followed him. Obergraben Strasse held no surprises. He recognized the cars parked along the narrow street and waved to a neighbor before making his way up to their third-floor flat. A quick glance down the hall verified he was alone before he inserted the room key in the lock and pushed open the door. "Damn, Edmund. You planning on a night out on the town?"

Edmund stood before him, attired in a vintage three-piece single breasted, two-button brown tweed jacket, matching waistcoat and trousers, light lavender shirt and a patterned silk tie. Completing his outfit was a pair of polished brogue shoes, all from the exclusive outfitter, Stewart Christie of Edinburgh. The look of the tailored, dark-brown herringbone pattern with hints of burnt-red and peacock-green? Effortless. Smart.

In truth, Geoff expected no less from the dapper, Edmund MacDonald, doorman of The Nicholas. There was much more to the man than his cover at The Nicholas and his clothier suggested.

Sergeant Edmund MacDonald, B Squadron, 22nd Special Air Services Regiment, had been awarded the Military Medal for gallantry on a deep insertion mission into central Iraq during the First Gulf War. He declined to discuss his time in Iraq, his wound, or the source of his considerable bank account. None-the-less, Lange trusted him implicitly.

"Guten abend, mein heir," MacDonald said, unfazed by Geoff's reaction. He hefted a tumbler of whisky in greeting. *"Möchten sie mit uns ein getränk trinkin?"*

Geoff recognized the greeting and the word *drink*. He replied in one of the few words of German he knew, hoping he'd conveyed his desire for a stiff drink. *"Danke."*

Chapter Seventeen

"*Sie haben die Frauleins verfolgt, jah?*" Vinny Cade asked from his place of repose.

MacDonald burst out laughing. "*Nein, falsches Geschlecht.*"

"I don't suppose you care to translate?" Geoff asked, addressing the second member of his team. Sprawled in an overstuffed chair, one leg draped over an arm, Vinny sported a huge Cheshire Cat grin at the exchange.

"Nope." Vinny couldn't suppress a chuckle at Geoff's discomfort.

Geoff cocked his head. *Vinny spoke German in addition to his fluent Czech?* He screwed up his lip, acknowledging they were one up on him. He remained at their mercy. *Damn.* Without a clue of what they'd said, it didn't take great insight to understand he'd been the butt of a great joke. "Okay, knock it off. Where's Taylor?"

"Grocery shopping," Vinny answered.

"He's doing what?"

"Are we to survive on beer and bratwurst?" Edmund asked, with an aggrieved look on his face.

Vinny relented. "Nah, he's out doing whatever the hell he does."

Geoff nodded, surmising the answer to the, '*Whatever the hell he does,*' reference.

"While you were out, Nick contacted us," Edmund added while he poured Lange a tumbler of Arran 10 Year whisky. "Asked us to check out their chauffeur. Guy named Dusa."

Geoff set his tumbler on a coffee table. "Not much to go on. Got a last name?" The query about Dusa troubled him. There were too many moving pieces, and despite being on the ground in Dresden for two weeks, he still didn't have a firm grasp on all the players and where they fit into the puzzle. Král and this Dusa guy topped his list for, "Persons of interest." Someone had to be passing information that was allowing Král to stay one step ahead of their operation. Was it Dusa or someone in the embassy? In any event, Nick had to watch his step. The cartels showed no compunction in eliminating any threat, be it real or perceived, to their operations.

"He sent a pic."

Geoff started at MacDonald's voice. "What?"

"Nick sent a pic of the chauffeur," MacDonald repeated. "Taylor's running a check on him. I suspect he's meeting with the Station Chief."

"What about the background they ran on Vasek?" Geoff responded, passing over Edmond's probable guess and the implications. That was a good move by Ferguson. "He may be able to eliminate one of our variables."

Edmund topped off his glass. "Clean. Wish a could say the same for the whisky. I'm afraid it's not up to scratch."

"What about the Laphroaig you brought?"

Edmund gave a shake of his head and replied in his natural Highlander's brogue. "Auch. That's gaun to Nick. I'm thinkin' he's aboot to be needin' it."

Vinny heaved himself out the chair and grabbed a Bavarian pretzel and a pot of brown mustard from the dining table. "We have enough to stir things up?"

Geoff hefted the full glass to his lips. "Not yet, but Nick may have gotten just enough to smoke them out." With Vasek eliminated as a potential problem, he'd have to sit down with Ferguson and see what they could come up with to entice a possible mole to slip up and expose himself.

Vinny dipped his pretzel into the pungent mustard and took a bite. "How's that?" he asked between chews.

"I met our cutout while biking," Geoff said. "Guy in full cycling gear. Had the brushoff when he pulled up next to me at a stoplight."

"Recognize him?" MacDonald asked.

"Nope." Geoff unfolded the slip of paper he'd been passed and handed it over. "The guy was smooth. Nick has the go-ahead to approach the DEA's lead agent in Prague. Dexter Coleman."

Chapter Seventeen

"Whoa," Vinny reacted. "From what little I know about that guy, I wouldn't trust him any farther than I could throw him."

"I suspect you could throw him a fer distance," Edmond said. "And furthermore, I don't like the idea of using Nick or the team as bait to smoke out the bad guys."

"I can't say I disagree with either of you," Geoff said.

Geoff looked a Vinny. "Pack your bags. We've got to watch Nick's Six." There was also more to his concern. He knew Nick's history; his wounds, both mental and physical still festered, and if unbound, they could be his friend's and the mission's undoing.

Chapter Eighteen

STARÉ MESTA
PRAGUE, CZECH REPUBLIC
TUESDAY 13 OCTOBER

Nick craned his neck to examine "'The Hanging Man,'" one of the Old City's iconic bronzes. He appreciated the artistry and the message it conveyed. The work wasn't another sterile set-up to attract the tourists.

"Sigmund Freud is Czechoslovakian, not German as most think," Katerina Vasek explained to her attentive group. "His place of birth is Príbor, east of here near the Polish border." She gestured to the bronze. "The artist has depicted him dangling by his left arm from that long pole, seemingly pondering whether to hang on or let go. It is an image drawn from one of Freud's own phobias, the fear of his own death."

Nick studied "The Hanging Man," pondering the story and his own fears. Foremost? His fear that he wouldn't be able to stop Král. A close second? What he might find out about his family. He glanced over his shoulder at their Mercedes

Chapter Eighteen

Sprinter van. Dusa stood curbside next to the front door patiently waiting for them to leave for their next stop. He couldn't get a read on the muscular chauffeur and hadn't heard back from the Dresden support team.

Exasperated, he pursed his lips, blocking out Vasek's voice. The tour was all well and good, and she was pleasant and informative, but these attributes didn't put him any closer to finding the answer to Gilmore's order. *Find out what's going on, then eliminate the threat.*

The only guidance he had received so far was that he had the go-ahead to approach Dexter Coleman, the DEA's lead agent in Prague. Nick rolled a kink out of his neck and looked down the street, concluding that meeting might not be so wise if it exposed his entire operation. But the overriding consideration? Another day had been ticked off their travel visas and he didn't want to face questions from Marie or the others on why he hadn't made any progress. Perhaps his meeting with Coleman would get things moving.

"Shall we go on to our next stop?" Vasek said, ushering the group toward the van. "We are to see the famous Golden Lane and its ancient shops. You may recognize the street. Parts of your *Knightfall* series were filmed there. Then we're off to Castle Prague and the Daliborka Tower before we stop for lunch."

Her mention of *Knightfall* was met with quizzical looks, so she clarified. "It is a Netflix series about the Knights Templar and their search for the Holy Grail."

Nick decided to bail her out, eager to get moving. "M…" He caught himself before he said, Michelle. "Marie and I have watched it."

He shot a glance at George, who returned his look with a subtle shake of his head, sharing his frustration. The women appeared to be doing better at containing their thoughts, as was Tom. Then he noted Tom hanging back. *Am I imagining, or has he seen something?*

Nick was grateful when Vasek whisked them through the Golden Lane, perhaps sensing that her group wanted to move on to Prague Castle and the Tower. That was a positive, but he still didn't have any idea what had caught Tom's attention.

"The Tower dates to the late fifteenth century and is a source of legend," Vasek said. "It is named after its first prisoner, Count Dabiboka of Kozojedy. The Count was imprisoned for sheltering rebellious serfs who fled from the cruelty of a neighboring nobleman. Such behavior, while perceived as noble in our time, could not be tolerated in his."

Nick suppressed a groan at her inadvertent pun but didn't see anybody else react.

"And Nikola?" she added for his benefit. "The Count had an alleged accomplice who escaped imprisonment. Count Vilém Patykaovi." She paused, adding to the dramatic effect of her statement. "Perhaps he could be a distant relative, yes?"

Nick's attention was yanked from his examination of the castle's battlements by Vasek's revelation. He suddenly felt adrift, keeping the fragments of his past alive while trying to remain focused on his mission. Underlying this flood of mixed emotions was the fact that he understood, at some point, that he had to escape the bonds of his past: The scars of being orphaned, the conflicted feelings of seeking out friendships and then being rebuffed. Michelle had been a stabilizing factor in his life, but he still had no firm idea of where life would lead him.

A line from one of Michelle's favorite country comedians flashed through his mind. "Where will you be when you get where you're going?" He could hear Jerry Clower's southern accent as he recited the line in one of his monologues.

Vasek cast Nick a flirtatious look. "Perhaps I can assist you with a search of our archives?"

Chapter Eighteen

Marie picked up on Vasek's offer and the look before he could respond. "Why, thank you. We'd love to."

Their tour guide's tight smile conveyed her reaction to Marie's protective response. Vasek collected herself and replied stiffly, "Of course. Perhaps tomorrow afternoon? Your husband might also like to delve into the history of Patykaovi Castle?"

"A castle?" Nick repeated.

"Why, yes. There may be a connection to your family's past."

"Nikola, darling." Marie gave him a tug on his elbow. "We must catch up to the others."

Nick wondered if Marie had missed the mention of the castle and changed his focus. Ann and Jennifer had wandered away, while George…. he caught himself. He had to use George's and Tom's aliases within earshot of Vasek … Adam and Tomáš appeared to be discussing the castle's terracotta-colored roof. Marie seemed distracted by something she'd seen. *What the…?* Tom had spun on his heel and was taking a series of panoramic pictures with his iPhone.

"I have obtained exclusive tickets for the tower," Vasek said waving them in the air. "Please follow me."

Nick couldn't suppress a shiver and grabbed the railing as they descended a series of narrow limestone steps slicked with a sheen of water into a vaulted, claustrophobic chamber deep within the tower.

"This is the infamous dungeon," Vasek said, leading them to what appeared to be a well.

He took a hesitant step toward the gaping hole in the floor. Suspended above the black void of the opening was a sinister creature. Shackles were attached to its wrists and ankles, chains represented the thing's arms and legs, and a seat-like leather apparatus, the torso. These were all topped by an iron mask with a skull set inside. The entire apparatus was affixed to a pulley system attached to a ring in the ceiling.

"Of course, the skull is for effect, but the apparatus and pulley are not," Vasek explained. She leaned over the void and gave the device's rope a sharp, rattling jerk to emphasize her point. "The unfortunate prisoner would be lowered into the oubliette, a secret room whose only access was this opening."

Of course, Nick thought, tensing at the other displays scattered around the room and visualizing what life would have been like for his ancestors and their struggle for survival. They were surrounded by metal cages, assorted torture devices, and two gruesome tables festooned with sharpened iron spikes affixed to rollers. Leaning against the far wall were a half-dozen long wooden poles with half-moon shaped devices affixed to their ends. A chain secured with a rusted lock formed a sort of noose.

"Those are Leading Forks," Vasek explained. "The tables are problematic. They and the cages were placed here for the tourists. The forks were not. They were fastened around a prisoner's neck to lead him from place to place."

Nick had seen enough. He headed for the stairs. Before he could ascend them, Tom caught him by the arm and pulled him around a corner.

"We've got a watcher."

Nick nodded. "Same guy as yesterday?"

"Yeah."

"Crap," Nick said. "That didn't take long. I'll call Lange and have him set up counter-surveillance."

Chapter Nineteen

CHARLES BRIDGE
PRAGUE, CZECH REPUBIC
WEDNESDAY 14 OCTOBER

Nick stepped out from under the Alcron Hotel's portico into a cold, overcast morning punctured by intermittent rain showers. He set off for the Charles Bridge, hoping the rain would hold off. Marie had wanted to go with him, but he had declined, saying he didn't want to expose her or the team to any unnecessary danger or the risk of discovery. He said he'd catch up with them later and asked her to make his excuses to Vasek for missing the scheduled tour. He also needed time to think. He only had fourteen more days to come up with an answer to Gilmore's admonishment and, so far, he had nothing. Perhaps this meeting that Ferguson had facilitated would provide a clue.

He made his way to Liliová Street, passing an outdoor café with several couples enjoying their caffe lattés and pastries.

The café's single line of tables with their red-and-white checked tablecloths provided a splash of color to the dreary stone facades of the encroaching buildings. What sun there was hadn't yet penetrated the gloom of the narrow, twisting street. He looked at the dull reverse image of the neighborhood reflected in the café's windows and caught sight of a fleeting shadow. He didn't spot anything more and moved on to the next store where he again pretended to look at the window display. Something didn't feel right, but he couldn't place what was setting him on edge.

Nick increased his vigilance and proceeded down the block, turning left on Karlova, the street leading directly to the Charles Bridge and his rendezvous. A heraldry plaque portraying a twisted serpent embossed in bright-gold on a deep-blue background greeted him as he rounded the corner. Beside the plaque, a sign advertised yet another small museum: The Mad Barber of Prague. The image on the sign depicted a medieval man wielding a straight-edge razor about to slit the throat of an unsuspecting customer seated in his barber chair. Nick cast another look around, pulled up the collar of his Bomber jacket, and picked up his pace.

His eyes were drawn to the nearest of the Charles Bridge's three towers at the river's edge. The tower's decorative stonework was exquisite, replete with carvings of the Saints that reminded him of the baroque cathedrals of France. While not particularly religious, he made the sign of the cross.

He passed under the portico of the monumental gate, encountering a scattering of milling tourists and several early-morning hawkers setting up their stands. Nick ignored both as he counted down the arches of the ancient bridge, looking for a statue of the Crucifiction, one of thirty sculptures lining the causeway.

Dexter Coleman had left a coded message for him at the hotel the night before on where to meet and what he would be

Chapter Nineteen

wearing. That wasn't much help, since everyone appeared to be dressed the same. He slowed when he spotted the statue of Christ on the Cross, the two Mary's standing vigil at his feet.

His eyes darted toward a man clutching a loaf of bread in his right hand approaching from the opposite direction, his left leg brushing against the bridge's low retaining wall. The man slowed and stopped by Nick's left shoulder, tore a piece of bread from his loaf, and tossed it into the river.

"Partyka?" the man whispered to the river.

Nick nodded. The man matched the description he'd been given. A gust of wind caught his contact's hair, blowing a thick strand across his forehead. The man reached up and brushed it back into place, revealing intelligent brown eyes.

The man identified himself, masking his voice by speaking into the wind. "Dexter Coleman, Special Agent in Charge, DEA."

Taken aback by the formal introduction, Nick wasn't sure how to respond. "Nick," popped out of his mouth before he caught himself. *Damn. So much for Nikola.*

Coleman tossed another piece of bread over the wall, this time stirring to life several pigeons who'd been nesting beneath one of the arches. He addressed the river, unfazed by Nick's response. "You alone…Nick?"

"Yes."

"Too loud. Presume people are listening. Do as I do. Soften your voice and speak to the river."

Nick pretended to study the statue of Jesus, taking Coleman's advice in hand while wondering if the agent wasn't being paranoid. There wasn't anyone within twenty feet of them.

"Our AG exempted op went off the rails," Coleman opened. "I presume that's why you're here."

"It is." Nick ignored the rain shower pelting his head and shoulders, focusing on Coleman's words.

"Who are you working for? The Agency?"

He recalled Taylor Ferguson's advice. "'Give just enough to get him talking, but not enough to give away anything that could come back to harm either of you.'" "I'm not at liberty to say."

Coleman appeared to digest his response. "Fair enough."

"What happened?"

"Under the AGEO, we opened and operated a legit commercial business. To avoid looking too pure, we did a bit of black-market stuff." Coleman paused to light a cigarette, offering one to Nick.

Nick shook his head. "What kind of stuff?"

"Mostly cigarettes. In fact, we were able to offset most of our incurred expenses."

Mostly? He wondered what else Coleman may have ventured into but dropped his question. "Until the op ran off the rails."

"Yeah." Coleman pulled a handkerchief from a pocket with his free hand and blew his nose. "So here we are, meeting on this bridge in the damn rain."

"What happened?" Nick asked, testing to see if what Coleman told him matched with the reports he'd read in D.C.

Coleman leaned forward, his hands gripping the stone wall, studying an approaching motor launch.

Nick tossed out another query, trying to pry something loose from the DEA agent. "The money didn't add up?"

Coleman straightened and dropped the half-finished cigarette into the river. "The Interior Ministry seized seven million from a ten million-dollar-deal. Money that was supposed to go to us."

"A lot of booze and cigarettes."

"Narcotics. It was designed as a sting, but we were the ones who got fleeced. The money just vanished down a rabbit hole. I suspect it was converted to cryptocurrency and washed through the dark web. Washington shut us down."

Bingo. Just as the investigation had found. "Let me guess," Nick said. "The Interior Minister orchestrated the set-up?"

"Ondrej Holcorá." Coleman tossed another piece of bread over the wall. "Corruption is pervasive in this country, starting at the top. The Czech Committee for Intelligence Activita is supposed to be chaired by the Prime Minister, but it's actually controlled by Holcorá. I should have smelled the rat."

Nick understood betrayal, knowing firsthand the sting of being set up. He'd been betrayed by a supposed friend, his *friend* from the Treasury Department, Mark Arita. Arita had opted for a plea deal, turning on even more people, and was now on supervised release. A burst of anger flared and dissipated as fast. He had to maintain his focus. "You were set up?"

"Yeah. The collapse of the Soviet Empire in '89 destroyed what vestiges of central authority and law enforcement remained in the country. The TCO's filled the vacuum when the Russians pulled out, entrenching their own tidy operations with bribes to the police, customs officials, border guards, the judiciary, government officials. Hell, just about everybody, supposedly even Holcorá's wife."

He needed to pursue the Transnational Crime Organizations. "Which one is the major player?"

"The officials or the TCOs?"

"The TCOs."

Coleman sneezed and blew his nose again. "Damn cold. Could be several. Meycek, Cernik, Liska."

He made a mental note of Coleman's answers. The agent hadn't mentioned the Král Group. *Why?* And Meycek? An old nemesis.

"As near as we can determine," Coleman continued, "most of these groups maintained a veneer of legitimacy, at least within the locals' definition of *legitimate,* staying within their expected boxes. That was all well and good until a number of them, no longer satisfied with black marketing, gambling, trafficking, and gun running, decided to diversify."

Nick played through the various scenarios. So far, he hadn't learned a damn thing that he didn't already know or couldn't have surmised except for Meycek. He sensed Coleman was trying to blow smoke up his butt. Had this the guy even been brought in on the Sensitive Activity Review's findings? Nick's mind closed off Coleman's voice. *Who were the others and what was their motivation?* He recalled the mnemonic, MICE, that pertained to those who would betray their country: Money, Ideology, Coercion, Ego. He caught himself. What had Coleman just said? *No longer satisfied? Then what cou—?*

The sound of Coleman's voice plunged through his thoughts. "Meycek appears to be making a move."

Nick watched to see if Coleman's pupils dilated before he answered. "I'm acquainted with them and their parent, the Novorossiysk Business Group." The guy's pupils registered a micro-change. He'd hit on something relevant.

"Then the name of Meycek's lead agent in Prague might register. Aleksandra Grekov."

Nick managed to conceal his shock at the unexpected revelation. Not only was his former contact in Russian intelligence, Alex Grekov, still alive, she was in Prague. *Damn! Was she still working for the FSB? And if she was?* He suppressed a shudder. *Oh, man, if she's here, we've got an entirely different ballgame. What the hell were the Russians up to? And why didn't Austin know about this? Crap!* He thrust his hands into his pockets to hide his trembling fingers. *Could they be part of...?*"

He screwed up his lip to appear as if he were thinking about Alex's last name. "Can't say it rings a bell." Nick changed the subject. "What about the International Consortium of Journalists and that local outfit?"

"The Czech Center for Investigative Journalism?"

"Yeah," Nick answered.

"That murdered reporter had to have stumbled onto

something, but the Center went cold after...after what they did to her."

He felt Coleman's surge of emotion at the mention of the reporter's fate. "What was her name?"

"Brid Krejci."

Nick decided to leave well enough alone and move on. He needed to confirm what he had learned from Austin's latest update and his questions about what relationship Coleman may have had with the reporter, and what she may have confided. He changed his focus to Austin's findings from a buried FinCEN report. "What can you tell me about the Treasury Department's files on their Financial Crimes Enforcement Network and their Suspicious Activity Report?" He clarified. "Their leads linking a money laundering operation that they located on a deep website?"

"They're accurate," Coleman answered. "The laundering operation originated in Venezuela and is run through a dark network, including a bank in the Cayman's, another in New York, the Schaffhauser Global Investments firm in Bern, the Czech government's Ministry of Interior, and perhaps a fifth cut-out we haven't been able to trace."

Nick recalled there had been previous reports submitted by the U.S. bank, usually under pressure from the Treasury Department, that touched on isolated incidents, but there hadn't been a unifying factor and certainly nothing of this magnitude. Until now. He glanced at a couple of young men who were approaching before responding. "I'd say we need to determine what Ms. Krejci was after."

"I want to nail those sons-of-bitches."

"We will." Nick swiped the water off his face, grateful the rain was beginning to let up. Most of the tourists had scrambled for cover and he didn't like being one of the few left on the bridge. He tugged on his collar, feeling exposed. He needed to finish. "So, what about the Král Group?"

"Near as we can tell, they were reasonably legit by Czech

crime organization standards; that is, until they decided to expand their operations from their base of casinos and gambling."

"Drugs. Contraband?"

Coleman looked at the men who had stopped next to them. The newcomers pointed to a patch of clear sky and spoke a few words before starting to pull a guitar and a bass fiddle from their cases. "There are three others linked to Král's group you need to know about: a minor boss, Petr Hájek; his financier, Anićka Drabek; and one of his lieutenants. Guy named Karel Sokol. There's more on them, but this isn't the place."

"Understood," Nick said, the names not registering.

Coleman reached for his pack of cigarettes and tapped out another. "Before we wrap up, there's a name that's been floated by one of our informants. Same root as yours, but it's probably a blind lead."

"Let me be the judge of that."

"Patykaovi."

Nick managed to suppress his surprise at hearing his probable ancestor's name. *My God, could my target be part of my lost family?* "Got a first name?"

"That's all I have." Coleman turned to leave, then stopped.

"You got something else?"

"Nah, I'll be in touch."

Patykaovi. Nick's lips tightened, his focus no longer on dark web connections, the fate of that reporter, or the other new players Coleman mentioned. *Could the agent be hedging? What else does he know that impacts my quest for my family?*

"You know how to contact me?" Coleman asked.

Nick considered that minor detail. "No."

Coleman handed Nick a business card. "Number's on the back."

Chapter Nineteen

He pocketed the card without looking at it as Coleman started to make his way off the bridge toward the Malá Strana district.

Coleman stopped and turned back. "And Nick. Don't trust anyone. It'll keep you alive."

Chapter Twenty

BENEDICTSKYA APARTMENTS
OLD TOWN, PRAGUE
THURSDAY 15 OCTOBER

"Careful with that, you clumsy ox." Hemmed in by several stacks of packing boxes, Anton Král shot an angry look at the foreman supervising the relocation to his new office in the Modrony district. Two of the supervisor's men were struggling to lever the eight-hundred pound safe onto a wheeled furniture dolly. Jarred from his thoughts, his anger flared at Reznik's assurances that the move would go without incident. There weren't enough of them, and they had the wrong equipment. *If they damage the Etrog box, they will lose their thumbs.* He flexed his fingers several times, refocusing his anger.

His office, his network, and his operation may have been compromised. One of his reliable contacts had suddenly gone silent. Compromised by whom, he didn't know. One of his own staff, or perhaps a rival. The Liska mob? They had become a source of irritation. Then again, what of the Interior Minister, Ondrej Holcorá? He could turn on him at any moment, as he had with the American DEA agent. Or maybe it was this newcomer, Grekov? Perhaps it was his StB partner looking to extort him or even some fanatic who had stumbled across his family's history? The possibilities of betrayal seemed endless. His gut told him his family had been targeted, perhaps by that damn reporter.

Král pounded his fist on the desktop. "Enough!" The outburst prompted a startled worker to drop the box he'd begun to lift. He caught himself and addressed the man. "No, you are good. Continue your work."

Calming, he returned to his thoughts. Whatever the source, he had no choice but to uproot the traitor. He hadn't heard from his mole in the StB and Sokol had come up empty, his usual sources pleading ignorance. More likely, they were silenced. He thought it ironic that the least of his concerns were the Americans.

Král shut out the annoying voice of the foreman, considering what he must do to secure his operation, discarding several ideas before settling on one. One that would not only eliminate the person or the mob who had betrayed him, but also divert the attention of the Americans to whose presence Delezal had alerted him. How Delezal had come by this information remained a mystery, one that he would pursue in the coming week. He picked up his iPhone and placed a call to his most trusted associate. "Karel, we must speak."

Sokol didn't hesitate. "One o'clock at Lokál."

Of course, Král thought. Sokol would choose the best pub in Old Town since he wouldn't expect to pick up the tab. "Yes, that will do."

Setting up their meeting was the easy part. Now he had to decide on the best way to entrap the traitor. He stopped himself. *No, I must entrap all of my enemies, including the American's all in one brilliant stroke.*

Král began to formulate his plan based on a scrap of conversation from a secret recording. He would bait the trap with his stash of cocaine. Mendez had said his gift of 500 kilos of the uncut narcotic was meant to address unexpected contingencies. And so, it would. Of course, he cautioned himself, the Mexican would expect something more in return. What that might be, he'd worry about later.

The decision brought him full circle. Whom to target? He closed his eyes and leaned back in his chair, blocking out the noise of the movers' bumbling efforts. He would choose a path that would cause the least amount of danger to his syndicate to flush the traitors, anticipating the unexpected move would also distract the Americans from his real purpose.

He pulled open the top desk drawer after the two movers had left, extracted a small tape recorder, and pressed the play button: "What are the, um—" "I'm talking about the product destined for Sre—"

He uttered an angry curse, unable to make out the slurred destination. "*Sakra!*" He pressed rewind and replayed the tape, still unable to decipher the missing word. After his third failed attempt, he continued through the rest of the recording.

"You are taking fifty percent of my cut. I need twenty."

"You better guarantee me that business."

"I will, but you gotta deal with the Mexican, maybe that other guy."

"Man, you gotta have a cut-out. We can't be talking like this."

"Five million euros."

"*Jdi do prdele!*"

He shut off the recording at the crude Czech expletive. One of the men's voices sounded familiar, but it appeared to have been altered and he couldn't place it. The other was clear and had a distinct Middle-Eastern accent. He rewound and played the tape several more times. He wrote a few cryptic notes: Who was the Mexican? Could it be Mendez or another? And what business? He could only surmise *"the product"* was drugs.

Král set the recorder on his desk. Those three questions were important, but the most important was, how did the tape find its way to Delezal? And why?

LOKÁLS CAFÉ, PRAGUE

Karel Sokol hefted his pilsner glass of Svijany lager, one of the outstanding beers produced in a country known for its beer. He'd selected a table in the corner so he could have an unobstructed view of the café's entrance. The information he had received would please Král. He only wished his nephew had been able to catch a few more words of conversation between Coleman and his new contact than *"Contraband* "and *"There's more, but this is not the place."* He took a thoughtful swallow of his lager, wiping the foam from his lips. That wasn't much to go on, but it was enough. Their mole in the American embassy had again proved useful.

Turning the middle-aged secretary who'd worked as a trusted employee of the Americans for twelve years had been easy; just one visit to her home by Reznik had sufficed. For a small stipend and the continued safety of her family, all she had to do was pass on her boss's schedule. Nothing more. At least for now.

Král's other lieutenant, Delezal, a man he held in contempt but would use, had trailed the unknown person who'd met Coleman on the Charles Bridge to the Hotel Alcron, easily evading the man's amateurish attempts to detect his tail. It was almost as if the American was doing the checks only for appearance's sake instead of doing anything useful.

From there, it had been easy enough to slip a bribe to one of the desk staff. Their guest's name: Nikola Partyka. He and his wife, Marie, were one of three couples traveling with Prestige Genealogy and Heritage Tours.

Delezal had also obtained the names of the others and the interesting fact that the Partykas were staying in a suite, a fact he found out of character for the skinflint American operatives he'd encountered in the past. If the Partykas were indeed American agents, they had a large expense account.

Sokol's follow-up of his own source within Celní Kontrola confirmed the American's entry date and the reason for his visit to the Czech Republic. Nikola Partyka had arrived on the twelfth of October with his wife, and their tourist visas were valid until the twenty-eighth. This information was useful, but he still had to determine the exact nature of Partyka's visit to Prague.

Partyka's cover, Prestige Genealogy and Heritage Tours, while a new company, appeared legitimate. At least on the surface, Sokol cautioned himself. Hadn't Delezal said the American came to investigate their own botched DEA operation, and that he'd met with Coleman? What didn't fit is why did the Americans meet on the bridge instead of in their embassy? He studied the pitcher of lager. There was the top layer of foam, of little substance, and below, the solid amber colored brew. There had to be more once he'd skimmed off the foam.

Yet to be determined was if the other five members of the tour group were part of whatever this Partyka was up to. Delezal's initial background check had turned up nothing suspicious on the others, but Sokol knew that meant nothing. Not if Partyka was working for American intelligence. And the others? Delezal's words: "We didn't see any suspicious activity. They're acting like typical tourists."

"You're losing your touch."

Sokol jumped at the sound of Král's voice.

Chapter Twenty

Král pulled out a chair. "Have you ordered?"

"Not yet." Sokol filled a glass from the pitcher of Svijany. "I thought it best to wait. There are several new items on the menu."

Král picked up a menu to cover his voice. "We have a problem, but first tell me what you know about the Americans."

Sokol reiterated what he'd learned, but his boss appeared distracted, so he decided to move on. "Coleman also mentioned two names just before he spotted our men and ended the meeting." He lowered his voice. "The first was Patykaovi, the second—"

Král leaned forward to be heard, his hands gripping his glass. "What was that name, again?"

Sokol tensed at the dual threats of Král's response and the deep rumble of an approaching motorcycle.

"Patykaovi."

"Not, Partyka?"

"No, I am sure. It was Patykaovi. Does it have meaning?"

Král pushed away from the table. "Do not ever say that name again."

The steel in Král's voice cut off Sokol's first reaction, to explore the significance of this Patykaovi, but the trembling in his hands told him to leave well enough alone. At least for now.

He watched his boss storm out of café. He would have to wait to learn what his boss's, and perhaps his own, *problem* was. One thing was certain: Whatever this Partyka was up to, it had something to do with Hájek's ancestral line—and, possibly, Hájek had his own plans to subvert Král as the dominant kingpin of the Czech Republic's Transnational Crime Organizations. Family relationships could be messy.

Chapter Twenty-One

NUMBER 10 UVOZ STREET
PRAGUE ADMINISTRATIVE DISTRICT FIVE
THURSDAY 15 OCTOBER

Lieutenant Colonel Aleksandra Grekov reached for the new invoice and read through the figures for the latest shipment of sugar beets. In an ironic twist that her old nemesis, Nick Parkos, would appreciate, beets were again to play a role in shaping world history. Bashir al-Khultyer, the terrorist Parkos had finally eliminated, used cans of beets to smuggle the nuclear material for his dirty bombs out of Russia. And now? Sugar beets were providing the legitimate cover for her own operation.

Meycek imported the root vegetable that the Czechs refined into sugar. The logistics were daunting. Each shipment of beets harvested in Russia weighed in the thousands of tons. She'd also found it a formidable undertaking to shield Meycek's operations from those who sought to extort her. Not the least of whom was the Interior Minister, Ondrej Holcorá.

Chapter Twenty-One

Her mind drifted to the stories her father had told her when she was a child. He'd almost made the work of growing the staple in the rich, black earth of the family's old estate in Kursk sound romantic instead of what it really was, a backbreaking ordeal. In his old age, he had said he could still smell the dusty, sweet scent of their beets awaiting shipment to Moscow and Saint Petersburg while he recounted the stories of their family. The other memory that lay heavily on her heart was his special nickname for her, Myka.

She suppressed a mixed wave of sorrow and anger, turning her attention back to a pile of intelligence reports on her desk. She sifted through several before finding the one she sought. Moscow had confirmed the shipment.

"Comrade Colonel."

She looked up at the sound of Sergei Kuznetsov's voice. Her deputy stood respectfully in the doorway. "Ah, Sergei, please come in. We have much to discuss."

She waited until Kuznetsov had settled in the chair across from her. "It appears Král may be in need of our assistance. His sudden move to Modrony suggests his operations may have been compromised."

"Yes, Comrade Colonel," Kuznetsov affirmed. "There is little doubt that he has been betrayed."

"Do we know the source of his difficulties?"

"There are several possibilities. I would place one of his own at the top of the list."

"That would not be unusual in these Balkans where there is no loyalty. Even within families." Her lips tightened as she considered the other possibilities. "Who else?"

"Someone in the StB or the Interior Ministry. Holcorá and his wife's greed and treachery have shown no bounds."

Her thoughts touched on Holcorá before she addressed the immediate issue at hand. "Does Král suspect us?"

"He would be wise to include us on his list of traitors, but we are blameless."

"What about that damn Iranian we are trying to entrap?"

"We've got him on tape. A copy of which has found its way to Král."

"Will he recognize your voice?"

"Our technician altered it and I purposely slurred the supposed destination of the shipment."

"In that case, we may be able to ease Král's mind and place a traitor at his feet. More importantly, we must not allow the Iranians to compromise Alpite Import and Export with their ham-handed attempts to divert our arms shipments." Her eyes hardened. "If Král must also be sacrificed to save our operation, then so be it. We can replace him with another. Perhaps his brother-in-law, Hájek."

"Yes, Comrade Colonel. I will begin to formulate plans to handle any contingencies."

While pleased with Kuznetzov's initiative, she had to probe, to assert her authority.

"And what of our plans for Dusa?"

"He continues to report the activities of the Americans and Vasek. I have directed him to do nothing more at this point."

"I concur. What else?"

"Our tail may have been spotted."

She swallowed her annoyance at this revelation but kept her face expressionless. "As I thought might happen. We are not dealing with a bunch of simple-minded American tourists. Have you spoken to Ilia? I will not tolerate such sloppiness."

"He will not make the same mistake again."

"What assurances do you have?"

"I will know soon enough if he has to be replaced. I've ordered him to follow the Americans today and report anything suspicious to me this afternoon." He paused. "I have the photos he took."

"Have we identified any of them besides the ones the traitor, Strickland, provided?"

"We have all of their aliases, and headquarters is running their names."

"I doubt they will find anything new, but no matter. It will keep them from bothering us." She held out her hand for the photos. Spreading them on the desk, she sorted through the blow-ups Ilia had taken. She stopped at the fifth and smiled at the familiar face. *Ah, my friend, fate has brought us together once again.*

"Comrade Colonel?" Kuznetzov asked. "Is there something I have missed?"

"I know of this man." She held up the picture. "What name is he using?"

"Nikola Partyka."

"Clever." She changed the topic. "What of Coleman's meeting on the bridge?"

"Our directional microphone was unable to record their conversation. The rain helped mask their words and they covered well."

"There will be other opportunities." She pushed the photos into a pile. "Task Ilia with shadowing them."

"Král's man, Delezal, is an amateur," Kuznetzov said. "He is not nearly as clever as he believes, even though he did manage to ferret out the supposed names of the Americans and where they are staying."

"Information we knew before they even arrived."

Kuznetzov reached for the photographs. "We can easily manipulate this amateur."

She pulled the photographs toward her. "I will keep these." She lightened her voice. "Excellent work, Sergei. That will be all for now."

She studied the photographs after Kuznetzov left. Parkos hadn't changed, but he would barely recognize her, the transformation so complete from severe KSB agent... *to ... what, exactly?* she wondered. She leaned back in her upholstered chair. *And now?*

A tasteful two-piece suit and colorful blouse had replaced the stark dull-gray uniform she'd worn in Moscow. Her black hair, no longer constrained in a tight, asexual bun, flowed over her shoulders, and makeup accentuated her deep-set brown eyes and softened the tight, horizontal slash of her mouth. The small scar over her right eyebrow remained, although she used eyebrow makeup to mask the trauma of the childhood accident. *Would he even recognize me? Perhaps he will remember the scar?*

Parkos had proven to be a formidable adversary, defeating her attempt to shield the terrorist al-Khultyer. She looked forward to gaining a measure of revenge and would not underestimate him again.

The harsh honk of a car horn blared from the street, penetrating the serenity of her office. The sound reminded her of driving with the maniacs crowding the congested streets of Moscow, and the stark times spent in her squalid office at the Federal Security Service's Lubyanka Headquarters. And now? She had adapted to this new life with an ease that reflected the life she should have known on her family's Kursk estate. The life of one of Russia's nobility.

Her great-grandfather, Count Kuzmin Grekov, had been a prominent member of the Russian aristocracy and a general in the Czar's White Army during the Bolshevik Revolution. He had died defending the Crimean enclave. Her entire family would have also perished if not for the Americans. Her grandmother and two young children, one of whom would become her father, were evacuated by the destroyer, *USS Overton*. Years later, her grandfather had returned to Russia, his status no better than that of a serf working the land of their old estate the Communists had confiscated and turned into a collective farm. Her father and all the others had perished.

In her own tale of survival, she, too, had fled for her life after the al-Khultyer debacle, an act she had thought quite prudent. To her great astonishment, she had not been arrested but had been lavishly rewarded for her actions, including a promotion to Lieutenant Colonel. Her posting to Prague had also bought her a new life and a degree of relative freedom that she craved. Now, she managed Meycek Exports, an affiliate of the Novorossiysk Business Group. If she succeeded, she would be promoted to full Colonel and maybe even awarded The *Order of Honour* by Federation President Srevnenko. Occupying a position of incredible responsibility, she would restore honor to her family name. She felt no compunction to disavow her family's history or her great-grandfather's heroic actions.

She turned her attention back to the issue at hand. Král would certainly underestimate Parkos. *My actions also cannot be so overt as Král's. When we intervene, I will not endanger my operation as the American, Strickland's, actions have threatened to do.*

Strickland had bought into their ruse, no doubt encouraged by a substantial deposit to his Swiss bank account, or by knowing the true intent of her operation. She had told her superiors they would soon have to cut him loose or, better yet, have him erased. While still useful, she'd been informed by the Washington cadre that the FSB's mole in Director Gilmore's NSA had become a liability, and that he was now the subject of an internal investigation. Strickland had almost succeeded in permanently blackballing Parkos, but *almost* in this business was tantamount to failure, and his failure to eliminate Parkos would lead to his own downfall.

Moscow's directive was clear: *If there is even a whiff of discovery of our intentions, you will abort the mission, leaving nothing behind that could be traced back to President Srevnenko.*

Chapter Twenty-Two

JIŘÍHO Z PODĚBRAD
PRAGUE, CZECH REPUBLIC
THURSDAY 18 OCTOBER

"You ready for a morning of sightseeing?" Marie asked.

"Not really," Nick muttered, setting aside the Le Vin notebook and the handcrafted wooden ballpoint pen he'd purchased the day before.

She considered his response and dismissed his foul mood. She held her tongue, recalling that he'd said Michelle had given him the notebook to work on his family's genealogy. What effect, if any, would his research have on their mission?

They stepped out of the Alcron's lobby into the brisk morning air. Their destination? The quaint neighborhood of JZP, short for Jiřího z Poděbrad. They had decided to visit JZP's farmer's market and the eclectic collection of shops bordering the scenic park the night before. They, *well at least me*, she recalled, looked forward to spending a few hours in an

Chapter Twenty-Two

area of the city not frequented by the usual mobs of German and Chinese tourists.

Today was scheduled as free time for Prestige Genealogy and Heritage Tours, and The Curators planned to make the most of the opportunity. The team would split up, leaving the Alcron at different times, all heading for predetermined innocuous destinations. They would take circuitous routes to and from these sites to shake any possible tails and converge in the afternoon at the Plzeń Bar and Brasserie, a small farm restaurant on the outskirts of Prague. This would be the first opportunity to speak together without the chance of being overheard and recorded; that is, if they weren't followed.

Perhaps their outing would cast a veil of legitimacy on their cover as simple tourists. Marie paused, cautioning herself. Tom had already spotted one suspicious person at the Castle. To assume someone else wasn't aware of their activities would be self-deceiving. In any event, she concluded their relaxed morning held the potential to accomplish something that would advance the goal of their mission.

"I can think of better things we should be doing," Nick said.

Man, what a grump, Marie thought. Despite a few half-hearted attempts by Jennifer and Tom to loosen him up at breakfast, Nick remained under a self-imposed dark cloud, nursing his foul mood. Three days had passed and only thirteen remained to complete their mission. He had told her that he'd eliminated the Czech Minister, Holcorá, as a viable player. While Holcorá may be corrupt, he'd be insane to get involved with the Mexican, Mendez, and counter his own President's pro-American policies over those of the Russians.

Marie and Vinny Cade had worked out a plan for Vinny to provide counter-surveillance to see if they could smoke out their watcher, be it one of Grekov's or Král's men, or less likely, someone from the Czech security service. She didn't relish the idea of being used as bait. She'd been down that road before in the Philippines. And it had nearly cost her her life.

She suppressed a frown at the memory, looped her right arm around Nick's left elbow, and gave him a gentle tug that one might expect of a spouse urging on a reluctant mate. "Granted, but we all agreed."

"Harrumph."

She pulled a tourist map out of her purse and pretended to search for directions. Nick's *Harrumph* could be a positive. At least he'd acknowledged her. "This way."

The short metro ride gave her an opportunity to finalize her contingency plans. Since Nick, as the team leader, and she by default, were considered at the greatest risk, Vinny had preceded them and was already conducting counter-surveillance. The guy was so adept at his craft, she'd never spotted him despite the years she'd spent with the Agency prowling the streets of Manila.

She led the way from the JZP station. The sight that greeted her wasn't what she had imagined. *Crap.* The square was actually an urban park with a scattering of shops along the perimeter and almost devoid of people who could mask their movements. She voiced her concerns. "I don't like this. Come on."

They strode to the farmer's market set up under three parallel rows of tents on the eastern edge of the park. Along each aisle stood a dozen stands each with mounds of colorful vegetables stacked decoratively in blue plastic crates: orange carrots, red tomatoes, purple cabbage, green leeks. All pleasing to the eye but pretty much like any American market worth its salt.

She could sense her partner's thoughts. The evening before, Nick had shared with her the times he and Michelle had visited the farmers' markets in central Ohio and his hope of finding something unusual to take home.

Nick lagged behind and said to her back, "This place looks

Chapter Twenty-Two

like an open-air Whole Foods store, and I don't see anything I can take to Michelle."

Marie turned to face him. "She'll be fine, Nick. And didn't your friend, Jessica, say that she'd keep an eye on her?"

"She has mid-terms this week."

There had to be more to Nick's worries than he was voicing. Marie began to respond, but her iPhone buzzed in her hand. She made a pretext of taking a picture and read the one-word text: COUNTER.

The codeword was one of several from a list of football terms the team had put together at their final meeting at The Nicholas. In football parlance, *Counter* meant: Run the ball in the opposite direction from what the other team expects.

She tapped out a 'K' and dropped the phone into her purse. "We've got a tail."

"Damn."

She guided him out of the market and toward several small shops. Vinny had surveyed her intended destinations, identifying which shops had rear doors that were accessible to side streets, and other means to escape a would-be pursuer. "Follow me, I've been through this drill before."

"What drill?"

"Losing a tail. And don't look around. Act normal." She flashed a disarming smile. "Okay, well, maybe not normal."

"Give me a break," he muttered as she led him toward a line of shops a short walk from the market.

"We've gotta stay out of the park. Vinny and I have a plan. You hungry?"

"What?"

"Are you hungry?"

"Why?"

She pointed to the shops. "Our first stop is that boulangerie. See it?"

"I can smell it."

"Figured you would. We'll grab something, then pay a visit

to that tobacco shop a couple doors down. You need to buy some cigars."

"I do?"

"You owe Geoff big time."

"I do?"

"You sound like an owl. And, yes, you do."

They exited the boulangerie, munching on a couple of pastries, and stopped before the window of the florist's shop next door. She took the opportunity to scan the reverse image of the park. She didn't spot anything suspicious despite Vinny's update that their tail was still watching. "Let's go." She stopped, following Nick's eyes. "What's the matter?"

"Sunflowers."

"What's wrong with them?"

"My first op. The terrorist I stopped bought a bouquet of sunflowers before he would set off one of his dirty bombs. They were his daughter's favorites. The Russians killed her and his wife during the battle of Grozny."

"Al-Khulyter." Her face softened, reflecting on her own operations with the CIA. "That had to have been tough."

"Yeah, it was. The guy had his reasons." He pulled his eyes off the display. "We'd better get going."

They made for the tobacconist shop next door identified by a sign bearing *TOBÁK* in white, block letters on a light-blue background.

"I thought you couldn't stand these things?" he said.

"I can't, but in this case, they'll serve a purpose. Come."

Nick led the way into the store. The woody aroma of cured tobacco and the tinkle of a small brass bell welcomed them. "Welcome to heaven," he said.

The owner looked up expectantly from behind a glass counter displaying a huge variety of cigars. "May I help you?"

Chapter Twenty-Two

"Možná," Nick said. He switched to English. "We are looking for a fine Cuban cigar."

"Ah, Americans," the owner said, opening the top of his display case. "It is hard to find an excellent cigar in your country."

Nick's eyes landed on a box of Bolivar Limitades. "How about those?"

"An excellent choice. You must know cigars, yes?"

"A friend has tried to educate me."

The owner handed him the box. "He has done well."

Nick translated the label written in Czech for Marie: "'A robust smoke with notes of cloves, earth, and bittersweet chocolate.'" Under his breath he added, "What are you supposed to do with the damn things, eat them?"

"I wouldn't advise it," Maire said, casting a quick look toward the street. *Nothing.*

The owner held out a dark, medium gauge Bolivar to Nick. "Please."

Nick checked the wrapper. *Havana, 2014.* He gave the cigar a slow spin looking for any cracks or signs of the seams unraveling. Finding none, he noted the slight irregular shape, indicating the cigar had been hand-rolled. He gave it a squeeze, then held it to his ear and repeated the squeeze. Finally, he ran the cigar under his nose, giving it a long sniff. He turned to Marie. "What do you think?"

"You seem to be the expert," she said. "Wonder how many of these cigars have made their way to Prague via the black market. Maybe even by Král's organization?"

Nick saw the owner tense at her mention of Král. "No idea."

"If you want some others, we have the time," Marie said.

"I'll check the ratings. I figure we can't go wrong."

"We?" she said, "This is your deal."

Nick detected the edge in her voice, but figured she wanted to move on. He pointed out two boxes. "We'll get a mix. A couple each of the Bolivar and those two, the Cohiba BHK 52's and Montecristo Number 2's."

"Does your lady friend speak Czech?" the owner asked in Czech.

"*Ach, ne.*"

A mischievous smile lit the man's face. "Very good, then you should know that the Cohiba's have been rolled between the thighs of young Cuban virgins."

Nick tried to hold back a snort of surprise but instead a loud, horsey laugh escaped.

Marie jerked her head around at the sound. "What?"

"Nothing," he managed to reply through a choked laugh.

"Yeah, right. If that joke was about me, you're toast, buster."

"I'm innocent."

"Right."

Nick pulled out his wallet and handed over the cost of his purchase along with a hefty tip, thanking the tobacconist profusely for the six Cubans. Purchases complete, he headed for the front door. "Done."

Marie pulled her buzzing iPhone from in her pocket and glanced at Vinny's text. *RED.* "Not yet." She turned to the owner. "Do you have a restroom?"

"*Toaleta?*" Nick said.

The owner gestured to a narrow hallway leading to the rear of the store.

Nick started at the deep-throated roar of an approaching motorcycle.

"Down!" Marie yelled. She threw her body at Nick before he could respond, knocking him off his feet, sending his box of cigars flying. The air around them was rent by twin booms and the sound of shattering glass. Shards from the store's plate glass window and buckshot cut through the shop's interior, shredding the space where Nick and Marie had stood.

Nick heard the tobacconist cry out in pain as he caught a

Chapter Twenty-Two

glimpse of their assailants speeding off. Two hooded men dressed in black, the rider grasping a shotgun. Nick scrambled to his feet, ignoring the screeches of the injured shop keeper. He snatched his cigars off the floor and sprinted after Marie out the store's back door, emerging onto a narrow side-street.

Marie's phone rang out again. She pressed it against her ear. "Got it." She grabbed his arm and pulled him down the street. "This way. Vinny says it's clear."

He stumbled, then took off, catching up to her when she halted at the far street corner. "Damn, what the hell was that all about?" he gasped.

"Our tail. We've got to get out of here."

He caught his breath and flagged down a passing Yellow AAA taxi while Marie scanned the street for the shooter. He climbed in after Marie and addressed the driver in Czech so there would be less chance of them getting ripped off or ending up some place miles from their destination. *"Dobré ráno. Hotel Alcron, prosim."*

"You think the target was us or the shopkeeper?" Nick whispered.

"You're thinking a turf battle over contraband, and we happened to be in the way?" Marie said.

"Yeah. Why would either Král or Grekov risk such a blatant attack?"

"They've both been known to take risks in the past to send a message."

Nick turned back from the car's right passenger window to face her. Several expanding red ovals dotted the sleeve of her left arm and shoulder. "You're hurt."

"I'm fine, I took a couple pellets." Marie winced as she twisted to look at her wounds. "But whoever they are, those sons-of-bitches just ruined my favorite jacket."

Chapter Twenty-Three

PLZEŃ BAR AND BRASSERIE
VYSOKŸ, CZECH REPUBLIC
THURSDAY 15 OCTOBER

"Hey, y'all," Vinny said, announcing his arrival in his best Southern drawl. He cast an inquiring look at Marie. "Y'all didn't start without me, did 'ya?" he continued, satisfied she appeared to be okay, although he noted she'd changed her jacket.

Jennifer hefted an enormous white-ceramic beer stein with the Czech national crest emblazoned on the front. "We didn't want to miss happy hour."

"Pull up a chair," George said, while filling the stein they'd reserved for their teammate.

Vinny nodded a thanks and took a long, thirsty swallow while he assessed their surroundings over the top of the stein's rim. For the benefit of the ladies present, he suppressed a loud belch. "Man, the Czechs sure know how to brew their lagers."

Chapter Twenty-Three

Ann pushed a plate with the remnants of a savory potato pancake toward him. "Betcha can't eat just one."

Vinny examined the plate. "There is only one, ma'am."

"Details," Marie commented, wincing as she reached for her glass. "They're great beer food. You're lucky we saved you that one. Oh, and thanks for spotting our tail."

"The pleasure is all mine." He speared the pancake with his fork and popped it into his mouth while noting her wince. "Say, this is pretty tasty."

"You have an ID?" Nick asked, anxious to get down to business and learn something about who Vinny had spotted.

Vinny handed Nick a brown paper bag by way of an answer. "With Edmund's compliments. Business can wait."

Nick reached into the bag and extracted a bottle of scotch. "Oh, man. The Laphroaig 10- year, Batch 007."

Tom peered at the label from his vantage point from across the table. "007? Nice touch. I don't suppose you're going to share?"

Nick stuffed the treasure back into the bag and set it by his feet. "Nope." He spotted their young waitress and waved her over, looking to atone. "*Mužeme smaženy syr a grilované kolbásy.*"

"*Debrá volba,*" the waitress responded with a bright smile at Nick's use of Czech. "*Chléb je na dome.*"

"*A nějaky chrebickek,*" Vinny added.

The waitress collected the empty pancake plate, flashed Vinny a fetching smile, and departed with a saucy swing of her hips.

"All right, what did you guys just say?" Ann asked.

Nick deferred to Vinny with a circling hand motion worthy of Aladdin.

"We ordered some Czech classics," Vinny responded. "Deep fried cheese, pastry wrapped sausages, and open-faced sandwiches. We got major points for speaking Czech. Bread's on the house."

Ann cast a glance at the waitress busying herself at the counter. "That's it?"

"My thoughts are as pure as the fallen snow," Vinny protested.

"Yeah, right," Tom said as he emptied the table's pitcher. "Next one's on us."

Vinny pulled out his iPhone and set it on the table. "Ah reckon we ought to get on to business."

Tom rolled his eyes at Vinny's accent and leaned over to examine a picture on the phone's screen. "That matches the guy I spotted outside Prague Castle. Got an ID?"

"All I know right now is that he appears to be local," he answered, dropping his accent. "I sent everything I have to Dresden to see if the guys can get an ID."

"I figure it's one of Král's goons," Jennifer said.

Unsettled by the news, Nick summarized. "We've got another new player."

"Actually, we've got several," Vinny said, "including the ones who shot up the tobacco shop."

"Shot up?" George pinned Nick, then Vinny and Marie with accusatory looks. "What the hell happened?"

"I'll take this one," Vinny answered, cutting off Nick and Marie. "I spotted a couple guys on a motorcycle just before the rider opened up with a shotgun on the store and—"

"We were buying some cigars for Geoff," Marie interrupted. "Vinny got the alert to me just before the guy got off a couple rounds, shattering the store's front window. We're fine."

"Well, that's just great," Tom said. "They tried to take you out and missed. Then our mission has just gone to hell. They're on to us."

"Not necessarily," Marie said. "They could have been after the owner, and we just happened to be in the way."

"Bullshit," George said. "We have to presume, that whoever they are, those guys were after you and Nick."

At the mention of his name, Nick intervened, changing

the subject before it came out that Marie had been wounded. She had told him in no uncertain terms after she coerced him into taking out the superficial pellets with a pair of tweezers that she would not be sidelined by a couple of shotgun pellets. "That's my take. George, don't you have something on our chauffeur, Dusa?"

"Yeah, Ferguson got an ID. His full name is Dusa Volpinovich Novikov and the Prague Station Chief has linked him to Russian intelligence."

Ann's face darkened. "Is Vasek working with that son-of-a-bitch?"

"You said you spotted the same guy that was at the castle, so the Russians took a shot at you guys?" Jennifer added. "What-the-hell is going on? Where do they fit?"

Nick collected his thoughts. Ferguson had said Vasek was clean and that she'd done an occasional low-risk job for the Agency, but now he wasn't so sure of her allegiance. Were they being played? He chafed at not having access to all of his analytical tools. He still had his low- tech Venn diagrams to help him keep all these different players sorted out, but it wasn't enough and Marie had shot down his suggestion that he could keep the diagrams in their room's safe. Her rationale: "'Don't assume anything is secure. If you must, keep them with you and never let them out of your sight.'"

Nick checked their surroundings. "Ferguson says she's clean, but Dusa is another matter. Coleman also informed me that an old acquaintance of mine from the FSB is in town."

"And who would this *old acquaintance* happen to be?" George asked.

"Aleksandra Kuzminova Grekov," Nick answered.

"Not helpful," George responded.

"She was my FSB contact in Moscow for one of my ops. I was never able to put her in a neat box. Her allegiances appeared to be all over the damn place."

"Pardon me?" Marie's eyes widened. "Grekov? Did I hear that right? Isn't she the one running Meycek?"

"One and the same," Nick said. "Coleman dropped that little bomb on me yesterday. Hell, I thought she was dead."

"And now she's in Prague," Marie said.

"What's she up to?" Tom asked.

"No idea," Nick answered, "but you can bet it's nothing good. From what I knew before I left the Agency, Meycek had bought three empty apartments, presumably for their company's headquarters. There was nothing else. The nearest we could determine at the time was the apartments were placeholders. Meycek remained dormant with just the address. We moved on. That is, until now. I asked Austin to take a look. He ran our old contacts and discovered Grekov obtained permanent residency status from the Czechs last year."

Tom speared a piece of sausage with his fork. "Allowed her to set up shop."

"What's Meycek's cover?" Jennifer asked.

"Import/Export," Vinny answered. "Geoff touched base with Austin. They're bringing in thousands of tons of sugar beets and importing a bit of light industrial machinery. He couldn't find any significant export business."

"Makes sense. What do the Czechs have that would interest the Russians?" Jennifer asked.

"High tech engineering," Nick said, suppressing his annoyance at learning Geoff had talked with Austin, "but more to the point, running at just two percent of their total exports, Russia doesn't even rank in the top ten countries for the Czechs. Beets make sense, but the *Export* piece of Meycek Import/Export doesn't fit."

"Why would the FSB be interested in beets?" Tom asked.

Nick thought it was ironic that he was now dealing with beets again. Sugar beets made sense from a business standpoint, but what else was Grekov up to? His suspicions landed on light machinery imports. "They're not interested in beets, except to use them as a false-front."

"A false-front for what?" Jennifer asked.

Nick voiced his conclusion, even if it was a long shot. "Their so-called export business."

"Oh?" George responded.

Before Nick could elaborate, their waitress re-appeared with a smile and their order. She leaned across Vinny's shoulder to place a jar of mustard by his side. He noted Vinny anticipate the move and turn over his phone.

When she'd departed, Vinny said through a mouthful of sausage, "She's flirting, but you can never be too careful."

"She tried to play me once," Nick continued, ignoring the waitress, "and I can guarantee you, that's not happening again."

"Who? Grekov?" Jennifer asked. "Are you holding something back?"

"I'm sorry, I'm losing you guys. It's a fault of mine," Nick said. "Let's start with the premise that the FSB wouldn't be running a sugar beet business except for a very good reason."

"We all understand that, but where's the link?" Ann countered.

"Let me put in my two cents' worth," George said. "The DNI specifically mentioned Král and then this Grekov just happens to appear in Prague. You think that's just a coincidence?"

"The director also mentioned that drug lord, Mendez," Nick said.

"Where does he fit?" Ann asked.

"Not sure," Nick answered, "but there has to be a connection."

Jennifer nodded. "Point taken. There are no coincidences."

"That still leaves us with the primary question: What's going on?" Marie said.

"That's for us to figure out," Nick answered, "but my gut tells me we're seeing the smoke, not the fire."

"Granted," Ann said, "But again. What's the end point?"

"Beyond ferreting out what got the DNI's hackles up and stopping whatever the hell that might be?" George answered.

"We're being fed little bits," Tom said. "Just enough to send us off on a wild goose chase."

"Perhaps," Marie said, "but I don't think our tail—"

"Or tails."

"Or tails," Marie acknowledged, "They didn't count on getting caught."

"How can we smoke out at least one of the players?" Jennifer asked. "How about that guy Delezal. I have a sense he's the weak link in Král's organization."

Nick decided to assert himself, otherwise this meeting would go off the rails, just like Coleman's drug deal. He caught himself. *Whoa, that's it.* "What about a drug deal?" he said. "Especially if they're looking for money to fund an operation."

"Damn big operation," George said.

"Austin unearthed a shady network in one of the FinCEN reports he reviewed. Coleman confirmed it. The report identified a black network of correspondent banks connecting the Central Bank of Venezuela, an offshore outfit in the Caymans, a major U.S. bank, Schaffhauser Global Investments in Bern, and the Czech Interior Ministry. He's also checking into the possibility of a mysterious fifth cutout."

"Is that a problem?" George asked.

Nick sucked in his lower lip. "Don't think so."

Marie held up her hand. "Back to the finCEN report. Are they using crypto-currency?"

"Dollars," Nick answered.

"How much are we talking about?" Ann asked.

"Just under 300 million that was supposedly sitting in a

monitored forfeiture account overseen by the Fed in New York City."

Tom whistled, "Holy shit. You only see that kind of money in drugs and arms."

"Wait," Marie said. "You said *supposedly*. People don't just lose 300 hundred million."

George let out a snort. "That's what you'd think, although Medicare has done a pretty good job of losing money."

"Who's the end user?" Jennifer asked, ignoring the jibe.

"Could be anybody," George answered, "but if Holcorá's involved, it's someone in Prague."

"I may have something," Vinny said. "Yesterday, Lange sent me a head's up. He said there's a new guy working for the Czech Center for Investigative Reporting who's been looking into a possible money laundering op. At the time, I couldn't figure where it fit."

"Okay, you've got our attention," George said.

"This is where things get interesting," Vinny said. "Acting on a hunch, Ferguson called the Embassy. At his suggestion, the Station Chief fed the guy parts of what Austin had found."

George summarized everyone's feelings. "Shit. If that reporter starts snooping around and gets too close…."

"We gotta protect him," Marie said. "I know how it feels. The CIA guys in Manila saved my sorry ass. Took out the bastard who was going to kill me."

George settled the issue and addressed Vinny. "Got a name?"

"Anton Jezek," Vinny answered. "I'm working it and I've already asked MacDonald and Ferguson to join us."

"What are they going to be doing?" Marie asked.

"We've got a surprise planned for your tail," Vinny responded.

Nick cast Vinny a suspicious look. "Just what do you have in mind?"

Chapter Twenty-Four

TEREZIN GHETTO
THERESIENSTADT, CZECH REPUBLIC
FRIDAY 16 OCTOBER

Nick scanned the sterile main street of the former Terezin Ghetto. "They've wiped this place clean," he told Marie.

Marie didn't respond. Nick suppressed a wave of displaced anger toward his partner, for in truth, he really had not considered what he had expected to learn…or to feel. Would he encounter a fragment of his family's past, as Vasek had implied to Marie when the two had talked the other afternoon? He had no idea and his frustration mounted. His grandparents had told him that their son, his father, had escaped with them from Czechoslovakia as an infant, but what of his grandparents' lives during the Second World War? Why had they left their homeland? And what of the box he'd discovered in the attic after their deaths?

He had initially hoped the site might hold some historical

interest, but the grounds of the Old Fort, restored as a "Site of Remembrance," conveyed no emotional impact. There was nothing to portray the brutality, the degradation of those interned here, let alone the squalor of what the Gestapo had portrayed as the Paradise Ghetto. He could have been anywhere.

Aside from the stark, red-brick walls of the former eighteenth-century fort and the railroad siding overgrown with tall grass, there was nothing to suggest the atrocities that were perpetuated in this lifeless place. He considered the trip a waste of time, but the other Curators had insisted. What did they know that he didn't? Perhaps nothing.

The random, disjointed thoughts whirling through his brain settled on what Marie had said on the thirty-minute drive to the provincial town of Terezin northwest of Prague. *Nick, you'll have to visualize what happened there and how that links to our mission.*

Nick remained skeptical of the time they'd be devoting to another field trip and how it could possibly contribute to their mission, but he did caution himself. Marie had been a reporter for ABC in Manila before being recruited by the CIA and he respected her advice. She'd seen and reported on the Japanese internment camps on Luzon and walked the route of the Bataan Death March. *Internment camps. My, God!* Is that why my grandparents fled? And they arrived at Ellis Island with only a suitcase. Yet, they had brought the keepsake box. What was in it that was so important?

He knew from his limited research that the Terezin Camp, as it was first known, was set up by the Gestapo in November of 1941, primarily as a tool of deception. The Nazis had rounded up those Czechs older than sixty-five, the prominent Jews, city leaders, artists, poets, musicians, and decorated WWI veterans and imprisoned them all in the new "'Resettlement Camp.'" In reality, the camp was a transit point, and thousands were loaded onto railroad cars and sent East to

Auschwitz, Majdaek, and Treblinka. The lucky ones ended up in the labor camps, even those who'd bribed the Gestapo hoping to not be sent away on the trains.

Deception. He focused on the word and closed his eyes, trying to visualize what the ghetto would have looked and felt like so many years ago. Another image appeared in his mind. The oak box. Had it been spirited away or hidden here? And could it contain the answers to the questions that haunted him about his family's and his own past?

Marie and the others had left him alone with his thoughts. All, except Vasek.

"This way," Vasek said, guiding him to a former barracks that had been opened to visitors. "I will show you something."

He looked past Vasek. The void behind a pair of open doors gazed emptily back at him. Reluctantly, he followed her under an infamous sign that topped the entrance. "ARBEIT MACHT FREI."

"You recognize the sign. Yes?"

Nick caught Tom out of the corner of his eye saying something to Marie and the other four members of their group. Marie said in a loud voice that he and Vasek could hear. "I'll catch up. I want to give Nick his water."

She walked over, reached into her purse, and handed him a plastic water bottle while whispering, "We've got our watcher. Same guy that was at the Castle."

Nick twisted off the bottle's cap, took a swallow, and responded to the curious look on Vasek's face. "The others want to check out the museum. We'll catch up with them later."

Nick stopped just inside the barrack's doors, allowing his eyes a moment to adjust to the dark. Before him in the gloomy, damp room was a long row of crudely constructed, quadruple-tiered wooden bunks topped with worn straw mattresses. On the wall to his left hung two forlorn pictures. In the first, hollow-eyed women, two or three to each tier of the room's bunks gazed blankly at the camera, while others, huddling in worn and probably vermin-infested blankets, lay on the floor clutching their children. In the other picture, dozens of men and boys were sprawled across the loose hay covering a similar room's concrete floors. On several, he saw a Jewish star sewn on their tattered coats.

He was shaken by the emotional impact of the second picture. An image from his subconscious intruded into his thoughts. A vivid, distant memory, resolute, yet fragile, from a fleeting moment in childhood with his grandfather. He'd seen a similar picture in the attic and recalled the wooden box held by his grandfather. What had *dědeček* said? "'Someday, my child, you will know our family's history. But now, you are too young to understand.'"

Nick pulled his eyes away, shaken. Could any of his family have been here? Had they, too, suffered and died?

Vasek swept her hand across the barren room. "Fifteen thousand children passed through this camp. Ninety percent of them perished in the killing centers. In total, some thirty-three thousand souls perished here. The lucky ones, the Displaced Persons, were spirited away by sympathetic locals. It is a past we Czechs have tried to suppress. We've had our own history to contend with, the Nazis and then the Communists in '48. What could we have done?"

"Why did you bring me here?" Nick asked.

"Your name struck a chord when I first saw it on the email inquiring about the tour. Before you arrived, I researched your family. I told Marie some of what I found, but not all.

"In September 1939," she continued, "the Czech government of the Nazi-dominated Protectorate of Bohemia and Moravia restored your family's aristocratic title, which the Czechs had stripped in 1918. However, your family supported the resistance in World War II and fled to London to join our exiled President, Edvard Bernēs. The Nazis labeled them traitors and confiscated their land, their castle. Your great-grandfather and his family returned after the war but fled again in 1948 when the Communists took control. Those swine confiscated your family's castle. It is now being restored."

"Castle?"

She smiled. "Yes, the Patykaovi's lived in a castle. It is not as large as some, but still very impressive. We must visit it."

"How do you know all of this?" Nick asked, stunned.

"There is something else you must see," Vasek said, leading him to a small gift shop adjacent to the compound's main gate.

Nick surveyed the shop as they entered, suspecting it may have once been an SS guard shack.

Vasek said a few words to a uniformed guard and motioned for Nick to follow her to the rear of the shop. She led him through a door that opened into a small room, the walls lined with hundreds of leather-bound books. Behind a small, cluttered desk in the far corner sat an ancient woman, her face worn by the weight of memories.

"These are the records of those who passed through this place," Vasek said. "The Nazis did not have time to destroy all of them when the Russians came." She bit her lower lip before continuing. "All of the evidence."

The old woman stood, her fingers, gnarled by arthritis, reverently holding a thick volume in her hands. A small, gold Star of David dangled from a thin chain around her neck. "*Ahoj*, Katerina. I have located the record you asked about."

The woman set the inch-thick volume on a pedestal stand and opened it to a section she'd marked with a slip of paper. She motioned for Nick to join her. *"Tady, je vase rodina."*

Nick's brain tried to register what she'd just said. *"Here, this is your family".*

He reached out, his right hand trembling as he touched

the musty, yellowed page. His index finger traced down the lined columns: Name, date of birth, sex, home province, last address, date of arrival, transport number.

"Transport number," he whispered, trying to comprehend the enormity of this.

The woman studied Nick's face. "There are so many in these books. Those who were placed on the trains. Now, there are so few of us." She gestured to the volumes surrounding her, her narration continuing as if she were alone, speaking to the others who'd died here. "There are two other repositories for the remaining records of our people, both in Prague. One is stored in the Third Department of the National Archives. The registers are not complete. Most of the originals dating to 1784 were destroyed during the war."

Our people? My God, could my family have been here? Were they Jewish? How much more had his father kept secret? Could this be why his grandfather had changed their name? How much did my father even know? And what does the ancient box from my grandparents' attic contain?

"Your family holds a fascinating place in our history," the old woman continued. She paused at the expression of disbelief on Nick's face. "But access to most of the government registers is not permitted for genealogical research."

"How much time have you spent in this place?" he asked, groping for something, anything, to provide him with a sense of normalcy.

"A lifetime. I was just an infant."

Nick's finger paused over several names: Patykaovi, Petr. And directly below: Mrazik, Anya. His hand froze over the next name. Hájek, Václav. And another, Hájek, Jakub. Were these men close friends or did they just happen to have been rounded up at the same time as his family? Was he related to any of them? To the men he was investigating?

His thoughts fixed on the name, Anya Mrazik. It didn't hold any meaning for him, but there was a something else he'd seen that rocked him; the juxtaposition of a first and a last name that were written in the register that formed the name: Petr Hájek.

The old woman broke his trance. "Anya, translates to 'Grace.'"

Nick turned his attention back to the woman, struggling to sort through the implications of what he'd just seen, not only for the quest for his identity, but for his mission, their target, Král's associate and brother-in-law—also named Petr Hájek. "Who was Anya Mrazik?" he asked "Is she a distant aunt?"

Vasek spoke. "We're not sure. I will ask those who will know and explore the genealogy pro—."

"Are there others? Others who escaped?"

"You must rejoin your group." The old woman gently removed his hand and closed the book. "There is much we must talk about. Perhaps you can return."

"There are so many," Nick said. "And my family. I had no idea."

"The mystery is who you say you are, Nick." Vasek said, her eye's catching his. She placed her hand lightly on his shoulder, letting it linger.

Chapter Twenty-Five

CAFÉ SPÁLANÁ
PRAGUE, CZECH REPUBLIX
FRIDAY 16 OCTOBER

Marie set off toward Liliová Street with a reluctant Nick in tow. Her destination was the popular Café Spálana the front desk had recommended.

"Where are we going?" Nick asked.

She smiled. "It's a surprise. Come on, it's only a short walk and you need to get out of the room."

"Don't you think I've had enough surprises for one day?" he said.

Nick's response confirmed her suspicion that he had encountered something disturbing at that damned ghetto, something that had left a mark. The problem? He hadn't shared what had happened during the twenty minutes he'd been alone with Vasek. "You'll like where we're going. Trust me."

"Harrumph."

She had learned something about her new partner over the past three weeks. When he clammed up, that meant trouble. When faced with something that threatened to expose his deeper emotions, he would throw up a protective wall. Perhaps his wife, Michelle, could breach that barrier to probe what troubled him, but it wasn't her place to ask her. Marie was no shrink, but she surmised something must have happened to him as a kid.

After they'd returned to the Alcron, he hadn't said a word. Not a word about what Vasek had told him when she'd pulled him into the gift shop. Not a word about what troubled him. He'd just returned to the room, poured a stiff drink, sat on the couch, and stared into space. A possible clue to his ordeal was when he'd taken the ancient wooden box he'd brought to Prague out of the bureau drawer and held it on his lap. What it meant, she had no firm idea, but it must have something to do with what he'd seen.

On one level, she understood Nick's reticence to divulge what had happened, but their need to talk took priority over any other considerations. She had to trust him, but his actions left her deeply troubled. She suspected he'd learned something that could impact their mission and whatever that was, it had left him so shaken that he couldn't process what had happened. Her thoughts returned again to the meaning of that cursed…perhaps it was, box.

She'd probed him about the keepsake, but he dodged her questions, finally stating he didn't want to talk about it. That statement confirmed in her mind that that damned box did factor in to what he encountered in the ghetto and that she had no choice but to confront him about its significance.

Her musings were cut short when she noted Nick casting a wary look across the facades of the eclectic mix of attached three-story buildings pressing in on the narrow sidewalk. The claustrophobic feeling of the cramped sidewalk drove most of the pedestrians onto the meandering, equally narrow cobbled street.

"We're not going to have to bolt out a back door again, are we?" he asked.

"Nope." She stopped in front of a café that distinguished itself from the adjacent establishments by a milling crowd of young, jeans-clad, cigarette-smoking adults clustered around the double-doored entrance.

"We're here." She pulled open the right-hand door of Café Spálána only to be punched in the gut by the visceral thumps of a band's bass guitar. She scanned the shoulder-to-shoulder crowd of swaying, ecstatic patrons. Not the quiet place she'd expected. She turned to leave, driven back a step by a massive electric guitar riff.

"No, no, wait." Nick yelled over the noise. The guitar player broke off from a sustained cord only to be replaced by the drummer's slow stick-work that gradually intensified in sound and difficulty. "This is incredible," he hollered in her ear. "Wow, look at that guy's sticks flying over the drumheads. Man, that's blazing speed. He's gotta be the second coming of John Bonham."

She managed to make herself heard above the drums with a shout. "Who?"

"No—Led Zeppelin. They're rocking out on 'Moby Dick.' One of their classics." He turned to a man who appeared to be in charge and pulled out a 2,000-koruna bill. "*Stůl prosim.*"

The man accepted the bill with a bow and escorted them through the standing-room-only crowd to a tiny table set with two chairs midway down the right side of the café. He asked a couple who'd occupied the table to vacate and pulled the preferred chair out for Marie so she could face the band. "*Pro krásnou ženu.*"

She was incredulous at this turn of events. Her partner, a total skinflint, had just shelled out a huge amount of money.

What was that all about? "That was a hundred bucks. What did you say?"

"'A table please.' Works every time."

"I'm sure it does. What did he say?"

"I'm thinking he was more impressed with you than my hundred bucks. He said, 'For the beautiful woman.'"

Marie considered the statement, flattered by the compliment. "Yeah, right."

Nick spun his chair around to face the musicians on the elevated stage. The name of the group was written on the base drum's face. *Dlouhé Vlasy.* Long Hair. "This is awesome."

Marie flagged down a waiter and ordered a pitcher of beer, resigning herself to the compliment, the venue, and the noise. She also concluded there was zero chance Nick wanted to discuss business, and she had to admit, he needed to decompress.

With that thought, Marie doubted anyone would be able to overhear them even if she could persuade him to talk. Another blast of sound assailed her ears. *Hell, I can't even hear myself think.* She looked at Nick and concluded the venue was perfect. She was getting a better handle on how her partner's brain was wired.

"Incredible. Listen to that guy," Nick hollered.

She leaned forward to shout a reply. "Do I have a choice? I can't hear anything else." She held no doubt that her ears would be ringing for days.

"Incredible," Nick said. "What an awesome trap set. Three rack and two floor toms. Oh, man. You see that? The drummer just set his sticks down and is playing the toms with his hands, bongo-like. This is sooo cool."

She had no idea what Nick was talking about, but it did explain the origin of the rhythms he'd often tap out on the seatback in the van—much to George's great annoyance. *Well, I'll be damned, we've got ourselves a closet rocker.*

Long Hair's music ramped up. She cringed at yet another

assault on her ears. A classic music aficionado, she gave herself up to the pounding rock and studied Nick. He appeared oblivious to her presence. She topped their steins and permitted herself to relax. Perhaps the music would drive whatever demons that had possessed him this morning from his mind.

Marie found her opening when the band finally ended their performance of *Moby Dick*. "Sorry about this morning."

Nick started, "Sorry about what?"

"I was thinking about Vasek."

He stiffened. "What about her?"

She took a sip of her beer, bracing herself for what she had to say. This conversation could easily end in disaster. "Clearly, there's something you don't want to tell me."

"I'm fine. There's nothing going on."

"I'm not talking about her hitting on you, which is obvious to everybody except you." She managed to catch herself before she added something she might come to regret. She had no idea if Nick had reciprocated and returned Vasek's play in kind. And if he had? She might well drive a permanent wedge between herself and her partner. She didn't even want to think of the implications on his relationship with Michelle.

He looked at the stage. "I don't know what you're talking about."

"Bull-shit!" she responded, her frustration bubbling to the surface. "You came out of that gift shop looking like you'd seen a ghost. What the hell happened in there? What did she tell you?"

Nick let out a long breath and turned to face her. "It's not what she said. It's what they showed me."

Marie frowned, her head rocking backwards at Nick's revelation. "They?"

"There was an old Jewish woman in the back of the store. A survivor. She's the keeper of the camp's archives. The walls were lined with the records of all those who passed through that damned place."

"The Ghetto?"

"She was a little girl. Somehow she managed to escape death, but not the horrors."

Her hand went to her mouth. "Oh, my God. I had no idea."

"Not many do."

She could barely hear his muted response. She collected her thoughts. Going down this path wouldn't give her what she needed, at least not yet. And she didn't want to press him. She'd learn soon enough what he'd seen. She turned the conversation. "I don't trust her."

"Vasek?"

"Yes."

"Why?"

"Woman's intuition."

He shifted in his seat, his hand gripping the handle of his stein.

She noted his body language and didn't wait for a reply. "I can't shake the feeling that she's working for someone and playing you. You're the means to their end."

"That's crazy."

"Think about it," she said. "No, I'll point out the obvious. First, did you ever notice that when she crosses her legs, she doesn't bother to pull down the edge of her short skirt when you're around? Second, she's too old to wear those clothes. Third…. Should I go on?"

"Ah, no, but Taylor vetted her. Twice. And the Station Chief—"

"I don't give a damn what Ferguson or the Station Chief say. I've been through this. In Manila. And so have you. I shouldn't have to remind you about that snake, Arita."

"How do you know about him?" Nick asked.

"Geoff provided me with background on your last operation. Hell, Arita and his Chinese buddies almost succeeded in getting you thrown in jail for treason." She paused. "Listen, Geoff wanted to make sure I got a feel for your strengths and weaknesses."

When Nick met her last statement with silence, Marie wondered if she'd blown their partnership and any chance to get him to reveal what had happened in the shop. She didn't dare say what else she knew about Nick's father and Ferguson. Finally, Nick responded.

"Presuming you're correct about Vasek, who is she working for?"

"Grekov."

"You sound pretty sure of that," Nick said.

"I am."

"Who's her handler?"

"Dusa," she said, without really thinking of the alternatives. "Vinny said he's tied to Grekov."

"Good point."

She shifted gears. "Can I ask about what happened at Terezin?"

Her question was greeted with silence before he relented. "Yeah."

She gave an inward sigh and decided to take a long shot. "Did whatever happened to you have anything to do with that old box?" By the expression on Nick's face, Marie knew she'd hit the right question.

"Yes. Katerina said I should visit my family's castle."

Her eye's widened. "You have a castle?"

Nick managed a wry smile. "Yeah. It appears so."

The band began their new set, leading off with Zeppelin's *Dazed and Confused*. Marie sensed his mood change, and before she could ask anything else, he said, "Do you know the lyrics?"

"No, I'm into classical music."

"There's a line that applies," he said. *"Lots of people talk and few of them know."*

The words left her stunned. *Damn, Did I just completely screw our relationship or did he just open up?* She decided the latter and drained the last of her beer. "Will you tell me what happened this morning?"

Nick studied her face, then nodded. "Yeah."

Chapter Twenty-Six

ALCRON HOTEL
PRAGUE, CZECH REPUBLIC
SATURDAY 17 OCTOBER

Nick measured the reactions of the seven members of his team. He needed to take them in a different direction. While the role of Grekov and the Russians remained elusive, at least he had some understanding of how they operated based on his encounters with them during the al-Khulyter affair. He would focus on Král.

He also vowed not to tolerate any discussions about what he'd encountered at the Theresienstadt Ghetto or how what he'd found there would impact their mission and his own quest to discover the origins of his family. The only outcome from the evening he'd spent with Marie at Café Spálána that he'd shared with the others was that they were now on tap to visit an old estate in Moravia. He trusted her to keep the remainder of their conversation confidential…at least for now.

He could no longer trust Vasek after Marie's revelations about their tour guide. That insight prompted him to consider how Vasek had reacted at the end of their visit to the archives. He'd been totally clueless about her advances. That being the case, he and Marie decided to spring the request to visit his family's castle on Vasek at the last minute. It would make it more difficult for her or, more likely, Dusa, to alert their accomplices.

And Král and the two men whom the Czech may well have sent to unleash the two shotgun blasts in their direction? Nick still hadn't arrived at a plausible explanation for their actions. The risk seemed out of proportion to the outcome… unless Král's true intent really was to kill him.

What Nick did understand was that blunting Král, whatever he had planned, would be a bit easier if the team's next actions were successful. He had floated the idea of snatching one of Král's lieutenants to see what they could pry out of him. His lips tightened at the thought. Perhaps they could break open their investigation with one audacious act without having to butt heads with Grekov's FSB.

The team was scattered about his and Marie's suite after an early breakfast, intent on running a status check on their mission. In deference to their sensibilities, such as they were, he'd kicked his pajamas and a dirty shirt into a corner next to the couch. They all appeared relaxed notwithstanding the laundry, sipping coffee, chatting amongst themselves. They were also expectant, anxious to get their day started.

Geoff, Edmund, and Ferguson had driven in from Dresden the night before. While the team breakfasted, the three had swept the suite for bugs before Geoff and Edmund split to reconnoiter the Old Town square. They'd also placed several ultrasonic white-noise blockers by the suite's windows to deter anyone from using a laser microphone to record their conversations. Nick had been skeptical of these measures until Ferguson demonstrated that he could pick up and record their

Chapter Twenty-Six

voices from the minute movements of the room's windowpanes.

He understood the team sensed something big was in the offing that would impact their mission, but they still didn't know from what direction, or directions, the threat would present. *Threat.* That was issue number one in Nick's mind. They had yet to confirm the danger to the country that Gilmore felt in his bones. What event could be so catastrophic that it could menace the very foundations of the Republic?

While they all acknowledged the ultimate import of their mission, this morning they were focused on the immediate threat. They'd discarded the idea of targeting Dusa as too risky, but they did float some ideas about how to turn him to their advantage. They also discussed abducting Král's associate, Petr Hájek, but dismissed it as too risky.

"Before we finalize our plan to snatch Delezal," Nick opened, "I'd like to wrap up one loose end. Taylor, what have you discovered about this Formative Agent, Dyna Pospisil?"

"Popsicle," Ann said.

'Popsicle?" Nick repeated, not sure he'd heard her correctly.

"Yeh, we're giving nicknames to all of our Czech *friends*."

He managed to suppress an overt sulk and pulled out a yellow legal pad to cover his reaction about being left out. *That would have been fun. Nobody asked me about nicknames.* He stiffened. Being left on the sidelines was a non-starter. His body language earned him a glance from Marie.

Nick ignored her look, drew a series of large circles to create a Venn diagram, and wrote down, "FRIENDS?" in block letters on the top of the sheet. He had to get his arms around the various players while trying to keep all of them, especially their adversaries' nicknames, neatly filed in his brain. A visual learner, he needed to literally see all the variables to connect the dots. He jotted a few cryptic notes to solidify the mass of data he was struggling to assimilate.

"Popsicle claims she's been coerced," Ferguson said. "Abusive relationship, two kids to feed and clothe, threats of deportation. The usual stuff."

"You believe her?" Jennifer asked.

"She's scared," Ferguson said. "That gives her credibility. That, and she gave up Grekov."

Nick shot Ferguson an incredulous look, but before he could snap a retort, Tom spoke. "It's a good bet she'd say anything to save her skin."

"And her kids," Marie added.

"True enough, but I believe her," Ferguson said. "We promised to protect her."

"*We?* Who's this *'we' you keep referring to?*" George demanded. "It sure as hell isn't us. Have you recruited some of your buddies from the Agency? Or maybe some of those jokers from DEA?"

Ferguson brushed off George's anger. "The Agency. I ran it by Geoff."

"And that somehow makes it okay?" Tom chimed in. "What about Nick?"

"What did she give us in return besides Grekov?" Ann interrupted, leaving Nick wondering what else might be going on that he didn't know about.

"She's hearing rumors of a big drug deal," Ferguson said, ignoring Nick's incredulous look, and George and Tom's outbursts.

Nick clenched his jaw, trying to suppress his anger. What drug deal? Ferguson had pulled this kind of trick before, holding back information whether intentionally or not. He suspected *intentional*—a control issue that Ferguson couldn't shake. The other thing that countered his anger? Ferguson's instincts were usually on point, and Nick would ignore them at his own peril.

He rubbed his chin, wondering just how credible Popsicle's information was. He recalled the term Marie had used at The

Nicholas and wrote, *Chicken Feed*, to one side of his diagram. As he did so, another thought occurred to him. *Why had Coleman's drug deal gone south?* The fallout from the busted DEA deal seemed out of proportion to the attention it had attracted in Washington. Why was that? There had to have been more. He inserted himself back into the discussion. "I don't care how big a deal is in the works, it couldn't possibly constitute a major threat to the country. My question to all of you is: 'Where does it fit?'"

"What's the link to our known players, like Král?" Tom offered.

"Nothing hard," Ferguson answered, "but we haven't connected Popsicle to Král."

"What the hell, Taylor. That's another '*we*,'" George said. "You can't cut us out." He held up his hand before Ferguson could respond. "And don't feed us any BS about 'Need-to-know.'"

Jennifer set her coffee cup down and leaned forward in her chair. "Do we have a secondary source to verify what she's heard?"

"No," Ferguson responded, not appearing to respond to Jennifer's peace offering of her use of an inclusive *we*.

"Tom, you said something that got my attention," Marie said. "You said, '*known players.*'"

Known players. Nick tapped out a staccato rhythm on the legal pad with his pen, his head spinning. *Were there others?* There were so many unknowns, so many variables to unravel. And where did this purported drug deal that Popsicle had dropped on Ferguson fit? He couldn't believe this information—or disinformation, he cautioned himself— would just happen to fall into their laps. He had to trust the team.

He wrote "'Others/Drug Deal?'" within one of his diagram's circles. He might not be left with any choice but to place a call to Coleman. His gut told him that something indeed big was coming down, but it wasn't a drug deal. He could think of only one plausible explanation. The deal had to be a diversion. Presuming he was correct, then who wanted them diverted and for what purpose?" He rested the pen on his legal pad. "Thoughts?"

"My bet is dis-information," Jennifer ventured.

"If your premise is valid," Ann responded, "then I'd ask who fed it to her and for what purpose?"

"Exactly my thinking," Nick said, allowing his team to brainstorm. They were all seasoned operators and he valued … no, needed their input.

"We've got Grekov and Král in play," George said, "so, who else would benefit?"

"Someone who could manage to tie us up in knots," Jennifer said.

Nick pondered what they had said as another thought came to him. "Or is one of them working to play the other off against us and leave their playing field uncontested for another player?"

"A third party we don't know about? An interesting premise," Marie said, "but to what end?"

"The million-dollar question," Nick said. He looked at Ferguson while working the variables in his mind. "Taylor, has the Agency come up with anything that pertains?"

Ferguson leaned back, cupping his left hand over his chin, the first finger curled across his upper lip. He dropped his hand after a moment. "Tehran."

George spat his reaction. "What! The damn Iranians?"

"We have intercepts that suggest they're up to something," Ferguson replied.

Nick glared at Ferguson, recalling that in his previous operation, he'd learned Grekov had been in Tehran supposedly trying... He cut off the memory. "I want everything you have."

Ferguson nodded.

Marie filled the tense silence that followed. "I'd prefer to supply Ms. Popsicle with some false information of our own and see what we get."

"We don't have time for any playback," Ferguson said. He paused. "No, that's not entirely correct, but it'll be tight."

Almost exasperated beyond words at Ferguson's "I've got secrets I can't tell you unless I shoot you," mind games, Nick reinserted himself into the blistering exchange. "What are you thinking?"

"I had a couple of guys place a key logger on her home computer. Some of what we got was encrypted. The guys are using our soft and hardware analytics to capture the keystrokes using the L54096 encryption algorithm."

Nick suppressed his fury. He wouldn't allow himself to be diverted by Ferguson's use of techy smoke and mirrors to divert the rest of the team from what he might be doing. He'd deal with him later. He couldn't allow his mission to veer off course or allow Ferguson to operate off his own secret agenda that could well be counter to that of his own mission. His response mirrored the thoughts of the others. "We don't have time to play fucking games, Taylor. What do you have?"

Ferguson held his hands up in supplication. "Old habits."

"I don't give a damn about old habits." Vinny demanded. "Answer Nick's question."

Ferguson's eyes cast daggers at Vinny. "We have to take at least one person out of circulation, no matter who they are working for. In this case, it's Král's goon Delezal. I've made plans for his interrogation."

Those statements quelled the discontent in the room but did little to mollify Nick's anger. Right now, he didn't want to know what Ferguson's *people* had in store for Delezal. The clock was running, and he'd worry about the implications of what they, or Ferguson, had to do to break Delezal later.

He decided to wrap up their meeting, finalizing their plan to capture Král's lieutenant, Julius Delezal. "Vinny, contact Geoff. We'll need him and Edmund. Then you and George do some dry cleaning and set up our counter-surveillance to identify and counter any pavement and wheel artists Grekov or Král may employ." He turned to Ferguson. "Taylor, do you have any reliable people at the embassy? Folks you know who are familiar with the area and know of a place to stash Delezal?"

"I presented the basic outline to the Station Chief. He's got some ideas and assigned a couple of his people," Ferguson said.

"And?" he prodded.

"Extraordinary rendition," Ferguson added. "I don't know the site."

"Unsat," Vinny said.

"I've got a good idea where it is, but it's best you don't know. I'm afraid you'll have to trust me."

Nick stood, not at all sure he could trust Ferguson. "Let's get this show on the road."

He caught Ferguson by the elbow as the others filed out of the room. He was so angry, he could barely speak. Ferguson's "'You've got to trust me,'" statement was a complete non-starter. No matter how good Ferguson's intentions might be in the agent's own mind, Nick could not let him go rogue. "Damn it, Taylor, I can't… no, none of us can afford to have you going off half-cocked and not keep us in the loop. This isn't yours or the CIA's mission. It's mine."

Ferguson studied Nick for a moment. "Understood. The site's in Poland. A place I've used before when I was involved in the Extraordinary Rendition program."

"What about Delezal?"

"We won't kill him."

"Not good enough."

"We learned our lesson. No rough stuff."

Only slightly mollified, Nick ended their conversation. "Keep me informed."

Chapter Twenty-Seven

OLD TOWN SQUARE
PRAGUE, CZECH REPUBLIC
SUNDAY 18 OCTOBER

Sundays were supposed to be days of rest and reflection, or so Nick's grandparents had raised him to believe. There was no doubt that today would run counter to this conventional wisdom. Just how much? Only time would tell. And time remained a problem. Only nine days remained on his travel Visa and the clock wouldn't slow.

His day had started with a heart-to-heart with Lange about Ferguson, their conversation sweetened by the Bolivar, Cohiba, and Montecristo cigars he'd given his friend. Having received assurances from Lange that he would attend to the CIA agent, they gathered the team to review the specifics of the operation. Nick left the meeting forty minutes later to assume his assigned station in the Old Town square satisfied that all the various pieces of their snatch were in place.

Nick surveyed the activity around the entrance of the

White Horse restaurant from his vantage point beside the statue of Jan Hus that dominated the square. Like many, if not most, of the religious reformers of his time, Hus had been branded a heretic and burned at the stake. A tangential thought worked its way into his brain. *And if this operation failed, what of his own fate?* Nick doubted he'd be burned at the stake. But the outcome might be just as lethal if he failed, to himself and to untold others, if the Director's suspicions about Král, Mendez and the hints they'd received about a possible arms deal held true. Perhaps they would learn something from Delezal to justify the risks they were about to take.

He had spent the previous afternoon observing Czech mannerisms to ensure he wouldn't be flashing *American Tourist* across his forehead and felt appropriately attired in a Kenvelo shirt-jacket, dark jeans, and a turtleneck sweater. He couldn't leave to chance that another watcher, like one of Grekov's goons, might also be observing Julius Delezal's movements. He gave a tug on the bill of the dark-wool Greek Fiddler's cap he'd purchased from a small kiosk near the hotel, made his way from the cover of Hus's statue, and crossed the cobbled pavement of the Old Town square toward his next vantage point.

A heavy rain in the late afternoon had driven most of the tourists away and the square's granite cobblestones glistened in the late afternoon sun. The shadows lengthened and deepened, a harbinger of the cold night to come. A solitary ray of light breaking through the cloud cover splashed the square's buildings in golden hues before it succumbed to the night, the moment lost. Somewhere to his left, Marie monitored his movements.

Nick paused at the steps of the Our Lady Before Týn cathedral. The church's twin Gothic towers, now illuminated by floodlights, anchored the square to his left. He decided to mix with the trickle of people making their way out of the church after evening Mass to provide some additional cover while he headed toward the restaurant. Situated on the ground floor of the Golden Unicorn House, Ferguson's informants had indicated Delezal dined at the White Horse every Sunday night. The upper floors of the corner building had been converted into a small boutique hotel simply named the Old Town Square Hotel. To his immediate right, Zelenza Street terminated in the square.

Nick shifted his gaze, focusing his attention on the sign board to the left of the restaurant's canopied outdoor seating area. *Restaurace White Horse* was printed in large letters above a white unicorn against a blue-gray background. From his vantage point, he could hear the rhythmic beat of jazz coming from a duo performing inside. He tapped his iPhone and brought up several of their best images of Delezal. There could be no mistakes in identifying the target. He considered another variable. If Delezal didn't conform to his usual routine, they were screwed, setting their mission back days, if not longer.

A man emerging around the corner of Zelenza Street caught his eye. A brown fedora topped a round face and the guy's dark-red, windowpane patterned sports coat did little to conceal a ponderous belly. *It's gotta be him.*

Nick stuffed the phone back into his jacket pocket and tilted his head slightly to speak into a throat microphone secured under the fold of his sweater. "I've got a probable." The response to his alert sounded over the small ear bud hidden beneath his cap. Vinny's voice.

"Confirm. We had him exiting his car. Join us when he's inside."

Tom and Ann Belek sipped their wine, waiting for Nick's call. They were pleasantly surprised by the upscale menu and credited Delezal with a least a modicum of good taste. They had secured a table allowing them both to keep their backs to the sole security camera Lange had spotted earlier in the afternoon. They'd also made their reservations using Tom's first name, Tômas, and would pay for their meal in cash.

"What the hell is an acon?" Tom asked.

"Beats me," Ann said. "Maybe they forgot the 'r' when they translated. You thinking of getting the beef sirloin?"

"Maybe they did spell—," he heard Nick's voice in his earbud and stopped in mid-sentence while pretending to study his menu. "He's on his way. Fedora. Dark-red, checked sports coat."

They both averted their eyes as Delezal made his way past their table in the vaulted- stone Romanesque interior of the twelfth-century building and watched as the maître de escorted their mark up a spiraling black-iron staircase to a small table on the second floor. The staff appeared to recognize him. After the waiter removed one of the place settings, they assumed he would be dining alone. The team's job just got a lot easier. Dealing with a lady companion would have presented difficulties.

"You didn't answer my question," he said.

Ann examined the other diners' plates set on the surrounding tables. "Beats me," she repeated, "but my guess remains. It's *acorn*. Might be good."

"If you're a squirrel. What are you ordering?"

"The house specialty. Pork knuckle."

He topped off her wine glass, eyeing the bottle. *Damn.* Much as he'd like to polish off the bottle, he couldn't do so until Delezal left, and God only knew when that'd be. He also wondered how they could prolong their dinner.

Ann seemed to read his thoughts. "Prague is more like France than the U.S. The staff isn't going to hover or push us out to clear the table for another customer. We'll have to ask for the check. Order another bottle and enjoy the music."

He made to flag down their waiter, but lowered his hand

when he spotted Ann slip the menu into her purse. "Seriously, did you just lift the menu?"

"Who knows, it may come in handy."

He settled back into his chair, ordered another bottle of Merlot, and listened to the two jazz musicians while keeping a surreptitious eye on their quarry. He had no sooner taken his first sip of wine when Ann beckoned their waiter and ordered again. "What, you're still hungry?"

"Nah, just something for Ferguson."

Her answer left him flummoxed. "Ferguson?"

An hour and a partial bottle later, Delezal paid his bill and made his way outside, followed a minute later by Ann, doggy bag in hand, and a mystified Tom.

Nick spotted Delezal exit the White Horse a moment after receiving Tom's alert. He stomped his feet a couple of times to restore the circulation and checked in with Ferguson. While the odds were negligible, Ferguson, along with the two guys he got on loan from the embassy's Chief of Station, were conducting counter-surveillance. "We clean?"

"Looks good."

"Roger that." He looked in Ferguson's direction before turning back to face the restaurant. "Damn."

He swung his head through an arc and back again. *Where the hell did he go?* He spoke into his microphone. "I've lost him. He was right in front of me, then vanished."

"He's not on Zelenza," Vinny responded.

Another voice came on the line. One he didn't recognize. An embassy guy? "You think he's on to us?"

Lange inserted himself on the net. "Calm down, everyone. He must have ducked into one of those shops next to the restaurant. Check them out."

"On it," Nick answered. He emerged from the dark alley

next to the cathedral and walked along the store fronts, casting a cautious glance into each. Out of the corner of his eye, he caught a fleeting glimpse, or so he thought, of a man in a long, black coat and dark beanie who ducked out of sight back down the narrow alley he'd just exited. He froze mid-step and spun, ready to pursue. Marie's voice stopped him.

"Relax. I've got him. Second shop."

Nick halted. "Affirm. Granát Jewelry. He's at the counter. Looks like he's buying something."

"Perfect," Lange said.

True enough, Nick thought. Král would come looking for him, and if he checked with the shop owners, they might assume his guy had been mugged. A few minutes later, Delezal exited the shop, quickened his pace, and made toward Zelenza Street and his parked car.

Edmund and Vinny pressed their backs into the shadows of the recessed doorway of a shuttered antique shop when they spotted Delezal rounding the corner. Adam and Jennifer rose from the park bench they'd chosen on the rim of the square and followed their mark, prepared to create a diversion if he fought back.

Edmund breathed a sigh of relief as Delezal approached. If Delezal had suspected he was being watched, he would have ditched the car and taken off. He motioned Vinny to approach their target while he remained in the doorway, waiting until Delezal had inserted his key into the door lock of a 2019 red Skoda Octavia.

Vinny slipped around the rear of the vehicle, came up behind Delezal as he opened the door, and pressed the barrel of his silenced pistol into the Czech's ribcage. "*Pěkné auto, Julius.*"

Edmund strode down the sidewalk, reached his right hand

inside his coat, and positioned himself by the passenger door opposite the two men. His voice cut through Delezal's shocked silence. "My partner and I will be joining you for a short ride."

Delezal froze. The expression on his face expressed bewilderment at the juxtaposition of Vinny's compliment of "Nice car," the pressure of the gun barrel in his side, and the other man's use of accented English.

Edmund heard Vinny caution their target in Czech. "Don't do anything stupid that you might regret. Unlock the other doors and get in." He placed a quick call to Lange, who'd left the square to cross the Charles Bridge, making for a small apartment on Mostecka Street in Lesser Town. His call complete, he slid into the front seat next to Delezal and slammed the door while Vinny climbed into the rear. He pressed his gun barrel against Delezal's chest. "Off we go then, mate," he said in his Scottish brogue. "Buckle up, we dinnae want yer ta get hurt."

Chapter Twenty-Eight

MODRANY FLATS
MUNICIPLE DISTRICT 12, PRAGUE
MONDAY 19 OCTOBER

Anton Král spun from the rain-streaked window of his cramped office in the Modrany Flats, challenging his remaining two leg men. "Where the hell is Delezal?"

Ondréj Reznik and Karel Sokol both stiffened, staring at their shoes. He presumed each of them was hoping the other would answer. Král fixed Reznik with a furious glare. "I asked you a question."

"It wasn't me. I—"

"Don't feed me another one of your damned excuses. When was the last time you spoke to him?"

A shrug greeted Král's question. The muscles of his jaw tightened. "Did you even bother trying to contact him?"

Reznik responded with a sullen pout, crossing his arms over his chest.

Král had had enough of this narcissistic, immature lout.

Chapter Twenty-Eight

I'm done with him. There's plenty of muscle to hire in this city. He took a deep breath and exhaled through pursed lips, permitting his anger to abate as he contemplated how to dispose of Reznik. He smiled, his voice calm. "Karel, what do you have to say?"

Sokol straightened, the expression on his face reflecting his confusion at his boss's abrupt change in demeanor. Král noted it took a moment for Sokol to collect himself. The first part of Sokol's answer would be a calculated lie, the last would not.

"I texted him this morning," Sokol said, "but didn't get a response. He usually goes to dinner at the White Horse each Sunday. I'll head over there to see what I can find out."

He presumed Sokol had indeed lied, but nevertheless waved him toward the door, choosing not to examine his iPhone. "Go."

Sokol donned his hat and made to leave. Reznik remained fixed in place.

"Both of you."

Král leaned back in his chair after the door closed and laced his fingers together behind the nape of his neck. Delezal had vanished. *What am I missing?* He'd heard nothing from him since…when? Saturday afternoon, when he called for his routine check-in. And now? Was Julius a traitor, subverted by the Minister of Interior, Holcará, or…?

He lowered his hands and grasped his coffee mug with both hands, deep in thought. The name of the Iranian, Rajif Mohammadi, kept circling through his mind as did the disguised voice of the other man on the tape. Could it have been *Delezal's*? *Where did Tehran fit into the puzzle*? Did Petr know anything he'd failed to share?

The sound of a light knock on his door prompted him to look up. His financier, Anička Drabek, stood in the doorway. Král blinked, momentarily caught off guard, then recalled she was scheduled to meet with him. *What time was it?* He looked at his watch. Nine. Already? "Come in, Anička."

Drabek wore a tailored, dark-blue business suit and low black heels. Her intense eyes were the color of polished gunmetal and set off by black-rimmed, oval glasses, which in turn accentuated the sophisticated silver-gray highlights of her shoulder-length hair. The line of her jaw fell somewhere between austere and beautiful.

His eyes traveled to her right hand, which clutched a Vera Wang tote bag. Curiously, in her left, she held the pullout handle of a large, wheeled trolley. By the tug she gave it when she took her first step, the thing had to be heavy.

He set his coffee cup aside and gestured to the seat next to his desk. "Are you traveling?" He felt her eyes scrutinize him.

"How are you, Anton?" she opened, ignoring his question.

"Julius has disappeared," he responded without belaboring the point or addressing her non-answer to his question.

Her face remained expressionless, but he could sense her analyzing the implications of his statement, formulating her response. She could always read him. In this case, that was not all bad.

"What does he know of our business transaction?" she asked.

"Very little. Not enough to endanger our operation." He paused, then added. "I had assigned him to watch the American, Partyka."

He studied her, gauging her response. He'd been careful to conceal his true intentions about the Mexican operation from the others, especially Hájek, but he couldn't be certain Delezal hadn't surmised why he had asked questions about the wisdom of expanding their operations to pursue more lucrative, but more dangerous endeavors.

Drabek merely nodded.

He spun his chair around to face the credenza, refilled his

coffee from a thermal carafe, then poured a cup for Drabek and handed it to her.

She took a sip. "*Je to debré, dik.*"

"Where do we stand with Mendez?"

By way of an answer, she reached into her tote and handed him a hardbound, dark-green business ledger.

He opened the cover and glanced at the list of personnel equipment: uniforms, helmets, body armor, webbing. He flipped through several more pages and stopped to run his finger down a long column, skipping over the ammunition for each weapon:

2000 MP-443 Grach pistols

1500 AK-74s – bundled with magazines, accessories, and repair parts

300 AKM-75s, 600-round drum magazines

50 PKM machine guns, 50 replacement barrels

20 NSV 12.7mm heavy machine guns

20 60mm mortar tubes with base plates

200 RPG-75 anti-tank launcher tubes

50 SNARK satellite communication systems

10 Shakhim thermal imaging systems

He grunted approval. The total amounted to nearly thirty tons of armaments for the Mendez Cartel, which Drabek had procured through a succession of contacts in Slovenia and Armenia. Perhaps enough to equip a regiment and more than enough to wet Carlos Mendez's appetite. The total weight of the shipment was well short of the Illyushin-76's cargo jet's capacity of fifty tons or Mendez's projected needs. "And the aircraft?"

"Azerbaijan Air Freight is scheduled to pick up the merchandise at the Hradčany Airport the day after tomorrow. The crates are stored in a small warehouse next to the Coloseum Zlaty pizza parlor on the outskirts of town."

"Excellent," he said. The former airbase near the village of Ralsko in the north of the country provided the necessary cover for the mission. Built by the Luftwaffe in World War II, then expanded by the Soviets, the base had subsequently been abandoned when the Russians left. Few people ventured to the site, with its deteriorating revetments and fractured concrete runway, all except the teenage maniacs racing their custom motorcycles.

The four-engine Ilyushin, designed to land on unimproved airstrips, was perfect for the mission. All his team had to do was clear the runway of debris not already moved by the kids. The aircraft also had the legs to fly across the Atlantic to its ultimate destination in Central America. He had insisted to Mendez's personal agent, Major Alfredo Sanchez, that the aircraft commander should have blind orders and would not know of his destination until he was airborne and out of Czech airspace. Once over the Adriatic Sea, the pilot would open his orders, turn off his transponder, and set course for his true destination, lost to prying satellite radio-frequency interrogations that would have tracked the flight.

He tore the top off a sugar packet and stirred the contents into his coffee with feigned indifference before setting the spoon on the saucer. "And our payment? Did Mendez insist on using the Dark Web's vendor market?"

Drabek hefted the blue-tinted aluminum trolley and dropped it with a thud on the desktop. With a flourish, she unsnapped the cover and spun the case so Král could see the contents. "He wanted to finalize early and make a direct payment."

He stared at the bundles of American hundred-dollar bills. "My God. How much is in there?"

"Ten million." She pointed to a large clear plastic-wrapped package in the netted pocket of the lid. "And this is a gift to ensure further purchases."

"What's in it?" Hájeck asked while he studied the bags of light-blue tablets.

"Fentanyl. There are five, each containing one-hundred pills."

"The going street value per pill is nine-hundred Kurona. A fortune," he whispered in awe, not quite believing the unexpected largesse. *I will use this for the castle.*

Drabek reached into the suitcase and held up one of the banded bundles, shuffling the bills between her fingers like a new deck of cards. "Of course, this is mere loose change for his cartel. He lost six tons of cocaine worth 120 million last month when the U.S. Coast Guard intercepted one of his narcosubs off the coast of Florida."

He didn't care a whit about Mendez's loss. "And what of our other product, the cocaine?" Král asked.

"I've arranged to have it moved to our warehouse in Daćice."

"Excellent. Have the chemists cut it and repackage for distribution."

"Do we hold any of it back for collateral?" Drabek asked.

Král stiffened at her question. Had she surmised what his other plan was for the product? "Perhaps." He shifted the topic to one of even greater import to him. "And our money from the frozen Venezuela account?"

"Our moderator assures me that the funds have been converted into bitcoin and are making their way to us." She paused at Král's frown. "He used an anonymizing software package called Tor to hide our IP addresses and employed a secure hash algorithm to conceal the transactions. Each of the intermediaries has their own private encryption key."

For the moment, his concern about Delezal vanished in the blur of Dark Web speak. Then the reality of what the transaction meant and the threat posed by his competitors forced their way back into his thoughts. Perhaps he'd been too quick to approach Meycek Exports—and the company's probable link to the Russian security service. Had he really deceived himself into believing he could delude Grekov and the FSB as to his real intentions? And what of the Americans? They had to have spies infiltrated all over Mexico. Had they discovered his connection to Mendez and sent Partyka and his team to Prague to—?"

Drabek's voice intruded. "We must eliminate the known risks to our operation." When Král didn't reply, she elaborated, her voice calm and reassuring. "The Iranian, Mohammadi, and that reporter, Anton Jezek, from the Czech Center for Investigative Reporting who's been asking too many questions, are our biggest threats."

The fact that Drabek even knew of the Iranian had eluded him. He finished his coffee and considered refilling the cup from his decanter of brandy, not to celebrate, but to suppress the sudden doubts that threatened to consume him. The unexpected arrival in Prague of this Nickola Partyka threatened to expose his relationship with Mendez. And if the American was a long, lost relative? He spun his chair to face the rain-streaked windows of his flat.

"Yes. We must eliminate both," he answered, the details of his plan to eliminate Reznik firming in his mind. "I will see to it."

"And our own sting to neutralize the DEA Agent Coleman and the American Partyka?" Shall we discuss this?"

He considered her request. A crazy thought occurred to him. Were those two responsible for Delezal's disappearance? The Americans deserved more than an afterthought.

"Yes, now would be a good time."

Chapter Twenty-Nine

NUMBER TEN UVOZ STREET
PRAGUE ADMINISTRATIVE DISTRICT FIVE
MONDAY 19 OCTOBER

Aleksandra Grekov saved and closed out the intelligence report she'd been drafting for the Deputy Director of the *Federalnaya Sluzhba Bezopasnosti*, Colonel General Nikolai Turgenov. For his eyes only, the report detailed the status of their operation. She glanced at the figure standing at ease in her office doorway. The light from the setting sun showed through the casement windows to her left, casting Kuznetov's face in partial shadow. *How long had he been standing there... watching me?*

She pushed the laptop aside. There were certain things... the additional layers of subterfuge that Turgenov and those surrounding him in the FSB could not know, her backup plans for unforeseen contingencies, the secrets that she kept filed safely away within her mind. She recalled a popular quotation that she'd read in the Russian Orthodox Synodal Bible the night before. Proverbs 26:27: "If you set a trap for others, you will get caught in it yourself."

Sobered by her reflection, she weighed her options for dealing with Král. While the Czech was beset with problems, those problems he knew of and those that would soon ensnare him, she had more than her own share of issues to contend with, including a tenuous relationship with headquarters that could easily entrap her. "Come in, Sergei."

Kuznetzov slipped off his black leather coat and sheepskin Papakha hat and hung both on the wooden clothes tree by the door. He took a seat without saying a word.

She wondered if Kuznetzov had knowingly selected the hat to reflect his pride in his Ukrainian heritage as she did. Following the revolution of 1917, the Red Army had banned the headwear that symbolized the predominant Slavic-speaking Orthodox Christian Cossack regiments that had fought for the Czar. Her grandfather had also covertly supported the Chernetsovtsy Cossacks, a Jewish regiment fighting against the Bolsheviks.

While she felt Kuznetzov shared her sympathies, at least for the Christians, she cautioned herself against trusting him entirely. Her history with the FSB had taught her to exercise caution in all relationships, personal or professional. And the Novosibirsk Business Group oligarchs, her old benefactors? They were all descended from the old Czarist aristocracy. She would have to tread carefully to—" Kuznetov's voice lanced through her musings.

"The Americans have sent Král into a panic."

She stiffened at his dual impertinence of speaking first and catching her unawares by his pronouncement. "Would you care to elaborate, Comrade?"

"They have snatched Delezal."

She struggled to conceal her surprise at this revelation. "I've heard."

A look of consternation appeared on Kuznetzov's face as

she had intended. He shifted in his seat. "He knows enough about our role in Král's arms shipment to—"

She lifted her right hand cutting him off. "And what of Ilia?"

"I ordered him to keep tabs on Parkos. Our source at Hotel Alcron reported—"

"Nick is a worthy adversary," she interrupted. "One deserving our respect. The NSA has sent their *Komanda.*" She searched for the American term. "Their 'A-Team.'" She caught herself. If Kuznetzov was surprised at her use of Parkos' surname, he didn't let on. She studied him.

Kuznetzov responded to her remark with a reflective nod. "Our background investigation suggests that Parkos' accomplice, this Ferguson, might have driven this operation."

She happened to agree with him, but wanted to determine if Kuznetzov had resources that he'd failed to mention. "Why do you say that?"

"He disappeared after the abduction."

"He?"

"Ferguson."

"And coincidences don't exist."

"*Da.* They will learn of our involvement in directing the Slovenian and Armenian arms shipment."

Her hands tightened around the edge of her desk. "Did Ilia determine where the Americans have stashed the Czech?"

"No. Another couple from their supposed tour group created a disturbance, drawing the attention of the *Policei*. Our team had to break contact."

Grekov stopped short of responding. If Kuznetzov knew of the American's plan, why hadn't he assigned more agents? She answered her own question. He had as much to lose as she if Delezal talked. "The Americans will not keep him in Prague."

"Should we eliminate him?"

She surmised Kuznetzov meant Ferguson. Her disquiet

receded at his suggestion, sensing an opportunity. "A counter move is our best option. But first, I agree, we must also eliminate Delezal before he can be interrogated. If Ferguson is taken out, so much the better."

"Delezal will spill his guts."

"No doubt. While these Americans profess adherence to International law, they are no different from us when threatened. They will exercise no remorse when using enhanced interrogation techniques."

"I have something from our source in the Serbian military," Kuznetzov added. "A Gulfstream 500 owned by Concierge Jet Service landed at Poland's Osztyn-Mazury airport early this morning, ostensibly to refuel, but the tail numbers didn't match those submitted to Eurocontrol." He stopped. "You will know the airport by its previous name, Szymony, made notorious for supporting the CIA's extraordinary rendition flights."

"Excellent, Sergei. The Gulfstream is their preferred aircraft for an extraordinary rendition operation, as is their use of that regional airport. Those would have been my choices if I were in their shoes."

"The flight originated from the American air base at Aviano, but the flight plan was filed as originating at Venice's Marco Polo airport and terminating at London City Airport's Private Jet Center."

Her eyebrows knotted. She'd almost missed a crucial element of Kuznetov's statement. "How do we know this?"

"A Beriev A-100 AWACS picked the aircraft up as it popped up over the mountains north of Aviano and then tracked it to Varga…," Kuznetzov paused. "Northeast Poland."

She suppressed a wave of anger and set her pen down in a deliberate movement signaling her displeasure. "London City airport is near the Brit's Lakenheath Airbase. They may have landed in Poland as a ruse, then diverted to Lakenheath."

"And taken Del—"

"How long has the military known this?"

Kuznetzov sidestepped her question. "Our Slavic brothers in the Serbian military have permitted us to operate our surveillance aircraft from Batajnica Air Base near Belgrade. They are anxious to counter their government's overtures to NATO and want to solidify their overtures for membership in our Collective Security Treaty Organization."

"I suspect there was a short fuse on this operation," she responded, not interested in what inducements Moscow may have offered the Serbian military. "And they didn't have time to—"

"Perhaps the Serbs were hedging their bets to give the impression of cooperation."

She picked up her pen and jotted a cryptic note. "That would make sense … or perhaps the military is inept and failed to notify us in a timely manner. We must presume they spirited Delezal to one of their black sites. Where did the plane land?"

"Olsztryn-Mazury airport. Not far from the village of Stare Kiejkuty and a base they used for their black operations over a decade ago."

"If I recall, the Polish intelligence agency, the Agencja Wywiadu still uses the facility for training their cadres."

"Jedostka Weojskowa Unit 2669," Kuznetzov added. "But they will not present the greatest challenge. We have identified units from the 18th Reconnaissance Regiment that have been assigned to protect the perimeter of Strefa B, one of two ultra-secure sites within the base."

Her mind spun with possible scenarios. "Presuming the Gulfstream continued on its mission. Did the Air Force continue to track the aircraft?"

"Unknown."

"I will contact Turgenov." She paused, reading the skeptical look on Kuznetzov's face. "But not before you determine the status of the Gulfstream. Call London."

He nodded.

She changed the topic. "And the arms?"

"They will be shipped the day after tomorrow from the Hradčany Air Base. Azerbaijan Air Freight."

"Our old base is still of some use, then." Her voice remained neutral. She had just fended off another extortion threat from Holcorá, or so she hoped. And there were still the Iranians. She'd shared her thoughts about the Iranian, Rajif Mohammadi, with Turgenov, who'd advised her to *marginalize* the agent from Iran's Ministry of Intelligence, the VAJA. The transcript of a targeted surveillance of the Iranian embassy in Moscow by the FSB obtained by Kuznetzov suggested Mohammadi may have stumbled across their plan. The Iranians would like nothing better than to destroy the Americans by creating a war on their Mexican border even if it exposed their supposed ally, Mother Russia. And their puppet, Mendez? He, too, would be dealt with if he became overzealous and exceeded Moscow's guidance.

Grekov gave voice to her thoughts. "Can we design the operation to eliminate Delezal, lay the blame at the feet of the Iranians, and turn this debacle to our advantage?"

Kuznetzov cocked his head. "Perhaps. May I suggest that the best course of action will be to focus on Delezal rather than creating a web of deceit in which we may ourselves be entrapped?"

"Proverbs 26."

He responded with a rare smile. "*Da.*"

"Report back to me within the hour."

She opened a new message to Turgenov after Kuznetzov closed the door. What she hadn't divulged to her deputy was that she'd heard from the chauffeur, Dusa Novikov. Vasek planned a trip to Parkos' family castle, Castle Patykaovi. She clicked her tongue. Tak, tak, tak. Nick is indeed full of surprises. She made a note to order Ilia to observe the Americans. Perhaps Nick was to meet with Král and his partner, Hájek, and conspire against her?

Her operation had taken a new direction fraught with extreme risk, but she'd listened to Sergei's and her own advice. Advice drawn from their faith. Now she had to place her trust in Sergei and others to find Delezal. They would only have one shot to find the Czech before the Americans moved him to another, more secure, location. Perhaps even in the States. *And if I fail? My fate will be sealed.*

Chapter Thirty

OLSZTRYN-MOZURY AIRPORT
STARE KIEJUTY, POLAND
MONDAY 19 OCTOBER

Concierge Jet Service's Gulfstream 500, tail number N8073V, landed at the Olsztryn-Mazury airport shortly after two o'clock in the morning. The pilot's landing speed, approach angle, and flare were normal to avoid undue attention from the locals at such an unusual hour. But once they touched down, there were no more precautions.

The aircraft roared down the isolated 8000-foot runway. Not until the final stretch did the pilot slam on the brakes, deploy the spoilers, and reverse thrust. The screech of the brakes and the screaming from the twin BMW-Rolls Royce turbofan engines registered their protests, far from a sedate landing roll for the exclusive passengers onboard.

The Gulfstream wrenched to a halt just before it would have careened off the end of the runway enveloped in a cloud of acrid, blue smoke from the abused brakes. The nose gear's

Chapter Thirty

hydraulics dipped, absorbing the shock of the abrupt stop, the jet's twin front wheels resting on the tall grass edging the tarmac. A fuel truck pulled out from the woods and stopped next to the aircraft's starboard wing. The operators jumped out and began to unreel a thick-black hose, connecting the high-tensile braided conduit to the fuel port adapter, beginning the high-risk process of hot refueling to top off the jet's wing tanks. While the pilot knew he had enough fuel to reach London, he also knew from experience there could always be an unexpected change of plans. He'd insisted on the extra risk of refueling based on an abundance of caution and kept his engines running.

Taylor Ferguson glanced out the aircraft's oval window, recalling the last time he'd been here years before, a lifetime ago. The small airport, carved out of northeast Poland's dense pine forests, had been rebranded as the gateway to the Masurian Lake District to obscure its prior association with the CIA's Extraordinary Rendition program. He turned his attention to his prisoner and smiled at the expression of wide-eyed terror on Delezal's face. He unclipped his seatbelt. "Welcome to Poland, Julius. Unfortunately, I suspect you will not enjoy your brief stay."

He stood and pulled out his Beretta. "Of course, you understand we must take precautions."

The jet's crew chief approached at Ferguson's prompt, pulled Delezal out of his chair, jerked his arms behind his back to click on handcuffs, then gagged him. With Delezal secured, Ferguson gestured toward the door. "Shall we?"

Ferguson's eyes shot over the darkened airstrip. Nothing, but one could never leave anything to chance. He'd ensured the landing fee had been paid in cash to the local government representative from the Air Navigation Service Agency standing watch in the small airport's control tower, along with a generous stipend to ensure there were no records of this unscheduled landing. A representative from the Polish Intelligence Agency, the Agencja Wywiadu, standing beside the ANSA agent was more than enough to guarantee there would be no record of, or questions asked, about the Gulfstream.

A driver waited, leaning against the side of an idling dark-paneled van with blackened windows parked a safe distance away. The driver took a final draw on his cigarette, flipped it onto the runway, and crushed the smoldering butt with the toe of his boot when he spotted two men exit the aircraft. He nodded a greeting to Ferguson, yanked open the rear doors of his van, and shoved in the prisoner. Delezal tumbled into the rear compartment, landing on his left shoulder with a muffled cry. The driver ignored him and prepared to slam the door. He turned at the sound of Ferguson's voice.

"Make a hole."

The driver stepped aside to allow the jet's crew chief to slide a large, sealed cardboard box in behind Delezal's crumpled body. He didn't appear happy at this development. "What the hell is that?"

"A few things to unsettle our guest," Ferguson answered.

The driver uttered an expletive and made for the front of the van.

"There's nothing in the box that will hurt anything," Ferguson said to the driver's back. He studied his prisoner, then slammed the doors closed. "There's no way in hell he's going to get into any mischief back there."

Only slightly mollified, the driver acquiesced. "It's a short drive."

"I remember," Ferguson said. He climbed into the passenger

seat and buckled up, listening to the roar of the Gulfstream as it taxied to take off for God only knew where. He didn't need to know. Neither man spoke again as the driver set course for the secret Polish base home to Jednostka Wojskowa Unit 1669.

The driver exited left out of the airport, turning away from the small village of Stare Kiekuty. He kept to the speed limit, illuminating the road with the van's dim fog lamps to avoid prying eyes, and braked to a stop at the base's main gate twenty minutes later. Coils of razor wire topped the chain-link fence festooned with yellow signs: Prohibited Area. No Photographs. Violators Will Be Prosecuted. The locals knew this place. There was no need for the warnings.

A stern guard, his MSBS Grott assault rifle held at the ready, approached the driver to check his ID while another approached Ferguson's window. A third walked to the rear of the van and tried the doors. Ferguson tensed at Delezal's muffled shouts. This was not the time to have these Neanderthals causing trouble. He twisted toward the driver, who lowered his window and spoke a few words to the guard planted at the door. He picked up on the few words he understood. "Russian.' 'Scum.' The guard laughed, yelled to his two compatriots, and all three returned to their post. The main gate and a second, inner one, swung open.

The driver gunned the van, passed through the double-gated opening, and made his way down a series of darkened roads deep into the dense woods toward Strefe B, one of two ultra-secret installations situated within the secret base. Ferguson didn't recognize a single landmark and the gathering clouds of an approaching storm blotted out what light shown from the waxing crescent moon. He could only trust the driver, which he wasn't inclined to do until they pulled to a stop in front of a dark-gray, windowless, concrete block building.

The driver set the brake but left the engine running. "Quickly." He didn't wait for a reply and made for the rear doors.

Two people, Ferguson's accomplices from the Agency, appeared at the building's front door and made their way to the van. The first, Draegan Wójcik, joined the driver, pushed the box out of the way, and yanked Delezal out the door. The driver grabbed Delezal under the arms breaking his fall before he crumpled to the ground.

Wójcik ignored the prisoner, eyeing the large box. "This go, too?"

"Yeah," the driver answered. "We'll come back for it. Grab this guy's other arm."

The second agent, Enid Dabrowski, sauntered up to Ferguson, ignoring the ruckus behind her. "Well, I'll be damned. We heard you were the escort, but didn't believe you'd show your face in this neck of the woods after—"

Ferguson eyed Delezal, who was being dragged toward the front door of the detention center and cut her off. "You finished the painting?"

Dabrowski pulled up her sleeve to show the paint spots on her arm. She cast a glance at Delezal, who disappeared into the building. "Come on. I understand we're on a timeline."

"Hold on a sec." Ferguson headed for the rear of the van. "I need a hand."

Dabrowski eyed the cardboard box. "What's in it?"

"A few things to decorate our friend's studio. You got a place to dump that creep while we get set up?"

"Yeah. We also have something to help him sleep."

"Good."

Chapter Thirty

The flash from the room's overhead light woke Delezal from a fitful sleep. He groaned and rolled away from the glare. His entire body ached. He rolled his shoulders, grimacing from the pain in his left shoulder where he'd landed on it. Flexing his wrists, he noticed something had changed. The shackles had been removed. *When did that happen?* He inspected the raw circles where the metal had abraded his wrists. The wounds had been cleaned and dressed. He had no recollection of that, either. He massaged his temples and blinked his eyes, becoming aware of other things.

The aroma of freshly brewed coffee penetrated the dull throbbing in his head. The aroma was overlaid by the pungent odor of freshly applied paint. And he was in his own bed. At least he thought he was. His dulled mind began to register the colors of his blanket, his own feather pillow. He swept his eyes around the room, disoriented. The space looked like his bedroom, but it wasn't. The curtains were the same, but the wall color had changed. A soft pastel blue, calming. Lilting music began to play while he wrestled with these conflicting impressions. Surround sound. He paused. Rachmaninov's Second Symphony. One of his favorites. *How did they know that?*

Delezal shook his head. *How long have I been here?* He looked for his watch—gone. He sat up, struggling to work through what had happened. He'd been abducted. That much was clear, and it was likely done by the Americans. He wrapped his arms around his knees and shuddered at the prospect of what they would do to him. How much could he give up to save his life—from them and from Král?

He spotted a closed door. He swung his legs off the side of the bed, stood a moment, his right hand on the mattress to steady himself, then walked over and tried the handle. Locked. He scanned the ceiling for video cameras. None. He had to pee. He saw another door. Open. A bathroom? He took several steps before coming to a halt. A small table was set in the corner with two chairs, a white tablecloth, and a menu.

He walked to the table curious about the menu. *The White Unicorn's?*

His head jerked around as the door in the far wall opened. He no longer needed to study the menu or pee. The man who'd likely abducted him stepped into the room and smiled.

———

Ferguson activated a small USB flash drive voice recorder as he entered the interrogation room "Ah, Julius, I see you are awake. Did you sleep well?" He didn't expect an answer. "We have a long day planned."

"Who are you?"

"In good time. I'd suggest you first take advantage of a hot shower and indulge in your favorite toiletries." He switched to French. "*Il's sont particulièment gentile, sortout l'Huile prodiguese et l'Avène Eau Thermale, n'est-ce pa?*"

Delezal stared in response to his abrupt use of French. His prisoner's facial expression broadcast all he needed to know. Delezal hadn't understood a word of what he'd said. He shrugged. "*Ça ne fait rein.*"

The sound of a cart pushed into the room by a severely dressed woman with a white apron tied around her waist prompted both men to look in her direction. She smiled a greeting to Delezal, stopped by the small table and set out a dinner plate of beef carpaccio, dressed with arugula, balsamic onions, and grated Parmesan. An enticing aroma spread through the room as she placed a basket of crusty French bread to one side of the plate. A pot of coffee and a bottle of Primitivo Merlot and two wine glasses followed. Completing the setting was Delezal's favorite dessert, the White Unicorn's chocolate fondant.

Ferguson poured a cup of coffee and offered it to his captive. "We hope you approve of our selections."

Chapter Thirty

Delezal extended his hand, accepting the cup without a word.

"Cream or sugar?"

Delezal stared at his abductor, then started again, spinning at the sound of atonal whistling from the woman, who was now bent over making his bed. She straightened. "I've taken the liberty of laying out some fresh clothes, sir. I trust you will approve of my choice."

Delezal could only stare at a pair of trousers and a shirt from his home's wardrobe closet.

Ferguson lifted the bottle of Merlot, studying the label. "*C'est bon.*" He proceeded to open the bottle, give the cork a sniff, and pour a couple ounces in one of the wine glasses, before giving it a swirl and a taste, finalizing the ritual. "*Magnifique.*"

He set the wine down and switched to English. "Perhaps you do not understand French, or you are startled by our hospitality. Be that what it may, I believe you understand English and trust that you will have some time to reflect on what you would like to share regarding your employer's intentions."

The woman gave a small bow and left. Ferguson flashed an insincere smile and followed her out of the room. The room's door latch clinked softly, ominously, behind them.

Delezal dropped back onto the bed, hands pressed to his temples to stop the throbbing in his head.

Chapter Thirty-One

CASTLE PATYKAOVI
MORAVIA, CZECH REPUBLIC
TUESDAY 20 OCTOBER

Nick half-listened to Vasek's running commentary, only catching snippets during the 70-minute drive to the ancient castle. *Charles IV of Bohemia... ancient nobility... Count Vilém... occupied by the Swiss who fortified the barbicans during the Thirty Years War...* His mind remained focused on Taylor Ferguson despite Vasek's mention of an ancestor's first name. Ferguson had remained close-mouthed about Delezal's fate or where they had taken their captive...perhaps for the best.

Today was the twentieth. Only seven full days remained until they had to leave the country. And what of Ferguson? Once again, the CIA agent had left him marginalized despite his assurances that he'd stay in contact. How many days would it take to break Delezal, and would Ferguson keep his promise: "No rough stuff." With that final thought, Nick turned his attention to Vasek.

Chapter Thirty-One

"The earliest portions of the castle date to the twelfth century," she said. "In 1480 it was rebuilt in the Gothic style and in the 1580's, Count Patykaovi expanded the central keep..."

Nick looked out the window of their Mercedes van, his thoughts wandering to Vilém. He knew nothing of the Count and the name hadn't appeared in any of his limited research before he left Washington. A sense of foreboding enveloped him. What might the visit portend? Would he really learn something of his family?

They descended into a valley darkened by a dense forest of massive oaks and beech trees, the beeches scattering bursts of bronze within the gloom. The forest soon gave way to the blue-green foliage and the clean scent of spruce and fir trees as they climbed the twisting mountain road. They passed a mysterious grove of gnarled, moss-encrusted trees twisted into bizarre shapes by the weight of snow and ice of past winter storms before emerging into an open meadow.

The imposing walls of Castle Patykaovi dominated the vista beyond the open space, its flanks protected by the steep crags of the White Carpathian Mountains. The high-pitched shriek of a golden eagle soaring above the weathered turrets broke the silence with a forlorn call. Behind the raptor, smoke rose in a gray, lethargic column from a spiral chimney, the work of a skilled potter. Nick wasn't sure what to make of this first impression of his ancestral home looming in the distance.

Strands of mist clung to the great lawn, the castle towering, apparition-like in the distance as they made their way down the narrow tract bisecting the expanse of a broad meadow. *Why was that?* Could the castle be haunted by the lost souls of his distant family? He shrugged off the thought as absurd.

The van slowed to a stop, its tires crunching softly on the graveled forecourt. He slid open the side door, his right hand gripping the armrest as he prepared to swing his legs out. He paused, mesmerized by the captivating scene.

A gust of biting mountain air, the harbinger of an approaching storm, blew through the door, penetrating the thin lining of his jacket. He felt a sudden sense of foreboding, something that chilled him to his very core. He turned up the collar of his coat to ward off the damp air while dismissing his premonition before he stepped into the remnants of the morning mist. The ground fell away to his left, leading his eyes to what may have been an old moat. He noted a solitary car tucked away at the far end of the court.

"Nick?"

Vasek's voice startled him. He turned to her. "I'm sorry. What did you say?"

"Count Vilém was very wealthy and had a large staff that cared for the estate."

He closed his eyes, trying to visualize an image of his distant relative, Count Vilém Patykaovi being welcomed home by a line of expectant servants waiting at the portcullis to greet their master.

In the distance, a roll of thunder rebounded off the mountains like so many cannons heralding the arrival of a storm. Fat drops of rain fell on the far side of the courtyard, the leading edge of the deluge driving toward them. Vasek's voice broke through his trance.

"This way. Quickly. To the gate house."

She and the other women took off at a trot. Tom and George trailed, having appeared to have spotted something.

Nick followed the men's eyes. Several men, one leaning on a shovel, appeared to be studying him. He focused on the two. Groundskeepers? No. There was something about the men, particularly the one standing apart from the other, that demanded his attention. What was it? Something in his bearing, his gaze, struck him, but what accounted for the man's scrutiny? The rain intensified, pelting him with huge drops. Nick took off for the portico, the question lingering.

Tom ignored the rain dripping off the brim of his hat and gave a tug on George's elbow, while pretending to point out something just below the far rampart. "A couple of guys watching us. Two o'clock."

"Got'em," George said. "Let's go."

They slowed at the sight of the men toiling inside a small, low-walled enclosure. The one nearest the wall held a wooden bladed shovel and was attired in rubber work boots coated in mud, woolen trousers, and a long threadbare coat, all topped by an old Slovakian army hat. The other groundskeeper labored purposely, throwing globs of viscid muck over the stone retaining wall. The man ducked his head and plunged his shovel into the mud without acknowledging the visitors.

Tom studied the second man. The trimmed beard looked out of place. He would have expected something shaggier, one matching his clothes. The man looked familiar, but he couldn't place where he'd seen him. He motioned to Tom and caught up with Vasek. "Katerina?"

Vasek paused under the entrance of the portico. "Yes, Tômas?"

He pointed to the laborers. "Do you know what they may be doing?"

"Oh ... I should have said something."

He noted her eyes dart over his shoulder at something in the far distance before coming back to rest on the workers. He also detected a note of insincerity and the hesitation in her voice. Puzzled by her response, he nonetheless let it pass. Maybe she'd been distracted by one of the others.

"That is the site of an ancient Mikvah, a ritual Jewish bath," she continued. "This one may date back to the fifteenth century. And the men? They are often here digging through the muck. I've been told they are attempting to restore it. The Nazis desecrated the bath by turning it into a pigsty. It fared no better after the castle was confiscated by the Communists in the putsch of '48. They sent the few remaining staff to work in the East German uranium mines. Nothing more was heard of them."

Tom feigned interest in her narrative while he scanned the area. He detected movement at the edge of a narrow clearing adjoining the dense forest. There was someone else out there.

He lifted his camera to take a picture of the Mikvah and magnified the image. *Well, I'll be damned, could that be Král?* He didn't recognize the other man, but snapped several pictures then swung his camera a few more degrees toward the edge of the forest, repeating the process. A diminutive man wearing wire rims, a dark green parka, and baggy brown pants filled his viewfinder. *The little Russian creep that he had spotted before?* He turned his attention back to Vasek's narrative.

"It is alleged the Nazi occupiers threw many of the count's valuables in with the slop ... at least those not of silver or gold," she explained. "Those they stole. Perhaps they are looking for some treasure?"

"And nobody stops them?"

Katerina shrugged. "They are doing no harm. Perhaps the authorities have given them permission out of amused tolerance, although I'm surprised they haven't chased them out."

Tom grunted an acknowledgment, his attention distracted by one of the laborers. He appeared to be studying something he'd found in the mud.

"Why's that?" George asked.

"It's been long rumored that at the end of the war, the Nazis dumped a horde of gold down one of the estate's wells. Nobody's ever found it." She pointed to an overgrown path that faded into the forest encroaching the remnants of the castle's eastern moat. "A flooded quarry, a grotto, is farther down that path. I've never ventured there. Perhaps that is where the treasure is to be found. Yes?"

Tom gave George a subtle nod toward the woods. "Want to check it out?"

"Sounds good," George said. "Katerina, we'll catch up. Tômas wants to take a look at the quarry. He's watched too many episodes of the reality show, 'The Curse of Oak Island.'"

She hesitated, looking doubtful, apparently confused about Oak Island. "All right, but please don't spend long."

George cast an indifferent glance when they passed the gardeners. "You catch that guy's beard and fade cut?"

"Sure did. And his eyes, studying us. That's no day laborer."

"Wonder who the hell he is?"

"I'm thinking it's Anton Král."

George almost stumbled at Tom's revelation. "Král? You've got to be kidding. What the hell would he doing out here? And who's the other guy?"

"Beats me," Tom said. "We'll tell Nick after we figure out what our watcher is up to." He showed the last couple of pictures he'd taken to his partner.

"Well, I'll be damned," George said, "That's the Russian whose been tailing us. What the hell is going on?"

Chapter Thirty-Two

CASTLE PATYKAOVI
PROTECTORATE OF MORAVIA AND BOHEMIA
TUESDAY 20 OCTOBER

Nick cast a curious glance at Tom and George as they disappeared down a narrow footpath leading into the forest. He passed through the portal of the gatehouse, thinking the name of the structure was a bit overstated. Not quite the Black Gate of Mordor. He smiled at the thought of spotting Gollum as he strode across the narrow wooden bridge leading to the gatehouse, but he couldn't pause, intent on catching up with Marie and the others who'd disappeared into the castle.

He pulled up short as he entered a courtyard paved with large rectangular stones. Before him stood the five-story great tower.

Vasek gestured to entrance. "This way, Nickola. There are wonders to behold inside."

He dragged his eyes from the tower and followed her into

Chapter Thirty-Two

the castle's foyer. His first impression of the vaulted hallway was of gloom, barely mitigated by the dull half-light cast by a few dated electric wall sconces. His second? The dank, musty odor that suffused the air of this ancient space. Judging from the scattering of portraits lining the walls, the hallway may have once been an old gallery. *My family?*

Nick cast a glance at one bearded fellow clad in medieval garb: Stockings, tights, a voluminous cape draped over an ornate tunic. The man bore a faint resemblance to a picture of Král's associate, Petr Hájek. He wondered who the gentleman in the painting might be. He paused, pointing to the portrait "Katerina, do you know who the man in this portrait is?"

"I have been told it is a nobleman named Andrez Hájek."

Nick suppressed an exclamation of surprise wondering what other discoveries awaited. He picked up his pace, following the hushed voices of the women into a large room that appeared to have once been the great hall.

There were no suits of ancient armor, crossed muskets, swords, or halberds mounted over the fireplace. The space was instead laden with heavy oak furniture, the fabric tattered, the bold designs faded by time to a dull rust color. A monumental tapestry portraying a seventeenth-century court scene covered most of the far wall.

Vasek herded her group out the door. "Come, there is more to see, especially the Chapel of the Holy Cross, rumored to have been the repository of holy relics brought back from the Crusades."

Nick wondered how the relics squared with the hints he'd learned of his family's heritage, the heritage buried over the centuries and nearly erased by the Nazis.

"Nickola, your grandfather managed to hide—"

The appearance of an ancient man, an apparition emerging from the shadows, stopped Vasek in mid-sentence. A full, gray beard framed the man's face, lined by time and circumstance. A pair of round, mottled-brown glasses perched on a beaked nose encased his prominent eyes, giving him the wizened look of an owl. His clothes, accented by a three-buttoned '60's styled green and brown Glen plaid blazer and a mismatched tie were worn, but clean. He walked with a slight limp and sported a fashionable walking stick.

Nick stared at the man as he made his way down the hall. The cane striking on the stone pavers resounded unnaturally loud in the confined space. TAP. TAP. TAP.

The old man shuffled to a stop before Vasek and steadied himself on his silver-handled walking stick. He welcomed her in the traditional European manner, brushing a kiss on both her cheeks. "Katerina, my child."

Vasek smiled. "How are you, *Otec?*"

Nick's head cocked at a quizzical angle at the Czech word she'd used. *Father?*

"*Dost debr.* Well enough," the old man answered. "Who are these people you bring?"

"Friends." She extended her arm, palm open, gesturing to Nick. "This is Nikola, father."

The old man approached, resting his right hand on the handle of his cane, his intense gray-blue eyes scrutinizing Nick's face. *"Yes,* I see him in your eyes."

Him? Before Nick could respond, he continued.

"I knew your father, Nikola."

"My father?"

"Yes. Ezra, son of Nikola Patyka."

"Ezra? Patyka?" Nick struggled to contain the surge of emotion washing over him, the revelation threatening to submerge him in the depths of …. what, exactly? His grandfather's name was Nikola. His father's was Thomas. *Who was this Ezra?*

Chapter Thirty-Two

He hadn't come across the name, Ezra, in his genealogical research. He did know his grandfather had changed the family's name when they emigrated to the United States. *Could his father's birth name have been Ezra?* Perhaps the registers, the registers the old woman at the ghetto told him had been destroyed by the Nazis and communists, could provide him with the answer. "Who are you?"

"I am Pádriac Hájek, your uncle twice removed." The old man swept his hand over the portraits. "I care for this place. Our family's heritage. Our people."

Marie's jaw dropped in disbelief. Hájek? "You must be—"

The old man held up his hand, stopping her, and looked at Vasek. "Are these people to be trusted?" he asked in Czech.

She, in turn, looked at Nick for his approval, then answered. "Ano."

The ancient, as Nick decided to call him, still not trusting the others despite Vasek's affirmative hesitated, then continued. "I knew your father. He reached out. We…"

The ancient, hesitated, apparently changing his mind about what he was going to say, then went on. "Your grandfather fled to the United States in 1948 in search of a better life with an infant, your father."

"How could you have known him?" Nick asked in disbelief. "You said he was an infant."

The ancient hesitated, his eyes conveying the depth of his emotion. "Your father returned to Castle Patykaovi to right the wrongs perpetrated on our family and our country." His voice cracked. "And, for that, he lost his life."

Nick gasped, a sudden chill racing through his body, a gust of icy wind cutting through his jacket. *My father lived here?* He reached for the nearby table to steady himself.

The ancient's face clouded with concern. *"To jsi zamal, müj synu, ano?"* You knew this, my son, yes?"

Nick shook his head, struggling to comprehend what he'd heard. He gathered what faculties he still possessed and concentrated. Had he heard the ancient's name correctly? Hájek?

"*Ach, ty mluvíš Česky.* You speak our language," the ancient said. He waited for Nick to acknowledge his words before continuing. "But I will use my limited English for the benefit of the others. Perhaps you saw my grandson and the other restoring the Mikveh. But there is no golden treasure to be found there."

At Pádriac's words, another figure, a woman, appeared out of the shadows at the end of the gallery. "Uncle, are these the visitors you mentioned?"

He turned at the sound of her voice. "Yes, please join us."

Pádriac broke the ensuing silence when the woman stopped at his side. "Nikola, this is my niece, Ida. You may have seen her son working in the Mikvah. Petr lives in the city as does his sister, Natálya, but I am blessed to have Ida keeping me company in this lonely place. Otherwise, I would only have the ghosts to keep me company.

A wave of dizziness washed over Nick at Pádriac's revelation. *Ida? Petr? Natálya?* He had found nothing about these people.

Ida received Nick with a warm smile as one would greet a relative. "Nickola, I am so happy you have traveled all the way from the United States to meet your..." The remainder of what she planned to say caught in her throat. "...to meet our, family. There are so few of us who survived, and each moment is precious."

Pádriac rescued his niece, giving her a moment to collect her emotions. "Ida, I would like to spend a moment with your nephew. Perhaps you could show the others the rest of the castle?"

The old man turned, pointing his walking stick down the dark corridor, and took several steps. "Come. I will show you the real treasure."

The old man paused when the women followed. "Kate-

Chapter Thirty-Two

rina, would you be kind enough to assist Ida. Perhaps show our guests the cellars and the chapel?"

Nick's brows bunched when Vasek said something to Marie. He couldn't make out what she'd said or how Marie had answered. Marie motioned for the other women to join her and followed Vasek down the hall, leaving him alone, bewildered by this turn of events. There was nothing rational about what was happening in this place. He struggled to contain his racing thoughts, trying to compartmentalize, to reign in the anxiety that threatened to overwhelm him.

The old man had said his last name was Hájek. Was the man in the Mikveh the same Petr Hájek that Coleman had mentioned on the bridge? Were there others in his family Coleman didn't know of? The ancient hadn't elaborated. Perhaps he didn't feel the need. *Why?* He watched Ida and the other women disappear from sight, feeling abandoned.

Dazed, he followed the old man into the depths of the castle.

The ancient stopped in front of an oak door reinforced with massive iron staves. He motioned for Nick to enter, sweeping his walking stick over the expanse beyond. "This is our treasure."

Nick's eyes swept over the castle's library. Bookshelves sagging with ancient volumes. A solitary pillar candle flickered on a writing table. The sights conjured the image of a sacred space. The table, the candle, the open book—an altar. *Perhaps it was.*

Hájek tread softly to another table centered in the room, laden with more volumes lit by an antique, green-shaded desk lamp. To the right side of the desk sat an old, boxy computer and a printer. "These are the duplicate registers, first begun in 1787 under the mandate of Familiant Law to record the history of the Jews of Moravia and Bohemia." He pulled on a pair of white cotton gloves and opened a venerable book, its yellowed pages stiff and wrinkled with age.

Nick joined the ancient. A faint scent reached his nose, an earthy smell emanating from the registers as if reflecting the history of this place and those who preceded. He glanced at the faded, scripted entries in the book, then continued his assessment. Next to the book, was a closed volume with an image of a white lion. *My God, it's the same image that adorned the burlwood box.* He recalled what his grandfather had said about his heritage. "In time you will know." Before he could ask about the book or the lion, the ancient spoke.

"Only now are we attempting to find the lost generations." Hájek placed his hand flat on the yellowed page. "This is where I started. The Lanove Rejstriky and the tax map cadastrals for Moravia first recorded in 1657." Pádriac paused. "The cadastrals recorded the ownership of the lands.

"Most Jews in the earlier times did not have fixed hereditary family names and that has made it extremely difficult to trace relationships. Our family is more fortunate than most. We are of the old aristocracy. Our roots can be traced. These volumes and the other documents here were secreted away by your grandfather in the caves dotting the castle's grounds before he and his family fled to England to escape the Germans and their collaborators. Hidden from the Nazi State and, later, the communists, these manuscripts document our family's history."

"Ida was a little girl, a few years older than your father. When the Russians came, a sympathetic family whisked her away to safety, adopting her as their own. She became one of The Displaced. When her own parents lost their lives, her whereabouts were lost to the family, but she found her way back to Prague."

Nick didn't interrupt to ask any questions. *Where can I even*

Chapter Thirty-Two

start? His questions would be answered in time—and with patience. Hájek's words began to resonate.

"But enough of my side, the maternal side of the family. There will be time for that," the ancient said, sweeping his hand over the volumes of books. "Now, I must tell you of your heritage."

Nick could only nod as Pádriac began his story.

"In accordance with Familiant Law, only the first-born son had the right to marry and replace his father as head of the household. The provisions of this law provided the head of the household a license to own property and raise a family. You must understand that most of the marriages at this time were performed by the priests. But those performed by the rabbis without a state permit? A child of such a marriage was defined as fatherless and recorded in the registers under his mother's maiden name."

He recalled the name, Anya Mrazik, he'd seen in the Theresienstadt archives, beginning to assemble those remote connections within his mind.

The ancient confirmed his thoughts. "Nikola, you are a descendant of the male heirs. Proving that you are a direct relative of Count Vilém Patykaovi is not so difficult, unlike for those of the maternal side of our family descended from Anya."

"And the names I saw in the Theresienstadt ghetto?" he asked. "What of them?"

The ancient sighed, his hand brushing over the open manuscript. "Ah, that is the problem. And what of young Petr and his sister, Natálya, your cousins, my niece and nephew?"

Nick could hardly belief what he'd heard. Cousins? Petr and Natálya?

Pádriac pointed to a name on the ledger passing over Nick's confusion. "You see the name here. Yes? Anya Mrazik. Mrazik, the daughter of Petr Patykaovi, is the link to the maternal side of our family, from which I, my niece, and her children are descended."

Nick tried to focus on what the ancient was saying but his mind was elsewhere preparing himself for what might follow. He interrupted the ancient's narrative. "Pádriac, what of my father? How did he lose his life?"

The old man closed the archive and removed his gloves. "Ezra worked for your government. The CIA. I do not know the details, but he was betrayed and arrested by the communists."

CIA? Betrayed? He stood immobilized by Pádriac's words, his breath coming in short gasps, stunned by what he'd heard. His face flushed. He trembled with the mounting rage that coursed through his body, two words piercing his soul. *CIA. Betrayed.*

Each of Pádriac's words laid bare the suppressed memories of Nick's childhood. The bullying, the pain of having few friends, the self-imposed isolation—erecting the rigid walls that prevented people from penetrating his protective shell. And what of his own grandparents? What had they hidden from him? No, they had done their best and were faultless. They couldn't have known. He straightened and spoke. "I should have known."

Pádriac opened his hands in supplication. "Nikola, until Katerina reached out, I didn't know—"

Nick cut the old man's voice off with a slash of his hand and staggered out the door.

Marie appeared at his side and took his arm "Nick…"

He did not hear her, nor was he aware of being led from the castle. His words escaped, barely audible. "They will pay. All of them will pay for what they've done."

Chapter Thirty-Three

THE GROTO, CASTLE PATYKAOVI
PROTECTORATE OF MORAVIA AND BOHEMIA
TUESDAY 20 OCTOBER

Tom pulled up before the rest of the team passed through the castle's gatehouse and shot a glance over his right shoulder. The other man he'd spotted in the distance had ducked out of sight, probably scurrying into the safety of the forest. *That has to be Grekov's man, the one who's been following us.* "You catch that?"

"Our buddy?" George answered.

"Affirmative. I'm sensing an opportunity."

George nodded his agreement. "Sure wouldn't want to waste a chance for a nice, collegial conversation among friends."

"Collegial?" Tom snorted and nodded towards Nick. "Should we tell him?"

George looked at Parkos' back as he passed out of sight

through the gate. "No, we'll handle it. Let him enjoy his castle."

Tom led the way into the woods, pausing a few yards up the narrowing path. A ray of sun broke through the cloud cover, penetrating the canopy, casting a mottled patchwork of light on the forest floor. The dense mat of sodden leaves, damp from the morning storm emitted the rank smell of decay. "I'll work my way around to the left in case he tries to slip back around us. Stay on the path."

Without waiting for an answer, Tom pushed his way through a tangle of underbrush and made his way deeper into the woods. Five minutes later, he caught his first glimpse of the grotto. Its surface was blanketed with a thick layer of fog that obscured its edges. There was no sign of George or the Russian.

He took several cautious steps into the swirling mist at the forward edge of the denser murk beyond. A blurred shadow of a man caught his eye. The Russian.

Tom's boot caught the edge of a gnarled root and he stumbled, his left foot slipping across the top of a slick moss-encrusted rock. His brain registered the image of the remnant of a broken branch projecting from a downed tree. He twisted away from the jagged lance as he fell. Leading with his right shoulder, he landed with a thump on the ground beside the rotted trunk. The Russian spun at the noise.

"Man, I got lost and almost broke my damn neck. I should have stayed with my group," Tom yelled toward the Russian.

He saw the Russian's right hand reach for his coat pocket. The holster for his own weapon was wedged under his right side. *Shit.* He yelled again, this time for George. "Gun!"

The Russian spun. George reacted an instant before the Russian could pull the trigger.

The crack of the rotten branch splintering like a weakened baseball bat and a dull thud were the only sounds in the forest.

Chapter Thirty-Three

The Russian crumpled to the ground from the blow to the side of his skull.

George dropped the branch and approached the Russian. He leaned over, scrutinizing the sprawled body, picked up the pistol, and gave it a heave. The weapon disappeared with a muffled plunk into the fog-smothered waters of the grotto.

Tom got to his feet, brushed off the dirt and leaves from his jacket, then approached the inert form. He knelt, checked the Russian's neck for a pulse, then pried open an eyelid. "He'll survive." He patted him down, found a wallet, and held it out. "See what you can learn. I don't want to kill the guy and I doubt he'll be bothering us anymore. We'll let him make his way back to Grekov. It'll send a message."

"What about Dusa?" George asked.

Tom gave the inert Russian a couple of smacks on his right cheek, smiling when the man emitted a groan, regaining consciousness. "I've got another idea. Let's carry him back and drop him at the car. It'll be fun to see the reaction on Dusa's face."

"Man, you're one twisted dude." George said. "We've got what we want

Leave him. He'll have a hell of a headache but shouldn't be any the worse for wear."

Tom and George exited the woods as Nick and the rest of the group appeared at the castle's portico.

"Where have you guys been?" Nick demanded.

The tone in his voice set off alarms in both men. George answered. "We wanted to check out the grotto."

"Bullshit. What were you doing?"

George decided the best course was to confess. "We spotted the Russian whose been following us. We decided we'd have a collegial—"

Nick glared at the two, cutting off the rest of what George had planned to say. His face conveyed that he wasn't in the mood for any wisecracks. "Get rid of him. I want to send a message to Grekov."

Tom made to protest, but he cut him off again. "We only have seven days and I'm not waiting for that bastard Ferguson to break Delezal." He motioned to Dusa who was leaning against the van's left front door, his face a mask of indifference. "Or playing any more games with that son-of-a-bitch."

Bastard? Son-of-a-bitch? Vasek appeared to be dazed by Nick's words. She cast an imploring look at Marie, who stood riveted to the ground, stunned by the exchange.

Nick spun on his partner, the veins in his neck engorged, his face flushed with rage. "Stay the hell out of this. You have no idea…" He choked on his fury, unable to continue.

Marie recovered enough to respond. "We can't, Nick."

Tom didn't need any further explanation. He and George had to start running damage control. He set his face and jerked his chin toward the forest. "Let's go."

George slowed when they were well out-of-sight. "What the hell was that all about?"

"Damned if I know, but I've seen that look before."

"Yeah, me too. In the 'Stan.' Rage. That crazy-eyed look of blood lust following hand-to-hand combat."

They walked in silence to the grotto. The Russian hadn't moved but was now sitting, fingers laced together across the back of his neck, elbows resting on his knees, staring at the sodden ground. He didn't lift his head at their arrival.

Tom tossed the guy's wallet, emptied of everything but some cash. It landed near the Russian's left side. He looked up and tried to fix the two of them with gazed eyes.

"I'll be damned if I'm going to murder the guy," Tom

said. "He'll make it back. That's all the message we need to send to Grekov."

George snapped a picture of the Russian with his iPhone and headed back toward the castle. "What do we tell Nick?"

"No idea, but we need to talk with Lange about Ferguson and Parkos. Parkos has gone completely off the rails and this op is about to spin out of control." He shook his head and started back down the trail toward the castle. "My guess is that Král is no longer our target. Grekov is."

"Well, whatever happened in that damn castle," George said, "we've got a couple hundred yards to figure something out."

Chapter Thirty-Four

CIA BLACK SITE
STARE KIEJKUTY, POLAND
TUESDAY 20 OCTOBER

Taylor Ferguson snapped on the interrogation room's lights at precisely 0500. The harsh glare jarred Julius Delezal awake after only a few hours of fitful sleep.

He stepped into the room, followed by Edna Dabrowski and Draegan Wójcik. Dabrowski wheeled in a red, five-drawer Craftsman toolbox. The wheels emitted a high-pitched screech. An assortment of small hand tools and a Dremel high speed drill with a selection of bits were conspicuously arranged on top of the cart. Wójcik carried a vinyl-covered chair with leather straps affixed to its arms and front legs. An orange heavy-duty extension cord was curled, snake-like, on the chair's seat.

Ferguson appeared not to notice Wójcik drop the chair or Dabrowski as she disappeared back through the door. An insincere smile etched his face. "Good morning, Julius. I trust you slept well."

Delezal pulled his rheumy eyes away from the activity in the center of the room and faced his captor. He shifted his eyes again as Dabrowski reappeared pushing a second cart, this one covered with a white tablecloth and laden with an array of aromatic breakfast foods and a carafe of freshly brewed coffee.

Ferguson gestured at the second cart. "Breakfast has arrived, Julius. I am afraid we do not have the luxury of time, but first we must indulge in this wonderful repast while my colleagues prepare for the rest of our morning's activities." He picked up a fork, speared a kielbasa breakfast sausage, and bit off the end. "Would you care to join me?"

Delezal didn't respond. He focused on the other man, who had plugged the extension cord into a wall socket and was now connecting it to a transformer and a set of fifty-amp electrical clamps. He starred in disbelief at the man and clutched his pillow, making no move to leave the safety of his bed.

Ferguson took another bite of sausage, set the fork down, and patted the grease from his lips with a napkin. "No?" He dropped the napkin and poured himself a cup of coffee. "Then we shall begin."

Dabrowski took several rapid steps toward Delezal, yanked him from the bed, and dragged him toward the chair.

"No, no. Please. I will join you for breakfast."

"Why thank you, Julius." Ferguson pulled out a chair. "I so hate dining alone."

He waited until Delezal had settled into the chair across from him before he took his own and lifted the cover from a serving dish. With a flourish, he set the cover to one side of the table revealing a stack of fluffy, golden-brown apple pancakes lightly dusted with powdered sugar. He placed his hands over his heart. "Ah, these are sheer heaven." He lifted two pancakes with a pair of silver tongs and deposited them on Delezal's plate. "I thought that you would enjoy the Pacuchy z Jablkomi. Myself? I am starving and will indulge in the rest of these delightful kielbasa."

Delezal starred at the pancakes, not moving.

"Please, Julius, just try a bite. I'm sure you wouldn't want to offend the chef. But if you care for something else from the kitchen, please ask."

Delezal lifted a fork and sliced off a piece of one of the pancakes. He paused, then took a bite. He took another, feeling less threatened. "Would you happen to have some syrup?"

"But of course," he said. "Would maple do?"

Delezal nodded. "Yes, thank you."

"Excellent." He addressed Dabrowski, using a false name. "Anna, would you please find Julius some syrup?" He poured Delezal a cup of coffee..

When Delezal had polished off the pancakes displaying a surprising appetite considering his present circumstances, Ferguson set his empty cup on the table and pushed away. "I so enjoyed our breakfast, Julius, but we must get down to business. Certainly, you understand that I must learn Mr. Král's intentions."

"But I don't know anything about them."

Ferguson's voice hardened. "Do not play us for fools." He stood, walked to the Craftsman cart, and pondered the collection of tools. He selected a pair of needle-nose pliers from a six-piece mini-set. He had no intention of killing the Czech or even seriously harming his captive. The rules had changed.

The CIA had barred the use of enhanced interrogation techniques after the excesses of the early 2000's. That, and the CIA had determined coercive interrogation techniques were ineffective and not worth the hassle, especially after a particular CIA black site had been outed in a series of exposés, most notably those published in the *New York Times*.

He wasn't convinced that the kinder, gentler approach was

effective, but decided to go along. At least for now. He had hours—not weeks, not even days, to extract whatever information Král's lieutenant could provide. Parkos and his team needed something to break open their operation.

"Where am I?"

He chuckled at Delezal's outburst. "Very good, Julius. You are showing a bit of backbone." He set the pliers down. "I will save these for later." He addressed Dabrowski. "Could I have the photographs, please?"

Dabrowski opened the second drawer of the toolbox, extracted several pictures, and handed them over.

Delezal's eyes widened at the fleeting glance he'd been afforded of his wife and two little girls. "You bastard!"

"Yes, I suppose I am." Ferguson sounded a bit rueful. He set the pictures on Delezal's plate and spun it. "Secure him."

Dabrowski and Wójcik grabbed Delezal before he could react, sending his chair clattering to the floor. The photographs fluttered to rest beside it. Delezal struggled to reach out to his family, but the two dragged him, thrashing and screaming, to the middle of the room where they secured his arms and legs to those of the vinyl chair with the leather straps.

Ferguson's voice softened. "I had so hoped you would be reasonable and want to spare your family any unpleasantness."

Delezal jerked at his bonds. "You would not harm them."

"But Julius, you leave me no choice if you do not cooperate. It will be so painful for your wife to see what we do to Hana before it's Doniella's own turn to die. And you? You will have the image of their last moments on your conscience forever. It is your choice."

"I cannot."

He turned to Dabrowski, tiring of Delezal's intransigence. "Shall we start with a fingernail or a tooth?"

Dabrowski gave her chin a thoughtful pull, her left hand lingering. "Perhaps a fingernail. It's not so messy."

"No. No. Wait."

He smiled. "A wise choice, my friend. Give me a name."

"Alfredo."

"That is a cream sauce, Julius. Surely you can do better than that." He picked up a pair of vice grips, testing their action. "Perhaps you have a last name? I do not wish to hurt you."

Delezal screeched the answer. "Sanchez. Alfredo is his first name. He calls himself major."

"A Mexican, then?"

"Yes."

Ferguson stooped to pick up the pictures of Delezal's family. "Another name."

Delezal jerked at his restraints, then stopped as Ferguson waved the photographs. He shrieked a name. "*Tlatoani*."

Ferguson took a step. "And?"

"Anička Drabek. She handles the money."

Ferguson kept his face impassive. He recognized Král's financier's name, Anička Drabek. *Tlatoani* meant nothing. But *what the hell does a Mexican army officer have to do with Král?* He set down the pliers. "Very good, Julius. We shall first talk about this Major Alfredo Sanchez."

Chapter Thirty-Five

CIA BLACK SITE
STARE KIEJKUTY, POLAND
TUESDAY 20 OCTOBER

Sergei Kuznetzov positioned himself next to the Polish army Star-266 general utility truck, lit a cigarette, and leaned against the cab. His contact had commandeered the 6x6 vehicle and hidden it within an old, hardened aircraft shelter. He shifted his stance after a moment trying to relieve the muscle spasms coursing through his lower back. He'd spent the past hour with his driver clearing branches and debris from the 500-meter runway and setting out parallel lines of portable airfield landing lights to guide in Victor Ulyanov's plane.

The remote airfield, with its concrete runway riddled with large cracks festooned with tall grass and scrub brush and the base's deteriorating structures, was of no further use to the Poles. The base was a vestige of the Russian occupation of Poland during the Cold War and ideally suited for his mission.

Thirty kilometers from the village of Stare Kiejduty, it had once hosted a squadron of Yak-38 Forager VTOL aircraft similar to the American's old Harrier jets.

Russian army engineers had also built the Strefe-B interrogation site where the Americans were holding Delezal. Both he and Ulyanov had had ample time to review the interior arrangement of the building's rooms and had agreed on the most likely place for the Americans to hold their prisoner. These facts did little to diminish the tension coursing through his body, nor did the stress he'd been under just getting to this place from Prague. His training hadn't prepared him for this type of mission.

Kuznetzov stepped out of the hanger and scanned the night sky to the southeast, listening for the distinct sound of the AN-2 Cub aircraft, amazed that the ancient biplane, introduced by the Soviet's in 1947, was still flying. But he knew the aircraft was a favorite of the hunting outfitter companies in eastern Europe. Extraordinarily durable, it was easy to maintain and could land on remote runways. The plane's choice as Ulyanov's cover was ideal. If questioned, he would explain that he and his team had charted the aircraft for a hunting expedition, intent on bagging the limit of red stag deer and wild boar.

That was all well-and-good, Kuznetzov thought, if their operation wasn't unmasked. It would only be a matter of hours before the Poles noticed the empty stall for their missing truck. It would not do for them all to be captured.

He checked his watch, acknowledging that obsessing on the time would not have any impact on Ulyanov's arrival or his stress. He pulled up the collar of his fatigue jacket to ward off the chill, early-morning air and took a long drag of his cigarette. The Alpha Group's arrival and his fear weren't the only issues consuming his thoughts in this desolate place. There was also his discomfort about relinquishing control. He would nevertheless defer to Major Victor

Chapter Thirty-Five

Ulyanov, the leader of the five-man Spetsgruppa Alpha Group team.

Part of Directorate A of the FSB's Special Purpose Center, the Alpha Group specialized in covert and counter-terrorism operations. Ulyanov's 13th Group was based in Krosnodar, Krai on the eastern border of the Black Sea and had taken to the air mere hours after receiving their orders from Moscow. He shrugged. The Alpha Group was more than capable of executing its mission. *And protecting my sorry ass.*

The sound of an approaching plane prompted him to fix his gaze on the end of the runway. The old aircraft's approach speed was so slow, it appeared to hover before setting down and taxiing to the end of the strip. The roar of the aircraft's massive nine-cylinder piston engine abated as the four-bladed propeller wound down, leaving the surrounding forest eerily quiet. The only sound he heard was the wind whispering through the pine boughs—the wind, a harbinger of an advancing cold front.

The passenger door just behind the lower left wing sprung open, followed by a burly
giant of a man wearing camouflage hunting clothes. The man scanned his surroundings, yelled something to someone in the plane, and turned his attention to Kuznetzov. "I see you have the truck. Have there been any complications?"

Kuznetzov presumed this must be Ulyanov. "None. We are clean." He looked past the soldier at another four men exiting the plane. Like their leader, all of them were dressed in hunter's clothing, not Polish army uniforms. And they were carrying bows, not rifles. "But—"

Ulyanov offered his hand. "Our cover. You never know when one might need to go hunting other game, *da?*" His smile vanished.

"I don't disagree." He took a last drag of his cigarette and flipped the butt onto the runway. "There is no need to further complicate a difficult operation." He didn't voice what he was really worried about. If the Americans were killed, their comrades would—

Ulyanov cut off his thought. "You have a picture of this man?"

He reached into a pocket of his fatigue jacket and handed over the picture of Delezal.

"Good, it matches what we were shown. Now, my men and I must prepare." The Spetsgruppa officer spun on his heals to join his men before Kuznetzov could reply.

Fifteen minutes later, Kuznetzov, Ulyanov, and his four Alpha Group men, now dressed in Polish army uniforms, piled into the truck bed. Ulyanov joined the driver in the cab leaving Kuznetzov no other option but to scramble in after the others. He'd barely taken a seat on one of the wooden benches in the back when the truck set off with a lurch and grinding of gears. Because of Ulyanov's late arrival, there could be no further delays.

They'd timed their operation to arrive at the Polish army base's gate just before sunrise. Kuznetzov heard the driver downshift and sensed the truck slowing. He glanced at his watch. 0643. Enough time. The guards would be tired, less vigilant, while waiting for their replacements. He heard voices and caught a few words. *Russians. Scum.* Then laughter. The truck edged forward, then gained speed.

Kuznetzov relaxed. The guards must have given Ulyanov's ID a cursory look and waved them through the double gates. The hardest part of the mission had been accomplished and they were now driving deeper into the base toward Stafe-B. Kuznetzov leaned back against the canvas side of the cargo compartment and closed his eyes, his ears attuned to the activity of the operatives around him.

The Alpha Group team was now outfitted in the camouflage uniform and green berets of the Polish 18th Reconnaissance Regiment and armed with a lethal collection of weapons. He recognized a Vityaz SN submachine gun, Stechan APS pistols, and several modernized ASM Val rifles with integrated suppressors. He took a deep breath, striving to calm his frazzled nerves.

The truck lurched to a stop with another grind of its gears. He heard Ulyanov's order. "Go, go, go."

Kuznetzov hesitated. He had been a junior officer of the GRU's Unit 29155 when they had deployed to Afghanistan decades before, but this was different. Then, his unit had been safely billeted in a secure compound in Kabul out of harm's way. *Well, mostly out of harm's way.* A car bomb had killed one of his best friends. He checked his holster and followed the other four out of the truck.

He flashed a look at the building's stark façade, checking for security cameras. The old Soviet interrogation center was windowless so that nobody could peer in it. But the reverse was also true, unless… The distinct double clicks of charging handles and the chambering of rounds from the Alpha Group's weapons jerked him back. He noted the operative's flick on their fire selector switches, setting their weapons for semi-automatic.

He tensed as Ulyanov tested the door handle. Open. Ulyanov advanced into the building, signaling his comrades to follow. He felt the prudent choice would be to lag behind and let the Alpha Group do their job. It was a wise decision. A shout of alarm pierced the air followed by the sharp crack of a weapon.

The muffled fire of an ASM Val shattered the silence of the compound. Someone had seen them on a security camera. He willed himself through the building's front door. Movement. Ulyanov and two of his men disappeared down a hallway. The other two split off, making for their first objective. His eyes fell on a crumpled form on the floor within an expanding pool of blood. Two people burst into the room and bolted for the front door. He yanked his pistol out of its holster. "Halt."

The two, a man and a woman, slid to a stop, their heads sweeping the room.

Kuznetzov recovered from his surprise. "Drop to your knees. Now!"

The two didn't hesitate, prompted in part by the appearance of the two commandos who had finished the sweep of the kitchen and other rooms they'd been assigned. The first leveled his rifle at the man while the other approached their captives. The second shoved the man face down on the floor next to his dead companion. "Move and you're dead." He turned to Kuznetzov. "Join the commander. We will attend to these two."

Kuznetzov didn't require any further prompting. He stepped around the prostrate Americans and joined Ulyanov. In the middle of the room, still bound to a chair with thick leather straps was the object of their mission.

Delezal reacted to seeing someone not in a Polish uniform. "Help me."

Uylanov made no move to release the man. "What did you tell them?"

Delezal cast a pleading look at Kuznetzov. "Tell them? I said nothing. I swear."

Ulyanov gave a shake of his head, leveled his pistol at Delezal's right knee and fired. He lowered his weapon, smoke swirling from its barrel, and spoke over Delezal's screams. "Do not lie to me. I will repeat my question once more. If you do not give the correct response, I will kill you."

Delezal screamed again, lurching forward trying to grasp his shattered knee. "They forced me—"

"What did you say to them?"

"I...I may have said '*Tlatoani*.' They hurt me."

The word, possibly a name, meant nothing. "Who else?"

Chapter Thirty-Five

"Anička Drabek."

Ulyanov's finger tightened around the trigger, and he spit out the words. *Bespoleznaya mraź. On predal nas i Král.*

Kuznetzov suppressed a shudder at both Delezal's revelations and the expression on Ulyanov's face when he said. *Worthless scum. He's betrayed us and Král.* There was no telling what else the Czech could have said. Revealing the word *"Tlatonia"* was enough to seal the man's fate and Drabek was Král's financier. He had to presume, as Ulyanov had already surmised, that their operation had been compromised. That is, if Parkos was smart enough to make the connections, which he was certain the American agent was. He set his face and nodded.

Ulyanov raised his pistol and fired three times, relieving Delezal of his pain. He turned away from the bloody mess and faced Kuznetzov. "I have my orders. We are to leave the remaining American's alive to clean up the mess."

"But——" Kuznetzov stammered.

Ulyanov cut him off. "Gather the American's electronic devices, computers, files, anything of use." He checked his watch. "We must be at the airstrip in thirty minutes."

Kuznetzov turned to leave when he spotted a gold-link chain on the room's bed. He snatched the chain and stuffed it in his pants pocket. Delezal wouldn't miss it.

Chapter Thirty-Six

LUDICKÁ STREET
ADMINISTRATIVE DISTRICT FIVE, PRAGUE
TUESDAY 20 OCTOBER

Rajik Mohammadi, had finally overstepped. The Iranian's incessant meddling in her affairs risked unmasking the full extent of Moscow's operations in Mexico. That could not be tolerated. Aleksandra Grekov also understood that Mohammadi's actions jeopardized her own aspirations to set right the wrongs done to her family during the Stalinist pogroms. The program she oversaw to supply arms to Carlos Mendez could not fail: such failure would lead to her banishment or, worse, imprisonment and death.

Grekov slowed for a passing gaggle of chattering teenagers, pulled her iPhone from her purse, and entered the number of her associate. "I've got my watcher."

"I am parked just to the left," Viktor said.

She approved, but she'd also had no alternative but to enlist one of her seldom used street artists since Sergei hadn't yet returned from Poland. On a positive note? From the limited feedback she'd received, the mission to eliminate Král's lieutenant was a success. Of course, she reminded herself, "success" had many elements, depending on the objectives and the perspective of her superiors in Moscow, which she suspected Colonel General Turgenov hadn't deemed necessary to fully inform her of.

In turn, she felt no compunction to inform Turgenov of her specific intentions. He would assume she would take the appropriate measures to address the intelligence he had obtained from the FSB's targeted surveillance of the Iranian embassy in Moscow. "You will marginalize the Iranian," he'd ordered.

She dismissed these tangential thoughts, altered her usual route to her apartment, and strode past Café Tone without stopping for a pastry and coffee. Her purse tugged on her shoulder as she picked up her pace and ducked into the alley just past the store. Her Glock-17 semi-automatic pistol and a silencer accounted for the additional weigh. Taught well, she had disassembled and cleaned the weapon before leaving her office.

She slid into a recessed doorway, blending into the darkness, and pulled out her pistol, screwing on the silencer. A set of heavy footfalls alerted her to Mohammadi's approach. *Such clumsy tradecraft*, she mused. *But why was he even shadowing me?* She didn't have time to waste on conjecture as the Iranian neared. She stepped out of the shadows as he passed, jamming her the barrel of her Glock into his right side. "Rajik, my friend. There has been a change in plans."

The Iranian spun, his right hand darting toward his coat.

"Ah-ah," Grekov cautioned. "That would be ill-advised. Your weapon please." She dropped his pistol into her purse and prodded Mohammadi forward with a push of her own weapon. "We will have only a short drive. And be assured, I will have no compunction about killing you if you even move to escape."

Viktor stood by the open rear door of an old Volga GAZ, exhaust billowing from its rusted muffler. A second agent was in the backseat, ready to secure their prisoner. She nodded her approval at his initiative, shoved Mohammadi into the car, and slammed the door.

Their drive down Valentine Street only took minutes. The Smíchov district, now the focus of a major urban renewal project, still had its gritty parts that would serve her purpose. Viktor slowed to pass the evening crowd beginning to gather at the Meet Factory, a former meat packing plant, then stopped at the rear of an abandoned warehouse two blocks further down the street.

Viktor and his partner pulled Mohammadi from the car and hustled him inside, depositing him in a barren concrete room, dank with decay and the foul smell of urine. Grekov cast a quick look over the rear lot, ensuring no one had seen them, and followed the three inside.

"Ah, Rajik," she opened, "you have made a fatal mistake, double-crossing Mother Russia by attempting to divert our arms shipments to your own country's purpose. Did you think we would not know? Greed and clumsiness are fatal flaws in our business, are they not?"

The Iranian stared at her in defiance, but beads of sweat had appeared on his forehead.

"We might have been able to overlook you providing the ZPU2 anti-aircraft cannon to Mendez since he may not understand the nuances of our business, but you should."

"I swear, I did nothing," Mohammadi protested.

"No?" She pulled a small tape recorder from her purse. "Well then, you might find this interesting:

"You are taking fifty percent of my cut. I need twenty."

"You better guarantee me that business"

Mohammadi's eyes widened, his eyebrows straightening,

lifting his upper eyelids in fear at the sound of his voice on the recording. He lurched for the recorder. "How did you—"

Grekov didn't waver and motioned for Viktor to lower his weapon. "In good time, Viktor."

"Let me kill this *prolklinat* scum," Victor said. "You shouldn't dirty your hands."

Panic replaced fear in the Iranian's face. His eyes darted, looking for an escape.

She shrugged, having tired of the weakling. "Yes, go ahead. He is a waste of my time."

The muffled "Pops" of two silenced rounds spun the Iranian around, driving him to the floor.

She glanced at the expanding pool of blood around the Iranian's chest, then turned away. "Leave him for the rats."

Chapter Thirty-Seven

SAFE HOUSE
DRESDEN, GERMANY
TUESDAY 20 OCTOBER

Geoff Lange scraped off the last of the previous day's stubble, gave the bone-handled straight edge razor a vigorous swirl in the sink, then held the blade under the tap to rinse off any lather residue, preserving the blade's edge.

The rest of the team accepted his morning ritual with bemused tolerance, acknowledging the act reflected a refined aesthetic that also encompassed his membership— perhaps ownership of—The Nicholas, his respect for an excellent cigar, and his evenings spent in front of the club's hearth sipping a dignified scotch.

But Lange's thoughts were focused not on the satisfaction of a clean shave, but on Taylor Ferguson and what he might learn from his interrogation of the Czech, Delezal. He needed to get Nick something substantial. Notwithstanding the Czech Republic's ninety-day travel visa, Parkos' team only had six

Chapter Thirty-Seven

days left before their tour ended and, with it, their excuse for remaining in the country.

The sound of the team's secure satellite phone ringing the opening bars of the Jurassic Park movie theme interrupted his thoughts. *Edmund would grab it, if for no other reason than to silence the song.* He dried the blade with a white microfiber cloth, hung it on the stand next to the shaving brush, and reached for his bottle of sandalwood-scented aftershave.

A frown crossed Edmund MacDonald's face at the irritating tone. He was deep into creating the *mise en place* for their dinner, having tired of sauerbraten and *Fettbemme*, an open-faced sandwich composed of sliced pork lard and topped with gherkins that Vinny seemed to crave. Vinny had gone on an errand and Geoff was in the lavvy. He yelled toward the bathroom. "Ah'm cookin."

The phone repeated its song oblivious to Edmund's reaction. The Scot reached across the counter and grabbed the offending device. "Hullo...Hou ye doe'in mate?... Shite... Aye, he's right here. Hang on."

"It's for yir. We gotta bit of a problem."

Lange bolted out of the bathroom and grabbed the phone. "Lange."

"We're compromised," Ferguson announced. "Edna's with me. Wójcik's dead. So's Delezal."

"What the hell happened?" Lange listened without interruption, detecting the notes of desperation in Ferguson's voice. The guy had been burned in the al-Khultyer affair, but this was an entirely different ballgame. An operative was dead, and a covert action blown. He didn't even want to consider how.

"Shit, they could have killed us too. I don't know why we're still alive," Ferguson said.

"Could have been sending a message."

"Well, they sure as hell did that."

"Where are you?" Lange asked.

"In the woods."

Lange flexed his left hand, the dull-red scar extending to several of his fingers a constant reminder of the months he'd spent at the Walter Reed National Medical Center in Bethesda recovering. He didn't pursue Ferguson's answer and didn't offer any sympathetic words. He knew from his own experience in the Iraqi desert when he had been wounded and lost several of his team members that Ferguson didn't need or want sympathy. What he needed to do was re-establish the agent's sense of control. "You secure?"

"For now. I figure the Russians are more focused on getting the hell out of Dodge."

"Russians?"

"Six of them. My bet, a Spetsgruppa Alpha team. Five of them were wearing the same camouflage uniforms as the Polish 28th Reconnaissance Regiment."

"Any Poles injured?"

"Unknown. Near as I can tell, they don't have a clue about what just went down."

"The sixth guy?"

"He looked out of his element. I'll go over our files and figure out where he fits."

Lange agreed. He also didn't want to press, not sure of Ferguson's mind set. He cast a look at Edmund, who held up a pen. "You need anything?"

"We're good for the moment. My next call is to a local asset. You're my second. I've already notified Uncle. I've gotta get a cleanup crew here. An aircraft … No, it'd be best to—"

Chapter Thirty-Seven

Lange interrupted. "You get anything out of Delezal?"

"Crazy stuff about a Tlatoani. That mean anything to you?"

"Negative. We'll check it out." He grabbed the pen from Edmund and wrote down the phonetic spelling. LATONEA. *A city? Could even be a province, but where?* "Anything else?"

"Got a couple names," Ferguson answered. "Anička Drabek and some guy, named Alfredo Sanchez. Odd thing is, he called the guy, 'major.'"

"Unknowns?"

"I know about Drabek. I recall Coleman saying something about her being tied to Král's organization. Maybe his financier."

Lange scratched down the name on the scrap of paper and showed it to Edmund. The Scot shrugged and shook his head. "And the second?"

"Delezal said he was a Mexican."

"You said 'major'? *Federales* or Army?"

"Unknown."

"Did he say anything about Král?"

"Negative."

Lange moved on. "They get the tapes?"

"Nothing useful. I had a USB Flash Drive voice recorder. Stuffed it down my shorts when I heard the Russkies breaking in. Damn miracle they didn't kill me and find it."

"What about any computers?" Lange prodded.

"No idea. Listen, I'd love to talk," Ferguson said, "but right now I've got shit to attend to. That, and I've gotta find a place to charge this damn phone."

Lange frowned at Ferguson's last statement and terminated the call. *Could he have used an unsecured phone? Crap.* He set the satellite phone in its cradle and began assembling the fragments of information into something of use beginning with the assault force. He agreed with Ferguson. Spetsgruppa Alpha Group. FSB. But how the hell had they known about

Delezal, and why mount the op? That suggested a major leak.

There was something else going on as well, something that had scared the hell out of the Russians. So much so, that they had taken the huge risk of mounting the operation to take out Delezal. He looked at Edmund "Ferguson gave me another name. Major Alfredo Sanchez."

"A Latino? Think that's what got Gilmore stirred up?"

"Damned if I know."

"What about drugs?"

"Or arms. I gotta call Parkos. This is where that crazy brain of his could come in handy. Half the time I have no clue how he does it, but he can see connections the rest of us can't."

Lange's concern about Ferguson's phone were not misplaced. High overhead, a Russian Olymp-K intelligence satellite had intercepted the call. The day before, it had maneuvered to a new a geostationary orbit at 24.4 degrees west, positioning it closer to a cluster of civilian communications satellites on the chance it would intercept any up or downlinked phone calls pertaining to their operation.

Chapter Thirty-Eight

METROPOLE VILLAS
MALA STRANG, PRAGUE
TUESDAY 20 OCTOBER

Petr Hájek rested his legs on the coffee table fronting an off-white sectional sofa, the modern design of his apartment in stark contrast with the interior of the ancient family castle. He swirled the contents of his cut-glass tumbler and took a swallow of the double Old-Fashioned he had just mixed.

He'd chosen the drink as well as the lilting horn contretemps of Zelenka's Capriccio No. 5 in G, to sooth the din raging within his mind. It had been a long day, Anton insisting that they return to Prague instead of spending the night at the castle. In retrospect a good decision. He needed time and the solitude of his apartment to process all that he'd learned and determine where that knowledge fit into his current circumstance.

The American, Nikola Partyka, who had appeared out of

nowhere with a tour group, had taken them both unawares. Curiously, Anton hadn't commented on the group, or specifically, Partyka, other than to utter, "Damn tourists." If his brother-in-law did have any foreknowledge of the purpose of the American's visit to the castle, he hadn't let on.

One advantage Petr had was a brief conversation with the family patriarch, information both of them chose not to share with Král. The American knew only fragments of the paternal side of the family, but next to nothing about the maternal side, the generations descended from Adéla Patykaovi and thence through Anya Mrazik. The immediate problem he wrestled with was whether this American was really in The Czech Republic seeking his heritage or for another purpose? The question Partyka had asked about his father begged for an answer. Was there another connection between father and son that he was not aware of?

And if this Nickola Partyka was a legitimate heir, what of Natálya's baby? What would happen to her child's inheritance? And what of his decision to let Král keep the Estrog and the other family heirlooms? He paused at the implications of those questions, his internal query moving on to address another. Did it even matter where Král fit and what designs he had on the castle? There was only one answer to the question: Yes. On that somber note, his thoughts turned to his minor role in Král's organization, likely offered so his brother-in-law could keep an eye on him.

Petr dealt mostly in contraband cigarettes and cigars, the latter having taken a dangerous turn after the Likas Gang shot up the store of one of their dealers. He kept his distance from Král's intent to expand into narcotics, something he knew only fragments about, including a supposed supplier in Central America.

So why had Král even brought him in? As a promise to Natálya to create a family business and to be the front-man for the legitimate portion of the operation? To that end, he'd begun work on a proposal for a web based, on-line casino that would undercut their rivals' brick-and-mortar operations.

These reflections brought him to the fate of Julius Delezal. Delezal had told him of Král's interest in another lucrative business, hinting that Anton had approached elements of the Russian mafia. And now? Delezal had disappeared. Had the man been killed because he knew too much, or had he fled to save his life?

The music reached its climatic rondo as he finished his drink. There was only one viable option for what he must do. For his own sake and to protect his sister and her unborn child, he must extricate himself from Anton's organization. But one final question remained: Where would the American, Nikola Partyka, fit into his plans?

Chapter Thirty-Nine

MONDRANY FLATS
MUNICIPLE DISTRICT 12, PRAGUE
TUESDAY 20 OCTOBER

Anton Král lifted the ancient relic he'd rescued from the muck of Castle Patykaovi's mikveh. Time well spent. The two-centimeter object cast in the shape of a hand with the index finger extended was a Yad, a Torah pointer. Someone reading the Torah would have used this relic to follow the lines of text in the dim light of the synagogue. He rolled the tarnished silver artifact in his hand. It still had a remnant of its oak shaft. *What had become of...* He blocked the remainder of the thought. There was no purpose in dwelling on the past.

He set the Yad aside and moistened a corner of his handkerchief to clean a smear of mud from a shard of glazed pottery. The bright blue fragment, with a hint of orange and red scalloping along the curved edge, may have once been part of a Seder plate. He pushed away from his table and crossed the room to place both objects in the safe next to the silver Etrog box and several other objects he'd rescued from the muck. His hand rested a moment on the Etrog. *The secrets these relics held. The stories they could tell.* One day he would know then all.

He pulled his hand away, a frown crossing his face at the thought of the problems his brother-in-law could pose. His resolve stiffened at what he must do. One day, he, Natálya, and their child would live in Castle Patykaovi, not Petr Hájek.

He shut the heavy door, spun the spoked wheel locking the secrets away, and dropped into his chair, his thoughts focused on the events of the previous day. He'd been shocked at seeing a tour group appear at the castle. Discomfort had turned to disbelief when he'd recognized the American, Parkos. *Why hadn't Vasek warned me?* Adding to his discomfort, he'd also spotted the Russian agent, Ilia, who had appeared at the edge of the forest. *Who had tipped him off? Dusa or Vasek?*

The Russian, Ilia, was a *blázen*, a fool, permitting himself to be spotted by the Americans, two of whom had followed him into the forest. The Americans had returned a short time later, only to head back into the forest after a confrontation with Parkos. Whatever had happened, he needed to make sure there were no loose ends, especially any that would lead back to Grekov. That is, if Dusa hadn't already alerted her to the confrontation.

He'd followed the same path into the woods after Petr had gone to say goodbye to his family and found the dazed Russian stumbling his way back toward the castle. He'd taken care of the Russian first, dumping his weighted body into the deep waters of the grotto. He had no regrets about the Russian, who had sealed his own fate. What remained were the broader implications of the past several days' events and, Delezal's disappearance.

Král sorted through the various scraps of information at his disposal, struggling to determine if these developments were in any way related. Delezal topped the list. He'd been missing for almost two full days, last seen at the White Horse and the neighboring jewelry store. Sokol had spoken with the store's owner, who said his customer had bought a man's fourteen carat yellow-gold Cuban chain necklace. That in itself was strange, but the cost? 36,000 Koruna—close to 2,500 dollars. *What was that all about?* Did Delezal sell himself to the highest bidder? The Russians? The Americans? Holcorá? Or did he have a side business as a pimp or drug dealer? Král had no idea, but the purchase may well have led to his disappearance. If Delezal had chosen any of those paths, then he would leave him to his fate, but if— His iPhone rang. *"Ahoj."*

"We've got a problem," his enforcer, Reznik opened.

He stiffened. "Delezal?"

"No, Anton Jezek. That *voleh* from the Czech Center for Investigative Reporting."

Král's hand tightened around the phone. "What about him?"

"Our contact in the American embassy, the secretary, passed on a meeting he had with the DEA agent, Coleman. She said Coleman may have been having sex with the reporter, Krejci."

"What does that have to do with Jezek?"

"They were friends."

Král suppressed a wave of anger, exasperated at Reznik's obtuse response

and what his revelation could portend. "They were friends? What are you talking about?"

"Jezek and Krejci. They talk, yes?"

"Of course. What's your point?"

"One of my guys caught him snooping around the Hradčovy airport. Even had a pizza at the Colosevh Zlaty pizza parlor."

Chapter Thirty-Nine

Král shook his head, trying to make sense of Reznik's statement. Did he know about the arms deal? How could he have learned? More to the point, the arms shipment was scheduled for pickup tonight. "Who? Coleman or Jezek?"

"Jezek."

He clenched his fists. His options were limited, but he may have been too hasty in his decision to get rid of Reznik. "Deal with him."

"*Moje potešni.*"

Král's lips tightened, conflicted by Reznik's reply, "My pleasure." He disconnected the call and leaned back in his chair, dismissing his ambivalence at the possible outcome of his order. Reznik would indeed deal with the reporter, no matter how distasteful. Conscience could play no role in his decisions, but... He grabbed his phone, then set it aside, and focused on the immediate problem—Delezal.

Could Delezal have compromised the arms shipment? His entire operation? Just yesterday, Anička had not said a word. But that was before... No, there wouldn't have been enough time to... Could the tour director, Vasek, have been compromised? And what of Grekov and that damn goon of hers he'd had no choice but to eliminate? How would the Russians react? He slammed his fist on the desk.

The option of moving up the timetables or canceling the Azerbaijan Air Freight were both off the table. The arms shipment was scheduled to leave within hours. He took several deep breaths, his thoughts settling on a way to put both the Russians and the American's off balance and give himself enough time to... To do what, exactly, remained elusive. He straightened as a solution came to him. There was one option he had yet to put into play.

Král began to codify the details of his plan to entrap the American, Parkos, with 5000 kilos of Columbian cocaine he'd set aside for contingencies in addition to the 500 kilos Mendez had gifted him. Before the hour ended, he'd settled on his plan and punched a number into his phone.

"Yes, boss," his lieutenant, Sokol, answered.

"We must talk."

Chapter Forty

ALCRON HOTEL
PRAGUE, CZECH REPULBLIC
WEDNESDAY 21 OCTOBER

Nick checked his watch. George would be here any minute. He'd finally decided that he had to know what was in the ancient burlwood box and asked George if he could pick the lock. George's answer? "No problem." He resumed his pacing around the suite's living room, then sat down and picked up the small scratchpad to review his cryptic notes from the conversation he'd had with Lange an hour ago. His eyes stopped half-way down the page.

Lange had posed a provocative question: "What had gotten the Russians so stirred up that they had risked running an operation in Poland, a member of NATO?" He had inscribed his answer in capital letters: ARMS. But that fact wasn't the only thing contributing to his headache. Near the top of his list, right after Ferguson's debacle, was what to do about Král. Should he confide in Marie and tell her what he had learned of his family?

A wave of guilt washed over him. He'd really shaken her at the castle but hadn't taken the first step to explain what happened. What he really needed to do was talk to Michelle to sort out his feelings before he apologized to Marie. But that option wasn't possible.

Marie studied her partner from her vantage point of the suite's couch. "You okay?"

"I've been better."

"What's going on?"

Nick set aside the scatchpad and chose the safest way out, not divulging what he'd been thinking about. "Ferguson."

Marie cocked her head. "Care to elaborate?"

"A Russian Spetsgruppa team raided the black site."

She rocked backwards at Nick's revelation. "Shit! Is Ferguson dead?"

"No, but one of his people is, and they murdered Delezal."

"They were in the middle of a damn Polish military base," Marie said. "How-in-hell did they know where to…" She stopped in mid-sentence. "My God. They ran an op in Poland? That's nuts. What could Delezal possibly have known that they'd risk an international incident over?"

"Unknown. Geoff's working his angles, but my gut is telling me it's arms." Nick poured a couple fingers of scotch in glass and held out the bottle. "This might help."

Marie stood, grabbed the bottle, waving off a glass. "Yeah, it might just. Arms? Hell, if Král was setting up an arms shipment with the Russians, two questions beg answers: "Why and where?'"

"I'd add a third. Are these tied to what got the Director stirred up? He focused on something that would present a clear and present danger to United States."

"No kidding. What's next?"

Chapter Forty

He stifled a comment as she raised the bottle to her lips, instead sorting through the variables and what he knew. "Delezal gave up two names, maybe three."

"Anybody we know?"

"One. Anička Drabek, Král's financier. He likely dropped her name first to delay whatever Ferguson had planned for him. The next one is somebody I've never heard of, Major Alfredo Sanchez. That one mean anything to you?"

"Major implies the military, but that doesn't help. He could be anybody from anywhere, even assuming that's his real name. We've got to presume Delezal gave it up the same time as Drabek."

"A drug cartel?"

"Could be, since we know Král has been expanding his business and would be looking for suppliers." She gave a puzzled shake of her head. "But again, I'd ask, 'Where do the Russians fit?'"

Nick shrugged. "Maybe the link is to the last name, or whatever it is, that Delezal gave up. Tlatoani. It sounds like a place name."

"Hang on." Marie grabbed her iPad and typed in a search. "A genus of frogs? That doesn't make any damn sense. Did Geoff give you a spelling?"

"Yeah, T-l-a-t-o-a-n-i. With a capital 'T'."

"Got it. It's the Nahuatl language name for the ruler of a Mexican pre-Hispanic state."

"Nahuatl?"

Marie held up her hand. "Give me a sec." Her fingers flew over the keyboard. "Nahuati is a language spoken primarily by people living in central and southern Mexico. Aztec derivation."

Nick started as he connected the dots. "We may have our answer for the Director."

"We do?"

"Yeah, we do." He set his glass down.

"Are you going to let me guess or are you planning on telling me? Hell, you're acting like Ferguson."

"Sorry, it's a fault of mine. I started stringing things together in my head formulating an answer without explaining how I got from point A to point C without going through B."

"Apology accepted."

"Let me put what we know together. Drabek is a known, so let's focus on the other two names. We'll begin with the question, 'Why would Delezal give up them up?'"

"He figured they would be important enough for Ferguson to spare his life."

"Oh, man," Nick responded to the implications of what Marie had said.

She lowered the whisky bottle, her celebratory drink aborted. "What? Ferguson?"

"No, it's what Coleman called me about yesterday. I didn't put it at the top of my priority list. He said we had to meet about what he'd found out from that reporter, Jezek."

"What about? Drugs?" Marie asked.

"Maybe, but I'm thinking weapons. It fits with something Geoff told me. I've got a meeting with Coleman in an hour," Nick replied. "Shouldn't take long. I'd like you to touch base with Geoff and fill him in."

"But—"

"No, buts," Nick stated. "I've gotta do this alone. Trust me."

"Nope," Marie said. "I'm calling Vinny. We'll watch your six." She turned at the knock on their door.

"That's George," Nick said. "I asked him to come over."

"Anything going on?"

Nick hesitated. "He's going to help me open my box."

"Gotcha." Marie stood and let their partner in while telling him, "I'm just leaving. Don't screw it up."

Chapter Forty

"Not a chance," George responded before taking a seat on the couch. "Let's see what you got."

Nick placed the box on the table. "I didn't want to open it myself."

"Smart," George said, lifting the box to examine the mechanism. "Easy, that's an old half-mortice." With that, he pulled out his tool bag, selected a U-shaped device, and picked the lock in a blink of an eye. "You want to do the honors?"

Nick reached for the box, then withdrew his hand. "Would you mind if I did this later?"

"No problem," George said, standing. "Figured you'd want some space."

Nick stared at the box after George left, wishing Michelle was at his side when he opened it. He tightened his lips, making a decision. If not Michelle, then, Marie. But when? He hid the box on the floor of the front closet behind their suitcase, grabbed his coat, and headed out the door.

Chapter Forty-One

109 KRIŽÍKOVA STREET, PRAHA 8
PRAGUE, CZECH REPUBLIC
WEDNESDAY 21 OCTOBER

"Nice," Nick said, stepping off the red and white Number 12 tram at the Križikova Street stop. He did a slow semi-circle, taking in the neighborhood just east of the Vltava River before making his way past his first waypoint, the Můj Šalek Kávy coffee shop. The aroma of the shop's coffee roaster enticed him to look in the window.

He pulled himself away from the display of pastries and made his way down the street before stopping at number 109. He nodded a greeting to Derek Coleman, who'd positioned himself on the sidewalk festooned with golden fall leaves, sipping coffee from a paper cup.

Nick surmised the site, located in an art deco building in the upscale Karlín district of Prague with its coffee shops, trendy wine bars, and indie art galleries, might have been purchased as a front for Coleman's discredited drug operation.

Chapter Forty-One

In any event, he figured Coleman knew what he was doing. *Or, not,* he cautioned himself. One positive? Vinny and Marie were conducting counter-surveillance. His partner was covering his ass again using her experience to watch for signs of danger he'd most likely miss.

"Follow me." Coleman cast a surreptitious glance over his right shoulder before ushering Nick into the secure building.

Nick cast his own glance from the stoop before following Coleman into a dim first floor corridor and clumping up a set of wooden stairs to the second floor. *Committed.*

Coleman eased his pace when another man holding a device that looked like an old walkie talkie exited a doorway at the end of the hall.

"It's clean," the man said as he passed and proceeded down the stairs.

"Bug detector," Coleman explained. "Can't be too careful. This way."

Nick thought the term was appropriate, considering the musty odor permeating the claustrophobic room. *At least there were no electronic bugs. That's a positive.* He ran a skeptical eye over the space, not so sure about the six-legged varieties.

"Something bothering you?"

Nick started at the question and the look on Coleman's face. "Thinking."

Coleman waved Nick to a chair. "Good, because we've got a lot to think about." He dropped into one of the room's other chairs, continuing before Nick could speak. "We've identified the final cutout in the money-laundering operation I told you about last Wednesday."

Nick recalled the conversation on the Charles Bridge—the findings of the Treasury Department's FinCEN report. The Venezuelan forfeiture account at the New York Federal Reserve holding some $289 million, a network of banks in the Cayman's, New York City, Bern, and a possible final cutout.

"I've got names," Coleman said. "CMM Banking in New

York City, the Cayman International Investment Group, and Schaffhauser Global Investment. The fourth in South America didn't pan out. The fifth one we studied appears to be somewhere in Eastern Europe and may be linked to Alpite Import and Export, LCC."

He mouthed a WOW. "Král's company. What did you find?"

"A tidy crypto-market that may be linked to arms sales on the dark web. We used DATACRYPTO, a web crawler/scraper software application, that can identify crypto-markets. Once we had that, we looked for the hyperlinks via the crawler, then extracted what turned up using the scraper."

Nick disregarded the web-speak, focusing on one word: Arms. That squared with what Geoff had said about a possible link to a weapons deal. He tuned out more of Coleman's technospeak until a familiar phrase surfaced.

"...we identified the moderator—"

Nick clamped his jaw. *Who the hell is "we?"* "Hold one, have you been working with Ferguson?"

Coleman stiffened. "I work with a lot of people, including Ferguson. Do you want answers or not?"

Nick wanted answers. "Who's the moderator?"

"The administrator managing the entire setup." Coleman said. "And that person is none other than Anička Drabek, Král's financier."

Nick's mind jumped to a possible link, his ability to connect disparate bits of information to a common source, and why Gilmore had tasked him with this mission. "You find any links to Meycek Exports?"

Coleman cocked his head appearing to make his own connections. "Not yet, although I won't be surprised if we can't find one."

Nick leaned forward, his interest piqued "Why's that?"

"I've been doing some off-line work."

He suppressed his surprise, working to keep his face

Chapter Forty-One

expressionless. *Offline? This guy is really good or completely out of control...maybe both. Or does he have his own——?*

"I couldn't figure out why Král always seemed to be one step ahead of me," Coleman continued, bursting into Nick's analysis.

Nick decided to focus on Král and probe about Grekov later. "What's the link?"

"I'm getting to that," Coleman said. "I've identified the mole—my secretary, God damn her eyes. She—"

"Tell me about her later. What happened?"

"Something didn't feel right, so I gave her a sidestep to see if she'd bite. Scheduled a couple of meetings concerning Alpite to see who else might show up." He paused. "The Station Chief provided the leg men."

Nick nodded. That explained part of the "we," but it left him wondering if Ferguson also had his hand in Coleman's plan.

"Spot anyone?"

"We spotted two. One of Grekov's people and Král's enforcer, a guy named Reznik. The Station Chief has a file on most of these louts."

"You're drawing a lot of attention. That's a problem."

"Right," Coleman acknowledged.

"If they think they've been spotted, their boss's operations will go dark. We'll be screwed."

"Good point."

Nick decided not to belabor the point and moved on. "You isolate her?"

"Who? My secretary?"

He nodded.

"No, I—" Coleman hesitated. "No—we, might find it useful to keep her in play to throw Král off, maybe pull in some other players we don't know about." He paused a moment, fixing his eyes on Nick. "I've had several meetings with an investigative reporter from the Czech Center for Investigative Journalism, Anton Jezek."

"That's what you told me." He waited for Coleman to elaborate.

"Brid was on to something and paid for it with her life."

Nick made a mental note that Coleman had used the reporter's first name. There was more to their relationship than he had let on. What could Coleman have shared with her? Could their relationship have led to the DEA's own operation being compromised? He refocused on the immediate issue. "Any idea what she'd found?"

"Brid never said," Coleman answered.

Nick struggled to maintain his composure. *What the hell did you tell her, buddy? Did that information lead to her death and your own operation being....? Damn, can I even trust you?* He straightened, biting off what he wanted to ask. "What did you learn from Jezek?"

"He drove up to Ralsko following a tip that Brid gave him."

Nick clenched his fists, tired of Coleman's obtuse answers. "Never heard of the place."

"Doesn't surprise me. It's hardly a tourist mecca."

"Where is it?"

"About an hour drive north of here."

"What's so important about it?" Nick said, striving to drag the answers from the agent.

"There's an old Soviet air base nearby that may factor into what they found," Coleman answered. "At one time the base supported three battalions of nuclear-tipped Scud missiles and a Mig-21 squadron."

An air base. That meant lots of bunkers. Places to hide stuff. Nick began to make the connections, his mind focusing on his next steps. Could Král or, hell, even Grekov, be planning to use the runway as a waypoint for an arms shipment to Mendez?

"How about the town?"

Chapter Forty-One

"The townsfolk were tightlipped, but one guy mentioned seeing a lot of unusual activity near a small pizza restaurant, the Coloseum Zatlÿ."

"That's it?"

"That's it."

Nick sorted through what he'd learned. "We need to throw a protective ring around Jezek."

With that decision made, Nick made a mental note to tell Geoff that Coleman was likely compromised. To what degree, he didn't know, but they had to proceed with caution when dealing with the agent. He'd also ask Geoff to run a sanity check on his plan to go to Ralsko.

Chapter Forty-Two

OBERGRABEN STRASSE, INNERE NEUSTADT
DRESDEN, GERMANY
WEDNESDAY 21 OCTOBER

Geoff Lange terminated Vinny's call and his update on Nick. Fortunately, there were no mishaps and neither Vinny or Marie had spotted anyone trailing him or Coleman to their rendezvous in the Karlín District. They also appeared to have been acting *normal*, whatever the hell that meant—especially after what Marie had told him of Nick's meltdown at the castle.

On one level, perhaps more, Lange's combat experience gave him insight into the whirl of emotions rocking his partner's psyche. He, too, had experienced those emotions while in Iraq after losing teammates, almost losing his own life, confronting the unknown, and experiencing outcomes that defied rational explanations. The stressors were endless and unpredictable. Guys would withdraw. You didn't know what

Chapter Forty-Two

they were really thinking...or what they might do when stressed again.

He reached for his humidor, having arrived at a decision. This wouldn't be the first time he'd had to drop someone from a mission, no matter how critical their position. If Nick was so unsettled by his encounter with that old man and what he'd learned, his judgment might be impaired enough to jeopardize the mission.

He proceeded through the ritual of lighting the cigar. There was something deeper going on with his friend—something that both he and Marie hadn't been able to pry out of him. What had Marie said about the aftermath of their visit to Nick's family's castle? Nick saying, "Get rid of him—the Russian agent. And Dusa? "Send a message to Grekov. Stay the hell out of this, you have no idea."

What Marie hadn't learned was why Nick had directed his fury at Ferguson. Was it something the agent had done...or something the agency had done, and Ferguson was just the hapless lightening rod? What the hell had that old man told him?

He blew out a slow plume of smoke and focused on the immediate problem. Nick had made a bad call in a moment of passion which, thankfully, George and Vinny had ignored. The team had to move on. *So how best to do that?* And what about Ferguson? He took a long draw on his cigar.

Nick wasn't the only one concerned about the CIA agent. Lange wouldn't permit Ferguson to derail the operation, particularly after the fiasco with Delezal. He set his jaw, acknowledging that he shouldn't have pushed for Delezal's abduction. But what was done, was done, and they'd have to deal with the consequences. His thoughts turned back to Nick.

He remained mystified about the origins of Nick's rage, but no matter what had triggered it, wanting to kill the Russian crossed the line. There were other ways to send a message. Could it have something to do with his family?

Perhaps that's what had driven Nick's decision to explore his family's genealogy, and what had appeared at the time to be a spontaneous decision to use a tour group as their cover. Gilmore had warned him to keep a close eye on Parkos. Did the Director know something that he hadn't passed along? No, the stakes were too high—whatever they were. "Damn."

Edmund turned from his food preparation at the expletive. "What's troublin' ya' mate?"

"We need to keep a closer watch on Nick."

"The castle?" George asked from his seat across the room.

"That's what I'm thinking," Lange answered. "I need to pin Nick down on what happened, but he's gone off the grid. Not answering his calls."

"What about Marie?"

"No luck."

"Want me to talk to Vinny?" George asked. "Maybe he knows where they went."

"Yeah, do that." Lange checked the time and pushed himself out of his chair. "I've gotta make a run to the consulate and update the Director. Call me if you learn anything."

"I thought you wanted to avoid that place," Edmund said.

"I do, but I don't trust sending a message," Lange said. "No telling whose hands it would pass through before it made its way to Gilmore. That, and I need to pick his brain to see if the name Tlatoani rings a bell." He also needed an update on Strickland. Presumably Nick's old supervisor was still under surveillance. The trick would be keeping the guy in play to see if he'd expose Král's intentions.

"Good point," Edmund said. "Think he'll alert our team in Mexico?"

"Hope so," Lange answered. "There are a lot of disparate elements in play, but we're getting close to fitting all the puzzle pieces together."

"The Russians, Král, whatever the hell Ferguson is up to,

and not even accounting for what Nick and Marie are doing," Edmond said.

"There are no coincidences," Lange summarized, snuffing out his cigar. He'd almost made it out the door when his phone buzzed. "Lange."

"Geoff, Nick. Got a sec?"

Chapter Forty-Three

RALSKO, CZECH REPUBLIC
WEDNESDAY 21 OCTOBER

Nick fought the memories of his last botched surveillance operation where he'd been knocked unconscious and imprisoned only to be rescued by Lange and his team. It'd been less than a year ago. With those thoughts at the forefront of his mind, he acknowledged there was minimal risk in what he and Marie intended to do. Just a couple of American tourists off the beaten path, exploring the small towns in the north of the Czech Republic. Besides, he couldn't back out, not after what he'd learned from Coleman. What they might find in this rural town could well be the key to blocking Král's plan to ship armaments to Mexico—if they weren't too late. He turned from the car window as the afternoon shadows lengthened across the rural countryside.

They had gotten off to a late start, leaving the rest of the team behind with instructions to develop the plan to protect the reporter, Anton Jezek. Nick had gotten Geoff's reluctant approval with a caveat: "Don't get caught doing anything stupid."

"How far?" he asked Marie, his question perfunctory. His thoughts continued to wander, settling on his guilt about dragging Michelle into the dark web of his past operation to take out the Chinese cell operating in Washington. The Chinese agent, Lin Wu, had threatened to harm her if he didn't cooperate. He sensed Marie casting him one of her penetrating looks, stopping his trip into self-pity.

"We're about ten kilometers out." She flipped on the headlamps of their 2017 Skoda Octavia sedan, throwing a thin beam over the two-lanes of highway 268. They'd chosen the unobtrusive, light-gray vehicle because it was the most popular family car in the Czech Republic and wouldn't attract attention. The bean-counters in D.C. would approve of their choice. Cheap.

"There, see that?" Marie said.

Nick followed Marie's left index finger toward an old castle perched on top of a nearby mountain. The ruins, backlit by the setting sun, dredged up a quote from a letter written by Vincent Van Gough to his brother, Theo, that Nick had seen at the Galleria Luceran or, as he called it, the Peanut Building. The words resonated: "I also believe that it may happen that one succeeds and one must begin by despairing, even if one sometimes feels a sort of decline. The point is nevertheless to revive and have courage, even though things don't turn out as one first thought."

"We're almost to the cut-off to the old Soviet base," Marie said. "You want to check that out before we head into town?"

Nick looked away from the castle and focused. Unlike his last time out, he had an experienced operator accompanying him. If Marie detected something was off, he'd defer to her judgment. "No, let's start in town. Jezek said there was word on the street that a drug deal was going down."

"You believe it?"

"No, but it's a small village. People may talk."

"You're thinking Král planted a rumor to help cover the real reason for all the activity in this backwater?"

"Wouldn't surprise me. He's hiding his real intentions."

"And those would be?" Marie queried.

"That's the problem. The arms are obvious, but I have a sense other factors are in play."

"Details," Marie responded with a shake of her head. She slowed to a stop in front of a small restaurant in the district of Hradčany, Pizza Coloseum Zlatÿ. "How 'bout we start here. You hungry?"

Nick surveyed the scattering of drab buildings surrounding the pizza joint and a couple of cars making their way down the narrow street. Literally a one-stoplight town. A two-story warehouse adjacent to the restaurant caught his eye. "This is the pizza place Coleman mentioned." He gestured to the warehouse. "Jezek said there was a lot of activity going on next door."

"Let's get a quick bite, then check it out," Marie said. "We'd be too conspicuous if we just start snooping."

Nick opened his door, not having to feign hunger. The enticing odor of fresh-baked bread and toasted garlic permeated the air and drew him into the small restaurant. He scanned the interior: vaulted wood ceiling, stone pillars supporting arched openings, a fire blazing in an open-fronted pizza oven, curved stairs at the far end of the bar leading to the second floor. Great atmosphere. *Now, if the pizza held up to the setting.* He pointed to a small table festooned with a straw-wrapped chianti bottle, red candle wax flowing down its sides. "How 'bout that one?"

A waiter attired in black pants, red shirt with a double row of brass buttons, and a black kerchief tied loosely around his neck approached with a smile after they'd settled into their chairs. He handed them two menus, opening with passable English. "May I help you?"

Chapter Forty-Three

"*Anu, děkuju,*" Nick said and continuing in Czech asked, "Do you have a good red wine?"

"Ah, we do indeed," the man said, brightening at Nick's Czech. "I'd recommend our pinot noir."

"That will do very well."

Marie picked up her menu and scanned the entries, not understanding a word. "Should I just close my eyes and point?"

"Why would they print it in English? This place isn't exactly a tourist Mecca," Nick said, while perusing the offerings. "You can't go wrong. Go for it and point."

Marie ran her eyes across the eatery and the other three patrons while pretending to choose. "Got a watcher."

"The older guy smoking a cigarette?"

"Yeah."

Nick shot a glance at the man sitting alone near the door. "Maybe, but there's only one other couple here and we're a curiosity in this backwater."

The waiter re-appeared, holding a tray with their bottle of wine and a basket of ciabatta bread. He proceeded to open the bottle, set the cork on the table, and with an expectant glance at Nick, performed a small pour.

Nick picked up the cork, giving it a sniff, swirled the glass, then took a sip. "*Vynikjící. Děkuju.*"

The waiter gave a small bow. "Welcome to Ralsko." He changed to Czech adding, "*Nás pritel*," before he turned and disappeared into a back room. Nick filled Marie's glass and hefted his own. "*Pro vaśe zdroví.*"

Marie cast Nick a curious look.

"We've been made," he said. "The guy by the door." He reached for her hand as if she were his spouse or lover. "To your health, my friend."

She lifted her glass in return and said in a conversational voice. "You don't think he's one of Král's guys?"

"I doubt it," Nick said. "Nothing escapes these folks and

he just made eye contact with me. That's unusual. The Czechs are a taciturn bunch and make a point of ignoring strangers."

"And we're strange?"

"Oh yeah, no doubt." Nick lowered his voice. "I'm thinking he might be open to a conversation." He turned to the man and lifted his glass. He spotted the waiter, waved him over, and said something in his ear.

Twenty minutes later, their pizza consumed, the bottle of pinot still half-full, Nick pushed away from the table. "We gotta go."

Marie picked up the tab. "Damn, 1,500 Koruna. That's close to seventy bucks. You'd think they'd give you a break."

"Give him a big tip. He helped us."

Marie, pulled two 1000-koruna bills from her wallet, placed them under the bottle of pinot, and followed Nick to the door. "This better pay off."

Nick smiled. "It will. In spades." He slowed as he passed the man.

"You are American, yes?" the man asked, his voice masked by the menu he held up to his face.

Nick nodded. "I have family not far from here."

"My father fought the filthy Russians," the man stated in Czech, now masking his words behind his stein of beer. His eyes drifted to the couple across the room and cast them a suspicious look. "Next door you will find something."

Nick kept going without acknowledging the man, but the words excited him. Once on the sidewalk, he translated the brief encounter, and made for the far side of the warehouse.

Marie tried the warehouse's side door. Unlocked. She pushed it open.

Nick passed her and found a light switch. He flicked it on, bathing the interior in dull light thrown by the overheads. *What the hell?* The old man's and Jezek's leads? So much B.S. "Crap, it's empty."

Marie scanned the interior. "Maybe not," she said

sweeping her right arm across the floor. "Take a look at the concrete. Those deep scrapes. They're new."

Nick dropped to his knees to examine the floor and what also appeared to be multiple parallel wheel tracks carved in a thick layer of dust. A *forklift?* "You're right."

He stood and followed the tracks to a large metal roll up door, located the control box to activate the chain hoist, and pressed the green button. He ducked under the door, ignoring the cringing metallic shrieks, stepping onto a large loading dock and scanned the area. He yelled over his shoulder. "We've got a problem. From the looks of the tire tracks, there were two semis."

"Damn, those have to be our weapons," Marie said. "Hang on." She pulled out her iPhone and took a series of pictures."

Nick spun and ran past her, heading for the car. "We need to get to that damn base."

Marie roared past the outskirts of the old air force base and several blocks of dull-white, five-story barracks before finding the main gate. She recalled the satellite pictures she'd seen of the base and picked the most likely road to the airstrip. Several minutes later, she braked to a halt at the edge of the runway with a taxiway leading to the first set of revetments.

Nick was first out, Marie joining him as they jogged from one group of crumbling concrete revetments to the next, sweeping their flashlights across the cavernous spaces. The old structures were uniform in their decay with rusted, twisted rebar protruding from the peeling blue, water-stained walls. They examined each structure in turn, their footfalls echoing in the dank interiors. Nothing.

"I wonder if we're wasting our time," Nick said. "I assumed they staged the weapons out of sight, but I'm thinking they just off-loaded them by the runway. No sense hiding them."

"Want to ask our local if he heard a plane?" Marie asked.

He took a deep breath. "Nah, the shipment's on its way." He pulled out his iPhone to notify Lange "We need find out where that damn plane went."

Chapter Forty-Four

MUNDRONY FLATS
MUNICIPLE DISTRICT 12, PRAGUE
THURSDAY 22 OCTOBER

Anton Král leaned back, his chair emitting the satisfying crunch of new leather. He had received verification that the Illushin-76 aircraft had safely departed Czech airspace after crossing the Baltic Sea and turning off its transponder. He was now waiting for Mendez's confederate, Alfredo Sanchez's call. He looked at his watch and did the math. 1000 hours in Prague, 0300 in San Miquel Dueñas. For better or worse, his shipment should have arrived in Guatemala.

Once there, the shipment would no longer be his concern. Fate, fickle as it could be, would determine what happened to the arms and the consequences of their use. He had also decided that he would no longer deal in the lucrative, but treacherous arms trade. There were too many variables he could not control.

A frown crossed his face as the adage by the American

sociologist, Robert Merton, "The Law of Unintended Consequences," wormed its way into his thoughts, the singular thought driven by a call from his source in Ralsko. The man had reported that a couple of strangers matching the descriptions of Parkos and his partner had been in town, an impact to his operation that he had not foreseen. The old man and his wife, who had also spotted the journalist, Anton Jezek, asking questions, now had seen the other two snooping around after having an early dinner at the Pizza Colosseum Zlatÿ.

He lifted the scrap of paper on which he'd written another note from the day before—intelligence he'd received from a source in Grekov's organization, who had been unmasked by his lieutenant, Karel Sokol.

What he'd learned had shocked him to the core, throwing his mind into turmoil. Grekov somehow had obtained information that Parkos could be Hájek's cousin? How did she come to know this? Impossible…or was it? A dark motive caused him to shutter. He had dismissed the American he'd seen at the castle, but could Grekov have surmised that Hájek—or even himself, and the American, Parkos, were conspiring against her?

To what purpose had Grekov done this? To use him to eliminate Parkos, thus keeping her own hands clean? He decided not to focus on her motives and concentrated instead on the significance of the American's *nom-de-guerre*. Was Partyka derived from the hereditary title, Nikola Patykaovi? The ramifications went beyond his dealings with the Russians, they impacted his designs for the castle.

Could this Partyka, or Parkos, he corrected himself, be a direct descendant of Ezra Partyka, son-of-Nikola Partyka, son-of-Petr Partyka, or was he a charlatan? Could he trust an informant in whom he placed little confidence? The three names swirled through his mind: Nikola Partyka, Nikola Patykaovi, Nick Parkos. Král pushed away from his desk and strode across his office to the open safe. He eyes passed over

Chapter Forty-Four

the Etrog as he pulled out the green hard-bound ledger he used to track his wife's and Petr Hájek's genealogy.

He returned to his desk and opened the ledger to study the descendant tree he'd begun, tracing Natálya's linage in a sequence of ascent from her mother, Ida, to her uncle, Pádriac Hájeck, and ending with Count Vilém Patykaovi, where the Count's family tree had split to three children, two sons and a daughter. The second son had died in battle in the Hussite Wars against the Catholic forces of the Holy Roman Empire. The other son's decedents continued as documented in the Lancove Rejstrciky and the tax maps denoting ownership as prescribed by Familiant Law. And possibly to this American, Parkos.

Was he an impostor? Král thought not. And where did that leave the maternal side of the family and a possible claim to the castle? In the seventh century, the women accounted for nothing. Natálya was descended from Adéla Partyka, the family's matriarch and Anya Mrazik, her great-great grandmother, daughter of Petr and sister of Nikola Partyka. Only through the diligence of the family's patriarch, Pádriac Hájek, was he able to trace the lineage.

His jaw tightened as he added Parkos' name to his ledger. As near as he could determine, this Parkos was Hájek's and Natálya's third cousin, removed. The links were tenuous at best, but worth validating. He spent the remainder of the morning delving into those few documents provided by Petr's uncle after he'd married Natálya. Parkos' great-grandfather had been killed by the communists and Parkos' grandparents had fled to the United States in 1948 with their infant grandson, Tomas, Parkos' father. And the old man had said that Tomas had returned to Czechoslovakia as a member of the CIA and had been detained and murdered by the communists. Král emitted a slow breath. *And what of my own father?*

His father, like so many others, had been detained and likely murdered by the communists. He never knew his fate with certainty. And his elderly grandfather? He'd fought the Germans first joining the Ušiak-Murzin Unit when he was only fourteen years old. That was before its leader, Jan Žižka, a Slovak, had aligned himself with the Russians. His great-grandfather had escaped to France in August of 1944, returning home after the war to re-establish the family line despite the risks to his life.

He considered the new entries he'd written. *And what of this possible conjoining of the family after all of these years?* "Serendipity?" he mused aloud. "Perhaps. Or perhaps something else, something of greater consequence that portends my future?" He spun his chair and looked out the window at the dull building adjacent to his own, fighting a wave of introspection, a trait with which he was not often burdened.

He closed the ledger, resting his hand on the cover. And if Parkos were a relative? He clenched his fists in consternation, catching himself, not wanting to dwell on the fact the American agent might indeed be a relative—the rightful heir to Castle Patykaovi? He concluded there were only two choices—embrace this Parkos or eliminate him.

Král recalled something he'd learned as he strove to construct his empire. He had to understand the variables, those things that were within one's control and what unknowns may lay beyond, and with that foundation, to control what is within oneself and treat with indifference all else.

Sound advice. Irrespective of the veracity of what he'd found, he had to divert the attention of the Americans—especially if they suspected he was involved in an arms sale to Mendez. That would get their attention. This was not just another drug deal. International drug sales would add another layer of concern to the American watchdogs of the DEA, but those sales would not directly threaten the security of the Americans, as would an armed revolt at their border.

With that thought, he focused on Grekov and the Russian

weasel, Ilia, who he had disposed of at the castle. That was one less of Grekov's people to contend with, but the chauffeur, Dusa Novikov, and perhaps others remained. So where did Ilia fit? Could Grekov possibly have thought that I met with Parkos at the castle to conspire against her? *"Do prdele!"*

The Czech epithet reflected his anger and frustration. He took several deep breaths and refocused. Delezal. He had gone to whatever fate awaited him, so why not use him? Why not feed misinformation to this reporter, Anton Jezek? Once that was done, he could set a trap for Parkos. Perhaps not to kill him, but to scare him off.

The other factor that played into his decisions was a cryptic text that Anička had sent. In it, she'd verified the fund transfer via a convoluted dark network passing through Schaffhauser Global Investments to his Swiss account at the discrete Kohler and Favre Bancaire Privee: $289,331,020.17. There had been no greedy hands skimming his money off the top.

He pulled out his tape recorder and thumbed "play," focusing on this plan to eliminate both Parkos and Jezek:

"You're taking fifty percent of my cut. I need twenty."

"You better guarantee me that business."

"I will, but you gotta deal with the Mexican, maybe the other guy."

"Man, you gotta have a cut-out. We can't be talking like this."

"Five million euros."

What other guy? Král asked himself. Rajif Mohammadi? Srevnenko? A rival organization like the Liska mob? He scowled at another recollection. The Liska's had blown their amateurish attempt to shake down the tobacconist, almost killing Parkos and his partner in the process. The botched shotgun attack had put the Americans on alert. It would be reasonable for them to presume their cover had been blown. Well, if so, I may be able to further divert their attention.

He played the recording again. He suspected that one, if not both, of the voices were electronically altered. He listened to the tape several more times. There was no obvious voice alteration like that used by a confidential witness, but whomever had recorded the tape had added subtle distortions, changes of amplitude, tone, and pitch. He set the recorder aside. They could have also used sophisticated software to clone a voice. Not many had the resources to do that. His suspicions focused again on Aleksandra Grekov.

His head jerked up at the buzzing of his iPhone. Sanchez. He slid his finger over the device to answer. "Yes?"

"I must go to the hospital to see your aunt but be assured she is okay."

A weight fell from Král's shoulders. *The pre-arranged code sent by Mendez's associate.* The shipment had arrived. He could now focus on Parkos and Grekov. That, and he had to finalize his plan on how to eliminate the reporter, Jezek after setting him up with information about a pending drug deal. He picked up his phone and placed a call summoning his enforcer, Reznik.

Chapter Forty-Five

ALCRON HOTEL
PRAGUE, CZECH REPUBLIC
THURSDAY 22 OCTOBER

Geoff Lange handed Marie her iPhone after studying the pictures she had taken at Ralsko. "Two semi's, perhaps fifty tons of cargo each, since an arms dealer would hardly be concerned with the EU's maximum weight limit for big-rigs. We've got a probable arms shipment and the names of Mendez and Sanchez. It doesn't take a leap of the imagination to connect the dots."

George inserted himself into the discussion. "There are only a few aircraft with the legs to reach the Americas with that kind of load: An Illusin-76. Perhaps a 747. If I recall, their max load is around forty tons."

"Let's back up a moment," Nick said, aborting a comment from Ferguson. Geoff had briefed him on Ferguson's busted operation in Poland, but he needed to focus on the immediate problem. "That's a lot of weaponry, especially for a cartel."

"Perhaps, but you'd be surprised how fast the weight adds up."

"I'd say it could be the first shipment of many for a bigger operation," Geoff said. "Something that had caught the director's attention."

"Do have we any hard intelligence that supports your scenario?" Marie asked.

Geoff considered Marie's statement. "Not yet, so let's focus on what we do have. A 747 is out. They can't operate from that airfield. Král needed a military aircraft. I'm placing my money on a civilian variant of the Candid—" He paused. "That's NATO's designation for the Ilusin-76. The manufacturer has repurposed the military aircraft for civilian use, and it's flown by several dozen international carriers. The one that immediately comes to mind is Azerbaijan Air Freight. Král also might contract Silk Way Airlines. Presuming we're dealing with an IL-76, its range, carrying a maximum weight of cargo, is 3000 miles. Not enough to reach Central America without refueling."

Marie spoke up. "Knowing that, they probably used two semis to speed up the loading process, not two aircraft."

"Correct," Geoff said. "Multiple aircraft would have attracted too much attention from the locals, and more than one might tip the hand of another player providing the assets."

Nick leaned forward in his chair. "Interesting. I'm thinking Grekov. We're presuming the cargo is heading to Central America or Mexico."

Geoff didn't equivocate, knowing Nick's history with Grekov. "It's heading to Central America, then trans-shipped to Mendez in Mexico."

"How about the Houthi's in Yemen?" Marie ventured.

"Don't think so," Geoff said. "They've got their network with Iran and—"

"Another Iranian connection then," Marie countered.

George inserted himself between the two. "At this point, it doesn't matter. I'll contact headquarters and have them work the flight tracker sites to see if they can determine where the damn thing went. Even if the pilot turned off his transponder, he'd have to turn it back on to land and refuel, and again at his destination. I'll also see if I can find out if either of those companies has any long-term contracts with companies in the Czech Republic."

"I need a better feel for Mendez," Nick said.

Taylor Ferguson handed Nick a single sheet of paper. "Here ya go. Everything you wanted to know about the Tlatoani."

Nick bunched his eyebrows as he scanned the report titled: "Carlos Mendez: Psychological Profile," and picked out the salient points. "I don't see anything here that surprises me. The guy's a thug. A man of the people. Yeah, right." He grunted and handed the analysis to Marie who scanned the body of the letter before dropping to the conclusions at the bottom of the page: Mixed personality disorder – Narcissistic/sociopathic. Ego-dystonic, hyperthymic-mania, expansive to cover his underlying insecurity. The last bullet stopped her. "Listen to this. Fashions himself as the ruler, El Tlatoani, the rebirth of the Aztlán empire, the Culhau peoples, the Mexica, a term that dates to 1325."

She handed the sheet back to Ferguson. "I'd say the last line is operative. "The Mexica portrayed themselves as a people predestined for empire."

Ferguson pulled another document from his briefcase and handed it to Lange. "My summary of the Delezal interrogation. I have no idea what he gave up to the Russians. We're working to retrieve our hidden recorder. That is, if the Russians didn't find it."

"We have to presume our operation has been compromised," Nick said. "Coleman did tell me that the reporter,

Jezek, had heard rumors circulating of a Mexican/Grekov connection."

Ferguson looked at his feet, then at Lange. "We have collaborative intercepts from our National Collection Services—SIGINT/HUMINT."

Geoff stifled a barbed retort, his anger directed at both men. Nick, for not telling him about Jezek's information, and Ferguson. He shook his head. "We need to focus on Grekov. The Russians present the greater threat—whatever the hell it is they're planning. I'll speak with the director. Mr. Gilmore can focus on Mendez while we clean things up in Prague. He faced Ferguson. "See what you can do about getting the Office of Special Projects and your buddies at the embassy engaged and plant sensors in Grekov's office."

"Král's fronting for them," Marie added.

"Who? The Russians?"

"Yes."

"Deliberately?" Nick prodded.

"We can't dismiss the possibility," Marie said.

"Concur," Geoff said. "We need to go after both. Are we all in agreement?

"I don't disagree," Nick said

Geoff cast Nick a curious look at the ambivalent response but decided to move on and deal with him out of earshot of the others. He stood, signaling the meeting was over. He turned to Nick. "A moment."

"What the hell's going on?" Geoff demanded after the room cleared.

Nick shrugged, a gesture that set off Geoff's mounting frustration with his friend. "Damn it, Nick, you've walked me out on a limb and it's about to snap. What haven't you told me?" His question was again met with silence. "Ever since you visited that damn castle, you've—"

"It's none of your business," Nick said.

"Why would you even say something like that?"

Chapter Forty-Five

"Why do you think?"

"You're keeping something bottled up inside, probably concerning your family."

"I don't like you trying to get into my head. You're not my shrink."

"I wouldn't dare try to get into your head and I'm sure as hell not your shrink, but you've left me without many options. What I'm questioning is your state of mind."

Nick again responded with silence, staring at the floor. Geoff stood. He had neither the time nor the patience to continue. "Get your damn act together or you're out." He paused, thinking of another way to penetrate Nick's wall of obstinance. "Listen, do I need to send you back to Michelle and let her deal with all this crap?"

Nick straightened. "No."

Geoff's admonition also served to strengthen Nick's decision to show Marie the contents of the burlwood box. He owned it to her.

Chapter Forty-Six

NUMBER 10 UVOZ STREET
PRAGUE ADMINISTATIVE DISTRICT FIVE
THURSDAY 22 OCTOBER

Aleksandra Grekov pondered another Russian proverb, a variation of the one she had shared with Kuznetzov. She set aside the cryptic message, one of two delivered the previous hour by the embassy's courier. "Don't dig a hole for someone else, or you will fall in it yourself." *True enough.*

The courier had made the short walk from District Six. While it would be safe to assume he'd been shadowed by a member of the Czech security forces, she felt her cover as a legitimate business, Meycek Imports, still held some validity with the local authorities. Not so much the embassy, now manned by a skeletal staff as relations between Moscow and the Czech Republic continued to deteriorate.

Aside from the fact that the chancery occupied the former headquarters of the Gestapo, the Czechs had linked two members of GRU Unit 29155, who had also been tagged for using the novichok nerve agent in a botched attach on two Russian dissidents in Salisbury, England, to an attack in the Czech Republic. The two were seen leaving the site of an explosion that had destroyed an army ammunition storage site near the city of Vrbětice. Besides expelling more than half of the Russian's staff, the Czech president had also renamed the square fronting the Embassy to Boris Nemtsov Plaza. Nemtsov, a Russian citizen and vocal critic of Srevnenko, had been assassinated in Moscow.

The gesture by the Czechs would almost be funny if it had not so offended the sensibilities of the ruling elite in Moscow. She would likely get dragged into whatever form of retribution headquarters choose.

Grekov gave her head an irritated shake at permitting her thoughts to wander. She refocused, knowing all these developments taken within the context of her real mission presented a credible threat to her own safety. Not having diplomatic immunity, she could easily be arrested and imprisoned—and likely forgotten by her government, dismissed as a liability, and, an embarrassment.

She re-read the courier's document, only sixteen words long, the sentence gleaned from millions of communications intercepted by their Olymp-K satellite: "I must go to the hospital to see your aunt, but be assured she is okay."

The message, sent by Carlos Mendez's deputy, Alfredo Sanchez, confirmed that Král's arms shipment had reached Guatemala. She considered it madness to foment conflict at the American border to distract their attention from the Kremlin's designs on the Ukraine, but the weapons were no longer her problem—at least for the short term. FSB operatives would monitor the trans-shipment of the weapons to Mendez. How they were used was not her concern. Her particular issue was that there were more shipments in the pipeline from their sources in Slovenia and Armenia, including heavy weaponry, shipments that she had to ensure were linked to Král, not to Moscow....or to her.

A hint of a sardonic smile crossed Grekov's face. Král had no idea she'd facilitated the transactions with Mendez through suppliers in Belarus. She set aside the message and picked up the second document from Moscow Central, her smile vanishing as quickly as it had appeared. This report summarized the intelligence from the Spetsgruppa raid on the CIA's safehouse in Poland and Delezal's fate.

The document raised any number of issues, but topping them all was her own list of those things she must address. Forty-eight hours had passed, and Ilia had not reported back from his surveillance of Castle Patykaovi. She shouldn't have sent him.

Dusa had reported that Parkos had a major confrontation with his partners, then the other two men in Parkos' party retraced their steps into the woods. She could only surmise what had happened to Ilia. In any event, she had to accept reality. Ilia had been spotted and eliminated. But was it by the Americans? She could not dismiss a suspicion that wormed its way back into her mind. While improbable, Parkos and Král could be conspiring against her and Král had killed Ilia. But why would they conspire against her? The answer remained elusive, but her question was superseded by an even more immediate problem: Her own safety.

She picked up her fountain pen and underlined two names in the report's summary: Tlatoani/Mendez and Anička Drabek. Then she began to work through the probabilities. Kuznetsov's version of events jibed with those submitted by the Alpha Group's team leader, Ulyanov. A positive.

She then focused on the questions she had jotted down on a piece of water-soluble paper that she'd flush down the commode before she left the office for her apartment: *Was the mission worth the huge risk they'd taken?* Perhaps. Time would tell. *And what had the Americans learned?*

Chapter Forty-Six

Neither Kuznetzov nor Ulyanov had any firm idea of what Delezal had divulged. For reasons she could not begin to fathom, Ulyanov had permitted the CIA agent, Ferguson, to live. She shook her head in disbelief. Why the hell would he do that? Guidance from his command?

She sorted through the implications of her second question. The Alpha Team had collected a couple of laptops and several recording devices in hopes of extracting further information. So far, the FSB's Technology Office had not found anything useful. The laptops only contained social media posts and music from a site called GarageBand. She'd let Moscow figure out if there were any encrypted messages buried within the babble.

But should she let Moscow determine her fate? What other intercepts could Turgenov have that he chose not to share? Could the same satellite that had intercepted Sanchez's call also have intercepted a frantic call by the American agent, Ferguson? And if so, what had Moscow learned?

Grekov set Moscow Central's analysis aside, overcome by a rare sense of foreboding.

She started at a sound coming from the hallway outside her office. There should be no one else in the building at this hour. She opened the bottom drawer of her desk where she kept her pistol. Voices, laughter, then the sound of a vacuum cleaner. She released her grip on the weapon, chastised herself for her paranoia, and closed the drawer.

It was inconceivable that the Americans would conduct an interrogation and not record it. She had to presume that Delezal had divulged her name and her role in the arms shipment. She could only guess how Moscow would react...and when? No, that wasn't true. If her actions compromised President Srevnenko, retribution would be quick.

What had Colonel General Turgenov said? "If there is even a whiff of discovery of our intentions, you will abort the mission, leaving nothing behind that could be traced to the president."

She wrote down a timeline on her paper, beginning her own defense for the accusations of incompetence that were sure to come from headquarters:

20th – Ilia sent to Castle Patykaovi/Dusa's short-fused alert of Parkos' trip

20th – Spetsguppa raid

20st – Ilushin-76 aircraft lands Ralsko - Too late to abort

22nd – HQ rpt received

Events had moved too swiftly to cancel the Azerbaijan Air Freight flight, but that excuse wouldn't prevent Turgenov from deflecting blame from his own role and lay the blame of a failed mission at her feet. Grekov's hand tightened around her pen, her knuckles blanching. And what of Comrade Turgenov? As the cliché said, "The silence is deafening."

Did Turgenov's silence indicate she was being shielded or marginalized? But if Turgenov did have advance knowledge that the mission was compromised, why hadn't he ordered her to abort? She already knew the answer to her rhetorical question. She gazed over the rooftops toward the embassy compound in District Six. Perhaps the web of deceit she had woven to cover her own intentions had also ensnared her?

That realization prompted her to consider her options, their foundations based on an absolute she'd carried with her all these years—her quest to restore her family's honor and that of her great-grandfather, Count Kuzmin Grekov. Her hand, of its own volition, wrote; Myka, her grandfather's nickname for her. She'd often wondered about her nickname. Why a name of Jewish origin? We were Russian Orthodox.

"Mykalia" was Hebrew for "Who is like God." Papa had changed it to Mikayla. Perhaps he had a premonition years before his death at the hands of the Bolsheviks. He had returned to the family estate in Kursk, humbling himself, working as a serf, while a commissaire lived in their old home.

Chapter Forty-Six

It was a miracle he'd survived, but then he had been arrested by the Cheka, torn from her, and sent to the gulags, where he perished.

And my grandmother and her infant daughter, my mother? They had been rescued, like thousands of others in the small boats, by the American destroyer, *Overton* during the evacuation of Sebastopol on the 14th of November 1920. They had been put ashore on the Turkish island of Prinipo, south of Constantinople, and for reasons she had never been able to fathom, made their way back to Russia to join Papa. They too, had lost their lives, leaving her orphaned.

Over the ensuing years, she had made several futile attempts to trace her genealogy, a task made even more difficult by Stalin's bloody purges and his systematic efforts to destroy all family records of the old aristocracy. What little she could find was via risky searches of the internet where her inquiries could be tracked by the FSB counter-intelligence office.

Lost in her own musings, Grekov was staggered when an unexpected epiphany rocked her internal narrative. *My, God. Is that what Parkos had discovered at that damn castle? His own family and his relationship to Petr and Natálya Hájek?* If that were the case, she would have to reach out to the American to save herself.

Chapter Forty-Seven

MODRANY FLATS
MUNICIPLE DISTRICT 12, PRAGUE
FRIDAY 23 OCTOBER

Král held the tarnished silver relic he had found in the muck of Castle Patykaovi's mikveh. He sensed a peculiar warmth emanating from the hand-shaped Torah pointer, the Yad a symbol of his faith. A faith that had also been buried, but that he had rediscovered in the search for his own identity.

He glanced to his left, his eyes settling on another object, the sculpted anthropomorphic being that he had placed on the credenza. The ten-centimeter, gray-stone statuette was a replica of the Golem, the ghoulish effigy of the Monster of Prague that stood guard at the entrance to city's Jewish Quarter.

In Czech legend, Rabbi Judah Loew had created the monster in the sixteenth century, molding it from the clay of the Vltava River. Loew had then carved the word *Emet*,

Chapter Forty-Seven

"Truth," on the creature's forehead, before crossing out the "E" to create a new word, *Met*, "Death." He then released his monster to create mayhem and protect the Jews of Prague from the Hapsburg King, Rudolf II's pogrom.

"Perhaps Rabbi Loew should have permitted Golem to continue his reign of terror?" Král asked the empty room. He uttered a grunt at the thought, accepting the fate of his people through the ensuing centuries. He pulled his eyes away from Golem and set the Yad on his desk blotter, angered that he had permitted his mind to wander, the myth of Golem and the relic's significance both supplanted by what he'd learned of the Hájek family's heritage—doubt replacing his past certainty about where his child would fit in the family's truncated history.

"Why didn't Natálya tell me?" Král asked the ghosts haunting his soul. The anger at the injustices endured by his family boiled to the surface, inflamed by what he'd discovered in the Nazi archives at the Terezin Ghetto. The top of the worn ledger's page read: *Politische Abt. Aufnahmerschreiber:* Political Dept. Recorder. Halfway down the page, dated April 12, 1944, he'd spotted the name Jakub Hájek. The old man had never mentioned his younger brother's name. Was it due to guilt at having survived when his brother had died at Birkenau?

When no answer was forthcoming to his question or from the spirits, Král pivoted his attention to something of substance, those individuals who could have led Parkos to the castle and what little Hájek had told him about Parkos' visit to the fortress's library.

He sorted through several possibilities, but only one name fit: Katerina Vasek, the tour director who had also taken Parkos to the Terezin Ghetto. While the possibility remained that there was no connection with the American's visit to the castle, his instincts told him differently.

While Vasek's Prestige Genealogy and Heritage Tours was

likely a cover, based on where she had taken the Americans, Parkos could also be legitimately researching his past. And hadn't Delezal reported that Vasek and Parkos had visited the small shop that housed the Ghetto's archives and the collection of ancestral documents? He'd gone there himself several years before in his own quest for his family's past. A past that had almost been extinguished by the Nazis.

Shaken by his recollection of what the old woman had shown him, he grasped the Yad, seeking a sign from the relic to help him decide what he must do to extricate himself from his association with Mendez and Grekov.

He'd again verified that nearly 300 hundred million U.S. dollars had been deposited in his account at the Kohler and Favre Bancaire Privee in Bern, the Venezuelan government funds that had been secured in a monitored forfeiture account at the New York Federal Reserve Bank. He chuckled at the word, "monitored." Not so much. He wondered how long it would be until the American bankers realized their funds had vanished? And when they did? Their full investigative forces would be unleashed with a vengeance to find both the perpetrator and their missing money. With that sobering thought, he made a note to discuss the matter with Drabek.

Král moved on to address the specific actions he needed to take to extricate himself from the morass of lies and deceit he'd created that now threatened to entrap him. The first was to summon Sokol and finalize the sham drug deal. If it worked as designed, Parkos would be convinced that the arms shipment was really a cover for a major drug operation and divert his attention to the Iranians. If his ploy failed, at least he would have distracted the Americans long enough to buy some time to counter the damage done by Delezal...whatever that was.

He ran through the possibilities of what those damages could be. Could Delezal have been abducted? And if so, by whom? The Americans? The Russians? Each of these possibil-

Chapter Forty-Seven

ities created their own problems. With that realization, he turned his attention to a problem that required his immediate attention. According to his source in the American embassy, Coleman's secretary, the DEA agent had arranged several meetings with the reporter, Anton Jezek. The secretary didn't know the nature of their discussions, but her information about the meetings was enough.

Král pursued another angle, the tour director, Vasek. He hadn't used her, but one visit by Reznik to her family had been enough to ensure she would comply with any request he demanded. He paused. No, it would not be necessary to threaten her again, but he could ensure certain information about a pending drug deal would reach her and that she would, in turn, pass it on to the reporter, Jezek.

He reached for his iPhone and scrolled down his list of contacts. Finding Sokol's number, he placed the call. The next was to Reznik, with whom he outlined an audacious plan to eliminate Jezek. Like Rabbi Loew's Golem, he would release terror and confusion amongst his enemies.

Chapter Forty-Eight

WENCESLAS SQUARE
PRAGUE, CZECH REPUBLIC
SATURDAY 24 OCTOBER

Geoff Lange leaned forward, resting his elbows on the third-floor windowsill of their fixed surveillance position in the Grand Hotel Europa. He adjusted the focus of his binoculars and swept the expanse of Wenceslas Square. The square, Prague's second largest, was actually a broad boulevard and former horse market located in the Nové Mēstu District. Only a short walk south from the team's hotel, the square was a popular gathering spot, as attested by the throng of Czechs gathering there to take advantage of the crisp, cloudless fall day.

"How long will we be doing this?" George asked from his perch on the room's king bed.

Lange didn't break his concentration to answer. "Ask long as it takes."

"I'm not sure the time we spent yesterday running

Chapter Forty-Eight

surveillance is paying off," Vinny added, his statement eliciting affirmative nods from Jennifer and Ann.

"Patience," Lange said. "Our intel is solid." His sight rested on a single individual, almost indistinguishable from his fellow citizens except for the man's bright-red Česko ice hockey jersey celebrating the Czech's victory over the old Soviet Union in the 1969 world ice hockey championships. He compared the man's face with a photograph on the table beside him, studied both for a moment, and confirmed his sighting.

Coleman's tip had proved correct. According to the DEA agent, Anton Jezek was chasing down a new lead in his investigation of Král's operations, something about a large drug deal. He'd also said he had evidence that a huge sum of money had made its way through the dark web, possibly to an account in Switzerland opened under Král's name. Money that Lange surmised would be used to purchase more weapons.

The problem Lange's support team was facing? Coleman couldn't provide the specifics on when Jezek would meet his contact, or who that contact might be. Lange grunted as he continued to watch Jezek weave through the crowd, making his way northwest down the sloping boulevard toward Old Town. "Got him."

George left his perch on the bed and peered over Lange's shoulder. "Where?"

"See him? Red jersey," Vinny said, holding the man centered in his own binoculars. "Just passed Da Copo's. Hold on. He's reversed course. Appears he might be running an inverse surveillance route."

"If he is, it's pretty weak," George said. "He's gone by a number of outstanding cafés. Damn, he just passed Oliver's. I'd think he'd at least go into one of them and watch for threats."

"Poor tradecraft," Lange acknowledged. He swung his

binoculars through an arc toward Nick and Marie who were seated under the outside awning of the Plzenska Rychta pub. "He's not very good, but it appears someone may have spent some time trying to teach him a few basics about how to run a surveillance detection route."

"The open question is, who is he meeting?" George said. "Hard to know what to look for."

"See that?" Vinny said.

Lange pulled his eyes from his binoculars. "See what?"

"He's frightened," Vinny said. "He's picked up his pace and is looking over his shoulder. I'm thinking he spotted a tail."

Lange noted where Vinny's binoculars stopped, focused on something or someone twenty meters behind the journalist. "Shit. Give me that photo of Král's enforcer."

"Reznik?" Jennifer said as she sifted through a pile of photographs that Ferguson had given them. She selected one and handed it over.

"That's him," Vinny affirmed. "You see any others?"

"No," Lange answered, "but our guy just ducked into that coffee shop a few doors down from Nick and Marie. He just bought us some time. Get down there and establish a floating box. We've gotta protect his ass." He swung his binoculars toward the Plzenska Rychta pub. "Time to bring Nick and Marie in."

Vinny pushed himself out the chair he'd set next to Lange's. "Pair up in threes?"

"Seriously, you're dropping a Yogi Berra quote on me?" Lange responded.

"Couldn't help myself," Vinny said as he and George disappeared out the door, followed by Ann and Jennifer.

Chapter Forty-Eight

Nick took a perfunctory sip of his Urquell pilsner, masking a grimace. He had selected the brew from a long list of offerings because of the advertisement in large block letters on the café's white awning, not because he knew anything about it. Mundane thoughts about his beer selection were quickly replaced by one of import. Today was the twenty-fourth, and while he'd been reminded their visas were good for thirty days, their cover under Prestige Genealogy Tours was rapidly drawing to a close. He caught himself. *One issue at a time.* He could always come up with an excuse to extend his and Marie's stay. But what about the others?"

"Will you be wanting a refill?" Marie asked.

He shot his partner an appraising glance and decided she was teasing. "Nope."

A smile lit his face as the laughter from a cluster of brightly-clad children kicking around a soccer ball reminded him of his wife. Michelle had played soccer for the Trojans of Centerburg High in Ohio and had briefly toyed with the idea of trying out for A&M's women's team.

His affectionate thoughts of Michelle made him realize that his shock at Lange's dressing down the day before had been replaced by gratitude for his friend's unexpected gesture of kindness. Nick pulled out a selfie Michelle had taken at an Aggie football game. On the back she'd written "The Twelfth Woman" alluding to A&M's "The Twelfth Man" student section. Below it she'd added. "I love you."

How did Lange know? Nick knew the answer. Lange had surmised what had really underpinned Nick's screwed-up attitude several days earlier and had gotten Michelle's letter delivered in a diplomatic pouch. And those few words Lange had said when he handed him the envelope? "I've got your back. I've been there, too."

He replaced the photo when a spectacular scissor-kick from one of the girls sent the ball skittering in his direction. The girl, perhaps ten or eleven, stopped in mid-stride wondering what he would do, perhaps afraid he'd be angry. Flashing a broad smile, he picked up the ball and tossed it back into play. "*Kuvēlá kopa!*" The girl gave him a happy wave and ran off after her friends.

"What did you say?" Marie asked.

"Great kick," Nick said. He jumped at the sound of Lange's voice in his earpiece and looked in direction Lange had indicated. "On it."

Marie reached across their table for the breadbasket while tapping the front of her chest. "Damn thing cut out," she whispered. "What's going on?"

Good question, Nick asked himself, but in response, he pushed up from the wrought-iron chair, stretching his arms over head. "Geoff spotted Jezek. The team's on their way down." He held up his hand as he received another message. "On it," he said through the throat mike tucked under the collar of his turtleneck sweater. "Our guy just ducked into Da Copos. Reznik's on his tail."

"Thirty-five bucks," Marie said, dropping a five-hundred and three one-hundred korona bills on the table. "That ought to cover it."

"Perfect," Nick said, heading toward the coffee shop. "Geoff wants us to linger by Copa's front door while the others set up a floating box to contain Reznik."

Marie hooked her arm under Nick's elbow. "Hey, you're getting pretty good with the lingo."

"Harrumph."

Jezek emerged five minutes later holding a paper cup of coffee embossed with Da Copa's logo. He paused for a sip, then headed toward Old Town with the team trailing him. They paused when the reporter stopped by a flower stand.

"What the hell?" Jennifer said into her throat mike. "That's Vasek."

"Vasek?" George repeated. "Where?"

"Behind the roses," Ann responded.

Chapter Forty-Eight

"Jezek just spotted her," Jennifer said. "He's working his way down the aisle for the meet."

"Reznik's on the move. Just pushed some kid out of his way," Vinny stated, his voice calm over their net. "I'll cut him off," he added sidestepping to a halt to avoid a mother pushing a baby carriage across his path. "Damn, no good. George, pick him up."

Nick took off. He knew George wouldn't make the intercept from his position at the far edge of their containment box, but he might just make it.

Marie recovered from her surprise and sprinted after her partner closing the distance, before veering to her left.

Nick missed her move, concentrating on Reznik. He cut to his right, shortening the distance, catching Vinny and Ann out of the corner of his eye. Two people blocked the entrance to the shop. *Damn!* He pushed the startled shopkeeper and her customer, who were standing at the register, out of his way.

"Knife!" Ann screamed, swinging her arms downward at the bewildered shop owner and customer. "Down. Down." The women just stared as she ran toward Reznik.

Jezek froze, his hand clutching a bouquet of roses, his head swinging toward the man with a crazed expression running down the aisle toward him. He spun, took a step to escape, and stumbled over a pot of carnations. He crashed to the floor and scrambled on hands and knees for safety under the flower displays.

Reznik hesitated at the unexpected warning, his serrated eight-inch knife poised for what would have been a fatal thrust to Jezek's exposed neck.

Ann's warning had provided Vinny enough time to vault over a low table separating him from Reznik. He caught his balance and lunged forward, delivering a vicious downward hammer-fist to the startled assassin's forearm. Reznik yelled a curse, his weapon clattering to the floor. Vinny followed his strike with a lightening blow of his left fist to Reznik's nose before the assassin could react.

There was no missing the crack of breaking bone and Reznik's howl of pain. The Czech took several wobbly steps, then sprinted out the back of the shop, hand to his ruined nose, making for the safety of the twisted, congested streets of Old Town.

Marie ran toward Vasek, the tour director's hand covering her mouth in horror and shock from the violence that had engulfed her. "Katarina, it's Marie. Come with me."

Vasek froze, casting an imploring look at Jezek.

"He'll be okay. Come," Marie hollered. She grabbed Vasek's arm, pulling her toward the shop's front door.

Nick's earpiece rang with Lange's voice. "What just happened?" Nick made a quick assessment. "Jezek's safe. Vinny took care of Reznik. The bastard ran out the back door."

"What about the others?"

"Everyone's good. We're getting out of here."

"Roger that," Lange said. "Meet me in the room."

While Nick kept Lange informed, George approached Vinny, his head on a swivel, looking for any further threats. "You good?"

"Yeah," Vinny answered, "I can't say the same for Reznik's nose." He peered under the table. "You can come out now."

Jezek rolled out from under the table and stood. "Who are you guys?"

"Friends," Nick said as he cast an incredulous look over Jezek's shoulder at Ann and Jennifer. They were browsing along the far counter amongst the vases of flowers without an apparent care in the world. "What the—"

"There's nothing to see here. Move along, folks," George said.

"Ah, got it," Nick said. "I'll stay behind and play clueless tourist."

Marie walked by with her arm now securely around Vasek's shoulder. "No need to play clueless there, partner."

"Seriously?" Nick said.

Vinny interrupted. "Spot anyone else?"

"No," George responded, "but we gotta get the hell out of here. He caught Nick's eye. "All of us."

Nick nodded. They had to disappear. He gave Jezek a guiding shove to the small of his back while waving his right index finger in the air like a propeller. "Jennifer!" He pointed to Jezek. "Time to clear out."

Jennifer nodded, grabbed a bouquet of carnations, wrapped her arm around the reporter's waist and walked him out of the shop, mimicking a romantic couple. Ann joined Marie, shadowing Jennifer, followed a moment later by the men who took circuitous routes back to the Hotel Europa.

Chapter Forty-Nine

GRAND HOTEL EUROPA
WENCESLAS SQUARE, PRAGUE
SATURDAY 24 OCTOBER

Nick arrived at the hotel first, trailed five minutes later by Ann, Jennifer, and their new charge, Katerina Vasek. That wouldn't do; he knew that Lange would be enraged if Vasek learned of his support role. One glance at the bewildered look on Vasek's face, though, confirmed his decision. The entire team needed to debrief, and they couldn't cut the tour leader loose, leaving Vasek to her own devices to fend off whatever threats still might exist after the failed assassination attempt. He motioned for the three women to lag behind before he made his way from the ornate lobby to the Europa's third floor. "Best for me to go in first."

Lange turned at the sound of the door opening and rose from his post by the window. "How are—?" He threw a furious look at Nick, then at Ann and Jennifer before his piercing glare settled on Vasek, who was cowering behind Jennifer's right shoulder. "What the hell is she doing here?"

"Exercising damage control," Nick answered, ignoring the musty smell of the room and the 60's décor. "We need to protect her." He paused and looked at Vasek. "And she needs to level with us about who she's working for."

Marie made her way past the group blocking the door and entered the room followed by George and Vinny. "And she has to know the danger she's put us and herself in."

"That monster who attacked us." Vasek's voice wavered. "He… he came to our home and threatened my family."

Lange dropped into his chair. "How so?"

Vasek choked back a sob. "He appeared at my door last week. He said would hurt my little girl if I didn't do as I was told."

"And that was?" Lange prodded.

"That I would be given a message that I was to pass to that reporter."

"Anton Jezek," Lange stated. "Do you know him?"

"The reporter? No," Vasek answered. "I have never seen him before. The other man, he showed me a picture, then gave me a phone number that I would use to contact him about certain information I'd come across."

"Gotta be one of Král's people," Vinny said.

"What did he tell you to say?" Nick asked.

"That I was a friend of the reporter's colleague, Brid Krejci, and that I had information about a drug deal."

Nick raised his eyebrows at her last statement. Mentioning Brid made sense, but how did Reznik and presumably, his boss, Král know Jezek's phone number? That spelled trouble. He also understood it wouldn't do to press Vasek. She was clinging to Marie's arm, struggling to control the trembling that racked her body. "Marie, can you take Katerina home?"

Before Marie could reply, Vasek emitted a wail as her legs

collapsed. She dropped in a heap onto the edge of the room's king bed. Marie managed to catch her before she slid to the floor. "We should leave," Marie said while holding Vasek upright. "We'll keep her out of sight."

George approached the bed to help Marie. "Best I go with them."

Vasek surprised everyone by straightening her shoulders and waving them off. "No!"

"Hold on," Lange said, halting George in his tracks. "Let her stay. Ann, pour her a glass of water."

Nick cocked his head at the exchange and asked, "Where's Jezek?"

"We cut him loose," Jennifer responded. "He said he had a safe place that he and his buddies in the OCCRP use when the heat's on."

Lange didn't appear mollified but stopped at the look on Nick's face. "Okay. Catch me up, starting with Reznik."

"He escaped," Nick said.

"We let him go," Vinny said. "He's a worthless piece of crap, an enforcer. I doubt if he knows anything."

Lange cocked an eyebrow at Vinny's characterization, even if it happened to be accurate. "He could have told us what other arms he's been twisting."

"Point taken," Vinny acknowledged, "but I doubt if he'd talk. Besides, we've already had enough drama with Delezal's abduction."

Nick decided to ask Vasek one more question. "Can you describe the other man?"

Vasek took a sip from the glass Ann handed her and looked at Nick. "Narrow face. Beard. Black eyes that reminded me of a rat."

Nick turned to Lange. It wasn't much to go on, but he took a stab. "Sounds like the description Ferguson gave me of one of Král's lieutenants. Guy named Sokol."

"Are you and Dusa on Grekov's payroll?" Marie said.

Vasek started at Marie's statement. "Grekov? Who is this Grekov?"

"A Russian," Marie said.

"But Dusa?" Vasek added. "He is our driver. Harmless."

Nick shook his head, "No, he is working for the Russians."

"But, why?" Vasek asked. "You are tourists, how—"

Nick gave a quick shake of his head, signaling the others not to answer. "Listen, Katerina, you've been tangled in a web spun by people who won't hesitate to harm you or your family if they learn they've been double-crossed. We know you've done some small jobs for the Embassy. My question to you is this: Are you working with Czech intelligence?"

"No, no. I—"

Nick changed tack. What was so important about the drug deal that drove Král's attempt to kill Jezek?

"Král? Who—"

"Never mind him," Lange said. "What did the man tell you about the drug deal?"

"That it is was worth millions and something of what the other reporter had learned." Vasek said. "Something…something about the Iranians."

Iranians? Nick pursed his lips, trying to mask his surprise. Lange's body language told him all he needed to know about his partner's reaction. He too, had been caught unawares by Vasek's revelation. Nick surmised they were left with little choice but to take the bait tossed out by Král. "Did you hear where the deal would go down?"

Vasek's face clouded in confusion. "Go down? I do not know what you mean."

"Where the deal would take place," Marie clarified.

"Ah, yes. Thank you. He told me to say a place near a city south of here. Dačice. He named a warehouse…" She paused, cocking her head in thought. "Yes, he said the Prodán Industrial Park."

"Did Jezek say anything to you in the flower shop?" Nick

asked. Vasek shook her head, but at her response, George pulled a piece of paper from his pants pocket and handed it to Lange. He glanced at it, and held it out to Nick. "Can you read this?"

Nick scanned the reporter's scrawled note. "Jezek was on to something. It matches what Katerina said and we've got an address."

"George and I will check it out," Vinny said.

Lange straightened and addressed Marie while pointing to Vasek. "Get her out of here and sit on her. I don't want her contacting her buddies."

"Where to?" Marie said.

"You'll think of something," Lange responded.

"Can we trust her?" Ann asked after Marie and Jennifer had ushered Vasek out the door.

"Damned if I know," Nick answered, "but some of what she said collaborates what Coleman's been hearing. My gut tells me she's clean. Ferguson ran her background twice and Coleman vouches for her."

"You believe both of those guys?" Lange asked.

Nick dropped into Vinny's empty chair. "Yeah, they both have too much to lose."

"Do we have a choice?" Lange asked.

"About what?" Nick responded. "About trusting Coleman and Ferguson, or going after the drugs?"

"Coleman and Jezek. Ferguson's been doing some good work," Lange added without elaborating.

Nick suppressed his urge to ask about the nature of Ferguson's "good work," and decided to address their immediate problem. "I'd say we have to re-think what we're up against. We've been focused on weapons shipments, but are the arms the diversion? And why would Král take the risk of killing Jezek?" Nick continued with his train of thought, connecting the circles of his mental Venn diagram. "Or it could be about

Chapter Forty-Nine

what Coleman told me on the bridge that Austin collaborated."

"And that is?" Lange asked.

"Austin's been doing his homework back at the Agency. Filled me in on the details of a money laundering operation he's been investigating. Nearly 300 million in impounded Venezuelan government funds have vanished from a secured account at the New York Federal Reserve Bank. At first, he didn't think it pertained to our op, but he discovered the electronic fingerprints of Král's financier, Anička Drabek, on the dark web." Lange made to stop him, but Nick held up his hand. "I've got a meeting set up with Coleman."

Lange's reaction to this latest twist escaped as a hiss. "Shit! All of our assumptions may be wrong. This hit may have had nothing to do with weapons. It could well be about what Brid Krejci really uncovered and why she was murdered, not simply collateral damage in a weapons deal."

"Yeah, the pieces no longer fit neatly together," Nick said, his mental diagram coming apart at the seams. "I don't think we've been left with much of a choice, even if we are being set up. We gotta move on what Vasek gave us. That, and we have to figure out what the damn Iranians have to do with this. We also need to bring the DEA in."

"Saving Coleman's reputation?" Lange asked.

"Yeah, in part."

Lange acquiesced. "We need to circle back to the drug deal. What do we know?"

"Only the bits we just learned," Nick said.

"Is it enough?" Ann asked.

"It fits with what Coleman has heard," Nick replied. "The open question is whether this drug deal is bogus or legit."

Lange picked up his binoculars, placed the covers on the lenses, and slid them into their case. "We can't waste the opening we've been given, whatever the hell it is."

"I'll notify Coleman," Nick said.

"What about Ferguson?" Ann queried.

"Later," Lange said. "We already have enough on our plate without adding any drama from the Agency."

Chapter Fifty

PRODÁN INDUSTRIAL PARK
DAČICE, CZECH REPBLIC
SUNDAY 25 OCTOBER

Nick cast a final look into the side-view mirror and exhaled. They had completed the ninety-kilometer drive south to the city of Daćice without incident, arriving at dawn. He needn't have worried about the operation unraveling before it had even begun. Lange had briefed the entire team except for Tom and Edmund. The Scot had returned to the rented apartment in Dresden, which he now equated to The Nickolas back in Georgetown, and Tom had remained in Prague to help keep tabs on Vasek.

Nick shot a glance into the rear-view mirror at the new guy, a floater, occupying the rear seat, then to the taciturn driver, deciding it best to keep his mouth shut. The last thing they, or he, for that matter, needed was for him to give vent to his anxiety.

Dexter Coleman directed the driver to make the turn into

the Prodán Industrial Park and drove a block before pulling into an empty parking lot. The rest of the team followed at five-minute intervals. They scattered their vehicles, parking in separate lots, all a short walk to their target, a small warehouse mid-way down the main road of the complex.

The park appeared to be quiet as a tomb, but that very fact left Nick further unsettled with a sense of incipient danger. Were they being set up? He had already been discomforted by Lange's uncharacteristic reticence before they left the Alcron. He voiced his disquiet "I don't have a good feeling about this. Too easy."

Coleman didn't respond, but the new man in the rear seat grunted his response as he exited their car. "You never know."

The new man was one of the DEA agents from Dresden and unknown to the locals and Coleman had brought him in as an extra precaution. The floater ranged ahead, his eyes darting from one side to the other, alert for the unexpected as he made his way down the deserted compound to a loading dock projecting from the rear of their target. Rounding the far corner of the dock, he disappeared from view.

Nick and Coleman followed at a distance. The other members of The Curators remained out of sight, making their own way to the warehouse from different directions. After what to Nick seemed an eternity, the floater's head popped into view and he waved his hand. *All clear.* Nick spoke into his throat microphone to the others. "Clear, let's go."

George, the team's breaking and entry expert, approached the solitary door near the loading dock that led to the building's interior. He knelt to examine the lock, then unrolled a leather tool case exposing a collection of specialty implements. He selected a raking pick and set to work. In less than a minute the lock clicked open. No entry alarm sounded.

Nick made a mental note of how easy it was for George to pick the lock and made to enter, but George held up his hand, signaling a halt. He opened the door and scanned the interior

Chapter Fifty

for motion sensors, cameras. Anything suspicious. "There doesn't seem to be a security system, or if there is, it's been deactivated."

Nick made his way around George into the building, followed by Vinny and Coleman. He halted after a few steps, his nose crinkling at a faint medicinal odor. *Iodine?* He spotted several large white boxes with the familiar blue and orange FedEx logo. He opened the top of one, picked up an empty white plastic drum, and read the label: "Caffeine, anhydrous. 2.5kg."

Coleman looked over his shoulder, commenting on Nick's discovery. "Cutting agent. The resulting mix is nasty...incredibly addictive."

Lange, Ann, Jennifer, and Marie passed them, giving the boxes a cursory look as they began their own search of the premises while the floater remained outside looking for trouble.

George was the first to spot the drug cache. "Over there!" He pointed to a tarpaulin- covered pile some three feet tall and fifteen feet long at the far corner of the warehouse's packing room.

Vinny responded to George's shout, crossed the room, and lifted the corner of the tarp. He motioned to his partner. "Hey, George. Grab the other edge. Let's see what we got." Together, the two threw off the tarp, revealing dozens of rectangular, white-woven polypropylene bags stacked on wooden pallets.

"Damn," Nick exclaimed at their discovery. He did a quick count of the stacks. "Good, Lord. There's got to be over a hundred."

Coleman finished his own count. "I'd say it's closer to one-hundred and twenty."

George grabbed one package at random and hefted it. "A good hundred pounds."

Nick did a rapid mental calculation while he busied

himself untwisting the wire loop securing one of the bags, exposing another clear plastic wrapper enclosing what could have been sugar. "Damn, that's close to six tons."

Jennifer's voice sounded through an open door to his right. "I've got the lab."

Nick trotted over to the open door of a large room dotted with eight tables, each topped with a ductless powder containment hood. He exited the room and noted Lange inspecting a pile of discarded blue-nylon rope and stacks of old burlap bags piled against the wall to his right.

"Hey, look what I found," Marie said, exiting the lab, holding out a sheet of paper she'd discovered in a desk drawer.

Lange made his way to her, accepting the paper. He pointed to the writing. "I don't have a clue what it says, but it looks like some sort of invoice written in Arabic."

"Let me see that." Vinny took the paper.

"You can read that chicken scratch?" Nick asked.

"No," Vinny said, pointing to a single character, "but I learned during my time in The Stan to look for these three dots over this letter. That's Farsi, not Arabic." He looked at the signature block. "Rajiv Mohammadi. Any idea who this guy is?"

Lange rubbed his chin. "No, but we have had a trickle of intel suggesting the Iranians have been active in Prague."

"Drugs? What the hell for?" Vinny asked.

"None of this is making any sense." Nick stood up. "But let's stay focused on what we've found, then get the hell out of here." He re-crossed the room, knelt beside the bag he'd opened, pulled out his iPhone, and took a picture. He checked the photo, replaced the camera in his pocket and fished around for his pocketknife. Pulling open the blade, he proceeded to cut a small opening in the clear plastic cover of the bag. A trickle of opalescent product cascaded onto the floor. He pinched a small sample and rubbed his fingertips

Chapter Fifty

together. Smooth, not granular. He held the substance to his nose. The product emitted an aroma like iodine. He touched his index finger to his tongue. Bitter.

Coleman knocked Nick's hand aside. "Are you nuts? Get your hands off that crap before you kill yourself. You've been watching too many movies." He extracted a drug detection device from a satchel he'd slung over his shoulder. A new field-testing unit had replaced the old chemical based colorimetric methodology that had, at best, a seventy percent accuracy. The new handheld device measured a tad over three by four inches and used a laser that could send its beam through the plastic covers of the bags. Coleman shot a look at Nick. "Never touch an unknown."

Duly chastised, Nick watched Coleman enter a series of commands into a tiny keyboard activating the device. He then keyed in another set of commands, aimed the device at the opening Nick had cut, and pressed another button.

"Bingo!" Coleman announced when the green laser indicator light flashed, followed by a red horizontal line flaring across the screen. "Cocaine." He studied the screen's diagnostics. "About seventy-five percent pure, cut with that caffeine we found." He selected another, smaller bag with a different label, cut it open, and tested it. He rocked back on his heals. "Crap."

"What?"

"I'm picking up methoxetamine."

Nick peered at the box's readout, unable to comprehend what it read. "What the hell is that?"

"It's a new psychoactive product. Bad news."

Nick turned his attention to Lange, who'd appeared holding a box full of plastic bags stuffed with light-green pills, each with a large "P" stamped on them.

Coleman looked at the bag. "Fentanyl."

"How many?" Nick asked.

"Those bags usually hold one-hundred."

Lange pushed the bags around, getting a count. "I'd say there's fifteen bags here."

Nick waved his hand across the hoard of drugs. "What do we do with all of this stuff?"

"I'll take care of it," Coleman answered while he pulled out a cable and attached one end to the USB port of his device and the other to a thumb-drive to back up his data. "It's best you folks get out of here."

Lange pulled Nick aside. "I don't know where the Iranians factor in, but we have to talk to Ferguson."

"Do you know how to find him?" Nick asked.

"I've got an idea."

Nick ventured a guess. "Cleaning up the mess at the black site?"

"That's done," Lange said. "My guess is he's gone underground. I'll find him."

Chapter Fifty-One

109 KRIŽÍKOVA STREET, PRAHA 8
PRAGUE, CZECH REPUBLIC
MONDAY 26 OCTOBER

Nick made his way down the narrow hallway to the musty room where he had met Dexter Coleman. Hard to believe that clandestine meeting had been only four days ago. Same place. Different issue. Now he had to figure out where the Iranians fit, if at all. Perhaps Ferguson would have the answer, but things weren't off to a good start. He checked his watch.

Ferguson should have been here, but he made a concerted effort to give the guy the benefit of the doubt. Then Nick's thoughts turned to what Ferguson knew about the fate of his father. Sent by the Agency on a mission to Prague, a mission in which he had lost his life.

He dropped into the faded, threadbare chair he'd used before, resigned to Ferguson's tiresome passive-aggressive, "I can't tell you without shooting you," attitude. Even collaborating on multiple operations, Ferguson remained a mystery. At the very least, he didn't appear to be burdened with any sense of empathy. Nick still knew nothing about the man that lay beneath that thin veneer of secrecy. A cynical and bitter man, except for—

Alerted by the sound of the door opening, he braced his arms on the chair to stand and greet the agent.

Ferguson burst through the door, his face contorted with anger. "Why the hell did *you* leave me out in the cold?"

Nick dropped back down landing on the cushion with a thud at Ferguson's entry and his pejorative use of, "You." He recovered enough to counter with a stinging retort. "You recall our conversation at Langley? I'll remind you. I said—"

"I know what the hell you said, Parkos," Ferguson said, calming. "You asked; 'Why should you trust me?' And I answered, '"You shouldn't.'"

Nick pivoted to focus on the issue at hand. "What do you know about a guy named Raji Mohammadi?"

Ferguson stiffened at the Iranian's name. "What the hell does he have to do with Grekov and Král?"

Nick gestured to one of the room's other chairs. "I'd hoped you'd tell me."

Ferguson hesitated, then settled into the proffered chair. "Is this Coleman's idea?"

"What idea?" Nick responded.

"To go chasing after phantoms."

"Phantoms? What the hell are you talking about?"

"We got an intercept…" Ferguson held up his right hand, while pulling out a small tape recorder from his inside coat pocket with his left. "Don't ask." He pushed the power button:

"You are getting fifty percent of my cut. I need twenty."

"You better guarantee me that business."

Chapter Fifty-One

"I will, but you gotta deal with the Mexican, maybe that other guy."

"Man, you gotta have a cut-out. We can't be talking like this."

"Five million euros."

"*Jdi do predek*"

Nick nodded at the Czech expletive. "Appropriate."

"What is?" Ferguson asked.

"Go fuck yourself."

"What the hell!" Ferguson shouted, his face flushing again.

Nick responded with a laugh. "Relax, Taylor. I translated the Czech. And, no, it wasn't aimed at you."

A laconic smile crossed Ferguson's face. "Well, that's a start."

"Have you identified those guys?"

"One is Mohammadi. Got him with our voice recognition program. The other one's voice has been electronically altered, but I've got some idea who it is, and that could tie up your whole investigation in one tidy bow."

"Really? Then who is the mystery person?"

"Yeah, really," Ferguson replied. "Based on what our analysts found, we think it's the Russians."

"Damn. I guess that makes sense if they're using Král to shield their own operation."

"That's plausible, but my question is what the hell are the Iranians mixed up in? Arms?" Ferguson answered his own question. "That's plausible given their track record, even if it runs counter to whatever Grekov is up to."

"That's not going to end well for Mohammadi if he's messing with Mother Russia."

Ferguson grunted his affirmation. "But the open question remains: Where do the drugs fit?"

"Money," Nick replied.

"I'll give you that," Ferguson affirmed, "but since you were the Transnational Organized Crime expert for the Balkans before you left the NSA, why don't you tell me? You ever come across anything about the Iranians?"

Nick scrunched his lips in thought. "No, I didn't, and their involvement doesn't square with what Coleman has told me."

"You trust that guy? The one who botched his own scam and lost ten million dollars?"

Ferguson followed his rhetorical questions with another one. "How much do you suppose the drugs you found in Dačice are worth?"

Nick responded to this query with silence as he added up the stash. Then his eyes widened.

"Yeah," Ferguson continued. "Millions. So, what happened to the product you discovered?"

"Coleman told me that he'd take care of it."

"I'm sure he did."

Nick's mind spun at the possible connections. His whole operating premise about who was behind the arms shipment had just been blown to hell. Was Ferguson right? Had he been chasing a phantom, caught in an elaborate web of deceit that had been woven by, well, by whom? *Coleman, Král, Grekov?*

He considered Ferguson's premise that the entire deal with the drugs was staged by Coleman. *So, what was his connection to the Mexican?* "Suppose the—"

Ferguson cut him off. "Mendez, or El Tlatoani as he prefers to call himself, is a pawn."

"How do you know what I'm thinking?"

"Over these past couple years, I've started to figure you out. You're following one of your logic trails, creating one of those damn Venn diagrams in your head. Did Lange happen to tell you that Strickland's been arrested?"

The revelation rocked Nick back in his chair. "Strickland?"

"Besides undercutting your work for years, he's been indicted for treason. He's been working for the Russians."

Chapter Fifty-One

The revelation left Nick momentarily speechless. "How's that pertain to us?"

Ferguson paused for effect. "We may have something linking Grekov...or, less likely, Král...to Mohammadi."

Nick pondered Ferguson's words, then grasped the arms of the chair as those revelations triggered an unexpected connection within his mind. *Lying by omission?* His voice trembled, trying to control the torrent of words threatening to spill from his mouth. "Why the hell didn't you tell me?"

The expression on Ferguson's face reflected that Nick's question had caught him at a complete loss. "Tell you what?"

"Does the name Tom Parkos mean anything to you? An agent who died in this country years ago."

Ferguson's brows knitted. "No, it doesn't. I would have made the connection." He dropped his head back, staring at the ceiling. "I had heard an agent died over here, but his name was Steve Benik."

"Beník, shortened from Benedictus," Nick replied. He paused to control the flood of emotion that rolled through him. "It means 'blessed.' He's my father."

"Steve was your dad? But what does he have to do with this?"

"Everything."

"God, Nick. I'm sorry..." Ferguson's voice trailed off. "I had no idea."

"What happened to you?" Nick asked.

A rueful, defeated smile crossed Ferguson's face. "There are 133 names inscribed in white marble honoring those who died in the line of service. Your father is one of them. "Shit, I'll probably be number 134. It's my curse, my problem to solve." He straightened. "We see the world differently, Nick, but in some ways you're a lot like me."

Nick made to respond, but Ferguson stopped him. "No, let me finish. Like me, you are a prisoner of your past trying to break free. You've spent your entire life building walls. Let me give you a piece of unsolicited advice. "You know as well as I that you can't quit."

Nick didn't respond, wondering once again if he could trust anything that Ferguson said, especially what he might know about his father. Perhaps he was telling the truth. He nodded his agreement. "So, where do we go from here?"

"Let's begin by figuring out where Grekov fits."

Chapter Fifty-Two

HOTEL ALCRON
PRAGUE, CZECH REPUBLIC
MONDAY 26 OCTOBER

Nick struggled to sort through his disjointed thoughts in the solitude of his hotel room. The confrontation with Ferguson had prompted introspection, as had his call to Austin this morning. The latter held a bit of promise for his investigation, but he set that aside. He reached for his wallet and extracted a folded piece of notepaper on which Michelle had written down a quote from Emerson: "Do not go where the path may lead, go instead where there is no path and leave a trail." *How did she know?*

He replaced her note, reached for a bottle of water, took a sip, and began to reassess his previous assumptions about the roles of Anton Král and Alex Grekov in his investigation. Then there was what the ancient one had told him at the castle about his cousin Petr. His thoughts darted from one possibility to another. But where did Coleman fit? Or were there still others at play he didn't know about?

As if in answer, the afternoon sun emerged from behind a cloud, throwing a harsh flare of light through the suite's window before he could entertain a plausible explanation for Coleman's actions. The sunlight splayed across the room, illuminating the suite's coffee table and the burlwood of his keepsake box with a golden glow while accents flashed off several glasses and his bottle of Laphroaig scotch.

He resisted the urge to pick up the box or pull the curtains, steeling himself to what he must do about Coleman. If he found any sign of duplicity, he would turn his findings over to Director Gilmore and let him take it from there with the Attorney General. He would also talk to Marie about the agent. But even with that decision, his internal deliberations left him exhausted and perhaps without recourse to deal with the DEA agent. He set the water bottle aside and moved on to less treacherous ground.

If Král was behind the arms shipment, the drug deal, and the theft of nearly 300 hundred million dollars from the Federal Reserve Bank, he would have no choice but to destroy Král's network and have to disavow his family—the ancient, Ida, Petr and Natálya. On the other hand, if he determined Grekov was the instigator of the arms deal, he could possibly salvage something of his nascent relationship with his extended family.

He began to gather his scattered thoughts into something resembling a coherent pattern working within the context of those variables, all the while recalling Dexter Coleman's final admonition when they had ended their first meeting on the Charles Bridge: "Don't trust anyone. It'll keep you alive."

Taking those words of caution to heart, he reached for a blank piece of hotel stationary and drew a Venn diagram. He wrote, "Grekov," on the top of the page focusing on the Russian as Ferguson had suggested.

Chapter Fifty-Two

While Grekov had provided some assistance in his operation to track down and stop the terrorist, Bashir al-Kultyer, her actions at the time were hardly altruistic and were often conflicting. He had little insight into her motivations, but he'd concluded that she had done just enough to assist him while shaping some other agenda known only to her. He also wouldn't put it past the Russians to do their best to foment problems on the Mexican border to help distract President Stuart from focusing on the Ukraine.

The impact of the country's relationship with Mexico— dealing with the drug cartels, especially El Tlatoani— and the partially constructed border wall sent his brain reeling in another direction, Ferguson's words working their way back into his thoughts: "You've spent your whole life building walls."

There was truth in those words. A lot of bad things had happened during the tortuous path of his life, but most of what he'd anticipated had never happened. His decision to seek clarity in his quest for his genealogy had been a start, but this effort had spiraled into disarray, creating an exponential increase in the complications that seemed to plague his life.

"Screw it." He forced aside his plunge into the caliginous depths of his mind and picked up the ancient burlwood box. He didn't bring this damn box all the way to Prague to not discover what secrets it held. He examined the filigreed brass escutcheon surrounding the keyhole, the three tiny brass studs that held it in place, and the clasp.

He took a deep breath, lifted the clasp, and opened the lid, exposing a faded, dark-red, felt lining. The contents lay haphazardly in the box. The first object that caught his eye was an ancient piece of mottled parchment, stained brown-yellow with age, that appeared to have been torn down the middle. *Why would someone do that? Did someone else possess the other half, or was it lost forever?* He studied the ancient writing, unable to decipher what it meant. The script did not appear to be

Latin or Moravian. The blocked shapes of the letters suggested Hebrew, confirming his family's distant ties to Judaism.

He set the parchment aside and studied the other objects. A silver amulet inscribed with Hebrew letters and an exquisite earring, coiled gold wire forming the circular hoop that ended in a miniature ram's head. He set the two pieces of jewelry aside, his eyes widening at what lay below, his right hand suspended above a folded piece of embroidered fabric edged with two sets of thin stiches, one gold, one pink.

He extracted the delicate fabric, gently unfolding it to reveal a three-by-four inch exquisitely embroidered scene. Judging from the figures' elaborate costumes and setting, it might represent a wedding scene from the seventeenth century. He set the embroidered fabric aside and lifted the final item in the box, a piece of paper quartered by two creases, each with small tears at their origins.

He grabbed his pen afraid to touch what he'd found with his finger tips and gently opened each fold. Nick gasped at what he beheld. Some sort of official document, the words topped by a golden crown and enclosed by two surrounds: one, a vine of flowers, and the other, of Hebrew letters scribed in gold.

His head jerked up at the sound of the suite's door opening. Marie. He quickly replaced the items into the box and closed the lid. "What had you been up to?" he asked, hoping the tone of his voice covered his furtive dive into his past.

"Mostly, no good," Marie responded, settling down on the couch across from him. She glanced at the keepsake box, then studied his face. He was hiding something. Over time, she had discerned that Nick appeared to possess three identities: the cognitive thinker, the introvert, and the extrovert. Seeing him

Chapter Fifty-Two

across from her, his face etched with a combination of fatigue and stress, she could not decide which of the three was dominant or, for that matter, which one she preferred.

She went through each trait in turn. The Introvert? Reclusive, thought-oriented, perceptive, but his fundamental nature hidden beneath protective layers that obscured his spirit. The Extrovert? Gregarious, a quip always available at the tip of his tongue, action oriented. Or lastly, The Thinker? Consistent, logical, impersonal.

No doubt his recent experiences had hardened him. He could have just used people and discarded them, as she presumed he'd been, but for some reason he didn't. Perhaps the kindness and compassion shown him by his grandparents had overcome his rage and hurt at losing his mother and father while so young? And this was where her own ambivalence came into play. The imponderables, Nick's moods, dictated by events outside her control, left her vexed.

She recalled something a psychologist friend had told her years before. Children who were left stranded in life from the loss of one or both parents often tended to self-isolate when overwhelmed, learning to solve most of their own problems after they'd been left alone as a child. That fit.

Her analysis halted at hearing a fragment of a sentence. "I need to take care of—" How long had he been speaking to her? She heard a familiar name. Král. "How do you intend to do that?" she asked, hoping to pick up the thread of what he was talking about.

"I've already handled it. All I have to do is connect with him," Nick answered. "I'm close."

Marie followed Nick's eyes to his keepsake box, his gesture providing her the opening to turn the conversation to one that would address her fundamental question of what was going through her partner's mind. "We—"

"Here, let me show you something," he said without any hint of rancor, cutting her off.

He leaned across the table to grasp the keepsake box. "What I found will explain a lot. A lot I should have told you about long time ago."

His hands froze on the clasp, at a metallic zipping sound rending the air by his head, followed in a milli-second by another sound, that of a bullet crashing into the wall behind him.

"Down!" Marie shouted.

Nick threw himself onto the floor, covering his head with his hands before Marie's warning even registered. A second round followed, splitting the air with a buzz akin to that of an angry hornet—the same sound he had heard at Cape Lisburne, Alaska when a sniper had taken a shot at him. He lay inert waiting for a third shot, his eyes improbably focused on the details of a short, rectangular brown arm of the suite's patterned carpet. *If I hadn't reached for the box at that very instant—*

He raised his head, peering at the stellate-rimmed holes in the room's plate glass window, stunned that someone had just tried to kill him, then to his partner. "Are you okay?"

"I'm fine," Marie replied. "What the hell just happened?"

Good question, he asked himself. He brushed off a mix of powered glass and tiny shards from his left arm and rolled over onto his right side to examine the twin holes in far wall, pushing off with his forearm. "OW!"

He searched for the source of the stinging prick and found it at the head of a thin bright-red line of blood flowing toward his elbow. He picked out a small piece of glass that had punctured his arm resulting into another zip of pain. "Damn it."

He swiped his hand across his arm, a sticky, red smear replacing the line, his concern with his minor injury replaced by one of greater import. He began his analysis, the process pushing through his initial fear.

Nick's assessment first touched on the tobacconist's shop, when he and Maire had to dive for cover to escape an assailant's shotgun blast. He'd concluded that was a chance accident, being caught in the wrong place at the wrong time. But now? Then there was the attack on Jezek and, third, the drugs. He didn't believe in coincidences. There had to be a connection, but—

Marie interrupted his internal dialog. "How's your box?"

He glanced at the keepsake, its contents spilled across the floor. He picked them up and replaced in the box and set it on the table, turning his attention to the immediate problem. Were they safe? He ventured a look at the window. Nothing.

Who just tried to kill me? Perhaps it was Král, looking to recover after his aborted play to take out Jezek, but that just didn't compute. "I'm fine. My gut's telling me that Grekov isn't behind this. It must be someone else."

Marie lifted her head, examined the room, then pushed herself into a sitting position, resting her back on the couch. "Really? Who?"

"I'd say we've just gotten the attention of another TCO kingpin."

"What? You're kidding, right? A new player?"

"We took millions of dollars-worth of drugs out of circulation," Nick said, "and Coleman mentioned the Likas group."

Marie bunched her eyebrows at the juxtaposition of the group's name and Coleman. "There's a remote chance Coleman is creating a smoke screen." She shook her head. "No, I'd focus on someone else looking to make a play."

Nick chewed on his lower lip, considering this. Various possibilities came to mind, including an improbable scenario that the drugs were designed as bait to distract him from discovering the real perpetrator of the arms shipments. "I'm wondering if someone is looking to leverage our investigation into Král's group to their own advantage and pin this attack on him."

"God, that's all we need." Marie stood and made her way to the window where she peered at the building across the street. "The sniper took his shot from that third-floor window."

Nick climbed to his feet, walked to her side, and had a look. One room's left hand casement window and a covering shutter were flung open. A sheer-white curtain billowing through the opening affirmed the probable site where the sniper had set up to take his shot. The rest of the building's windows were closed, as were perhaps a quarter of their shutters. His examination continued downward to the first floor's barred, faded-green double doors and the adjacent display window inscribed with "Studio R." A massage studio. He surmised from the barred door and windows that the building was abandoned. An ideal spot for a sniper.

He turned and studied the ragged holes near the door frame, his sense of exhalation at having survived covering the tumult of emotions laying beneath the surface of his mind that were primed to explode. There was one thing he could do. He lifted the box. "This may have something to do with it. Let me show you what I found."

Chapter Fifty-Three

NUMBER 10, UVOZ STREET
PRAGUE ADMINISTRATIVE DISTRICT FIVE
MONDAY 26 OCTOBER

Aleksandra Grekov sat behind her desk, her body rigid with suppressed anger, her dark eyes smoldering. The latest intelligence report from the embassy lay like a viperous serpent by her right hand. And now? As if the intelligence report wasn't bad enough, word had reached her from her contact at the Alcron's front desk of an assassination attempt on Parkos. She had immediately dispatched Kuznetzov to investigate and braced herself to receive his report of the event.

She lifted her eyes and studied her deputy. He stood before her, hands clasped behind his back, face expressionless. Whoever did this would surely stir up a veritable hornet's nest of anger from the Americans. The ramifications of the measures she must take to track down the assassin extended far beyond the impact of Parkos' investigation that impacted on her own fate. "What more have you discovered?"

Kuznetzov offered two deformed bullets cupped in his right hand.

Grekov accepted them without comment, casting them only a glance.

"7.62mm," he said handing over several pictures of Parkos' damaged room. "Judging from what information I've been able to obtain, the shooter used a semi-automatic Dragunov sniper rifle."

"And the shooter?" she asked, not concerned about the type of weapon or what might happen to their source at the hotel.

"Judging from what I can surmise about the trajectories, his position was likely on the third floor of an abandoned building directly across the street from Parkos' room. The place is swarming with *Policie*. I could not approach."

She recalled how Parkos had come to her aid in the city of Neum last year, but only felt a fleeting moment of concern for the American agent. "So, we know nothing specific of this assassin?"

"Nothing," Kuznetzov admitted. "No, that is not entirely correct. Someone knew the exact location of Parkos' room and that he was there. Not only was the sniper aware of Parkos' movements, but the gunman also had to be acquainted with the neighborhood and able to set up with minimal notice and then escape. He's a local, operating with his own network."

"We will narrow down our search. There has to be a least one other informant in that nest of traitors on the Alcron's staff coordinating with the sniper." Grekov leaned back in her chair. She doubted Král was responsible for the attack on Parkos after factoring in her underlying suspicion that Parkos and Král might be conspiring against her. As Kuznetzov stated, there had to be another party she had failed to detect.

Chapter Fifty-Three

What organization was behind the attempted assassin and why did they try to kill Parkos?

Grekov set those vexing questions aside. She had to review her own contingency plans and take immediate action to protect herself, irrespective of this new threat. "Sergei, find out who was behind this attack and the unknown informant at the hotel. And when you do, I will request a five-man element from GRU Unit 29155 to attend to the messy details. This assassin and whomever else is complicit must be eliminated."

"It will be done, Colonel," Sergei affirmed. "With your permission?"

"Yes, see to it," she responded. "And check with our source in Czech security. Perhaps our asset in the *Státní Tajná Bezpečnast's* counter-intelligence unit can provide a lead."

Grekov picked up the intelligence report after the office door clicked shut. The contents and those of another message she had received were no less sobering and drove her next moves. Their mole in the NSA, Edward Strickland, had disappeared, missing his scheduled drop in Washington's Rock Creek Park. He had left none of the subtle markers to indicate his desire to contact them, or notify them of potential threats, and he had not been seen at his home. The FSB station in Washington had made the reasonable presumption that the American had been detained.

Grekov spun her chair and placed the report in her safe on top of the other, equally disturbing message. Mexico's former Defense Minister, Juan Carlos Alvarez, had been arrested for conspiracy to distribute cocaine, Fentanyl, and methamphetamine. Her problem? Not trusting the mercurial El Tlatoani, Alverez had been selected by Moscow to be the real point man in their intricate plan to ship arms to Mexico. And if Alvarez even hinted at what little he knew of Moscow's goal of destabilizing the American southwestern States to save his own skin…?

Who had tipped off the authorities to arrest Alvarez? The

American DEA? Mendez? Or had Strickland folded and spilled his guts to the FBI to save his own ass?

She had to contact Moscow Sta— No, I cannot do that. These new developments had dropped her on a desolate island where she would have to use her own cunning to save herself. She took several deep, calming breaths, then began to address all the variables and how they fit into what she must do, Moscow be damned.

Grekov paused as one of her memories of her erstwhile colleague from times past, Nick Parkos, floated to the surface of her mind. She would draw on the American's analytic approach to solving an insolvable dilemma by connecting the pieces of disparate information to find the whole. She snatched a blank piece of paper from her printer and drew a series of interlocking circles.

She studied the final product after nearly an hour of work. Reznik had gone underground. Delezal was dead and buried. That left Král's remaining lieutenant, Karel Sokol, and the financer Anička Drabek. In the final analysis, though, there were only two options. She had to abort the Alvarez/Mendez mission and erase any trace of the Mexicans' links to herself and the FSB. To that end, she drafted a message for her superiors recommending measures be taken to remove both as sources of embarrassment. Once that plan was set in motion, she would personally take care of the scum, Sokol, saving Král the trouble. She paused in her assessment, focusing her anger on Taylor Ferguson. The American agent had caused her no end of trouble.

Chapter Fifty-Four

SAFEHOUSE
OBERGRABEN STRASSE INNERE, NERSTADT
DRESDEN, GERMANY
TUESDAY 27 OCTOBER

Nick gazed out of the car's window during the ninety-five-minute drive from Prague to the team's safe house across the border in Dresden, Germany. George, at the wheel of their old Skoda Octavia sedan, and Marie, who had scrunched into the rear seat, exchanged few words. He was grateful they were providing him the quiet space he needed to think while they traversed the open plains and dense forests north of Prague toward the rugged Giant Mountains and the headwaters of the Elbe. From there, they crossed the border and followed the river's course to Dresden.

The breathtaking scenery of the northern Czech Republic had been lost to Nick except on a subliminal, calming level, permitting his mind to wander before his thoughts settled on a quote from Louis Pasteur that he used to have pinned above his desk at the NSA.

Dans les champs de l'observation, le hasard ne favorise que l'esprits préparés.

In the fields of observation, chance favors only the prepared mind.

With the quote in mind, Nick rummaged through the glove compartment, an act that earned him a puzzled look from George. He found the notepad and pen he had placed there before his and Marie's exploratory trip to Ralsko the previous Wednesday, flipped open the cover, and wrote down the six cardinal investigative questions he had learned years before in his criminology classes at Ohio State: Who? What? Where? When? Why? How? Focusing on these fundamentals, he began to gain control of his racing thoughts.

The second and third on his list were easy enough, as was the How. The "Who" remained elusive. He focused on the "Why?" The latter boiled down to three motives: Money, drugs, and arms. *Big stakes.* He permitted his mind to wander. *What else?* He tapped his pen on the page. *Don't ask the question if you're not prepared to hear the answer.*

In this case, he had no idea what the answer could be or where it would lead. He was still mulling that basic issue when the car slowed and pulled to a stop along the curb of a quiet residential street.

"We're here," George announced, exiting the car. He led the way to the doorway of a light-gray limestone building set among a collection of colorful, baroque town homes. Nick made for the trunk to retrieve their luggage and his burlwood box, but George stopped him. "We'll get those later. They're safe enough." He opened the door that led to a common hallway and a flight of stairs. "No elevator. We walk."

Edmund greeted the trio at the door to the safehouse. "Ah, our wayward travelers." He stood aside permitting the three to enter. "If you'll be needin' the loo, it's to the left."

Chapter Fifty-Four

Nick's eyes traveled over the living room of Lange's safehouse. He spotted an overstuffed chair set in the corner and dropped down into the deep cushion. He caught a few snippets of George's whispered conversation with Lange, but not enough to understand what they were discussing. Him, most likely, but no matter. The foundations of a nascent plan to redefine the new risks that he, and by extension, the team faced had begun to coalesce into a coherent pattern, beginning with an assessment of the multiple variables in play.

He settled back in the chair, recalling what Ferguson had revealed in his meeting at the Križíkova Street building. Strickland had been arrested. Could the attempt on his life be linked to his old supervisor? His lips tightened at the implications, first concluding that line of reasoning would lead him to Grekov. No, the risk to her own safety would be too great for her to be the perpetrator.

He pulled the notepad from his hip pocket and studied what he had written after the six cardinal questions: Pattern, Leads, Tips, and Theories, seeking to uncover the fallacies in his prior assumptions that had led to the attempt on his life. Marie turned and held out a cut-glass tumbler before he could proceed.

"Ardbeg. One ice cube," she said. "We figured you could use something with a bit of a kick, considering everything."

Nick leaned forward to accept the drink. "I sure could. Thanks."

Edmund cast an appraising eye at Nick's hand as he grasped the tumbler. "Yer lookin' a bit peely wally, *mo charaid*."

Nick took a grateful sip, bemused by Edmund's use of Gaelic no matter what the words meant. The Ardbeg's blend of peat and peppery heat burst on his palate. He took another sip and set the glass on the chair's arm, hoping the others hadn't noticed his trembling hand.

"What a fine whisky won't remedy, you won't find a remedy for what ails ya," Lange advised, paraphrasing the

Irish saying before adding, "Sit back and enjoy your drink, then we'll get started."

Nick hefted the glass in acknowledgment and downed a third of it, while formulating a response. But before he could open his mouth, he happened to look down at his pants leg, his eyes falling on a large, dark-red splotch where he'd rested his punctured forearm. *Damn, my new trousers. Michelle is going to tan my hide.* He fished out the ice cube from his drink, along with his handkerchief, and began dabbing at the splotch in a futile attempt to remove the stain. He paused at the sound of Edmund's voice.

"Let me take a look, mate. I've had more than my fair share of those."

Nick lifted his hand revealing the splotch looking much worse for his efforts, its edges now leaching beyond its original boundaries.

"Shouldn't be a problem," Edmund said after examining the stain. "I'll take care of it when we're done. Now, you were about to say?"

"I'm wondering if we've been focusing on the wrong people," Nick said at Edmund's prompt, prying his eyes off his pants leg. "Someone else with a different agenda from what we were sent here to investigate. Someone we inadvertently unmasked."

"Someone desperate enough to try to kill you," Lange added.

"Admittedly, that's a big deal for Nick," Marie said, "but shouldn't we stay focused on our primary objective?"

"Stopping any further arms shipments," Nick replied, inwardly agreeing that it was a big deal.

"I'd say that drug stash we found doesn't factor in except as a means to keep us distracted," George submitted.

"I agree," Nick said, rubbing his chin in thought, "but one thing we haven't spent much time thinking about is where

Chapter Fifty-Four

those 300 million bucks that disappeared from the New York Fed fits."

"And you have an idea?" George said.

"Sure do," Nick said. "When I talked with Austin a couple days ago, he told me he'd found evidence of Anička Drabek's fingerprints on several dark web transactions linking her to the heist."

"Makes sense. She's Král's financier," Edmund commented.

"True, but let's take a moment to think outside the box," Nick said, after dismissing the idea that his new-found cousin, Petr, was behind the heist. He caught the eyes of each member of the team in turn. "Let me throw this out. What if Drabek is doing a bit of free lancing?"

"Damn," Lange responded. "You may be on to something. And could she be partnering with someone else who fed information to Jezek?"

Nick took a contemplative sip of his scotch, the team's interaction providing him a rope to grasp as he struggled to keep from succumbing to the maelstrom of pent-up emotions that lay below the surface of his mind. "Good question."

"If that's the case, that could remove both Grekov and Král from our list of suspects, Marie added.

Nick amended her statement. "At least for the attempt on my life."

"How about Coleman?" George ventured.

"No…I don't think so," Nick answered, holding up his empty glass.

Edmund poured out another full measure and handed it back.

Nick took a swallow and tossed the notepad onto the table. "Forget about the money and the drugs. Let someone else worry about those. We need to refocus on our primary task."

"And that is?" Lange prodded.

"Stop any further arms shipments." Nick paused. "No, belay that," he continued, lifting a Navy term he'd heard Lange use. "We can't forget about the money, but if Drabek is—"

"We can use her to destroy Král's network," Marie said, finishing Nick's sentence.

"Unless those missing funds are used to purchase more arms, they are of no concern to us," Lange cautioned.

"I'm not ready to give up that bone," Nick said, addressing Lange. "Mark it down to that sixth sense you're always so ready to accuse me of possessing. I believe the word is, sagacious." He paused. "I'm not sure what I've said made any sense."

"A lot of what you say usually doesn't make any sense." Marie chuckled in response to Lange's eye roll.

"I didn't really say all that I said," Nick noted, accepting his drink.

George was unable to contain a loud snort, prompting the others to join in at another of Nick's Yogi Berra quotes. Edmund responded by topping off Nick's glass. "I'm interested in what you have to say about the money."

"I'm not saying that Král is not complicit on some level, but my gut is telling me that he's being played by the Russians and our new, mysterious third party. Someone who is likely internal to his organization."

"Really? Why's that?" Edmund asked.

"I'll add to my original premise," Nick said, "Besides the 300 million, Král probably has tens-of-millions more stashed away."

"In a Swiss account," Edmund added.

"And out of our reach," Lange noted. He opened his humidor, extracted a cigar, and set about lighting it. "My cut? Drabek and one of Král's lieutenants are tapping into Král's account for their own benefit."

Nick pressed his lips together. "Let's presume there are no other lieutenants beside the three we know about: Reznik,

Delezal, and Sokol. Delezal is dead and Reznik is the enforcer. He isn't smart enough to be a player. That leaves Sokol."

"But what if those funds are being used to buy more arms?" Marie countered.

Nick studied the faces of the team, noting Lange blowing out a large plume of smoke, a sign that the head of The Curators was mulling over what he had said. "That is literally the multi-million-dollar question. And operating on that hypothesis, we have no choice but to chase down Král's account."

"Aye," Edmund affirmed. "Or accounts."

"How do you intend to do that?" Lange asked. "Do you have some trick up your sleeve?"

"Actually, I do," Nick answered. "Coleman and Austin are both on it. And since I just pulled that rabbit out of my hat, how about a cigar?"

Lange raised his eyebrows at both Nick's answer and request. "Care to enlighten us?" he replied, handing Nick a cigar and a match.

Nick spun the cigar, applying the match to the tip, deciding it was well past time to let the team in on what he'd learned when he placed a follow-up call to Austin. He didn't respond immediately, occupied with getting the cigar to draw. "I called Austin yesterday. The Offices of Intelligence and Analysis and Terrorist Financing and Financial Crime have been able to trace several recent clandestine fund transfers pertaining to the missing Federal Reserve account."

"On the dark web?" Lange asked.

"Surprisingly, these weren't," Nick responded. "They were electronic fund transfers made via a network of nested accounts, money transmitters, and correspondent accounts."

"Makes sense," Edmund noted.

Lange appeared incredulous. "You understand that?"

"It's one of my many talents," Edmund responded.

Nick gave a thoughtful pull on his cigar while making a mental note to himself. *And that, my friend, explains why you can afford those thousand-dollar suits. You sly dog, you've got your own account set up somewhere.* He exhaled a plume of smoke and added his *Coup de Grace*. "And Austin told me that a whistle blower at the Swiss bank, Kohler and Favre Bancaire Privee, leaked the names and the specifics of several thousand dirty money accounts held by the bank."

"No shit," Lange sputtered.

"Yeah, no shit," Nick verified. "And one of those accounts belongs to Král." He paused at his revelation, a puzzled expression crossing his face at another epiphany.

Lange peered at Nick. "What?"

Nick waved off Lange's interjection while he searched the depths of his memory. At last he came up with the two names from the first encounter he'd had with Coleman on the Charles Bridge: Anička Drabek and Karel Sokol. What had Coleman said? "There's more on them, but this isn't the place." He bobbed his eyebrows while waggling his cigar. "I have our new players."

"Who?" Marie prodded in the stunned silence that followed his pronouncement and accompanying comical gestures.

Nick couldn't let go of his Groucho imitation. "You've said the magic word, 'Who.' And the answer is, Král's financier, Anička Drabek, and his lieutenant, Karel Sokol."

"Why them?" Lange asked.

Nick took a sip of his scotch, enjoying the moment, understanding on a deeper level that he and the team had taken the first step towards working through the trauma of his narrow escape from death. "The money."

With that final burst of frenetic thought, Nick was overcome by a tsunami of fatigue bred from the combination of scotch and stress. He slid down in the chair, welcoming its embrace. George and Edmund relieved him of his cigar and glass and slipped an ottoman under his feet while Marie covered him with a cotton comforter.

Chapter Fifty-Five

MONDRONY FLATS
MUNICIPLE DISTRICT 12, PRAGUE
TUESDAY 27 OCTOBER

Anton Král massaged his temples with his fingertips in a futile attempt to abort the onset of a throbbing headache. "Can my day get any worse?" he asked the empty office.

The cascade of troublesome news had begun just after one o'clock with word reaching him via a local news broadcast of the shooting incident at the Hotel Alcron. Parkos? A sixth sense that had kept him alive while threading his way through the perils of building an empire, prompted a call to his contact at the hotel. His source confirmed Král's suspicion that an attempt had been made on the life of one of their guests, a Mr. Partyka. His contact couldn't provide any details beyond seeing Partyka and his wife leave the hotel with their luggage and that the *Policie* were investigating.

He pondered the scant information while pouring himself

a hefty shot of the potent Czech liqueur, Becherovka. He downed it in a single gulp, poured another, and capped the bottle before focusing on what impact the attack on Parkos might portend for his operations. One fact was clear. He didn't order the hit. And since he wasn't behind the attempted assassination, there could be only one credible suspect, the Russian, Grekov. But why would she take such an enormous risk? What had Parkos uncovered? *The arms shipments?* His jaw tightened at the thought, compounding his headache. *That would lead to me.* He tilted his head back and downed the drink.

He began his reassessment with the fact that he had accepted Grekov's proposition to act as a go-between for an arms shipment to that crazy Mexican drug lord. *Why had I agreed to partner with her? Is she now protecting me by taking out Parkos?* Not likely, he answered himself. That brought him full circle. There must be another player threatened enough to try to kill the American, one who Parkos had stumbled across in his investigation. The Likas gang? The Iranians? The Interior Minister, Holcorá, or another operator he wasn't even aware of? That question prompted him to pick up his iPhone and enter the number of his trusted lieutenant. Perhaps he had heard of something.

Karel Sokol answered on the first ring. "Yes, Anton?"

"You've heard about the attempt on Parkos' life, yes?" Král opened.

"What!" Sokol rejoined, the incredulity evident in his voice. "When? What happened?"

"Two hours ago," Král replied before briefing his lieutenant on what little he knew.

Sokol's reply was emphatic. "It has to be Grekov."

Král cocked his head, frowning in consternation at the inflection he detected in Sokol's voice. "Perhaps, but there may be others."

"It has to be her," Sokol repeated.

Král suppressed his first impulse to confront his lieutenant,

Chapter Fifty-Five

deciding instead to give voice to his thoughts on the other possible suspects: the Likas gang, Holcorá, the Iranians. To each, Sokol had a prompt response. Král tapped his fingers on the blotter. Were his lieutenant's counter-points valid? Perhaps, but he sensed Sokol's replies were too fast, almost as if they had been scripted. He frowned and terminated the call. "Find out all you can and get back with me this evening."

Král set his iPhone down, deeply troubled, his eyes drawn to his safe and fixing on its spoked wheel. *My God, my funds! Could they have been compromised?* He shook his head. There was no rational explanation for his panicked conjecture. His funds were in a secure Swiss account that only he and...Drabek. No! She wouldn't. He couldn't shake the inferences he could draw from a conversation he'd had with Drabek the previous week expressing his concerns about the safety of his money, today's events, and his conversation with Sokol. Her responses, in retrospect, were too glib, as were Sokol's.

He pulled his eyes off the steel-clad safe and placed a call to his agent, the honorable Julius Steiner of the firm, Kohler and Favre Bancaire Privee.

"Herr Steiner," the banker answered. "How may I be of assistance?"

Král began the ritual. "*Dobry chen. Jmeji se*, Anton Král. I would like to inquire about my account."

"Certainly, Herr Král," Steiner purred while he accessed the bank's voice recognition system for their special clients. "May I have your access code, *bitte*?"

"4705643791."

"And your code word?"

"Kámen," Král replied.

"Very good. And what is it you wish to know, Herr Král?"

"I would like to verify my balance and any recent transactions."

"Of course. A moment please. Yes, your balance is one U.S. dollar."

Král barely recovered from this stunning statement, managing to utter a cryptic, "Thank you." He overcame a wave of dizziness. "Can you please verify the date of the completed transactions and the routing codes?"

"Certainly. Per your instructions, Ms. Drabek authorized the transfer of your funds in the total of $293,000,097 to the Bank of Armenia, the amount specified after deducting our standard transaction and transfer fees. I am pleased to say that your account earned $3,569,278 based on the Swiss Average Overnight rate of 0.70%. I hope you found that satisfactory."

He tried to process the banker's information and managed to say, "Yes, very. Thank you."

"We, of course, complied with your request," Steiner responded, "but I must say that I am personally distressed to have lost your accounts."

Accounts? Král rocked back in his chair, shaken as in no other time in his life. He recovered enough to ask, "And the other funds?"

"They, too, have been transferred." Steiner paused, then continued, his voice devoid of any emotional inflection, as if it were an everyday occurrence to affirm the status of the nearly 460 million dollars his accounts should have held. The banker cleared his throat in the strained silence that followed his recitation. "Herr Král, I am also most distressed that I must inform you of a serious breach of our confidential accounts by a disgruntled employee."

Král's sense of dread increased beyond what he thought possible. "I understand. Please continue."

"I am afraid the particulars of your, as well as other accounts, were divulged to the Organized Crime and Corruption Reporting Project. I understand one of the recipients was Herr Anton Jezek. Perhaps you have heard of him?"

Král tensed at the question. Was Steiner probing for what he may know of the reporter? "No, I am afraid not." The banker's revelation perhaps explained Drabek's actions and

Chapter Fifty-Five

provided him with a brief glimpse of hope. Perhaps Drabek had moved the funds because she feared if she delayed acting on the whistleblower's information, INTERPOL would act to seize his money—but why hadn't she conferred with him? And if she knew, who else could she have confided? He tensed at the answer—Sokol.

"Will there be anything else, Herr Král?"

Steiner's question penetrated the gray fog engulfing him. "Ah, no. Thank you. That will be all." He terminated the call, his head falling back, staring in disbelief at the ceiling, sickened. Financial ruin. My entire organization near collapse. My efforts to restore the castle, to will it to my unborn child. Gone.

He reached for the bottle of Becherovka, then dropped his hand. No, he had to have a clear mind to confront the very real possibility that the United States National Central Bureau of INTERPOL would issue a Red Notice warrant for his arrest and extradition if they managed to tie him to the disappearance of the funds from the New York Federal Reserve.

He pushed the bottle away and began to formulate a plan to counter, or at least mitigate, the damage, and if those measures failed, to fashion an escape plan that leveraged what he knew of Grekov's operations. Perhaps if he approached Parkos and gave up what he knew of Grekov, he might escape both the clutches of INTERPOL and whoever else was determined to destroy him.

Chapter Fifty-Six

673 LUKÁNÊ
PRAGUE, CZECH REPUBLIC
WEDNESDAY 28 OCTOBER

Nick set the burlwood box aside and turned his attention to the mysterious text he had received the evening before. "OCCRP. Urgent we meet. 1900. 38 Neurdova." The initials of the crime reporting network demanded his attention, but who had sent the note? And did it have to do with the attempt on his life, the attack on Jezek, his team's pursuit of Král, or something else entirely? He'd shared the text with Lange and Marie, both of whom were equally mystified.

The fact the sender knew his email address had escaped him at the time, but later, when that realization struck, it prompted a new line of thinking: Should he even go? His internal debate circled around something he'd heard his professor at Ohio State say years ago: "The highest risk is not taking one."

Could he choose to ignore the quote's advice, content with

the status quo, with nothing gained or lost? Or should he go, accepting the uncertainty of the meeting's risks of success or failure—progress of sorts with either outcome. He rubbed his chin, considering one more variable.

He had been operating under the charge of accepting risk when he had been captured and imprisoned the year before by the Chinese in Georgetown. "And how did that turn out?" he asked himself in counterpoint. Lange and his team had managed to rescue him, but the entire affair had also endangered Michelle's life. Those memories served to sober him.

He stuffed the iPhone into his hip pocket, crossed the living room, and pried apart the curtains. At the moment, he was safe enough, ensconced in the small cottage that Ferguson had secured on the outskirts of Prague. But, unlike Georgetown, he didn't have a clear idea of what or whom he faced in this clandestine meeting, but if the sender were his cousin, Petr? He had to go.

"See anything interesting?" Marie asked, joining him to peer over his shoulder.

"Perfect. It's started to rain," he replied, dropping the curtains.

"You sure you want to do this alone?"

"Yeah. I'm good. I'll be careful. Plus, Vinny and George are securing the perimeter of the meet site."

"When are you leaving?"

Nick checked his watch, then slipped on his coat. "In a couple of minutes. It's only a short walk and I don't want to arrive early."

"Makes sense," Marie said. Her eyes shifted to his backpack pushed into the corner of the couch. "Why are you taking your box?"

"I've been thinking about the sender."

"And?" Marie prodded.

"It may be Petr Hájek."

"Wow. You're thinking he may want to help us?"

"Possibly, I'm thinking that what may be driving him is the need to protect his—no—our family."

"And what you showed me in that box may be enough to turn him?" Marie asked.

"It's a long shot," Nick replied, "but he may have the other half of that torn document."

He hefted the upscale, linen version of a Czech army backpack he'd purchased preparing to slip it over his shoulders. He paused, then gave the pack a couple of short lifts by one of the straps, wondering why it weighed so heavily in his hand. The box and pack together couldn't weigh more than five pounds. Had Marie slipped her Beretta into one of the inner compartments? He set the pack down and opened the flap. "Do you think I'll need that?" he asked.

"You never know," Marie answered. "George told me it's a bad neighborhood."

Nick slipped on his Fiddler's cap and headed for the door. "I'll be careful. Let Vinny know I'm heading out."

Chapter Fifty-Seven

38 NEURDOVA
PRAGUE, CZECH REPUBLIC
WEDNESDAY 28 OCTOBER

"Just great," Nick muttered while stamping his feet on the bare concrete floor, striving to restore their circulation. "I just got suckered into a damn wild goose chase. Factoring in the debacle in Georgetown, I'm now 0 for 2." He chafed his hands to warm them. "So much for risk analysis."

He had literally been cooling his heels in the damp, bitter cold, listening to the steady patter of rain on the narrow driveway of 38 Neurdova before taking shelter in the home's small garage. The free-standing structure, its floor scattered with oil stains, was empty except for a few, forlorn lawn implements hanging on the walls. He checked his watch, pulled his sodden hat tighter over his head, and made for the street. *Enough of this crap. I'm out of here.*

He froze mid-stride. His heart lurched at the sight of an imposing, bearded mugger in an oversize, dark-blue pea coat and woolen watch cap emerging from the shadows. The man halted, feet braced apart, blocking his way. *Was that a gun?* Terror gripped Nick's throat.

He spun, lunging toward the garage's side door, reaching for the handle. A gloved hand seized his left shoulder, yanking him back. He stumbled, legs entangled. The assailant grabbed his backpack, jerking him upright. He struggled to pull free. His assailant's grip tightened.

"*Stopa!*"

Nick ceased struggling at the Czech command, managing to catch a glimpse of the mugger. "Petr?" he sputtered.

Hájek released his grip, but his eyes remained fixed on his captive. "This is not how I wished our meeting to begin."

"What-the-hell, you b—" Nick hollered.

"*Pojd, mám klíč. Prijít.*" Hájek cut Nick off before he could spit out the expletive.

"You have a key?" Nick echoed, too surprised to respond beyond parroting what he'd heard. Nor did he try to reach for his gun or make another attempt to escape. Neither would have been of any use. And, where the hell were Vinny and George?

"Yes, I have a key," Hájek said, opening the door. "Come, we have much to discuss. It will be warmer inside."

Nick followed Hájek into the home's small living room, stunned by this abrupt turn of events. The Czech flipped on the light switches and gestured toward a chair before busying himself pushing around the contents of a small liquor cabinet. Nick slid off his backpack and dropped it on the couch.

Hájek glanced over his shoulder. "You might wish to remove your jacket and cap."

Nick considered the suggestion and complied, taking the opportunity to collect his wits. "What's going on?"

"Ah, this will do," Hájek said, holding up a bottle of Czech Hammerhead whiskey. "An appropriate name, Hammerhead." He poured two stiff drinks, offering one to

Chapter Fifty-Seven

Nick. "An interesting question, cousin. I presume you want to know why I mentioned the OCCRP?"

"They're on to your operation," Nick said. "Related or not, I suppose this does make us cousins of a sort."

"My brother-in-law, Anton Král's, operations," Hájek clarified, "and that is why we are having this meeting. Anton erred in ordering the attack on the reporter, Jezek, and he has caused me considerable trouble."

Nick was incredulous, both at Hájek's admission and the probable consequences. "What do you know of his operations?"

Hájek chuckled. "Very little, but enough. You are finding that everything here is not as it seems, yes? You may be asking yourself, 'What does Anton Jezek and OCCRP have to do with us?' I will answer for you. I presume you know about the missing funds from the New York Federal Reserve Bank? ... Ah, I see from your face that is another mystery of which you are aware. Yes? But what you don't know is those funds have again gone missing."

"How do you know that?"

"I am not so naive as Anton thinks."

"And their use? Is he using the money to purchase arms?"

"Perhaps, by another party. But that, I cannot answer with certainty. You should know that I am not involved with any crazy Mexican drug lord." Hájek paused, then went on. "We must understand each other before we can arrive at solutions for the common problems that vex us both."

"Perhaps," Nick echoed, not sure what direction their conversation would take.

"You too, lost your parents and, despite the efforts of your grandparents, were left to your own devices. That is something we have in common."

Nick was thrown by Hájek's words. *How does he know so much about my family? Of course, the old man. He managed* to respond to this new twist. "I went into foster care, but I suppose you know that."

"Pádriac told me of your encounter at the castle," Hájek continued, holding up his hand to silence Nick. "And I know of your father and his *nom de guerre*, Steve Benik." Hájek hesitated, as if conflicted as to what he would say. "I only know he lost his life here. I do not know the circumstances."

Nick made no effort to interrupt, his mix of fear and anger replaced by a sense of intrigue, wanting to pull more from this Czech. He also understood there would nothing further to be gained by asking more about his father.

"You know, then, what it is to be abandoned." Hájek said in the heavy silence that followed. He emptied his glass, refilled it, and offered the bottle to Nick. "Perhaps the loss of your parents broke the little boy in you, but I suspect not the man that emerged. You are a survivor, like me."

Nick accepted the bottle, filled his glass, and took a contemplative sip.

"You have seen the castle, and Katerina said you spoke with *dēda*, Pádriac, our family patriarch." Hájeck continued. "We are both carrying the burden of our ancestors."

Katerina? So, she is involved despite her denials. Nick reached for his backpack, his mind racing at the implications. If Vasek was complicit with Hájek, then she had likely told him what the old woman showed him at the Terezin Ghetto. He swallowed a mouthful of the Hammerhead. "I saw the register at the Ghetto. The names. Anya Mrazik, Václav Hájek, Pádriac, Jakub."

"My family, descended from our common ancestor, Count Vilém, and generations later, Petr Patykaovi, our great-great-grandfather. Petr had two children that I know of, a son, Petr, of your family line and a daughter, Adéla, from whom my mother is descended."

Nick hadn't even considered that, or Petr's sister. "And Natálya?"

Chapter Fifty-Seven

A smile crossed Petr's face. "Yes, and she is with child."

The implications didn't escape Nick. If he were eliminated, Natálya's child would be next in line to inherit the castle. And before the child came of age, her father, Anton Král, would be the executor of the estate.

"Then it is possible her child would inherit the castle if I were discredited…or killed," Nick responded. "Petr, we are acting at cross-purposes."

"*Ano*," Hajek replied without amplification. "We have much to share."

Grasping at Hájek's open-ended prompt, Nick made his decision, his earlier premonition proving correct about the fate of the keepsake box. "Here, I want to show you something." He loosened the straps of the backpack and pulled out the Beretta, which hindered his access to the relic.

Hájek's eyes focused on the pistol. "You are planning to use that?"

"Is there a need?" Nick answered, his response bolstered by the knowledge that George and Vinny were out there, somewhere.

"*Ne*."

Nick double-checked the safety, set the weapon on the couch, and extracted the box, watching for Hájek's response.

His cousin set his drink on the room's coffee table and leaned forward. "Exquisite. That is a family heirloom?"

"I found it in my grandparents' attic after their deaths. I did not mention it to your grandfather."

"I recognize our family crest." Petr paused. "And I have reasons to believe Král, may possess the key and other heirlooms in his safe."

"What—"

"And your box? What does it contain?" Hájek interrupted.

Nick opened the lid by way of an answer and extracted the contents, spreading them on the table. The silver amulet and golden ram's head earring, the torn fragment of ancient parchment, the embroidered fabric depicting a wedding scene, and the official document topped by the golden crown.

Hájek's eyes widened at the sight of the ancient treasures, his eyes settling on the document. "May I?" He lifted the fragile paper. "This is a ketubah, an official wedding document. I have seen one like it in the *Židovské Muzeum*. It is priceless. You have been to the Jewish Museum in Prague?"

Nick again remained silent, fascinated by what Hájek had said.

Hájek set the document down and lifted the torn piece of parchment. "Pádriac must see these."

"Why are you doing these things—the arms, the money, the drugs?" Nick responded.

"I do these things for my...for our family."

"What do weapons shipments to a Mexican warlord possibly have to do with our family?"

"It's complicated," Hájek said, his voice devoid of inflection. "But I know nothing of an illicit arms deal."

"I do complicated," Nick rejoined. "Try me."

"The Nazis and the Communists destroyed our heritage, our dreams. Restoring the castle has already taken nearly five-hundred thousand dollars. What would you have done, what would you do if you were in my shoes?"

"Král would seek to destroy the stability of my country to save..." Nick stopped, unable to continue.

"To save our castle," Hájek said.

Nick needed to turn the conversation to one he could control. "Král has a traitor in his organization. The financier, Drabek, and maybe someone else."

Hájek nodded. "I had my suspicions about Drabek, but who is the other?"

Nick went with his intuition. If he were wrong, no matter. The information, even if false would serve to disrupt Král's network. "Sokol."

"Ah, you Americans. What am I to believe?"

Chapter Fifty-Seven

The scorn in Hájek's voice unnerved him, as did the Czech's apparent indifference to the mention of Král's difficulties. He needed another counter. "You're being played by the Russians... and your brother-in-law."

"I have no doubt of that," Hájek replied, sliding the torn parchment toward Nick. "Král possesses the other half of this document. He showed Natálya the contents of his safe and she shared that knowledge with me. We must make this document whole to find the answers to our questions." He paused and fixed Nick with his eyes. "Nikola, we are family. Would you betray that?"

The question left Nick conflicted. Could he protect his cousin, and by extension, his family, from Král and the Russians without compromising his own mission, his country, and his colleagues? "What about Drabek?"

Hájek's voice hardened. "She is of no further concern to you."

Nick accepted Hájek's response. It was not a lesser man's obstinacy. Petr understood his place and had no intention of having the family usurped by Král or his compatriot's designs whatever the latter might be.

"Do you know who tried to kill me? Was it Sokol or Král?" Nick countered.

"I have my suspicions and will handle the matter if I am correct. And that is why you must leave."

"Leave?"

Hájek stood. "I believe we are done."

Nick gathered the treasures and returned them to the box. "How do I contact you?"

"I will contact you," Hájek said, walking Nick to the door. "And remember, there is no safety in our meeting. *Memento Mori.*"

Hájek's last words wrenched Nick to a stop before he could cross the threshold. He knew the phrase, first voiced in the fourteenth century when the Black Death swept through Europe killing millions. "Remember, you too must die."

Sobered, he passed through the door, making his way toward the safe house. He hadn't seriously considered his future with Michelle this past two months. He'd spent too much time feeling sorry for himself. But he had to consider the fate of the others in his life. The driving rain cut through his open coat, chilling him to the bone. *Who would be next?*

Chapter Fifty-Eight

673 LUKÁNÊ
PRAGUE, CZECH REPUBLIC
WEDNESDAY 28 OCTOBER

Violence rarely issues a warning. When Nick arrived at the deserted safe house, he found Marie's cryptic note on the kitchen table, "Gone to see Geoff. Food in frig." He assumed George and Vinny were still running surveillance and would eventually turn up. With a shrug, he proceeded to empty the backpack, change out of his soaked clothes, and make his way back to the kitchen.

He set the Beretta on the table within easy reach, unsettled by Hájek's grim prophecy, *Memento Mori*. He busied himself with assembling a sandwich, spiced with a healthy side of introspection. The encounter with his cousin had prompted a jumble of conflicting emotions, leaving him torn between what Hájek had said about not betraying their family and the need to complete the mission.

He nibbled on the sandwich, doubting there was any point

in trying to turn Hájek and make him an American asset. Setting that decision aside, the broader question remained. Where did his loyalties lie? He was surprised that he felt no sense of betrayal in considering choosing family over... well, everything else. Nick mulled his remaining options. At best, the—

What was that? Nick tensed at an unexpected noise. It sounded like it might have come from the street. He dismissed it, unable to identify the source and returned to his meager supper. A heavy THUD followed by several dull thumps coming from the front of the house stopped him in midbite.

This time, there was no mistaking the noise. *Someone was pounding on the front door.* He grabbed the Beretta, released the safety, and racked the slide, chambering a round. He hesitated. Had the noises stopped? No, another thump. Softer this time. He made his way out of the kitchen alert for danger, unsure what to expect. An assailant would hardly announce his arrival—or would he?

He positioned himself to the right side of the door, Beretta poised, and turned the handle. He yanked the door open, using it to shield his body, and ventured a look. *Nothing.* Then his eyes caught sight of something at his feet. A man, sprawled face down across the front steps, his arms and legs racked by spasmodic jerks. The man turned his head. Nick swung his Beretta. "Taylor?"

Ferguson looked up, his eyes pleading for help. The agent tried to speak. Instead, a thin stream of saliva spilled from the side of his mouth.

Nick dropped to his knees, in part from shock, in part to assist his friend.

"Help me," Ferguson gasped, his words escaping in a strangled croak.

Nick scanned the street for threats. Seeing none, he set his weapon aside and lifted Ferguson's head off the step, not quite sure what to do next.

Chapter Fifty-Eight

"Poison," Ferguson gasped.

The word penetrated through Nick's shock, confirming his fears. He grabbed Ferguson's arms and dragged him into the living room out of the rain, turned the agent's head so he wouldn't drown in his own saliva, and kicked the front door closed. Ferguson vomited.

Nick stared at his friend in disbelief. *I've got to call someone.* He pulled his iPhone from his pocket and entered the number.

"Lange," his teammate answered.

"Geoff," Nick blurted, "Ferguson's been poisoned. He's here."

"Here?" Lange replied.

"At the safe house. He's seizing." Nick glanced at the sound of Ferguson's retching. "Oh, shit, he just vomited again."

"Look at his pupils," Lange ordered. "Are they constricted?"

"Yes," Nick answered a moment later, his senses now assaulted by both the sour stench of vomit and Ferguson's groans.

"Neurotoxin," Lange said. "Get him to a hospital. Marie's still with me. Where are the others?"

"I, I don't know," Nick said, trying to keep the panic out of his voice.

"Okay, I'll contact them and call for an ambulance. Don't let him choke. Roll him on his side. We're on our way. Hang in there."

Taylor Ferguson thought he heard voices. He picked one out and tried to speak. "Par–" He suppressed a scream at the piercing pain behind his eyes. He tried again. "Parkos." The name escaped as a sibilant wheeze before he was overcome with another bout of nausea. He retched and vomited again.

He lay there, panting, drenched in sweat, barely conscious, aware of fragments of things around him. Voices. A light. A blurred pattern on the wall. He tried to think, grasping for the remaining threads of his life. This much he knew. He'd been poisoned. He resigned himself to death, not panicked at the prospect despite the pain racking his body. *If this is death, then so be it,* he thought. *Nasty, but what had he expected? Perhaps it would be preferable to confronting the accumulated deeds of his life—the lies, the lives I've had taken, the— A voice?*

"Stay with me, God damn it!" Nick shouted. "Stay with me, you crazy bastard."

Ferguson gasped, struggling for breath, the voice he heard from so far away. "Parkos?"

"Yeah," Nick responded. "Don't you dare—"

Ferguson tried to speak, but again choked on his words. "Your fa—"

"My father?" Nick repeated. He leaned over, turning his ear toward Ferguson.

"Your father, Tom…he broke their…" Ferguson grimaced in pain, falling back before he could finish.

Nick reached his hand out to cradle his friend's head. "Broke their what, Taylor?"

Ferguson tried to lift a hand in response as Nick's face dimmed. Then everything went black.

Tears coursed down Nick's cheeks. "God damn you, Ferguson. Don't you die on me, you crazy bastard." But, as he had done so often in the past, Ferguson ignored him. Nick studied the agent's face. It appeared surprisingly serene in death, the visage prompting him to recall something Ferguson had said, a quote from George Adair: "'Everything you'll ever want is on the other side of fear.'" Nick choked back a sob, reached over, and closed Ferguson's eyelids. "Rest in peace, friend."

Chapter Fifty-Eight

George and Vinny burst through the front door, freezing in place at the sight of Ferguson's contorted body, Nick kneeing beside him. Vinny reacted first. "The ambulance is on the way."

Nick looked up, his voice devoid of emotion. "He won't need one."

Vinny knelt to check Ferguson's pulse and shook his head.

"Shit," George said. He grabbed a comforter off the couch and covered the body.

Vinny turned his attention from Nick to Ferguson. "That's not our only problem. We've got a hot zone."

"I'll get a cleanup crew," George said. "We can't have the locals involved."

Nick didn't move, oblivious to his partners' actions. What had Taylor tried to tell him about his father? Perhaps something about what had happened to his dad in Prague. He would never know. He covered his face with his hands, recalling something else Ferguson had once told him: "Be part of the solution, don't become part of the problem." He reached his hand out to the agent, then stood, his face set. The rules no longer applied. The Russians had left their signature, the nerve agent. Grekov would feel the wrath of his retribution for his friend's agonizing death.

Chapter Fifty-Nine

NUMBER 10, UVOZ STREET
PRAGUE ADMINISTRATIVE DISTRICT FIVE
THURSDAY 29 OCTOBER

"Are you crazy?" Aleksandra Grekov could barely contain her fury. "You killed the CIA agent, Parkos' partner? Why the hell did you do that?"

"Orders," the leader of GRU Unit 29155 replied, unmoved by Grekov's outburst.

Orders? Grekov struggled with a response to this automaton. At her direction, the Unit specializing in sabotage, subversion, and assassination had been brought in to take out Sokol who Kuznetzov had identified as Parkos' assailant. "Whose orders?"

The major shrugged. "Headquarters."

"What about the man you were sent to eliminate?"

"He was the man."

Grekov was thrown by that response. What was going on? Clearly something Moscow Central chose not to share. But

Chapter Fifty-Nine

why? What did Ferguson know that so scared headquarters? Could it be something to do with Parkos...or his father? Was this more of Turgenov's doing? The answer to all those questions would have to wait. "Does the name, Karel Sokol, mean anything to you?"

The major stared at a spot just over her head. "No."

Kuznetzov, who'd positioned himself behind Grekov's right shoulder, leaned forward and whispered something into her ear. Her jaw tightened, but her deputy was correct. She would get nowhere with this imbecile, even if he wasn't lying through his teeth. "You may go. Tell your superiors that I will clean up the mess you have left."

The major straightened and saluted. "Comrade Colonel."

Grekov dismissed him with a wave of her hand, not bothering to return the salute. She turned to Kuznetzov after the office door had closed with a soft click. "Sergei, please be seated. Let us find where the dog is buried and get to the crux of our problem," she said, paraphrasing an old Russian saying.

"I can see no rational reason why they would kill the American agent," Kuznetzov said.

Grekov didn't respond for a moment. "Did you know we killed Parkos' father?

Her deputy's eyebrows rose in surprise. "But why?"

"I've worked with Parkos before. In another mess Central created a year ago. We were partnered to chase down that crazed Chechen, Bashir al-Khultyer. You have heard of him?"

"*Da*. But his father?"

"I searched our files on Parkos and discovered something unexpected. Parkos' father, like Ferguson, was a CIA agent; his *nom de guerre* was Steve Benik. He lost his life under mysterious circumstances here in Prague. Supposedly a random act of violence by a drunken local. The KGB may have been responsible for his death, a violation of the unwritten rule between the KGB and the CIA that they would not kill each other's agents."

Kuznetsov appeared circumspect. "I suspect the local was framed, perhaps even tortured to admit the crime."

"It would not surprise me," Grekov said. "The files were heavily redacted."

"Do you think Parkos knows?"

Grekov emitted a sigh. "I suspect he might, Sergei. And that will make him doubly dangerous." She tapped her fingers on her desk. "There are things going on of which we are not aware, but in which we are now entangled. Whether we will be able to free ourselves from this web, only time will tell. Time we may not have."

She sat upright, squaring her shoulders. "*Spasibo*, Sergei," she said, dismissing him. "You have done well. We will continue this conversation tomorrow morning. Now, I must think."

She stared at the latest invoice for another shipment of beets after Kuznetsov had departed, then shoved it aside. She doubted she would need to concern herself with the dealings of her front company, Meycek Imports—or further arms shipments, for that matter. Her primary concern now? Her life.

Moscow's elaborate scheme—No, your elaborate scheme, she corrected herself—to funnel arms to Mendez was unraveling due to the efforts of Parkos and his team. And as Central had made perfectly clear, nothing of Moscow's involvement with the Mexicans could ever be traced back to President Srevnenko.

She spun her chair toward the cabinet behind her, extracted a full bottle of Stoli vodka, and filled a water glass. She drained a third of it, then began to sort out what had transpired over the past week, how those events impacted her, and what she must do.

Even if she survived the next week or wasn't ordered back to Moscow, she would not be surprised if she were assigned a

Kimpromat. A nursemaid, the most visible member of a new security service detail, would ensure she didn't defect. She would be a virtual prisoner. That, she could not allow. She downed another couple of fingers of vodka and exhaled a loud, prolonged sigh. *So, where do you stand with Colonel General Turgenov?* The mere fact that she could not answer this question told her all she needed to know, but still she clung to some remnant of hope.

For now, Moscow Central had not taken any overt actions to suggest she was in immediate danger, but unlike those who did not work for the FSB, she knew that meant nothing. A proverb her grandfather had told her as a child resonated: "In a quiet lagoon, devils dwell."

Grekov polished off the last of the Stoli, pushed away from her desk, and took a final look at her ornate office. She must disappear. And she had to do something about Král.

Chapter Sixty

673 LUKÁNÊ
PRAGUE, CZECH REPUBLIC
THURSDAY 29 OCTOBER

Geoff Lange surveyed the assembled Curators scattered around the living room of the safe house. Smoke rose in a lethargic column from the smoldering wood in the fireplace, Ferguson's death weighing heavily on all of them, but most of all, on Nick.

The only good news Lange could manage to come up with was that Nick had not shown any symptoms aside from some tingling in his fingertips of an incidental exposure to the neurotoxin, novichok. Ferguson's body would shortly be on its way back to the States courtesy of the cleanup crew sent by Prague's CIA station chief. Lange checked his chronometer. 2340. A long day nearing its end, but about to get more trying.

Nick appeared almost catatonic—no, torpid was a better

description, Lange concluded. His friend was overwhelmed by the events of the past three hours, which had included his clandestine meeting with a mysterious contact and Ferguson's death. His life had been turned upside down. Marie sat next to her partner, providing what solace she could, coaxing a few words from him and endeavoring to penetrate the matted layers of Nick's shock and grief.

Lange reviewed what he knew of the "incident," as the group was now calling Ferguson's horrific death. He had no doubt that forensic analysis would detect traces of novichok smeared on the doorhandle of Taylor's one-room apartment. And the use of that specific agent pointed straight to the Russians. But how had they known where to find Ferguson? A leak at the embassy? Who the hell knew? He certainly didn't. All he knew was he had to clean up this mess, complete the mission, and get the team out without any further deaths.

Lange's immediate problem, though, was that Nick had not revealed the details of his meeting earlier tonight. Lange reached for his cigar, noting Marie reacting to something Nick had said.

"Nick met with Petr Hájek."

Lange blew out a large plume of smoke. Hájek, not Král as he had suspected. What could they have talked about? He doubted it had anything to do with Ferguson's murder.

"Nick took his burlwood box to the meeting," Marie went on. "I asked him why at the time." She paused, casting a glance at Nick before continuing. "I think they talked about family."

"What about the text OCCRP?" Lange replied, noting Nick's slight frown in response to Marie's statement. He ventured a question. "Nick, what happened? Did you talk about family or something else?"

Marie touched Nick's elbow. "Nick, say something. We have to know."

Nick mouthed two words, his eyes fixed on the remnants of the fire.

Marie leaned over. "Nick, what did you say?"

Nick looked at her and said in a voice only she could hear. "*Momento mori*. Petr said, *Momento mori*—"Remember You Too Must Die." And Taylor…"

Lange responded before Marie could speak, passing over Nick's use of Hájek's first name. "*Mori* means death in Latin."

"Damn it, Nick, you're not responsible for Taylor's death!" Marie asserted, the edge in her voice seeming to break through Nick's emotional wall.

Nick lifted his head. "Yes, I suppose you're right." That admission appeared to give him strength. "We've got to protect him."

"Protect him? Who? Hájek?" Lange sputtered.

"Hájek. He was not behind Taylor's murder. We must protect him," Nick repeated with certainty. "Petr is my cousin."

Lange fell back in his chair. "Cousin?"

"I need a drink," Nick said. "I've got some things I need to tell you."

Nick's request rousted Edmund out of his chair, who then poured a generous glass of Nick's own Laphroaig whisky and handed it over. "Here ya go, mate. The 007. I think it suits the circumstances."

Nick managed a thin smile and took a swallow. "Tis nectar, Edmund. *Tapadh leat*."

"How'd ya know that?" Edmund replied at Nick's use of Gaelic for "Thank you," before answering himself. "Ah, yes, your wee lassie, Michelle. She's Scotch-Irish."

Nick hefted his glass in salute to his wife, then proceeded to summarize what he'd learned from his cousin about the arms shipments, Jezek's attack, and the confirmation of his suspicions that Král's operation had been undercut by Drabek and probably Sokol. Finally, Nick told them about what had happened to the funds that went missing from the New York Federal Reserve Bank, and what they were probably used for.

Lange knocked the ash off the tip of his cigar. The statements about the missing money intrigued him the most. It wasn't about the arms for the Mexican, Mendez. Král wanted the funds to restore the castle—and to that end, he'd made a deal with the devil. "What you're telling me, then, is your cousin should not be our concern?"

"Yes. Well, no. Not entirely," Nick replied, correcting himself. "Petr's not a major player. He is concerned that if something happens to his grandfather and mother and something happens to him, Král will become the administrator of the estate. We need to go after Grekov."

"How do you propose we protect him?" Marie asked.

"Petr?" Nick asked.

"Yes."

"First off," Nick answered, "we need to see what we can do about expediting the National Central Bureau for INTERPOL's request to issue a Red Notice for Král's arrest and extradition."

Lange took a thoughtful draw of his cigar, intrigued by Nick's use of Hájek's first name. He would need to consider the implications for the mission if Nick became too close to the Czech, but first, he needed to do a bit of adaptive planning now that the playing field had been clarified. "That may not be so bad. We could use it as cover to get Hájek out of the country."

"I don't think he'd go," Nick said. "His family and the castle mean everything to him."

"And you?" Lange asked.

"Time will tell, but that's not my focus. I want those damn Russians to pay."

"What about Drabek and Sokol?" Lange asked.

"Not our concern," Nick said. "Petr said he'd take care of them."

"And the 300 million?" George added.

"I suspect Drabek's and Sokol's motives are nothing more nefarious than greed," Nick stated, his resolve firming. "But Grekov? We can't let her, or permit the Russians to buy more weapons on the black market and ship them to Mexico."

Chapter Sixty-One

LUDICKÁ STREET
DISTRICT FIVE, PRAGUE
FRIDAY 30 OCTOBER

Nick made his way down Lidická Street pretending to window shop, but he was using the various shop windows as mirrors to check for anything that appeared out of place. He stepped into Potraviny, a tiny convenience store, exploiting it as a cover-stop, wandering the three aisles of sundries before pausing beside the front door to watch for any suspicious activity. Seeing none, he left the shop and continued to his destination, Café Tone. Lange hadn't liked the idea of sending him off on what could well be a fool's errand fraught with danger. Nick had countered that he had no choice.

Another unexpected text, the second in as many days, had sent him to Prague's Fifth District for another clandestine meeting. This text, unlike the first, had given him a hint of the sender, even though it consisted of just four words in addition to the meeting place and time: "Born at night, Chelya."

Grekov had translated those first three words, part of the Chechen national anthem from a note he'd found that was left behind by the terrorist, Bashir al-Khultyer, when she and Nick raided the terrorist's safe house near the city of Chelyabinsk.

And the meeting place specified in the text? Café Tone, a small coffee shop. Routine surveillance by the local CIA station over the past year had established that she passed the shop every day on the short walk from her business to her apartment.

Nick slowed his pace; otherwise he'd be early for the rendezvous set for 1700. He tensed as a car approached and slowed. A wheel artist and a gunman ready to blast him to oblivion? He made a step toward the open door of the Café Wine Bar located next door to his destination, then he caught a glimpse of the car's interior as it accelerated past him and exhaled a sigh of relief. A young woman was behind the wheel who'd been distracted by several children occupying the rear seat. Hardly Russian agents. No wonder George and Vinny, who were again running counter-surveillance, hadn't sent him any cryptic texts warning of danger.

He looked through the display window of Café Tone, surprised there weren't any tables. There were several customers in line at the counter. He didn't recognize her at first. Instead of the dull-gray, sexless outfit she had worn at the FSB headquarters in Moscow, Grekov was now attired in a tasteful two-piece suit. And, unlike in Moscow, where she had twisted her black hair into a severe bun, her hair was now touched with a hint of gray, and hung loose, brushing her shoulders.

He took a deep breath and entered, the tinkle of a small brass bell announcing his arrival. The other customer turned and smiled before completing his transaction and leaving the shop. Nick returned the man's smile with a weak one of his own and approached the counter, pretending to study the kremroles, the Czech version of a profiterole.

Chapter Sixty-One

Grekov turned to face him. He was again taken by her brown, deep-set, intelligent eyes. She had softened the horizontal slash of her mouth with an application of a subdued red lipstick—and there, above her right eyebrow, he noticed the scar.

Grekov smiled, "So, you remember my childhood scar?" She further startled him by giving him a welcoming hug, as if greeting an old friend. "You are not going to kiss me?" she teased. "We are old friends, are we not?"

Nick was non-plussed by her unexpected greeting but managed to collect himself enough to kiss her lightly on each of her cheeks in the French style.

She turned to the pastries. "They look wonderful. Choose one, then we must go and talk of old times." At her urging, he chose a kremrole.

"We have little time," she said when they were outside. "If I am not at my apartment soon, my *Kimpromat* will become suspicious." She glanced up and down the street as if preparing to cross, then placed her hand on the small of Nick's back guiding him toward a dim alleyway.

"Were you followed?" Nick asked.

"Perhaps. I often come here, though, for a pastry and a coffee before going home. I doubt they would be suspicious. Come with me."

Pastry in hand, Nick did as he was told, wondering who "they" might be. She led him into the dark alley, squeezing past a folding metal gate before emerging on Pecháckova Street, where she turned right. She reversed course at the next corner and led him back to Lidická Street.

She took Nick's free hand and gave it a tug. "Quickly, this way. We will cross the Palacky Bridge, then take a circuitous route to the Botanical Gardens. It will be safe to talk there."

Nick had no idea where the gardens were, but it didn't matter. He tossed the remnants of his kremrole into the Vltava River as they crossed the ancient stone bridge and made their way to the garden's massive greenhouse. A blast of hot, humid air greeted them when they entered.

Grekov swept her arm over the vista. "It is beautiful, is it not? I come here when I need to think."

Nick didn't respond, the heavy air weighing on his shoulders. He pushed away his discomfort. He couldn't succumb to one of the ploys she'd used in the past to disarm him. Grekov guided him to a wrought iron bench backing on a shallow pond festooned with four-foot-wide water lilies and a magnificent surround of tropical greenery.

"I have been betrayed by Moscow Central," Grekov opened. She didn't wait for a response. "I have been compromised."

Nick was taken aback by her revelation. And the edge in her voice. Frightened? Unlike her. *What the hell was going on?*

"Does the name Colonel General Nikolai Turgenov mean anything to you?" Grekov continued.

"The head of the FSB?" Nick replied, seething inside at the gall of this woman to say she was betrayed when she—and her damn Russians—had murdered Taylor.

"He is the man behind the plan to send weapons to Mexico." Grekov paused again. "I presume that is why you and your team are in Prague. Operation Diagonal."

Grekov's revelation stuck him like a thunderbolt. "How do you know that?"

"Your old supervisor, Strickland. He told us much before his arrest."

Nick held up his hand, the muscles in his neck tightening into angry cords. "At the moment, I don't give a damn about Strickland, the weapons, or you, for that matter. Who authorized the murder of my friend?"

Grekov sighed. "Yes, for that I am sorry. There was no need."

"No need?" Nick retorted, not impressed by her rare expression of contrition. "Who murdered him?"

Chapter Sixty-One

"A three-man team from GRU Unit 29155. They specialize in assassinations among other distasteful things."

"Did you know?"

"I swear, I did not. I suspect Turgenov ordered it, but to what purpose, I do not know. ...and that is why I must defect."

Nick rocked back, his hands gripping the back of the bench, his eyebrows shooting up in surprise. "Defect?" But then, he made the connection, connecting disparate points. "Ferguson's murder had something to do with my father."

Grekov started at his statement. "I... No, perhaps it might. I didn't make the connection, but the files identified another agent working with your father. The files were heavily redacted, but there is enough to suggest it may have been Ferguson. There is no mention of what they could have discovered. What I suspect is your father's death was a source of embarrassment to the former KGB."

Nick struggled to find the words. "An embarrassment? My father lost his life....and it's an embarrassment?"

Grekov didn't flinch at Nick's verbal assault. "His death violated an unwritten rule that the CIA and KGB would not kill each other's agents. The KGB framed a drunken local who admitted to killing your father to cover whatever truth lay behind your father's death. Now, for reasons I do not fully understand, Turgenov decided Ferguson had to be silenced."

He couldn't detect any sophistry in her reply, but still ... "It's been twenty-six years. You really believe that?"

"Yes. And I have no doubt there is much your own CIA has chosen not to share." She reached into her jacket and pulled out a small card. "This is how you can reach me."

The CIA? Nick struggled to find a reason, any reason, to prolong their meeting, to find out more. Something else that would keep her talking. "What about the weapons?"

"Not now, but I have much more I can tell you." Her eyes darted toward a young couple walking down the gravel footpath toward them. "I suspect that within days I will be summoned back to Moscow. I will not be returning to my office or my apartment. It is too dangerous." She held his eyes with an imploring look. "My fate will be just as bad as your friend's. At best, I will be left to rot in the Lefortova prison reserved for those suspected of treason."

She stood to leave, a fleeting, disarming smile lighting her face. "It would be best if you spent some time in the gardens before you join your two friends who have been following me."

Nick made to reply, but she waved him off. "*Dasvidanya. Udachee.*"

Dasvidanya? Udachee? Goodbye? Good luck? Nick said to himself. What did she mean by that? He looked up to ask, but she was gone. She remained an enigma, leaving him at a loss as to her motives. As she had done so many times befor

Chapter Sixty-Two

673 LUKÁNE
PRAGUE, CZECH REPUBLIC
FRIDAY 30 OCTOBER

"We gotta move," Nick stated, swinging his eyes across the team, judging their reaction.

"You don't think she's bluffing?" Lange asked, alluding to what he knew of Nick's uncertain collaboration with Grekov during the al-Khultyer affair. "It wouldn't be the first time."

"Ferguson was burned," Edmund interjected, touching on a topic that the team would rather not address considering the danger Nick had placed himself in with his meeting with Grekov.

"The broader question is, are we all compromised?" Lange asked, "And, if so, by whom?"

"It's safe to presume we're all at risk," Ann stated.

Nick clenched his fist in a mix of anger and frustration. His mouth set at his last memory of Ferguson, seeking some sense of meaning after what had happened, or what else could have defined his friend's life at the moment of his death. And that gave him pause to consider his own life and his relationship with his cousins or whatever remained of his family heritage. Those were nothing compared to what he had shared with Ferguson over the years. He gave voice to his feelings, what his friend would have said if their positions had been reversed. "Screw them."

"Say again?" Lange said.

"Something Ferguson would have said if he were in my place," Nick replied. "Screw them. I want those bastards."

"Understood," Lange said, "but Grekov told you the assassins were GRU. They're long gone. I should also remind everyone that when I was doing mission planning with my SEAL team, I always told them, 'Your enemy gets a vote.' It's fair to say that both Grekov and Král have kept us off balance and they'll have a vote in determining how we proceed."

"Aye," Edmund said. "They have been right clever."

"Up to now," Nick observed. "We've managed to disrupt both their networks, even if we were provided an inadvertent assist by Drabek and Sokol."

Vinny turned from the table where he was mixing a drink and asked, "Geoff, what's the flight time from here to D.C.?"

"Nine hours, give or take, depending on the headwinds. Nick, from what you've told us, I presume Grekov wants to defect."

"She said, and I quote. '… that is why I must defect,'" Nick affirmed.

"Nothing ambiguous about that," Lange replied. "What's our lead time?"

"I'd say, less than forty-eight hours," Nick said. "She's expecting to be recalled to Moscow within…" He checked his watch… "within thirty-six hours."

"Can we get an aircraft here in time for the extraction?" Vinny asked.

"No need," Lange answered. "Frogman is sitting on the apron at a small executive strip just outside Dresden. She has a range of 6,700 miles. The distance is just over 4,000 to Washington. No sweat."

Nick smiled at Lange's name of his private Gulfstream 550ER—Big Tough Frogman—a shortened, "BTF," emblazoned on the aircraft's tail. He had never asked how Lange could afford the sixty-million-dollar aircraft, let alone the money for the flight crew and maintenance. He set those questions aside for another day, not that it was any of his business. "If we can get Alex to Dresden, can we get her out tomorrow?"

"Alex?" Vinny asked.

"Short for Aleksandra. We have a history," Nick replied. "We shared some pretty tense moments during a past operation."

"No reason why we can't," Lange answered, ignoring Vinny's implication. "Do we all go or just Nick and one other to escort her to the States?"

That question prompted a word of caution from Jennifer. "Before we get to the team, there are those pesky little details to address. The first; does Grekov have family?"

"None that I know of," Nick answered.

"Good," Jennifer responded, "Number two. We can't just drop her off at Dulles and ask her to grab a cab to the Marriott."

"Let me address the second part of your question first," Lange said. "We can stash her at our safehouse in northern Virginia where we hid Nick and Michelle last year. The first part is a bit trickier, but I've been through this drill before with another asset we extracted from Syria."

"Asset?" Vinny said. "Hell, she—"

"Details," Marie interjected. "I figure while Nick is chasing down our asset, Geoff can place a call to Mr. Gilmore. The director can grease the skids with Secretary

Valardi. The Bureau of Conflict and Stabilization Operations falls under State."

"Conflict and Stabilization?" Edmund said. "What does that outfit have to do with asylum seekers?"

"I have no clue how they came up with that name," Marie said. "Oh, and another piece of trivia. They share the title with the Brits."

"They do?" Edmund responded. "Never heard of the bloody office."

"I only know because I worked with them on a defector who escaped from North Korea when I worked for the Agency," Marie explained. "In any event, the affirmation process for asylum seekers is straight forward enough…at least for the State Department's bureaucracy. Grekov's a high-level Russian asset. For someone of her value, all she has to do is be standing on American soil and present herself."

"That's it?" Vinny said.

"Pretty much. They'll ask her a bunch of questions just to make sure she's legit."

"I'll vouch for her," Nick said. "Not necessarily one hundred percent, but I know she was operating on a knife edge on our last operation, which explained why I could never get a firm read on her."

"How so?" Marie asked.

"She was playing both sides against the middle. Her grandfather was part of the old aristocracy, a White Russian general who lost his life in the Crimea enclave. Her family lost everything."

"Like Hájek?" Marie said, her statement earning an irritated look from Nick.

"How convenient," Vinny said, ignoring the look. "Unless she's a mole."

"Trust me, she's not," Nick said, grateful to move on from any questions that touched on his relationship with his cousin

Chapter Sixty-Two

and the subtle undercurrent of any possible conflicts of interest. "And if she doesn't commit to me tomorrow, we'll roll her up."

Lange caught Marie's eye. "One way or the other, we'll take one of the players off the board. Now, what about Hájeck?" he asked, following up on Marie's valid observation.

Nick paused at Lange's question about his cousin, making a conscious decision to not call him by his first name. "Now that we have blown-up the networks for the weapons sales, we may have to leave Hájek to his own devices."

"Okay, let's move," Lange said, inwardly relieved by Nick's statement. "We're out of here tomorrow provided Nick can get Grekov to commit. I'll call the pilot and have him prep Frogman, top the tanks, and file a flight plan."

"The entire team?" Edmund asked.

"Yes," Nick answered. "Our time here is done and we gotta get Grekov out. She gave me a contact number. I'll call her." He paused and looked at Lange. "What time are you looking at?"

"How much time to you need?" Lange responded.

"I'll tell her to meet me at the western drop-off lot at the botanical gardens. 1730."

"Roger that," Lange affirmed. "Ninety minutes to the airstrip. Wheels up at 1930 hours. George, you drive."

"Guess we need to be packing and tidying up the loose ends," Edmund said. "I figure the folks in Germany can close up the Dresden safe house."

"Speaking of loose ends," Nick said, "do we contact Coleman?"

"No," Lange answered. "He can take care of himself, and we still don't have a clear idea of the source of the leaks in our operation."

Nick wasn't convinced. He didn't like the idea of leaving Coleman out of the loop. "He said it was his secretary."

"Not good enough," Lange answered. "The fewer people who know about what we're doing, the better. I'll tell the director not to make any calls to Valardi until we're over the Atlantic."

Chapter Sixty-Three

NA SLUPI BOULEVARD
PRAGUE, CZECH REPUBLIC
SATURDAY 31 OCTOBER

Nick swayed in his seat as George changed lanes, weaving his way through the evening traffic along Na Slupi Boulevard paralleling the eastern bank of the Vltava River. The mission was on. Nick had confirmed with Grekov the specifics of the pickup site at the botanical gardens. Nick settled back into the rear seat of their trusty Skoda Octavia, scrolling through his text messages.

A message from Dexter Coleman popped up, arousing his curiosity. He was about to type in a reply when George spun the wheel, making a hard right turn, throwing him and his sore arm into the door. "OW! What the—" He got his answer before he finished his sentence.

"We've got a tail," George said into his throat microphone, ignoring Nick's squawk. "Light-blue Avia. Driver and one other… Good, I'll slow and let you catch up…I'll take the next right." He turned his head and spoke over his shoulder. "Vinny will take care of it."

"Vinny? He's trailing us?"

"Course he is," George said. "Gotta have a contingency plan."

"How the hell did they know?"

"Whoever it is, they may have just been keeping track of us with no idea of what's on our minds."

"Our mysterious informant?" Nick speculated.

"Don't think so. We've been buttoned up. Nobody, not even the DNI, knows what we're—"

"What?"

"Hold on," George said, catching sight of Vinny in the rearview mirror. He accelerated past a line of cars in the right lane.

Nick braced and swung his head around at the sounds of screeching of tires and the discordant blasts of angry horns. A jumble of cars, one run up on the sidewalk, jammed the traffic behind them.

"Vinny never could drive worth a flip," George observed with a chuckle. "Caused a real mess back there."

"But what about his car?"

George flashed a smile. "Stole it. I figure he's already disappeared into the crowd. He and the ladies will catch up with us just north of town."

Nick nodded at George's mention of Jennifer and Ann, deciding it best to keep his mouth shut and concentrate on his part of the mission. His iPhone sang out with an incoming text. He almost ignored it but decided to check it out.

"Grekov." He said in answer to George's unasked question. "She's almost to the pickup point."

The phone rang as it set it down, again singing out the first bars of Aerosmith's "Dream On." He looked at the caller

Chapter Sixty-Three

ID. Coleman. What the devil could he want that was all that important? He slid his finger across screen. "What's up?"

"We gotta meet," Coleman answered.

"What about?" Nick countered.

"I can't say over this line."

That statement caught Nick's attention, but whatever Coleman had to say was being overtaken by events. It could wait. "Listen, I'm right in the middle of something. I'll call you back," Nick said, doubting he would be able to do so any time soon.

George cast a curious look in the rearview mirror.

"Coleman," Nick answered.

"What did he want?"

"No idea. Whatever it is, he couldn't tell me over my phone," Nick replied, his statement eliciting a skeptical grunt from George.

"Aside from our pickup," George said, "I haven't heard of any new developments."

"Me neither," Nick affirmed. "I'll call him from the airport."

"Sounds like a plan," George commented before turning his attention back to the traffic.

"You never know in this business. He just might have something,"

A few leisurely turns and a couple of minutes brought them to their destination. George pulled over, keeping the engine idling. "See her?"

Nick scanned the lot. "No—wait, there she is. Just passed through the park's gate. She's heading our way."

"Roll down the window and wave," George said. "Make it look like we're picking up a friend."

Instead, Nick climbed out of the car after spotting Jennifer and waved for Grekov to approach. The wave also served to alert both Jennifer and Ann who had been shadowing the

Russian agent. Seeing Nick's wave, the two took off for their car so they could pick up Vinny.

Grekov turned and stood a moment, looking at the greenhouse, then she returned Nick's wave, and walked to the car.

"*Vse kohrosho?*" You okay? Nick asked, pushing the right-side seat forward to allow her to enter.

She pulled her gigantic purse out of the way to make room for him. "*Da.*"

"You will miss the greenhouse," Nick said.

"New adventures await."

Nick addressed George. "She's good. Let's get out of Dodge."

"Dodge?" Grekov said.

"Sorry, it's an American expression for: 'We have to get out of town,'" Nick replied.

"Jennifer and Ann verified they're on their way to pick up Vinny," George said, after pulling back into traffic. "They'll meet us in Benezov just north of here, then ride shotgun for the remainder of the trip."

There was no need for Nick to reply. He gestured toward Grekov's purse which, resembled the oat feeding bags he'd seen draped over a horse's muzzle. "That's it?"

"Any more would have been too obvious," she replied, opening the top for his inspection. "No weapons, just makeup." She smiled. "A strike for vanity, yes?"

"My partner is about your size if you need anything," Nick offered, not really having a clue if Marie would object. And if Marie cocked an eyebrow at him volunteering her wardrobe, he would reply with her own rejoinder: *Details.*

ACM CHARTER SERVICES TERMINAL
DRESDEN, GERMANY

Chapter Sixty-Three

"I see it," Nick said for Grekov's benefit, pointing toward an aircraft parked near an isolated hanger a couple of hundred yards away. Not unexpectedly, she'd had little to say during the trip.

"Got it," George replied as he slowed, nearing the gate. The private security guard, forewarned, waved the old car through without so much as a raised eyebrow. "Free and clear," George said.

"I hope so," Grekov said, leaning forward to get a glimpse of the plane. "Now is not the time to get detained by the German authorities."

George pulled up next to the Frogman. "Your ride to the States."

Grekov studied Lange's Gulfstream. "This is not the aircraft you used to transport Delezal to Poland."

Nick covered his surprise that she had specific knowledge of Ferguson's aircraft. "Nope, we're traveling first class. Come on, we'll get you settled while the rest of the team arrives."

"You're all leaving?" Grekov asked.

"Our business here is over," Nick said, leading her up the stairs.

Her first view of the aircraft's interior appeared to stun her. "Do all American spies travel in this fashion?"

Nick laughed. "No, this plane belongs to a friend."

"You know an oligarch?" Grekov asked, further nonplussed.

"Nah, in fact, that's him." Nick smiled at Grekov's reaction. She couldn't have been more startled in an afternoon full of the unexpected.

"Lange? He owns this plane?"

Nick was about to respond to Grekov's unexpected recognition of his partner when Lange's secure phone rang.

Lange turned his back and answered in a soft voice. "Lange."

"Geoff, this is Dexter. Is Nick with you?"

"Yeah, what's up?"

"Something big."

"Okay, give us a sec." Lange grabbed Nick by the elbow. "Excuse us, business" he said to Grekov. "Marie, can you entertain our guest?" He mouthed, "*Coleman*," as he guided Nick to his private compartment at the rear of the aircraft and closed the door. "I've got Nick on speaker."

Nick muttered, "Sorry, Dexter, I got busy," while thinking to himself, *He sure is a persistent son-of-a-gun.*

"So I've heard," Coleman said. "First off, I'm really sorry to hear about Ferguson. He had his moments, but he was a damn good agent. I presume you've got a lead on the bastards who did that, but that's not why I'm calling. We've got some major developments with our other player."

"Král?" Nick said.

"None other," Coleman replied. "The Chief of Station cornered me last night. The Agency used some of their SIGINT wizardry to break into his network and verified his complicity in the arms shipment to Mendez and his involvement with another player."

"Grekov," Nick said.

"No. Mexico's former Defense Minister, Juan Carlos Alvarez."

The name meant nothing to Nick, but he kept his mouth shut.

"My guess is Ferguson put two-and-two together," Coleman continued. "He fingered the Russians, and it ended up costing his life."

Nick wasn't so sure, based on Grekov's story, but again, he didn't comment. This was the time to listen, not pepper Coleman with questions.

Coleman filled in the blanks. "We're chasing down the

Chapter Sixty-Three

Russian connection, but that's not all. Král's cleaned house. Hold on. I'm sending you a couple pics. They speak for themselves."

Lange leaned over Nick's shoulder as the first picture appeared, mouthing a "Wow."

"You got them?" Coleman asked.

"Yeah," Nick affirmed, "the first one is ju—. Good, Lord," A second image appeared leaving him stunned. The two pictures were of Sokol and Drabek, bloodied and quite dead. "How'd you get these?"

"Would you believe Petr Hájek sent them to me? Figure he's looking to atone."

"From what Nick's told me, he's covering his ass," Lange said. "Hájek's feeling the heat from INTERPOL and distancing himself from Král's organization."

"That, and, like Dexter said, Král's cleaning house," Nick said. "Those two betrayed him."

"How so?" Coleman asked.

"Long story, but they stole funds from his Swiss account," Nick explained.

"Stole? Hell, Král stole the money from us," Coleman said "That, and all the millions he made off drugs. I can't say that I'm feeling a lot of sympathy."

Nick made his decision. While he was torn about what to do about Petr, Natálya's unborn child, and what he'd learned by sharing the walnut keepsake box with Hájek, he had no choice but to let the cards fall where they may. He could not compromise himself or The Curators. More importantly, he couldn't destroy Michelle's dreams of becoming an Air Force officer by appearing to be complicit in his cousin's activities and having her security clearance background investigation flagged as suspicious. "Understood. The balls in your court. Go after him."

Michelle? Nick was swept with a pang of guilt after Coleman terminated the call. *Dang, I've got to call her.* He closed his messenger app with its grisly pictures of Sokol and Drabek, and opened his "Contacts" to access Michelle's number. His happiness at the thought of talking to her faded at the sound of her recorded message. "Hi, you have reached Michelle …" He waited for the message to play out, then left his own. "Hi, kiddo. It's me. We're heading home. I'll call when we land. Love you."

Chapter Sixty-Four

THE NICKOLAS
3136 M STREET N.W.
GEORGETOWN, WASINGTON D.C.
MONDAY 2 NOVEMBER

"I never thought we'd both be coming here again," Nick said, guiding Michelle up the stairs of The Nicholas leading to Lange's private lair, scarcely believing two-and-a-half months had passed since Gilmore had summoned him.

"Did you make the right decision?" Michelle asked, apparently reading his thoughts.

"Considering everything, I think I did," Nick replied, knowing his answer included a slew of unvoiced caveats. He'd picked her up at the airport the previous evening and hadn't wanted to talk about the mission or what he'd discovered about his family, and didn't want to now. There would be time enough when they were home.

He also hadn't told her about the hints he had received from Austin that Gilmore wanted him to return to the Liberty

Crossing campus to assume his disgraced supervisor's old position. *Not likely*. He'd learned over the past months that he just wasn't cut out for that sort of work, especially if he had to face cleaning up the mess the traitor, Strickland, had left.

As for their mission? Král had been arrested and was cooling his heels in a Czech prison, awaiting extradition to the States. While Interpol wanted to keep him in Prague, the Czech government wanted to wash their hands of him. As for Grekov, she was hidden away in the Virginia safehouse and had already fingered her Mexican contact, Alvarez, who, in turn, was turning on his compatriots. There was little doubt that Alvarez would spill all he knew about Méndez, aka, El Tlatoani. As for the illicit weapons already in Mexico? A CIA special operations group had been tagged to work with the Mexican Special Forces to take down Méndez's headquarters and capture him. In Europe, another CIA team would attend to thwarting any remaining mischief the Russians had in mind, and Coleman had assured the team that he was working with Treasury and INTERPOL to secure the lost funds from the Federal Reserve bank.

Not bad for a couple of month's work, Nick concluded, before his thoughts turned to his cousins. He could only conjecture about Petr and Natálya's ultimate fates.

The Curators had wrapped up their debriefings at the NSA's Liberty Crossing campus that morning and were now gathering at The Nickolas for a final hurrah before they all scattered for some well-deserved time off. Well, most of us, Nick thought. Lange wasn't likely to catch a break, since he'd already gotten word from the Director that several new missions were lined up in the queue, including one in his former haunt, Somalia.

Nick and Michelle paused at the head of the stairs. "Looks like we're the last to arrive," Michelle said, surveying the room.

Nick verified her observation. Lange, clad in his dark-red

smoking jacket, occupied his usual chair in front of the fireplace, chatting with George and Vinny who'd pulled up a couple extra chairs. All three were shrouded in a pale-blue haze of fragrant cigar smoke. Austin Mack, assisted by Tom, busied himself laying out his usual fabulous spread of gourmet cheeses and hors d'oeuvres on a table by the library's front window. The team's three women were standing close by the bar, exchanging laughs.

"Let's grab a drink and join the ladies," Nick suggested. "They're probably relating war stories, but I've got a plan."

"A plan?" Michelle asked, the skepticism evident in her voice.

"Trust me."

"Hey, guys," Marie welcomed them. "We were just telling a few yarns."

"See," Nick said to Michelle.

"See what?" Ann asked.

Nick bobbed his eyebrows, Groucho style. "I'm innocent of anything you're thinking."

"You don't know what I'm thinking," Ann replied, "and in deference to Michelle, I'm not going to say what that might be."

Jennifer chimed in. "Actually, we were saying how we used our cross-country running skills to box in Grekov's watcher. It was a masterful performance, including lots of girl talk, swinging arms, and a spilled soda."

"Where were you?" Michelle asked

"Prague's botanical gardens," Jennifer answered. "We spotted Grekov's watcher hanging out in the orchid display, doing his best to blend in."

"With the orchids?" Marie teased. "You know I really love dendrobiums—"

Nick put on his game face. "Just the facts, ma'am."

"Seriously?" Jennifer said. "Dragnet?"

"This is the city, Los Angeles, California … I work here… I'm a cop," Ann chimed in.

"Ah, mission complete. This calls for a celebratory drink," Nick said making for the bar, leaving behind four bewildered women.

"What was that all about?" Jennifer asked Michelle.

Michelle shook her head. "My husband's weird sense of humor."

"I think he's hinting we should quit the shop talk," Marie said, watching her unpredictable partner pour a stiff measure of Marker's Mark bourbon into a glass. She turned back to Ann and Jennifer. "He's making a Manhattan for Michelle."

Michelle half-turned. "I wanted to ask you—"

"Your husband was a total gentleman, if that's what you're wondering," Marie interrupted.

"I appreciate you confirming that, but what I really wanted to ask was whether he found out anything about his family."

Marie spotted Nick returning and whispered in Michelle's ear, "Just ask him about his castle, but not here."

"Castle?" Michelle echoed in disbelief as Nick reappeared with her Manhattan.

Michelle pulled Nick aside. "You've got a castle? Seriously?"

"Yup, it appears so," Nick replied. "I'll beguile you with tales of knights in shining armor slaying dragons and rescuing fair damsels in distress after we get back to our room."

Nick and Michelle made sure they spoke with everyone, and were hardly able to share a moment alone together with the whirl of activity of The Curator's homecoming. Michelle finally pulled Nick aside and said, "Let's go downstairs and have a quiet moment. I've been wanting to try out those red-leather chairs under Major Nickolas' portrait."

"I'm sure the good major will be keeping a watchful eye on us for any shenanigans," Nick quipped.

Chapter Sixty-Four

They made their final rounds, saying their goodbyes before making their way to the fireplace to thank their host.

Lange stood, "How are you two doing?"

"Great, but we need to bail," Nick said. "We have an early flight tomorrow. Gotta get Michelle back to her studies."

"I could have flown you home in Frogman," Lange protested.

"Thanks, but no," Michelle replied. "We've imposed enough."

Lange knew better than to argue with Michelle, instead offering his hand to Nick. "Solid work, Nick. All in, all the time. I'll see you around." He gave Michelle a hug and an admonition. "Take good care of him."

Nick, like Lange, was not a fan of prolonged farewells. Those few words were enough. They struck home. He tossed Lange a salute, "'Move, shoot, communicate. You take care of yourself."

He took Michelle's arm and headed toward the stairs, pausing to cast a final look over The Nicholas' man cave before they descended. He wondered if he would ever see this gaggle of certified crazies again. "Night all," he said to himself, before slipping out of sight.

Their departure was noted, though, by Marie, Ann, and Jennifer, who exchanged knowing glances. "Good for them," Marie said, hefting her gin and tonic. "To the kids."

"To the kids," Ann echoed. "They're quite a match."

Edward spotted "the kids" as soon as they reached the bottom of the stairs and approached balancing a silver serving tray with a Glencairn glass filled with Laphroaig Ten Year, batch 007 scotch for Nick and a stiff Manhattan for Michelle. Between the glasses were four truffles from his purveyor, Lain Burnett, Highland Chocolatier. "A little bird sent a text saying ya might be wantin' these," he said, offering Michelle her glass. *"Lang may yer lum leek, lassie."*

"I wish you good luck and good fortune in the future, too,

Edmund." Marie stood on her tip-toes and planted a kiss on his cheek. "You are welcome in our home anytime."

They sat in silence after Edmund departed, Michelle giving Nick some space to collect his thoughts. After they finished the truffles, she decided it was time to ask about what he had learned from his quest for his family's roots. "Did you have a chance to find out what was in your keepsake box?"

Nick looked at the floor, mute, the memories threatening to overcome him.

Michelle waited a moment. "No matter how hard the past months have been, you would have regretted not knowing those parts of yourself."

Her statement, kind as it was, gave Nick pause as he pondered what he'd found in that five-by-eight inch burlwood box and everything he'd experienced in the Czech Republic: His cousins, Petr and Natálya and their mother, Ida; the family castle; the family patriarch, Pádriac; the Terezin Ghetto; and what he had learned about his father... *Where to start?* "It's complicated."

Michelle reached for his hand and gave it a gentle squeeze. "I do complicated."

Afterword

An author's intent when setting down to write a novel is to craft an engaging story replete with unexpected twists and turns that engages the reader from the opening to the final line. I trust that *The Curators*, the fourth and final novel of The Defenders series, has met that goal. You, my readers, will be the final judge if I have met that goal.

While I worked on the initial draft of *The Curators* crafting Nick's journey, a quote from Ralph Waldo Emerson came to mind: "Do not go where the path may lead, go instead where there is no path and leave a trail."

Indeed, Nick's and the other characters' journeys took any number of unexpected turns that emerged from my original outline. The changes to their character arcs, in turn, drove the story forward. For example, I had no intention of having Taylor Ferguson meet his unfortunate demise and Petr's sister, Natálya, did not even exist. Such is the life of an author, but it is also what makes writing fun.

I suspect at this point that you may be saying to yourself,

"Writing a 350 page novel is fun? Seriously?" Well, yeah, it's this journey which drives us authors. I should also point out that my friend and primary editor, bestselling author Jacquelyn Mitchard, kept telling me: "You've got to create a character that the reader is emotionally invested in." I should also point out, Jackie would rap my knuckles with her literary ruler if I drifted too far from the major theme of the novel.

To construct the setting for the novel, I did take some liberties, but trust that I conveyed a faithful representation of Prague. Count Vilém Patykaovi's castle is fictitious, being an amalgam of many found in the Czech Republic. While the Theresienstadt Ghetto and Therezin are all too real, the gift-shop is fictitious. The Extraordinary Rendition site, but not the interrogation building and the former Soviet Hradćany airfield in Ralsko are also real. And, while I wish such a place existed, Geoff Lange's man cave and The Nicholas are products of my imagination. My own 'man cave' for my writing? It's otherwise known as the guest bedroom overlooking Diamond Head from which I'm periodically evicted.

I've heard said that you shouldn't embark on writing a novel unless you're prepared to read it seventy-five times. And so it was. I'd finish my 'final' edit only have my editor and patient colleagues who were kind enough to review my draft find even more things to fix. To that end, I cannot say enough of the work of Alicia, Ally, Robertson and Rick Ludwig, author of the Maui Mystery Series. Their insights and suggestions made a significant contribution to my final draft. Maria Novillo Sararia, BEAUTeBooks, has again portrayed the essence of my novel in her cover, carrying over the design elements of the first three novels in the series. You can indeed read a book by it's cover. Crafting a novel is one thing, but actually presenting it to the readers is another. I am indebted to my publicist, Sharon Jenkins, Sharon@mcwritingservices, for her incredible work on my various author platforms and her patient insistence prodding me to virtually leave my writer's Man Cave to present my novel to my readers. Finally, I must extend a heartfelt, "Mahalo nui loa" to my mentor and publisher, Williams Bernhard, Babylon Books for his tireless efforts in releasing *The Curators*. His work was and remains instrumental in presenting my novel.

And so with those acknowledgments to those who assisted in bringing my novels to life, I bid a fond farewell to Nick, Michelle, Geoff, and Marie – it's been a fun ride getting to know you.

About the Author

A native of Columbus, Ohio, Kenneth Andrus attended Marietta College where he was recently recognized as a distinguished graduate. Graduating from the Ohio State University College of Medicine, he was commissioned in the United States Navy where he completed his studies in internal medicine, obtaining board certification. He subsequently completed a twenty-four year career retiring with the rank of Captain alternating tours at Naval medical teaching hospitals, the Fleet and the Fleet Marine Force.

Highlights of his operational tours included Medical Officer, Third Battalion Forth Marines; Surgeon 9th Marine Amphibious Brigade, Operation Frequent Wind; Medical Officer, U.S.S. Truxtun CGN-35, Surgeon, Commander Seventh Fleet; Command Surgeon, Commander U.S. Naval Forces Central Command Operation Desert Shield/Desert Storm and Surgeon, United States Pacific Fleet. Following his retirement, he continued to serve our veterans while working at Veterans Affairs.

Dr. Andrus began his writing career after his retirement from VA first penning a heartfelt book about his experiences as the father-of-the-bride for his two daughters. "Congratulations, Your Daughter is Engaged. Now What? A Father's Emotional Survival Guide." While still on active duty, the idea for his first novel began to form resulting in the publication of

"Flash Point, the first in the five book The Defender series. His second novel, Amber Dawn was published in March of 2021, and the third, "Artic Menace" was published in August of 2021. While working his draft for "The Curators," the forth in the series, he completed a novella "Twenty-one Day in December" to be included with several other Babylon Press authors and to be published in December of 2021.

He currently resides in Honolulu, Hawaii with his wife of forty-three years, Christine, also a retired Navy physician.

Also by Kenneth Andrus

The Defenders Series

Flash Point

Amber Dawn

Arctic Menace

The Curators

Made in the USA
Middletown, DE
07 August 2023

35882018R00231